GIRL GENIUS

THE CITY of LIGHTNING

the SECOND JOURNEY of AGATHA HETERODYNE
BOOK TWO

Story by Kaja & Phil Foglio
Drawings by Phil Foglio
Colors by Cheyenne Wright

OTHER BOOKS FROM AIRSHIP ENTERTAINMENT AND STUDIO FOGLIO

Girl Genius® Graphic Novels

The First Journey of Agatha Heterodyne:

Book 1: *Agatha Heterodyne and the Beetleburg Clank*
Book 2: *Agatha Heterodyne and the Airship City*
Book 3: *Agatha Heterodyne and the Monster Engine*
Book 4: *Agatha Heterodyne and the Circus of Dreams*
Book 5: *Agatha Heterodyne and the Clockwork Princess*
Book 6: *Agatha Heterodyne and the Golden Trilobite*
Book 7: *Agatha Heterodyne and the Voice of the Castle*
Book 8: *Agatha Heterodyne and the Chapel of Bones*
Book 9: *Agatha Heterodyne and the Heirs of the Storm*
Book 10: *Agatha Heterodyne and the Guardian Muse*
Book 11: *Agatha Heterodyne and the Hammerless Bell*
Book 12: *Agatha Heterodyne and the Siege of Mechanicsburg*
Book 13: *Agatha Heterodyne and the Sleeping City*

The Second Journey of Agatha Heterodyne:

Book 1: *The Beast of the Rails*
Book 2: *The City of Lightning*

Girl Genius® Novels from Night Shade Books

Girl Genius: Agatha H. and the Airship City
Girl Genius: Agatha H. and the Clockwork Princess
Girl Genius: Agatha H. and the Voice of the Castle

Girl Genius® is published by:
Airship Entertainment™: a happy part of Studio Foglio, LLC
2400 NW 80th St #129 Seattle WA 98117-4449, USA

Please visit our Web sites at www.airshipbooks.com and www.girlgeniusonline.com

Story by Phil & Kaja Foglio. Pencils by Phil Foglio. Colors by Cheyenne Wright. Selected spot illustrations colored by Kaja Foglio and/or Cheyenne Wright. Logos, Lettering, Artist Bullying & Book Design by Kaja. Fonts mostly by Comicraft– www.comicbookfonts.com.

This material originally appeared from January 2015 to November 2015 at www.girlgeniusonline.com.

Published simultaneously in Hardcover (ISBN 978-1-890856-64-9)
and Softcover (ISBN 978-1-890856-63-2) editions.

First Printing: May 2016   PRINTED IN THE USA

Agatha Heterodyne

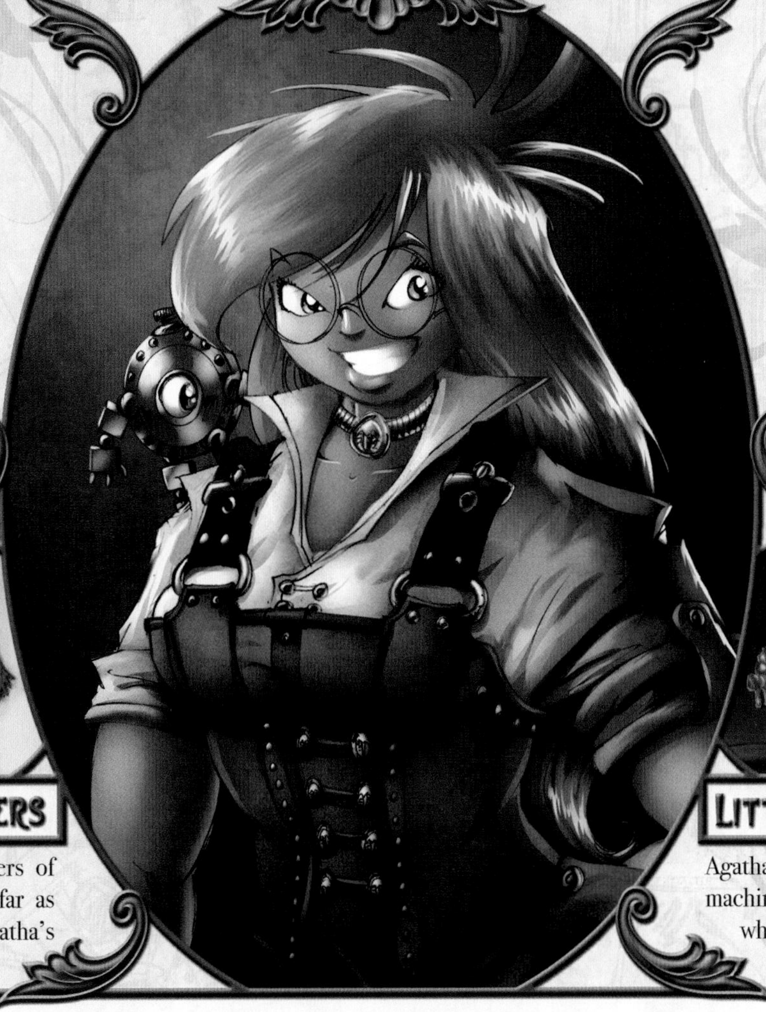

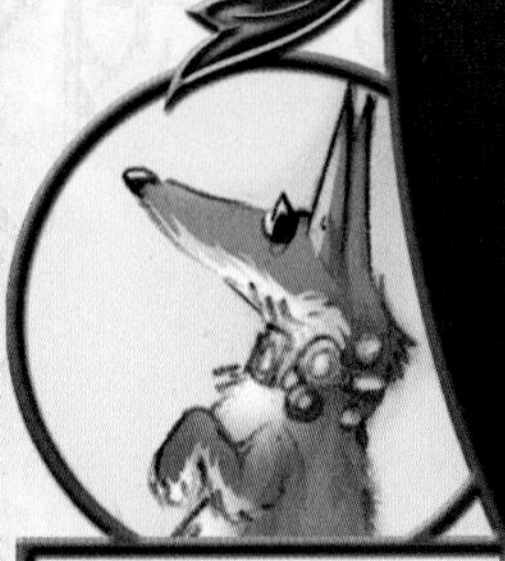

Wasp Eaters

Fierce little hunters of slaver wasps. As far as anyone knows, Agatha's is the last one.

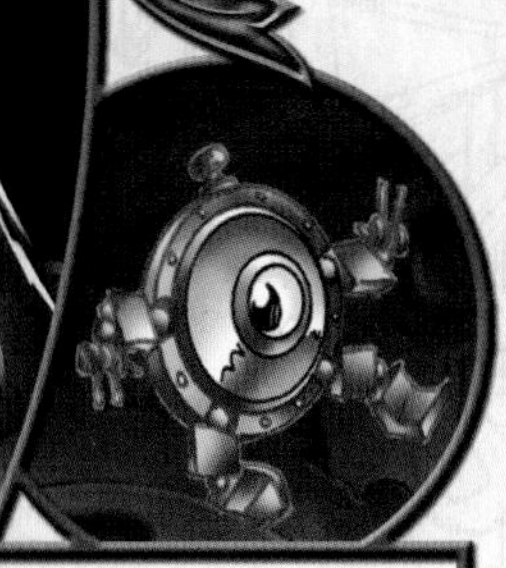

Little Clanks

Agatha builds helpful machines to assist her when she's working.

Agatha is the latest in a powerful line of mad scientists (or "Sparks" to be polite.) She has just established herself as the Lady Heterodyne: hereditary ruler of the fortress-town of Mechanicsburg.

The Town of Mechanicsburg

Mechanicsburg has been the refuge of the Heterodyne family for hundreds of years and is, therefore, a bit peculiar. It is currently trapped in a bubble of stopped time.

Castle Heterodyne

The mechanical fortress that looms in the center of Mechanicsburg is intelligent, with a rather ghoulish sense of humor. It was broken for many years, but Agatha and her friends managed to repair it.

The "Other"

The terrible, mysterious Spark who–a generation ago–terrorized Europa with devastating attacks. The Other made extensive use of mind control–adding to an already fearsome reputation. Although most people still don't know it, the Other was actually Lucrezia Heterodyne (née Mongfish)–Agatha's mother.

Lucrezia recently tried to replace Agatha's mind with her own, but failed.

Her physical whereabouts are currently unknown. An echo of her personality is still lodged in Agatha's head–kept in check by a clever mechanism built into a locket.

Geisterdamen

The fanatically loyal servants of the Other. They help spread slaver wasps across Europa.

Jägermonsters

A band of fearsome monster soldiers created by one of Agatha's not-so-nice ancestors. The Jägers have served the Heterodynes for generations.

Krosp I

The "Emperor of All Cats" and a failed experiment. Krosp has found that, although he is indeed the highest-ranking cat around, his "subjects" are more likely to fall asleep than carry out his orders.

Dimo

One of the smarter Jägermonsters. Dimo recognized Agatha as a member of the Heterodyne family before she came to Mechanicsburg.

Princess Zeetha of Skifander

The Lost Princess of the Lost City of Skifander. Zeetha has befriended Agatha, and has taken it upon herself to train Agatha in self-defense. She hopes that, in the course of their adventures, she will find her way home.

Violetta Mondarev

A "smoke knight" who never much liked her job. Since she began guarding Agatha, she's been having a lot more fun.

Ardsley Wooster

A spy for the British Queen Albia. Wooster has spent many years in Europa, keeping an eye on its rulers. He is now accompanying Agatha on her journey.

THE CORBETTITE MONKS

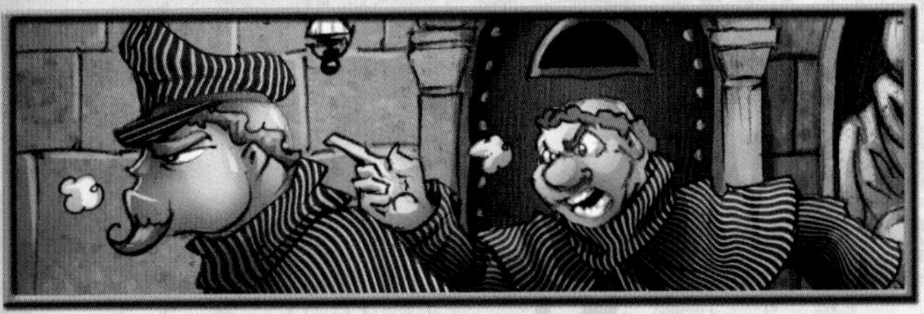

A monastic order that runs an extensive railway system, as well as defusing and containing dangerous artefacts left behind by the Sparks of Europa.

THE BEAST

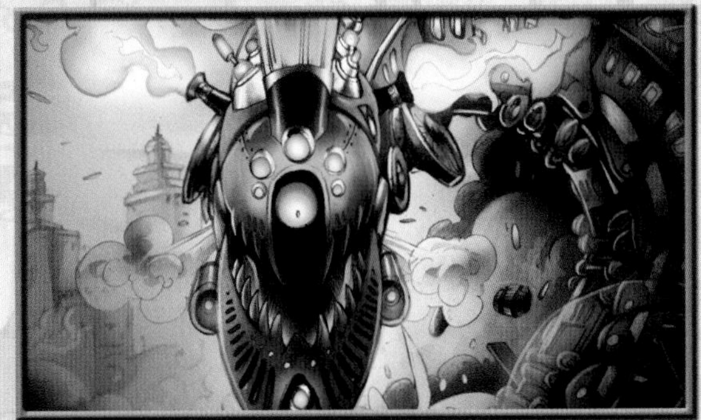

A monstrous, self-aware engine created by Agatha's ancestors for the Corbettite Railway.

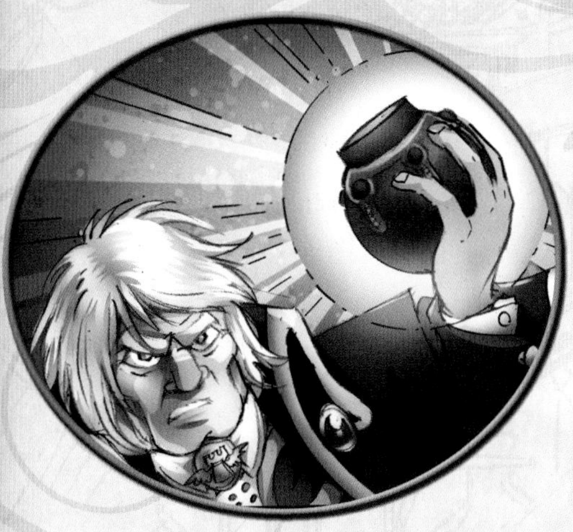

BARON KLAUS WULFENBACH

A powerful Spark, the Baron was the founder of the Wulfenbach Empire and the force behind the Pax Transylvania. Briefly, Lucrezia Mongfish had him under her sway, until he deliberately sealed himself inside the time bubble around Mechanicsburg.

GILGAMESH WULFENBACH

Gil is stuck ruling what's left of his father's empire. He and Agatha share a mutual attraction, but there's something very wrong with him at the moment, and Agatha knows better than to get close.

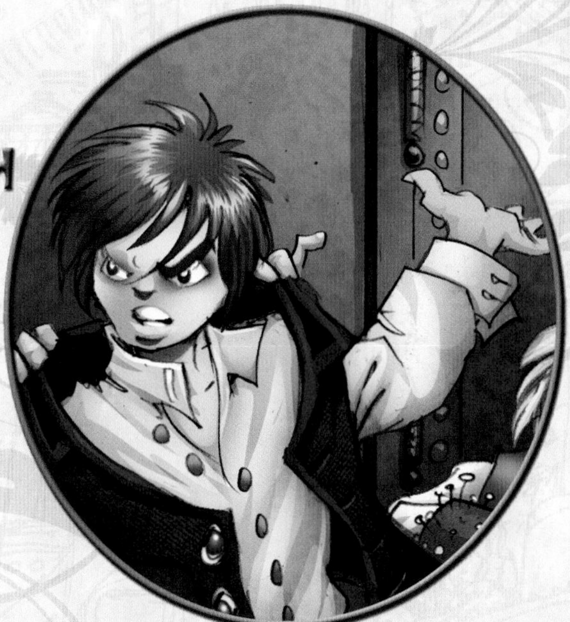

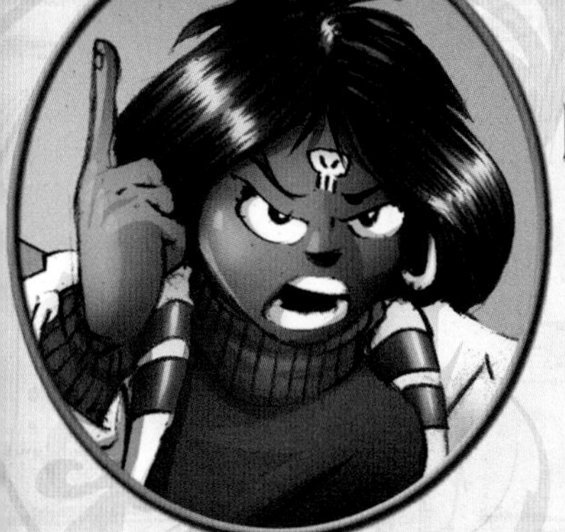

BANGLADESH DUPREE

Bang is a former Pirate Queen whose fortress and pirate fleet were destroyed under mysterious circumstances. She now works for the Empire.

AIRMAN THIRD CLASS AXEL HIGGS

Higgs is a Wulfenbach airman who seems to have some secrets. He and Zeetha have been in a romantic relationship since the Siege of Mechanicsburg.

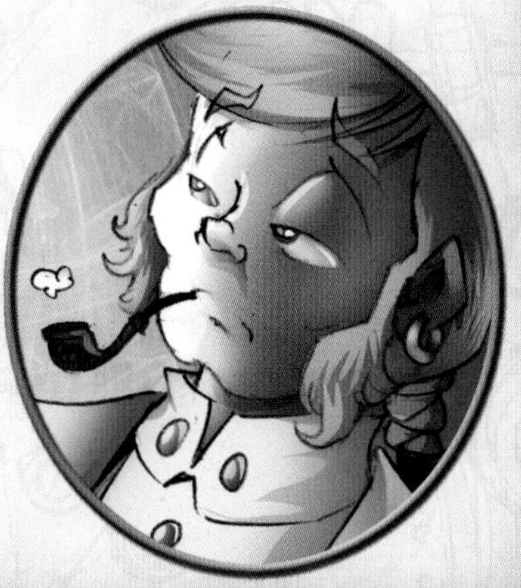

THE STORM KING

Long ago, the Storm King–Andronicus Valois–united the powers of the West against the fearsome powers of the Heterodynes. The Heterodynes and their monsters were successfully beaten back at the site that would become Sturmhalten, and arrangements were made for peace, cemented by a marriage between the King and Euphrosynia Heterodyne. This did not go well, and the reign of the Storm King came to a tragic end.

The LOYAL ORDER of the KNIGHTS OF JOVE

"The Order" is a secret society made up of descendants of the original Storm King's honor guard. They are involved in a plot to destroy the Wulfenbach Empire and restore the throne of the Storm King, and have close ties with the Mongfish family, especially Lucrezia.

TARVEK STURMVORAUS

Tarvek Sturmvoraus is the heir to the throne of the Storm King. Tarvek is a strong Spark, and worked closely with Agatha and Gil during the repairs on Castle Heterodyne. He is currently trapped inside Mechanicsburg.

MARTELLUS VON BLITZENGAARD

With his cousin Tarvek out of the picture, Martellus has declared himself the new Storm King. He plans to use a political marriage to the Lady Heterodyne to help strengthen his claim.

XERXSEPHNIA VON BLITZENGAARD

Seffie is involved in the machinations of the Knights of Jove, but to what extent? She loves her brother, Martellus, but isn't always very nice to him.

LADY MARGARELLA SELNIKOV

Violetta's aunt, and part of a group that hopes to free Tarvek from Mechanicsburg. Lady Margarella is now dead, killed by the Beast of the Rails when she accidentally set it free. She was searching the monostary vaults for something completely different, guided by cryptic notes in a stolen book.

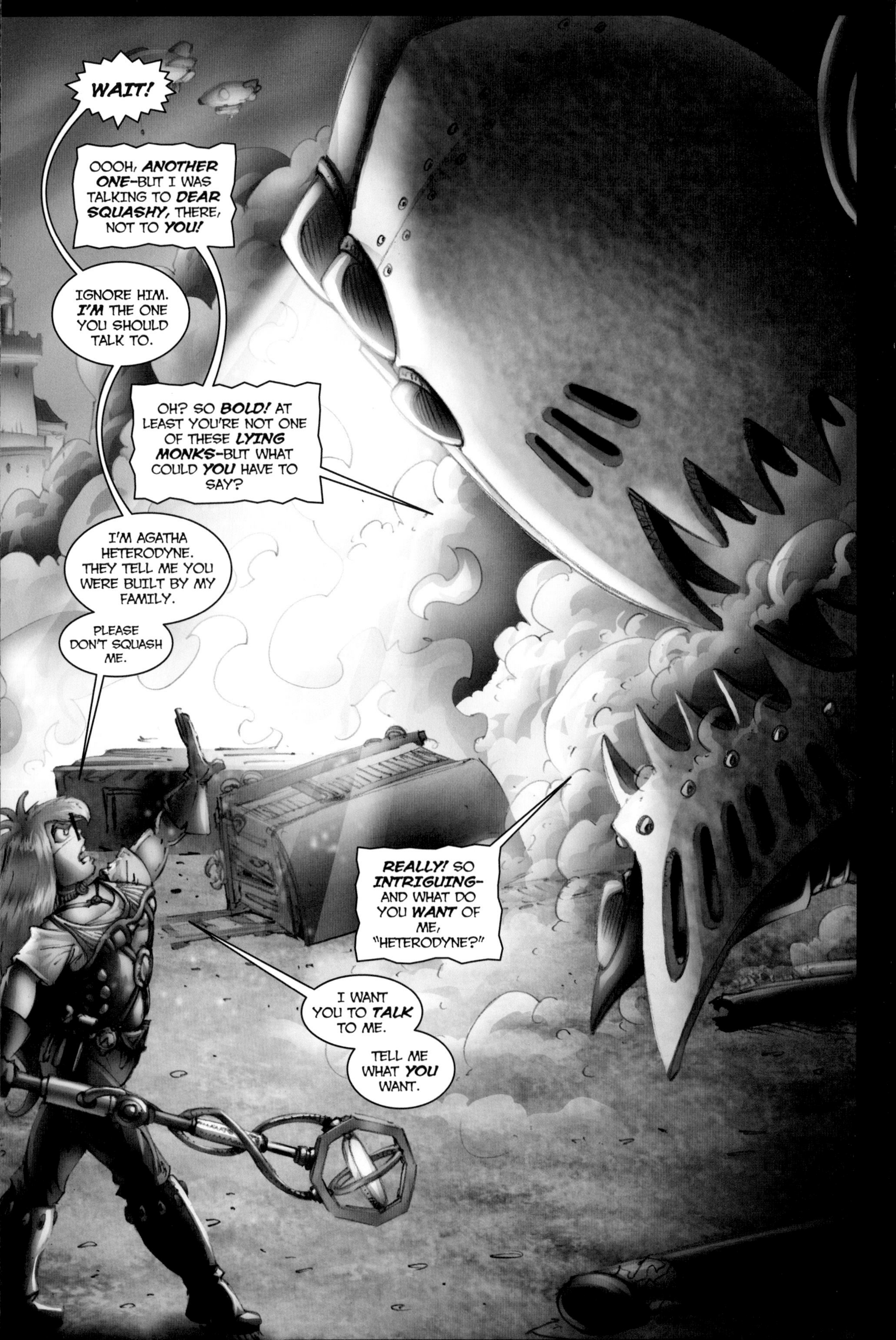
WAIT!
OOOH, ANOTHER ONE–BUT I WAS TALKING TO DEAR SQUASHY, THERE, NOT TO YOU!
IGNORE HIM. I'M THE ONE YOU SHOULD TALK TO.
OH? SO BOLD! AT LEAST YOU'RE NOT ONE OF THESE LYING MONKS–BUT WHAT COULD YOU HAVE TO SAY?
I'M AGATHA HETERODYNE. THEY TELL ME YOU WERE BUILT BY MY FAMILY.
PLEASE DON'T SQUASH ME.
REALLY! SO INTRIGUING– AND WHAT DO YOU WANT OF ME, "HETERODYNE?"
I WANT YOU TO TALK TO ME.
TELL ME WHAT YOU WANT.

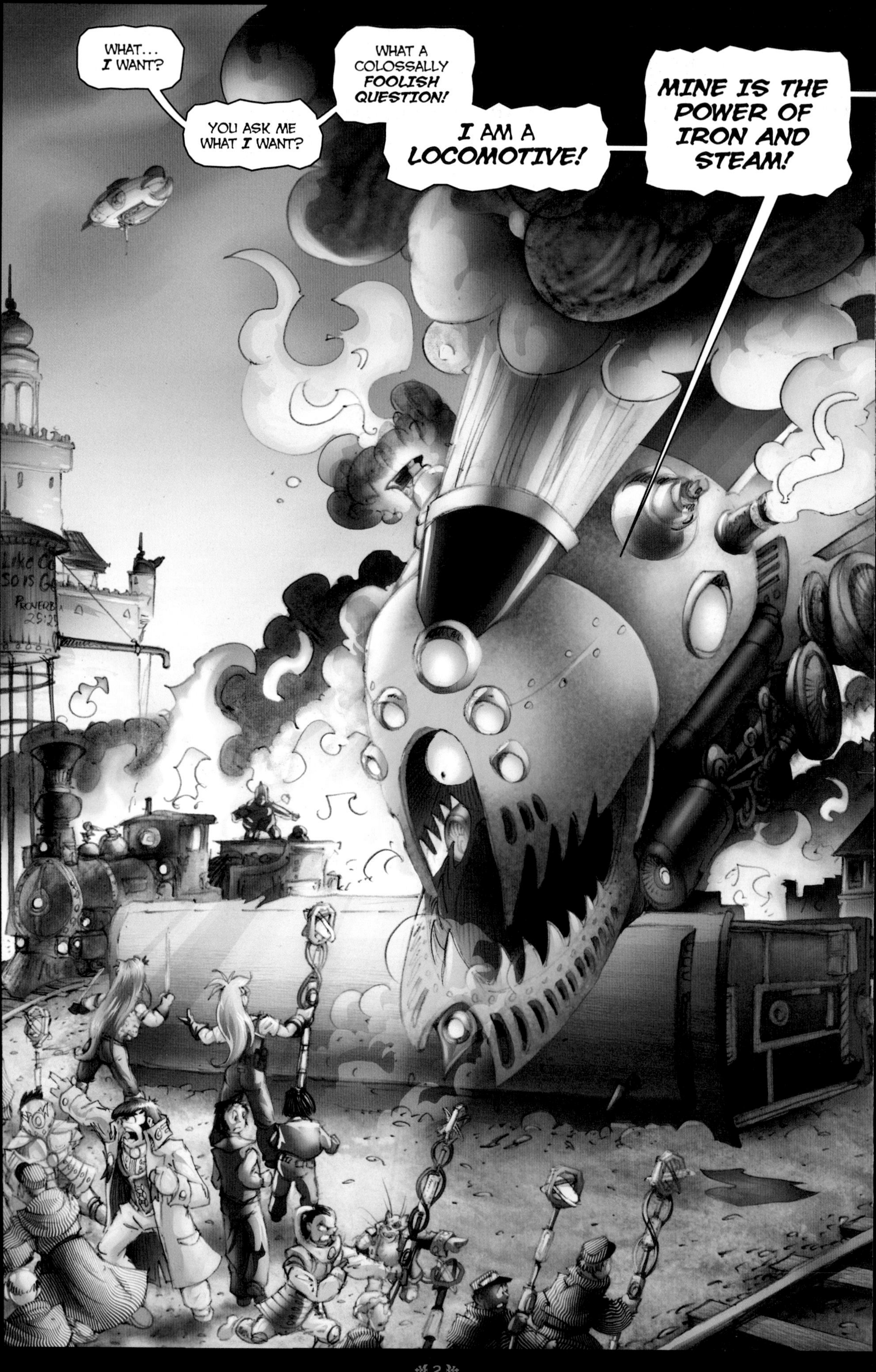
WHAT... I WANT?
YOU ASK ME WHAT I WANT?
WHAT A COLOSSALLY FOOLISH QUESTION!
I AM A LOCOMOTIVE!
MINE IS THE POWER OF IRON AND STEAM!

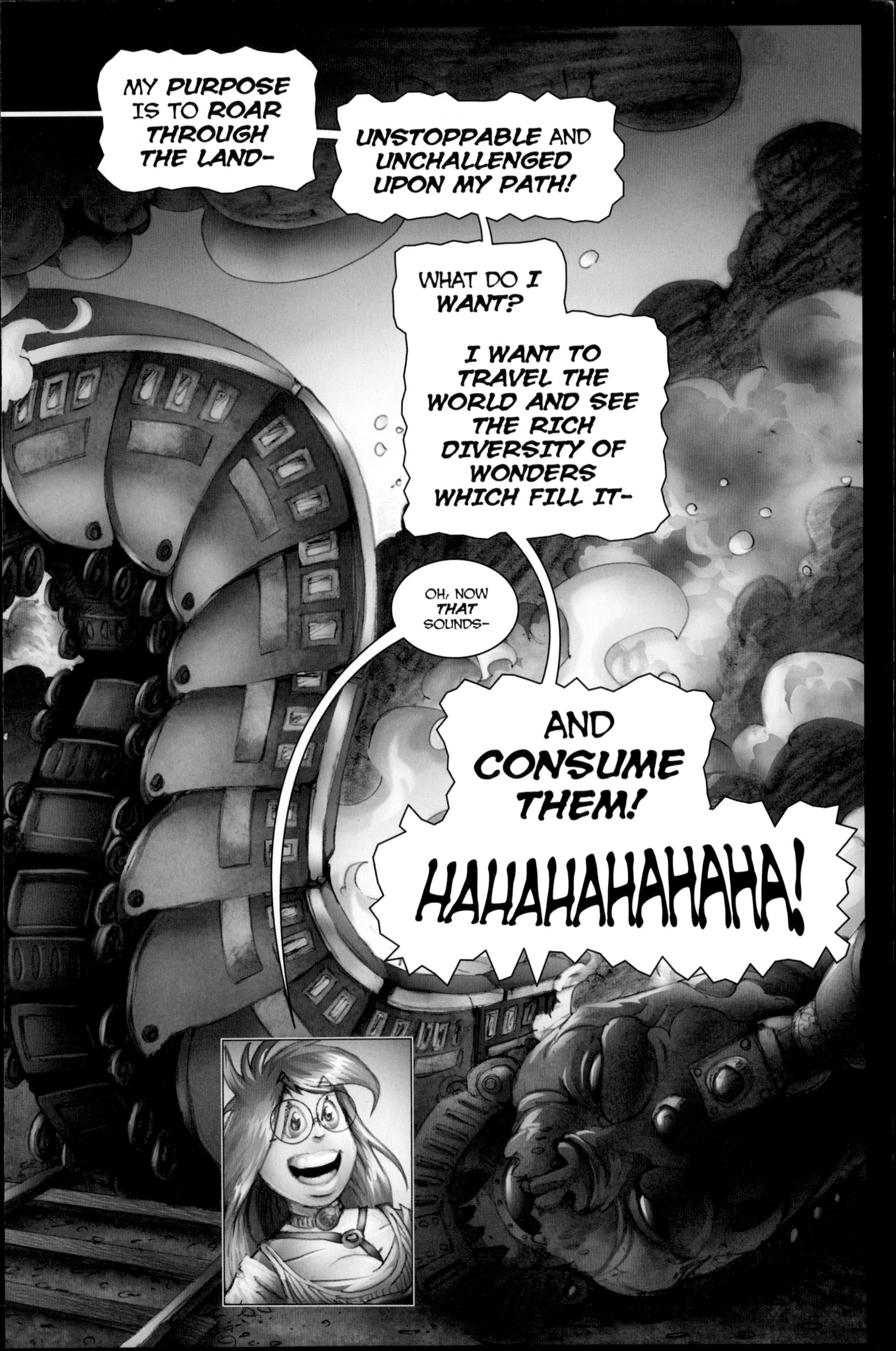
MY PURPOSE IS TO ROAR THROUGH THE LAND-
UNSTOPPABLE AND UNCHALLENGED UPON MY PATH!
WHAT DO I WANT?
I WANT TO TRAVEL THE WORLD AND SEE THE RICH DIVERSITY OF WONDERS WHICH FILL IT-
OH, NOW THAT SOUNDS-
AND CONSUME THEM!
HAHAHAHAHAHA!

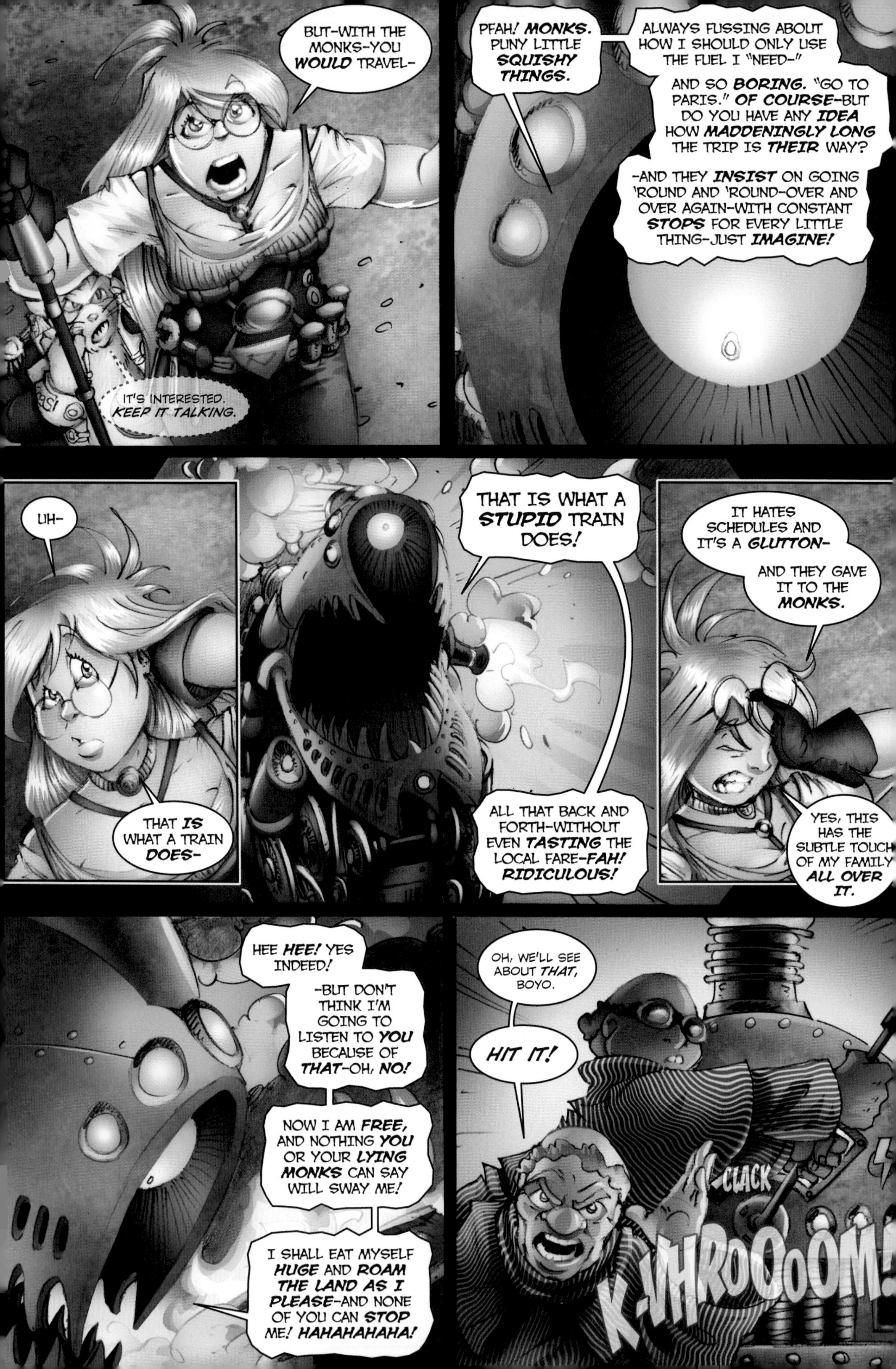
BUT-WITH THE MONKS-YOU WOULD TRAVEL-
IT'S INTERESTED. KEEP IT TALKING.
PFAH! MONKS. PUNY LITTLE SQUISHY THINGS.
ALWAYS FUSSING ABOUT HOW I SHOULD ONLY USE THE FUEL I "NEED-"
AND SO BORING. "GO TO PARIS." OF COURSE-BUT DO YOU HAVE ANY IDEA HOW MADDENINGLY LONG THE TRIP IS THEIR WAY?
-AND THEY INSIST ON GOING 'ROUND AND 'ROUND-OVER AND OVER AGAIN-WITH CONSTANT STOPS FOR EVERY LITTLE THING-JUST IMAGINE!
UH-
THAT IS WHAT A TRAIN DOES-
THAT IS WHAT A STUPID TRAIN DOES!
ALL THAT BACK AND FORTH-WITHOUT EVEN TASTING THE LOCAL FARE-FAH! RIDICULOUS!
IT HATES SCHEDULES AND IT'S A GLUTTON-
AND THEY GAVE IT TO THE MONKS.
YES, THIS HAS THE SUBTLE TOUCH OF MY FAMILY ALL OVER IT.
HEE HEE! YES INDEED!
-BUT DON'T THINK I'M GOING TO LISTEN TO YOU BECAUSE OF THAT-OH, NO!
NOW I AM FREE, AND NOTHING YOU OR YOUR LYING MONKS CAN SAY WILL SWAY ME!
I SHALL EAT MYSELF HUGE AND ROAM THE LAND AS I PLEASE-AND NONE OF YOU CAN STOP ME! HAHAHAHAHA!
OH, WE'LL SEE ABOUT THAT, BOYO.
HIT IT!
CLACK
K-VHROOOOM!

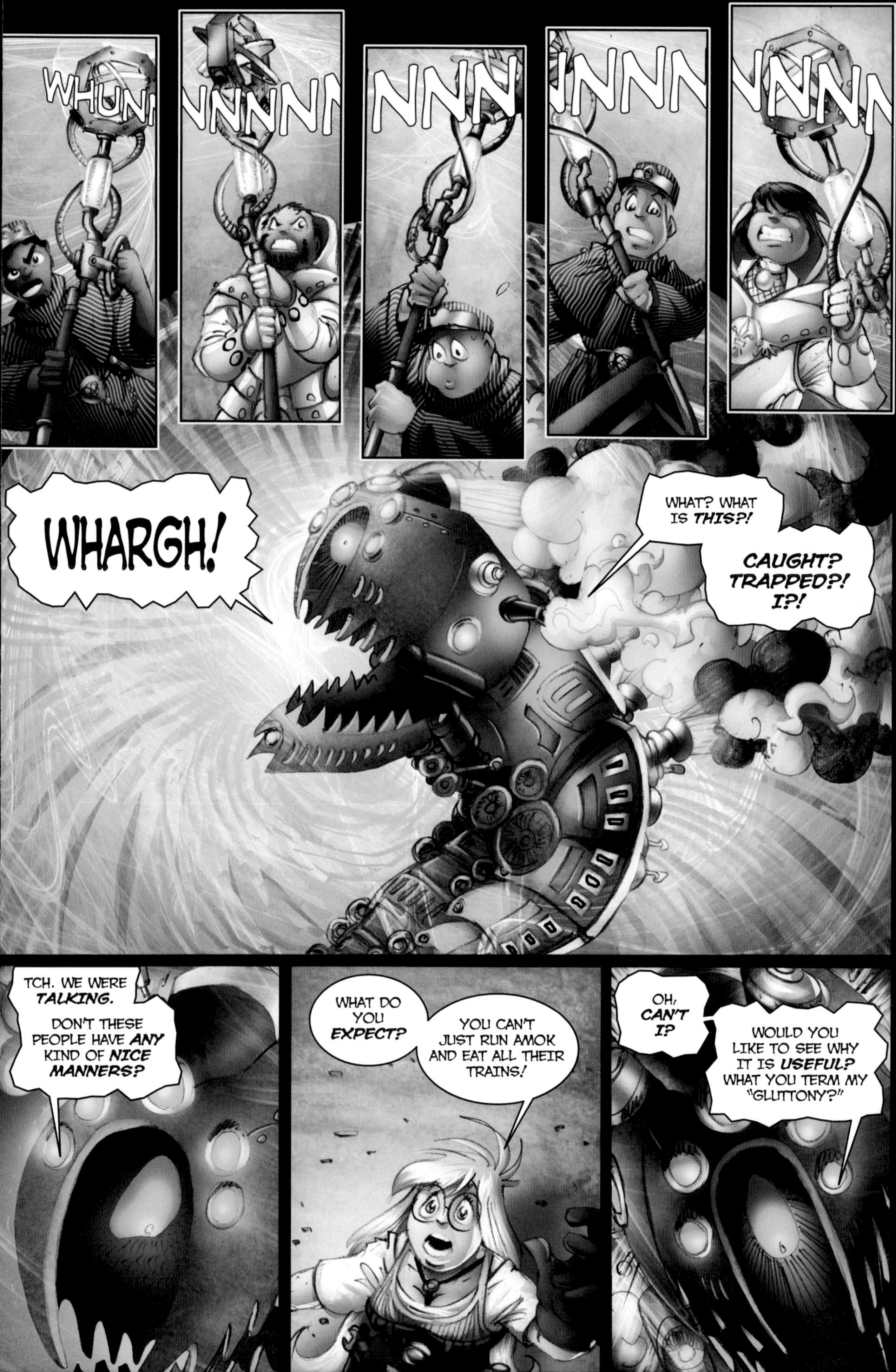
WHUNN
NNNNN
NNN
NNNN
NNNN
WHARGH!
WHAT? WHAT IS *THIS?!*
CAUGHT? TRAPPED?! I?!
TCH. WE WERE *TALKING.*
DON'T THESE PEOPLE HAVE *ANY* KIND OF *NICE MANNERS?*
WHAT DO YOU *EXPECT?*
YOU CAN'T JUST RUN AMOK AND EAT ALL THEIR TRAINS!
OH, *CAN'T I?*
WOULD YOU LIKE TO SEE WHY IT IS *USEFUL?* WHAT YOU TERM MY "GLUTTONY?"

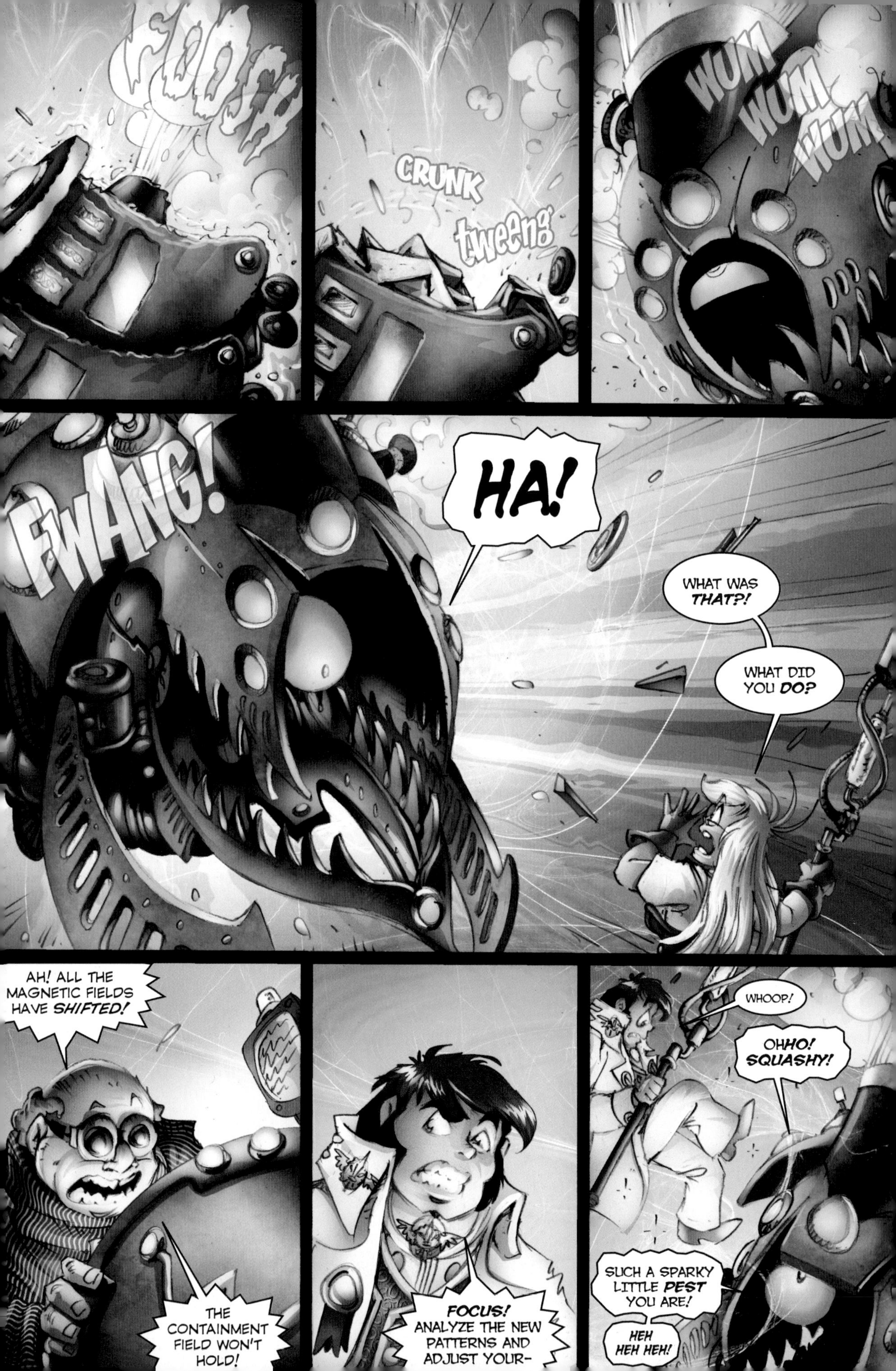

CRUNK
tweeng
WUM WUM WUM
FWANG!
HA!
WHAT WAS THAT?!
WHAT DID YOU DO?
AH! ALL THE MAGNETIC FIELDS HAVE SHIFTED!
THE CONTAINMENT FIELD WON'T HOLD!
FOCUS! ANALYZE THE NEW PATTERNS AND ADJUST YOUR-
WHOOP!
OHHO! SQUASHY!
SUCH A SPARKY LITTLE PEST YOU ARE!
HEH HEH HEH!

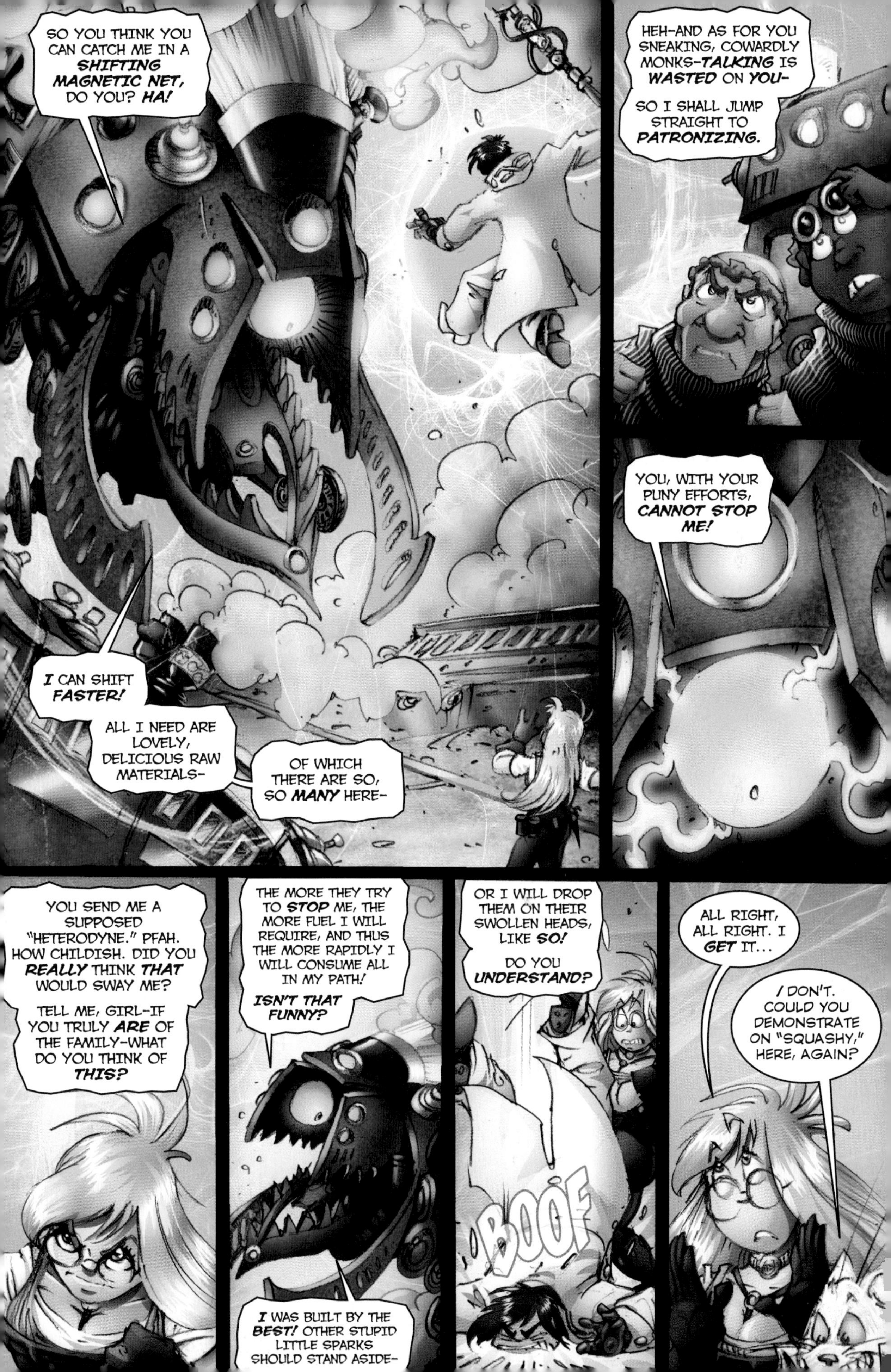
SO YOU THINK YOU CAN CATCH ME IN A SHIFTING MAGNETIC NET, DO YOU? HA!
I CAN SHIFT FASTER!
ALL I NEED ARE LOVELY, DELICIOUS RAW MATERIALS-
OF WHICH THERE ARE SO, SO MANY HERE-
HEH-AND AS FOR YOU SNEAKING, COWARDLY MONKS-TALKING IS WASTED ON YOU-
SO I SHALL JUMP STRAIGHT TO PATRONIZING.
YOU, WITH YOUR PUNY EFFORTS, CANNOT STOP ME!
YOU SEND ME A SUPPOSED "HETERODYNE." PFAH. HOW CHILDISH. DID YOU REALLY THINK THAT WOULD SWAY ME?
TELL ME, GIRL-IF YOU TRULY ARE OF THE FAMILY-WHAT DO YOU THINK OF THIS?
THE MORE THEY TRY TO STOP ME, THE MORE FUEL I WILL REQUIRE, AND THUS THE MORE RAPIDLY I WILL CONSUME ALL IN MY PATH!
ISN'T THAT FUNNY?
I WAS BUILT BY THE BEST! OTHER STUPID LITTLE SPARKS SHOULD STAND ASIDE-
OR I WILL DROP THEM ON THEIR SWOLLEN HEADS, LIKE SO!
DO YOU UNDERSTAND?
BOOF
ALL RIGHT, ALL RIGHT. I GET IT...
I DON'T. COULD YOU DEMONSTRATE ON "SQUASHY," HERE, AGAIN?

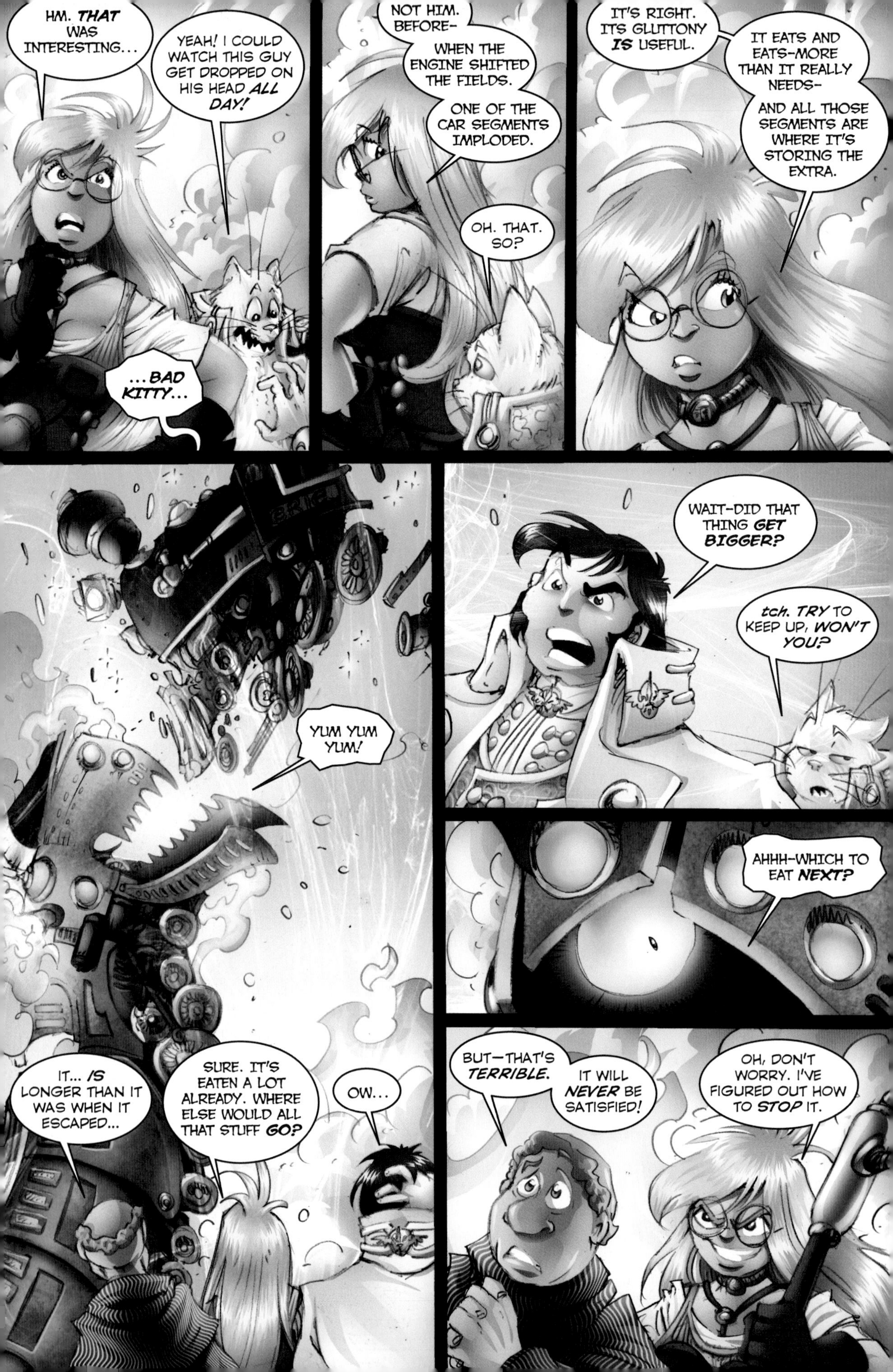
HM. THAT WAS INTERESTING...
YEAH! I COULD WATCH THIS GUY GET DROPPED ON HIS HEAD ALL DAY!
...BAD KITTY...
NOT HIM. BEFORE-
WHEN THE ENGINE SHIFTED THE FIELDS.
ONE OF THE CAR SEGMENTS IMPLODED.
OH. THAT. SO?
IT'S RIGHT. ITS GLUTTONY IS USEFUL.
IT EATS AND EATS-MORE THAN IT REALLY NEEDS-
AND ALL THOSE SEGMENTS ARE WHERE IT'S STORING THE EXTRA.
YUM YUM YUM!
WAIT-DID THAT THING GET BIGGER?
tch. TRY TO KEEP UP, WON'T YOU?
AHHH-WHICH TO EAT NEXT?
IT... IS LONGER THAN IT WAS WHEN IT ESCAPED...
SURE. IT'S EATEN A LOT ALREADY. WHERE ELSE WOULD ALL THAT STUFF GO?
OW...
BUT—THAT'S TERRIBLE.
IT WILL NEVER BE SATISFIED!
OH, DON'T WORRY. I'VE FIGURED OUT HOW TO STOP IT.

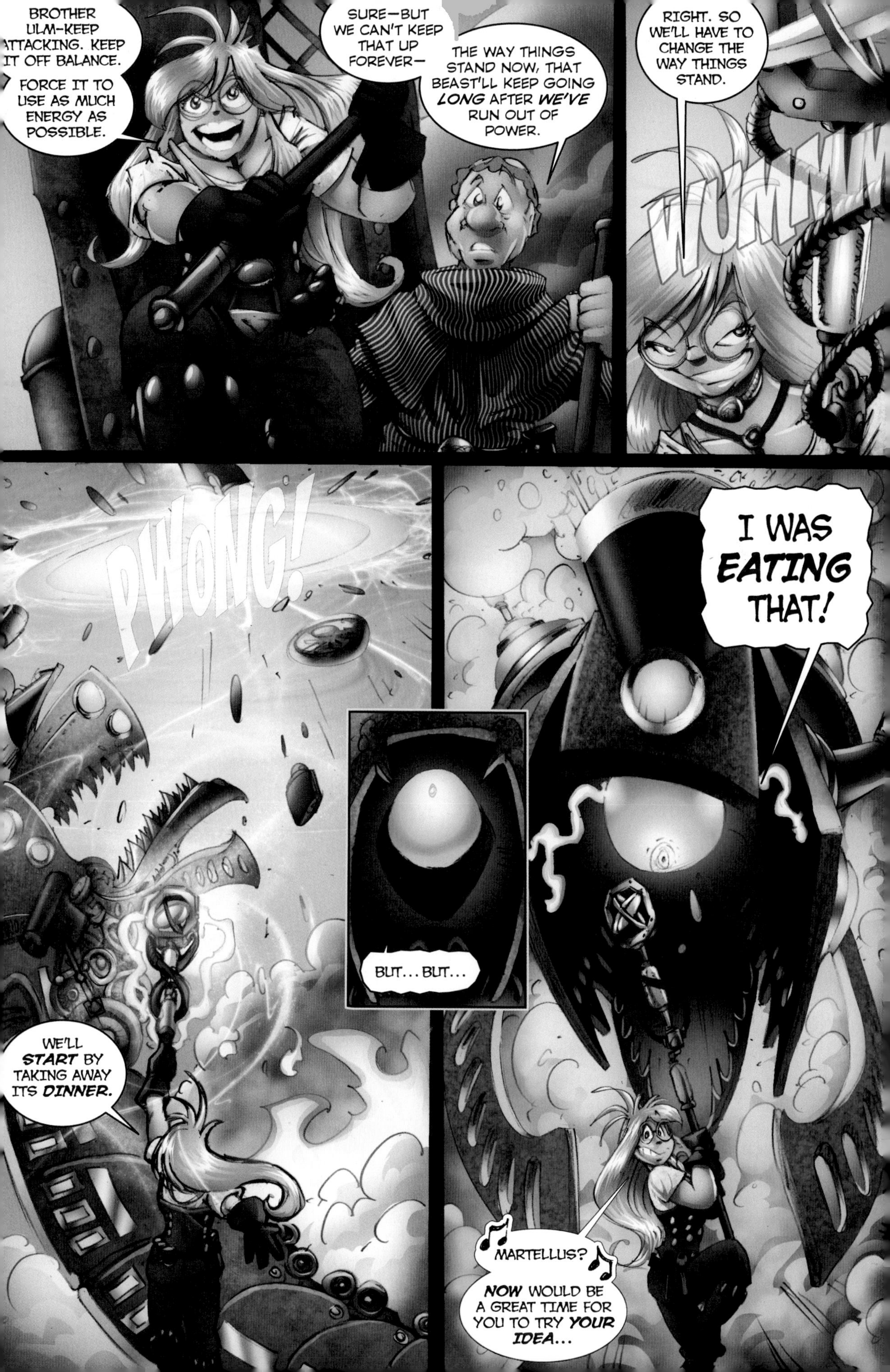
BROTHER ULM–KEEP ATTACKING. KEEP IT OFF BALANCE.
FORCE IT TO USE AS MUCH ENERGY AS POSSIBLE.
SURE—BUT WE CAN'T KEEP THAT UP FOREVER—
THE WAY THINGS STAND NOW, THAT BEAST'LL KEEP GOING *LONG* AFTER *WE'VE* RUN OUT OF POWER.
RIGHT. SO WE'LL HAVE TO CHANGE THE WAY THINGS STAND.
WUMMM
PWONG!
WE'LL *START* BY TAKING AWAY ITS *DINNER.*
BUT... BUT...
I WAS *EATING* THAT!
MARTELLUS?
NOW WOULD BE A GREAT TIME FOR YOU TO TRY *YOUR IDEA*...

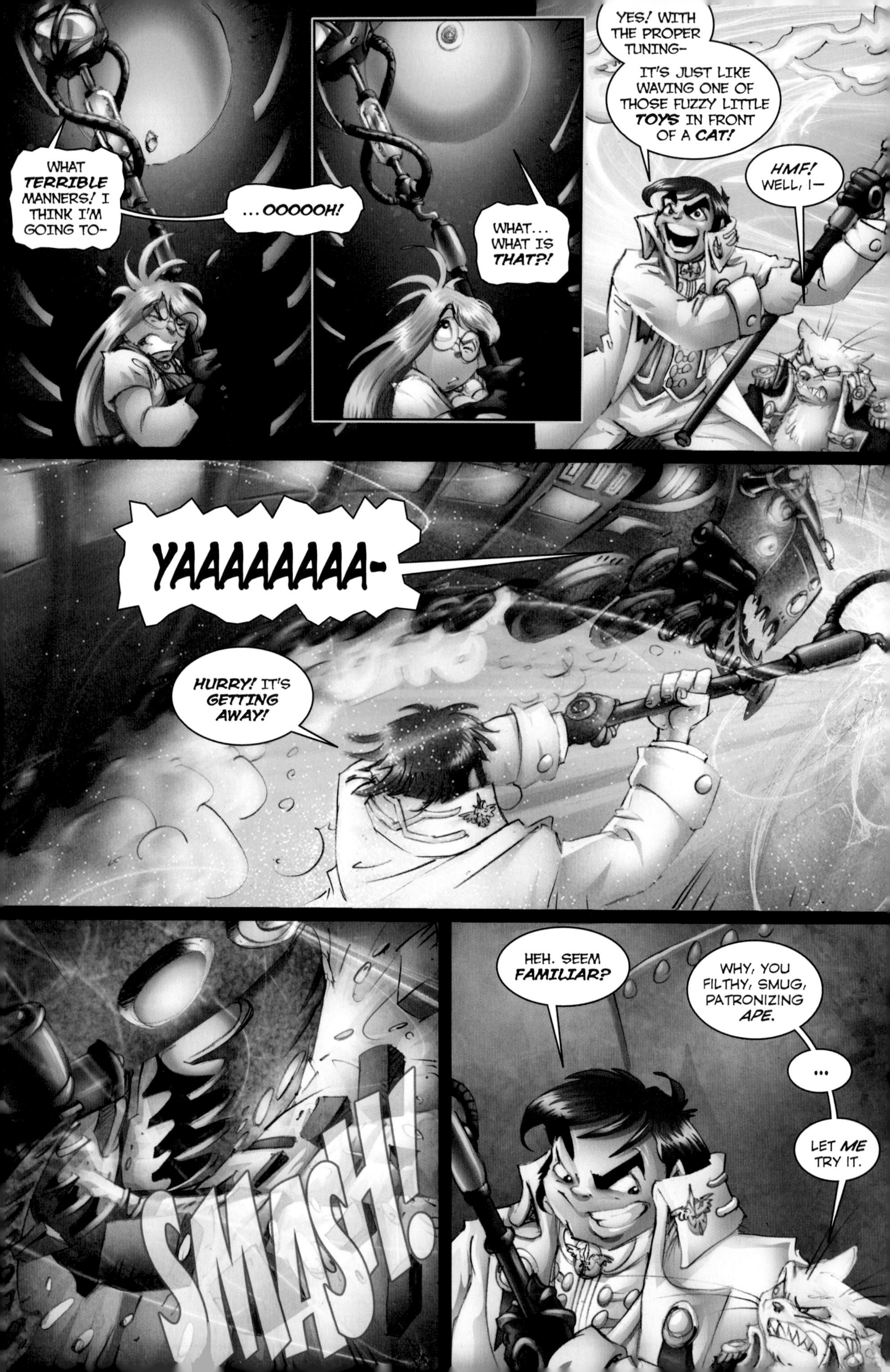
WHAT TERRIBLE MANNERS! I THINK I'M GOING TO-
...OOOOOH!
WHAT... WHAT IS THAT?!
YES! WITH THE PROPER TUNING-
IT'S JUST LIKE WAVING ONE OF THOSE FUZZY LITTLE TOYS IN FRONT OF A CAT!
HMF! WELL, I-
YAAAAAAAA-
HURRY! IT'S GETTING AWAY!
SMASH!
HEH. SEEM FAMILIAR?
WHY, YOU FILTHY, SMUG, PATRONIZING APE.
...
LET ME TRY IT.

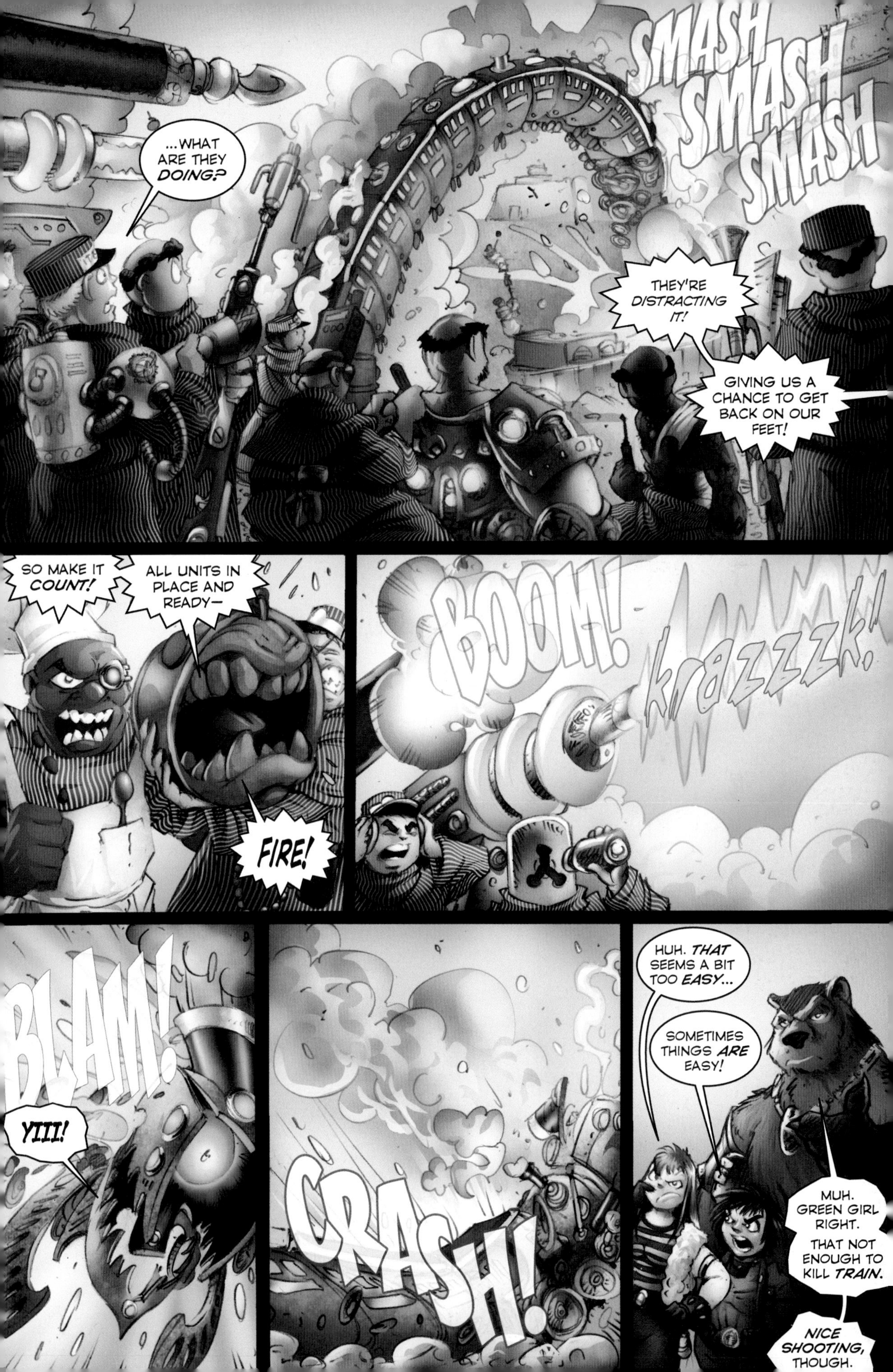
SMASH
SMASH
SMASH
...WHAT ARE THEY *DOING?*
THEY'RE *DISTRACTING* IT!
GIVING US A CHANCE TO GET BACK ON OUR FEET!
SO MAKE IT *COUNT!*
ALL UNITS IN PLACE AND READY—
FIRE!
BOOM!
krazzzk!
BLAM!
YIII!
CRASH!
HUH. *THAT* SEEMS A BIT TOO *EASY*...
SOMETIMES THINGS *ARE* EASY!
MUH. GREEN GIRL RIGHT.
THAT NOT ENOUGH TO KILL *TRAIN.*
NICE SHOOTING, THOUGH.

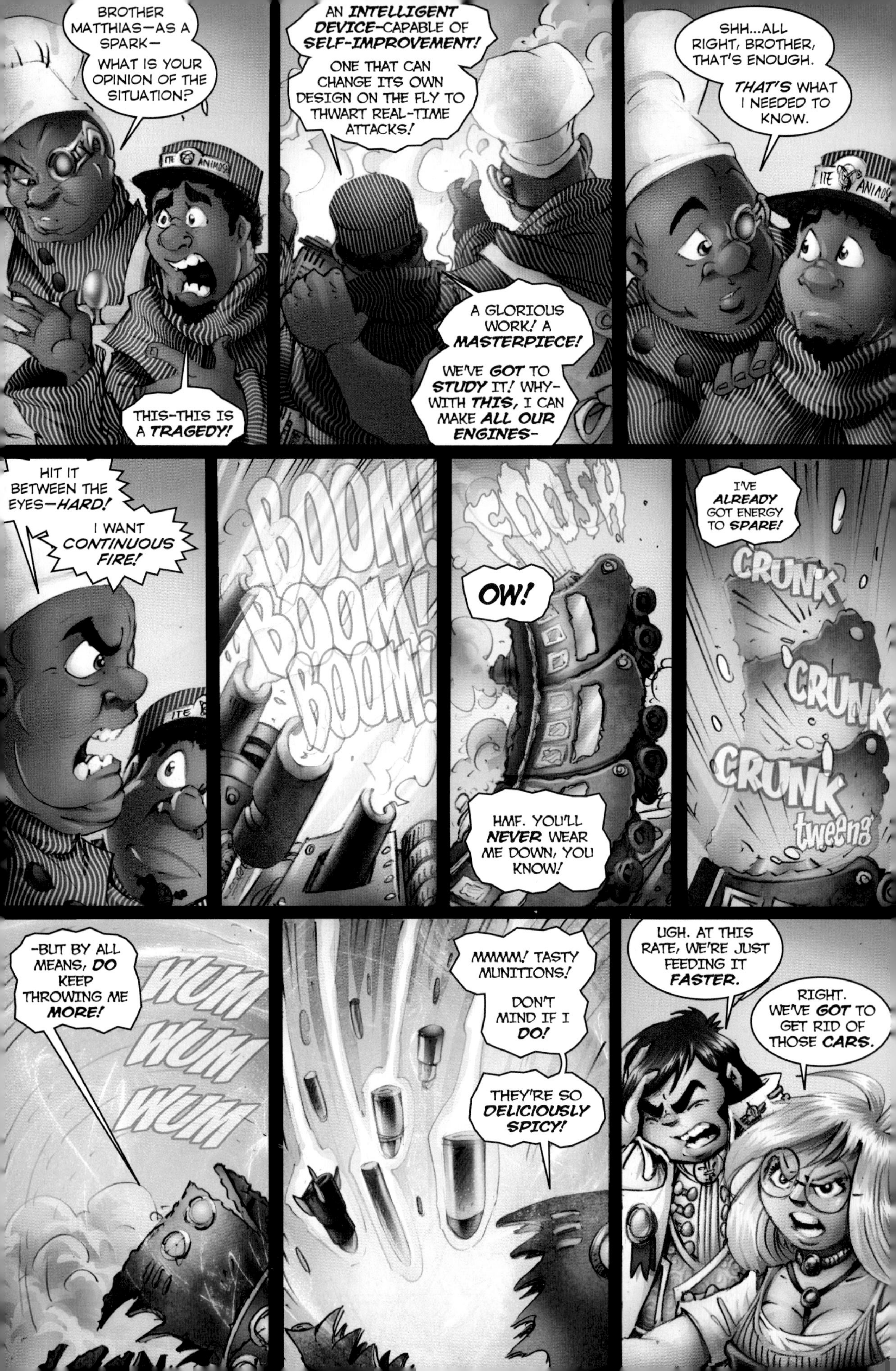

BROTHER MATTHIAS—AS A SPARK—
WHAT IS YOUR OPINION OF THE SITUATION?
THIS-THIS IS A TRAGEDY!
AN INTELLIGENT DEVICE-CAPABLE OF SELF-IMPROVEMENT!
ONE THAT CAN CHANGE ITS OWN DESIGN ON THE FLY TO THWART REAL-TIME ATTACKS!
A GLORIOUS WORK! A MASTERPIECE!
WE'VE GOT TO STUDY IT! WHY-WITH THIS, I CAN MAKE ALL OUR ENGINES-
SHH...ALL RIGHT, BROTHER, THAT'S ENOUGH.
THAT'S WHAT I NEEDED TO KNOW.
HIT IT BETWEEN THE EYES—HARD!
I WANT CONTINUOUS FIRE!
BOOM! BOOM! BOOM!
OW!
HMF. YOU'LL NEVER WEAR ME DOWN, YOU KNOW!
I'VE ALREADY GOT ENERGY TO SPARE!
CRUNK
CRUNK
CRUNK
tweeng
-BUT BY ALL MEANS, DO KEEP THROWING ME MORE!
WUM WUM WUM WUM
MMMM! TASTY MUNITIONS!
DON'T MIND IF I DO!
THEY'RE SO DELICIOUSLY SPICY!
UGH. AT THIS RATE, WE'RE JUST FEEDING IT FASTER.
RIGHT. WE'VE GOT TO GET RID OF THOSE CARS.

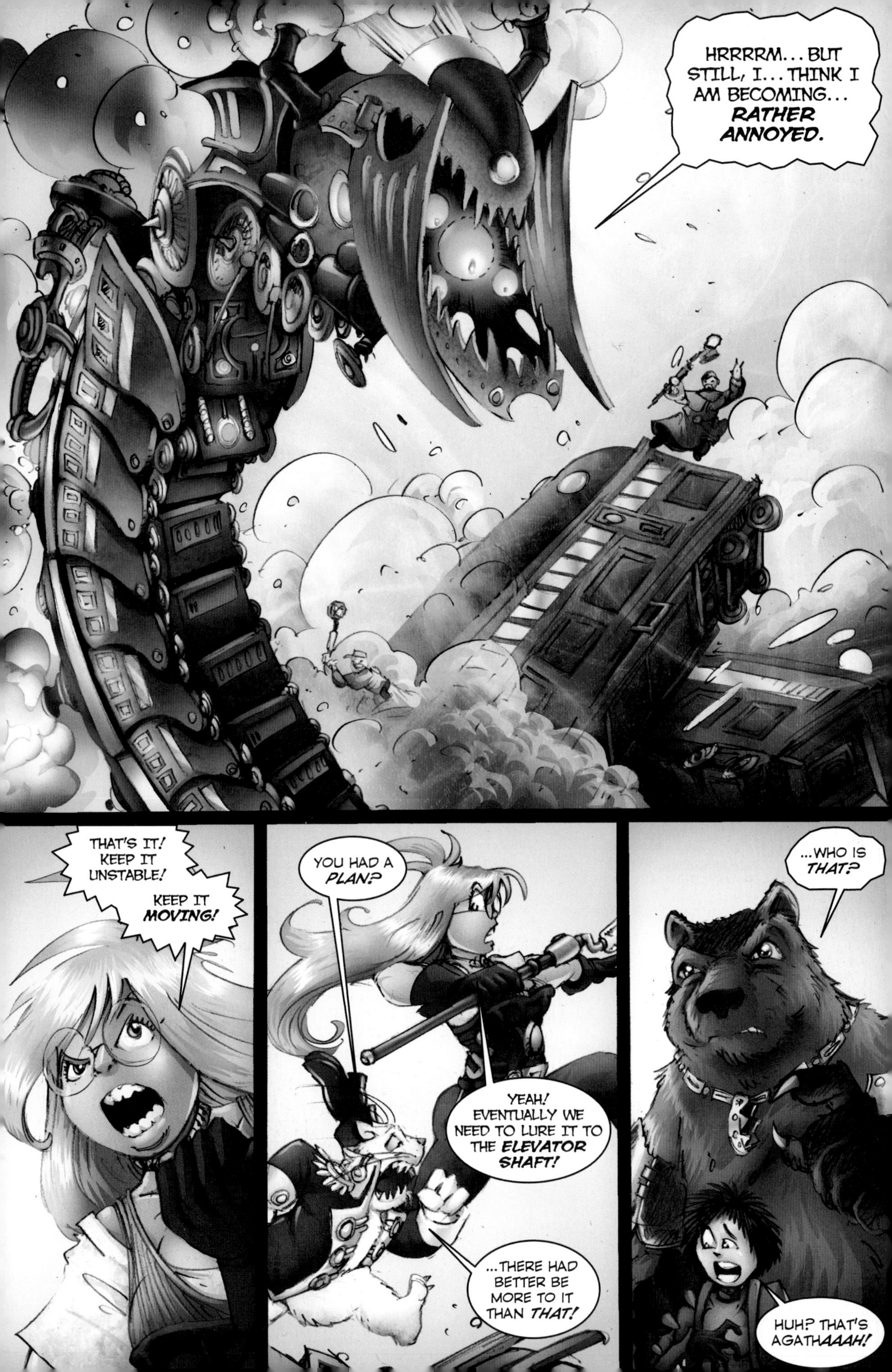
HRRRRM... BUT STILL, I... THINK I AM BECOMING... RATHER ANNOYED.
THAT'S IT! KEEP IT UNSTABLE!
KEEP IT MOVING!
YOU HAD A PLAN?
YEAH! EVENTUALLY WE NEED TO LURE IT TO THE ELEVATOR SHAFT!
...THERE HAD BETTER BE MORE TO IT THAN THAT!
...WHO IS THAT?
HUH? THAT'S AGATHAAAH!

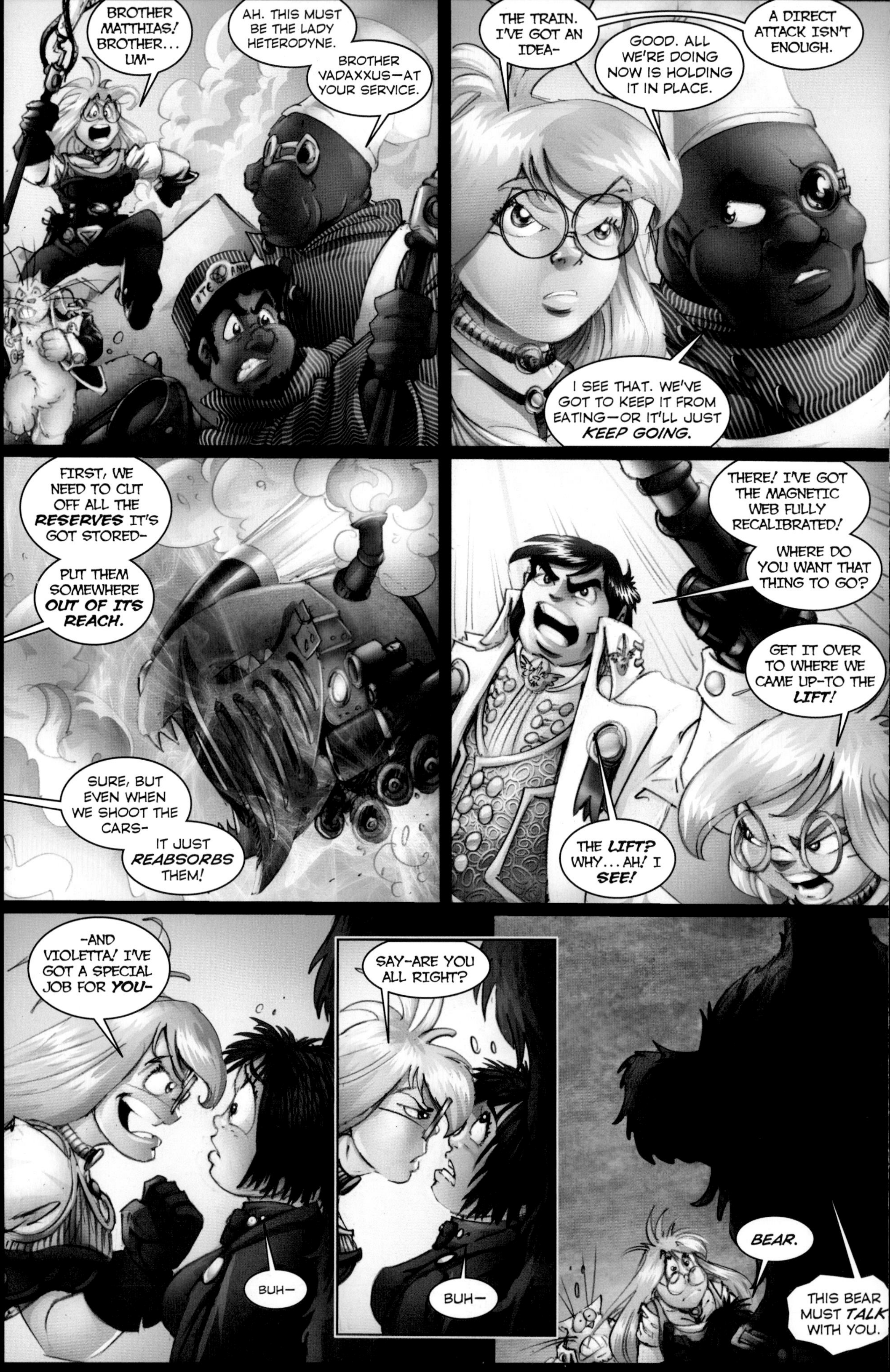
BROTHER MATTHIAS! BROTHER... UM-
AH. THIS MUST BE THE LADY HETERODYNE.
BROTHER VADAXXUS—AT YOUR SERVICE.
THE TRAIN. I'VE GOT AN IDEA-
A DIRECT ATTACK ISN'T ENOUGH.
GOOD. ALL WE'RE DOING NOW IS HOLDING IT IN PLACE.
I SEE THAT. WE'VE GOT TO KEEP IT FROM EATING—OR IT'LL JUST *KEEP GOING.*
FIRST, WE NEED TO CUT OFF ALL THE *RESERVES* IT'S GOT STORED-
PUT THEM SOMEWHERE *OUT OF ITS REACH.*
SURE, BUT EVEN WHEN WE SHOOT THE CARS-
IT JUST *REABSORBS* THEM!
THERE! I'VE GOT THE MAGNETIC WEB FULLY RECALIBRATED!
WHERE DO YOU WANT THAT THING TO GO?
GET IT OVER TO WHERE WE CAME UP-TO THE *LIFT!*
THE *LIFT?* WHY... AH! I *SEE!*
-AND VIOLETTA! I'VE GOT A SPECIAL JOB FOR *YOU-*
BUH—
SAY-ARE YOU ALL RIGHT?
BUH—
BEAR.
THIS BEAR MUST *TALK* WITH YOU.

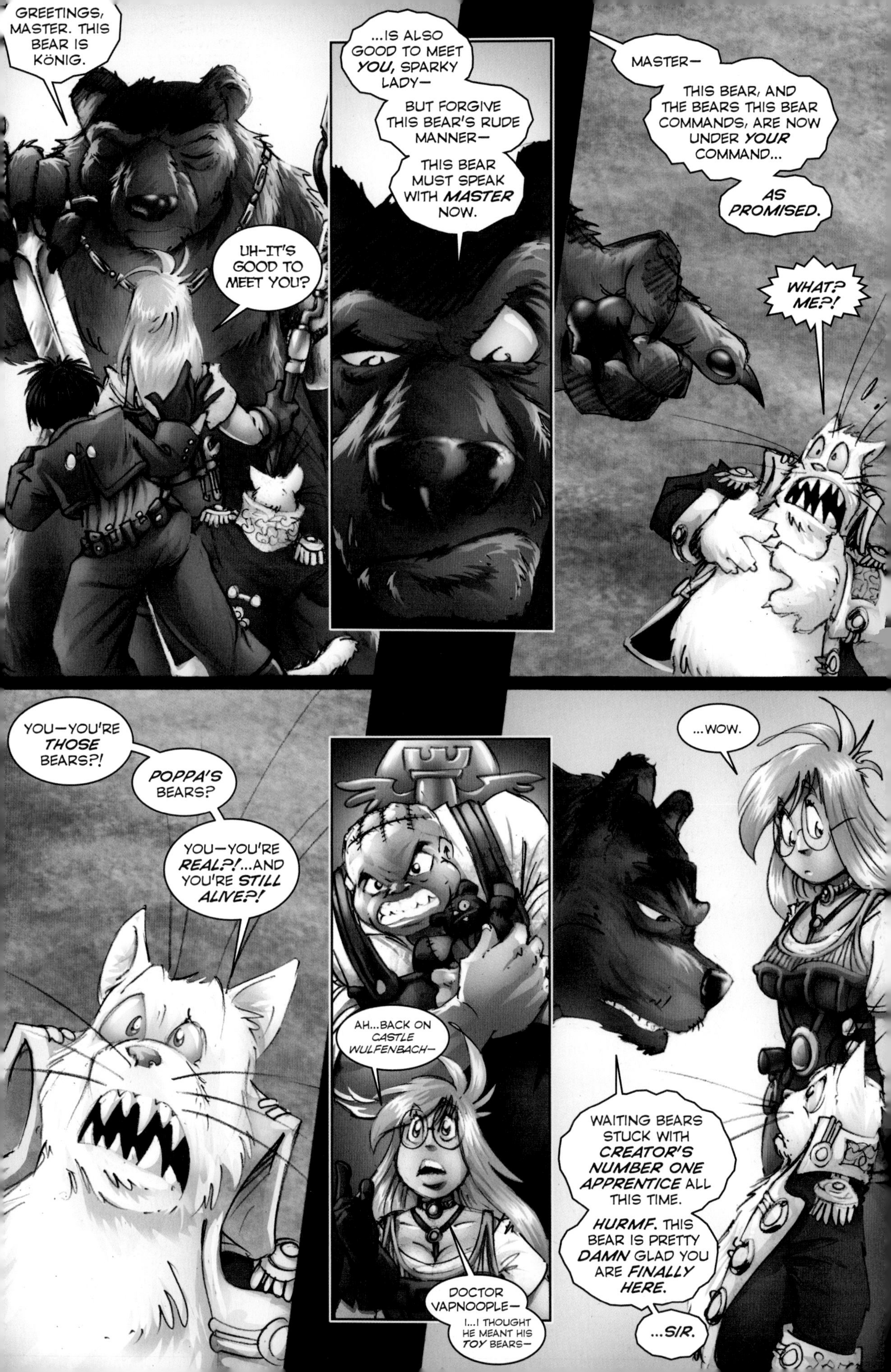
GREETINGS, MASTER. THIS BEAR IS KÖNIG.
UH-IT'S GOOD TO MEET YOU?
...IS ALSO GOOD TO MEET YOU, SPARKY LADY—
BUT FORGIVE THIS BEAR'S RUDE MANNER—
THIS BEAR MUST SPEAK WITH MASTER NOW.
MASTER—
THIS BEAR, AND THE BEARS THIS BEAR COMMANDS, ARE NOW UNDER YOUR COMMAND...
AS PROMISED.
WHAT? ME?!
YOU—YOU'RE THOSE BEARS?!
POPPA'S BEARS?
YOU—YOU'RE REAL?!...AND YOU'RE STILL ALIVE?!
AH...BACK ON CASTLE WULFENBACH—
DOCTOR VAPNOOPLE—
I...I THOUGHT HE MEANT HIS TOY BEARS—
...WOW.
WAITING BEARS STUCK WITH CREATOR'S NUMBER ONE APPRENTICE ALL THIS TIME.
HURMF. THIS BEAR IS PRETTY DAMN GLAD YOU ARE FINALLY HERE.
...SIR.

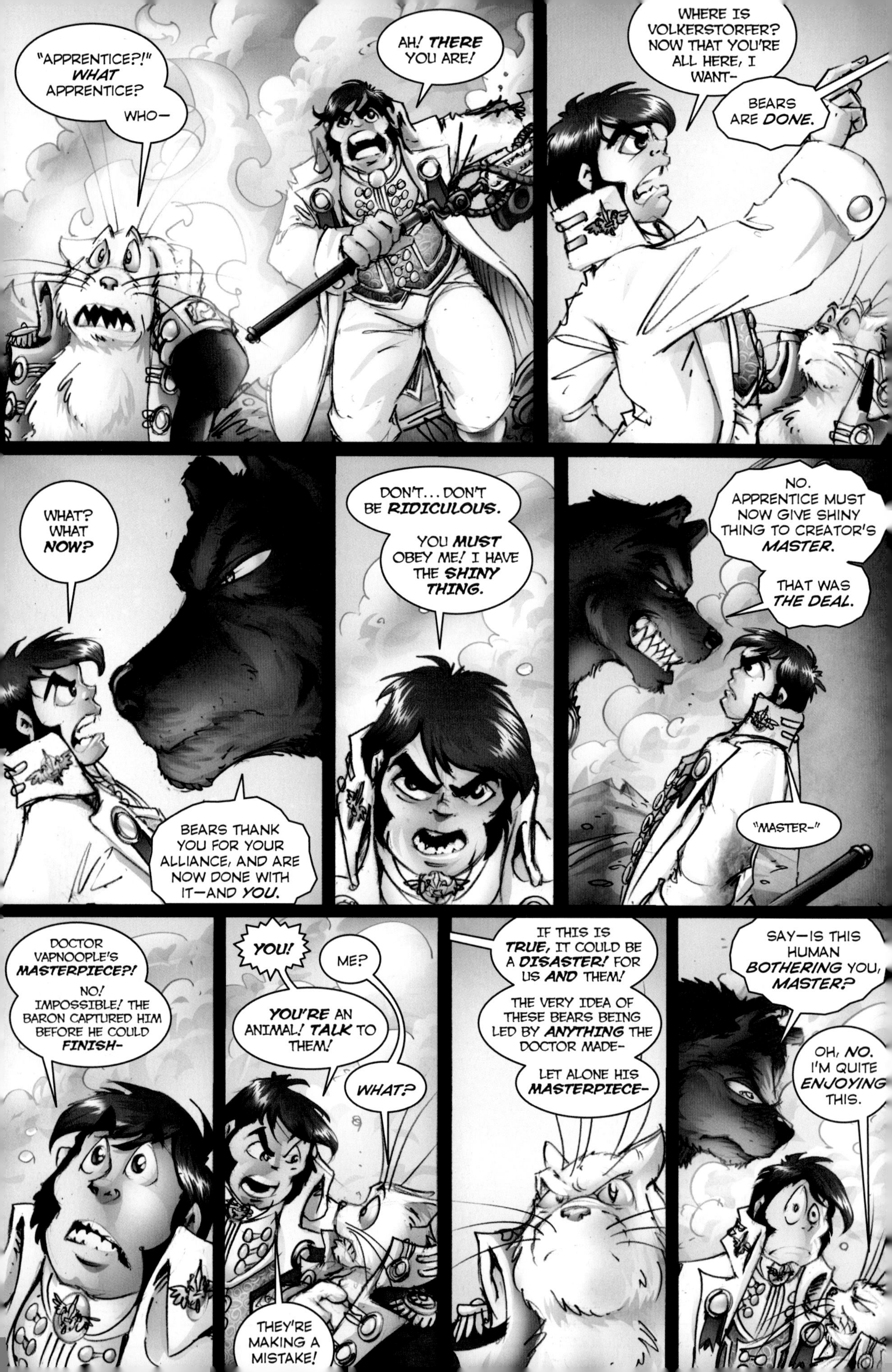
"APPRENTICE?!" WHAT APPRENTICE?
WHO—
AH! THERE YOU ARE!
WHERE IS VOLKERSTORFER? NOW THAT YOU'RE ALL HERE, I WANT-
BEARS ARE DONE.
WHAT? WHAT NOW?
BEARS THANK YOU FOR YOUR ALLIANCE, AND ARE NOW DONE WITH IT—AND YOU.
DON'T... DON'T BE RIDICULOUS.
YOU MUST OBEY ME! I HAVE THE SHINY THING.
NO. APPRENTICE MUST NOW GIVE SHINY THING TO CREATOR'S MASTER.
THAT WAS THE DEAL.
"MASTER-"
DOCTOR VAPNOOPLE'S MASTERPIECE?!
NO! IMPOSSIBLE! THE BARON CAPTURED HIM BEFORE HE COULD FINISH-
YOU!
ME?
YOU'RE AN ANIMAL! TALK TO THEM!
WHAT?
THEY'RE MAKING A MISTAKE!
IF THIS IS TRUE, IT COULD BE A DISASTER! FOR US AND THEM!
THE VERY IDEA OF THESE BEARS BEING LED BY ANYTHING THE DOCTOR MADE-
LET ALONE HIS MASTERPIECE-
SAY—IS THIS HUMAN BOTHERING YOU, MASTER?
OH, NO. I'M QUITE ENJOYING THIS.

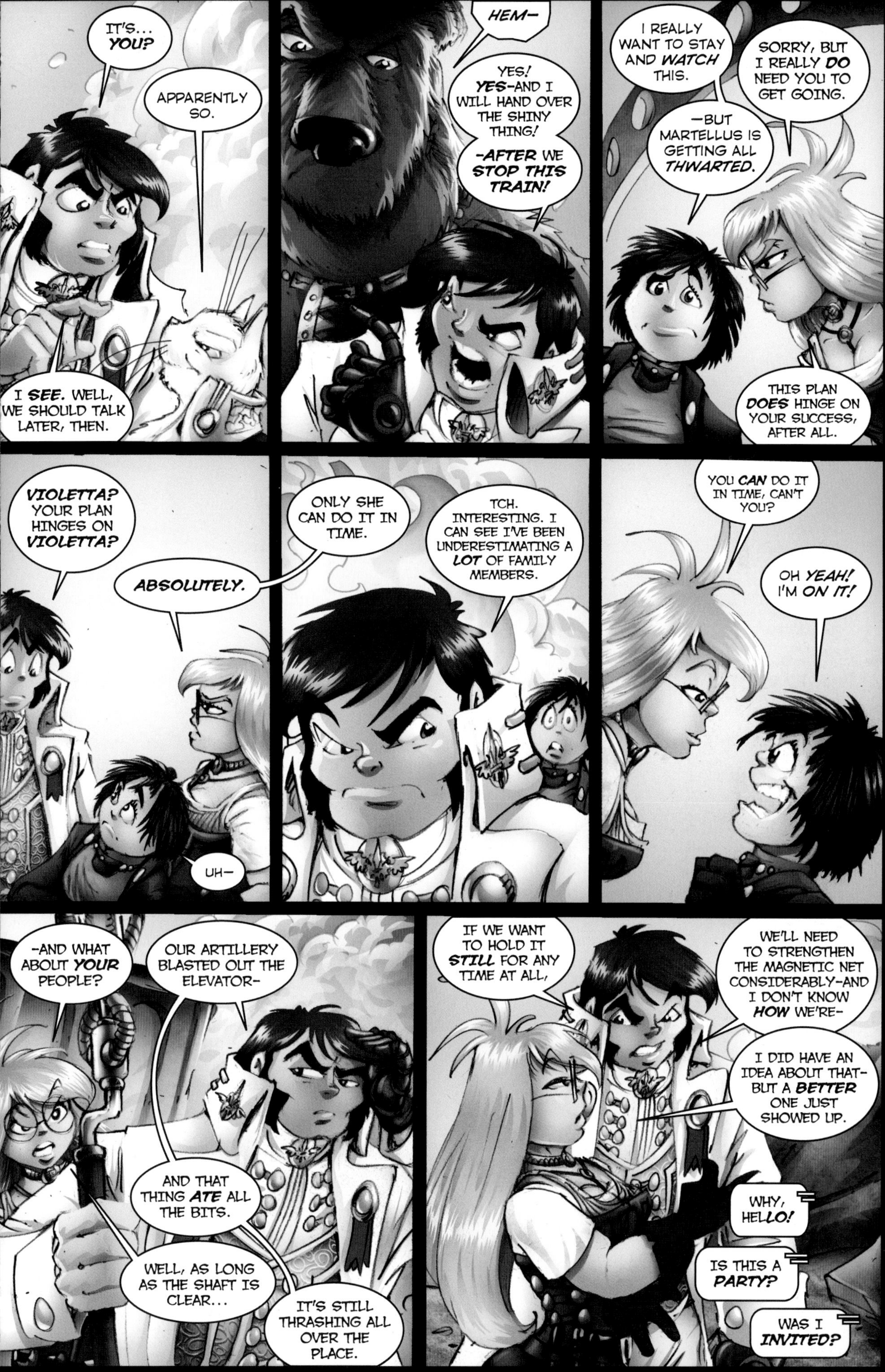
IT'S... YOU?
APPARENTLY SO.
I SEE. WELL, WE SHOULD TALK LATER, THEN.
HEM—
YES! YES—AND I WILL HAND OVER THE SHINY THING!
-AFTER WE STOP THIS TRAIN!
I REALLY WANT TO STAY AND WATCH THIS.
—BUT MARTELLUS IS GETTING ALL THWARTED.
SORRY, BUT I REALLY DO NEED YOU TO GET GOING.
THIS PLAN DOES HINGE ON YOUR SUCCESS, AFTER ALL.
VIOLETTA? YOUR PLAN HINGES ON VIOLETTA?
ABSOLUTELY.
UH—
ONLY SHE CAN DO IT IN TIME.
TCH. INTERESTING. I CAN SEE I'VE BEEN UNDERESTIMATING A LOT OF FAMILY MEMBERS.
YOU CAN DO IT IN TIME, CAN'T YOU?
OH YEAH! I'M ON IT!
-AND WHAT ABOUT YOUR PEOPLE?
OUR ARTILLERY BLASTED OUT THE ELEVATOR-
AND THAT THING ATE ALL THE BITS.
WELL, AS LONG AS THE SHAFT IS CLEAR...
IT'S STILL THRASHING ALL OVER THE PLACE.
IF WE WANT TO HOLD IT STILL FOR ANY TIME AT ALL,
WE'LL NEED TO STRENGTHEN THE MAGNETIC NET CONSIDERABLY-AND I DON'T KNOW HOW WE'RE-
I DID HAVE AN IDEA ABOUT THAT-BUT A BETTER ONE JUST SHOWED UP.
WHY, HELLO!
IS THIS A PARTY?
WAS I INVITED?

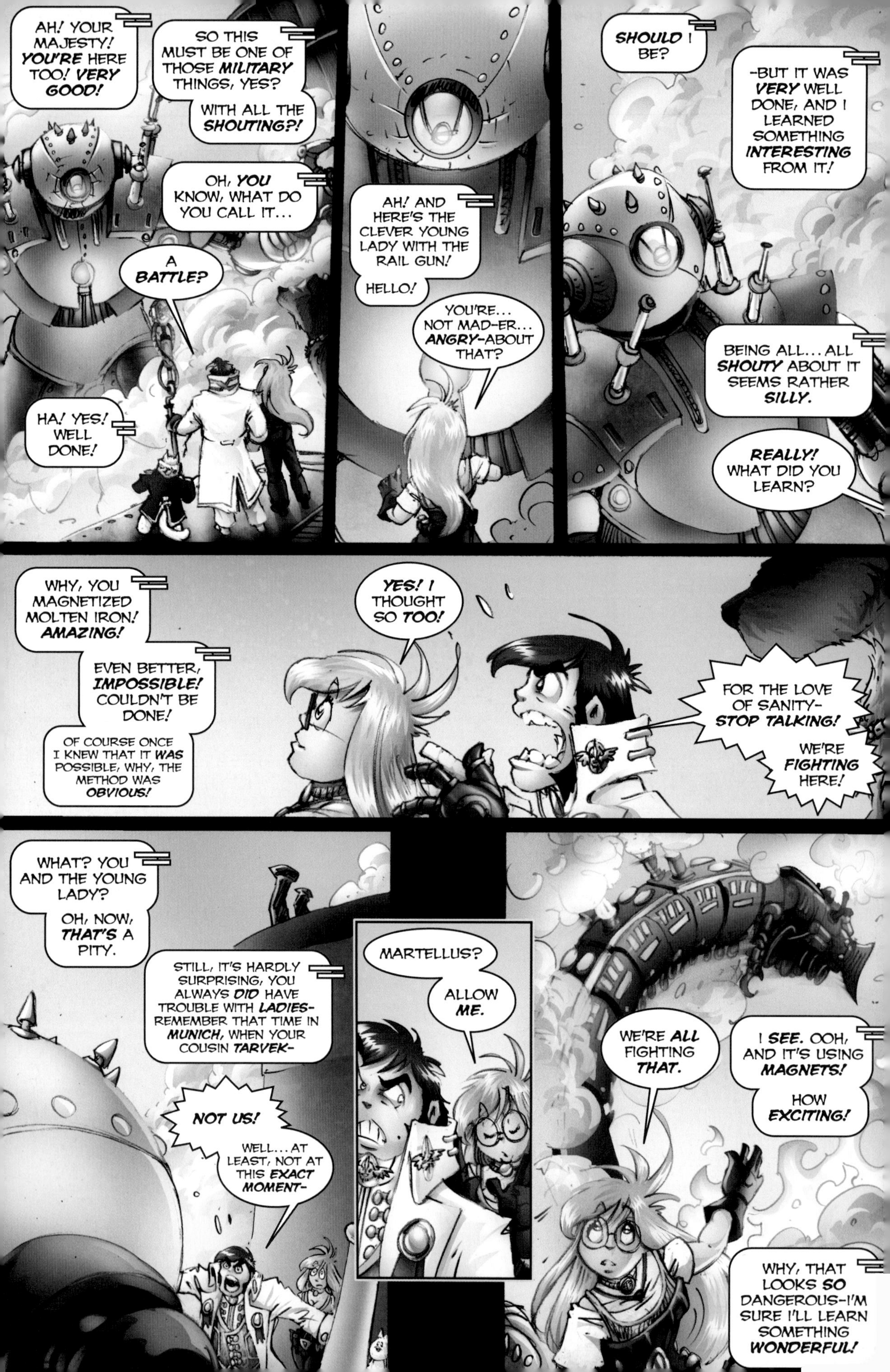
AH! YOUR MAJESTY! YOU'RE HERE TOO! VERY GOOD!
SO THIS MUST BE ONE OF THOSE MILITARY THINGS, YES?
WITH ALL THE SHOUTING?!
OH, YOU KNOW, WHAT DO YOU CALL IT...
A BATTLE?
HA! YES! WELL DONE!
AH! AND HERE'S THE CLEVER YOUNG LADY WITH THE RAIL GUN!
HELLO!
YOU'RE... NOT MAD-ER... ANGRY-ABOUT THAT?
SHOULD I BE?
-BUT IT WAS VERY WELL DONE, AND I LEARNED SOMETHING INTERESTING FROM IT!
BEING ALL... ALL SHOUTY ABOUT IT SEEMS RATHER SILLY.
REALLY! WHAT DID YOU LEARN?
WHY, YOU MAGNETIZED MOLTEN IRON! AMAZING!
EVEN BETTER, IMPOSSIBLE! COULDN'T BE DONE!
OF COURSE ONCE I KNEW THAT IT WAS POSSIBLE, WHY, THE METHOD WAS OBVIOUS!
YES! I THOUGHT SO TOO!
FOR THE LOVE OF SANITY- STOP TALKING!
WE'RE FIGHTING HERE!
WHAT? YOU AND THE YOUNG LADY?
OH, NOW, THAT'S A PITY.
STILL, IT'S HARDLY SURPRISING, YOU ALWAYS DID HAVE TROUBLE WITH LADIES- REMEMBER THAT TIME IN MUNICH, WHEN YOUR COUSIN TARVEK-
NOT US!
WELL... AT LEAST, NOT AT THIS EXACT MOMENT-
MARTELLUS?
ALLOW ME.
WE'RE ALL FIGHTING THAT.
I SEE. OOH, AND IT'S USING MAGNETS!
HOW EXCITING!
WHY, THAT LOOKS SO DANGEROUS-I'M SURE I'LL LEARN SOMETHING WONDERFUL!

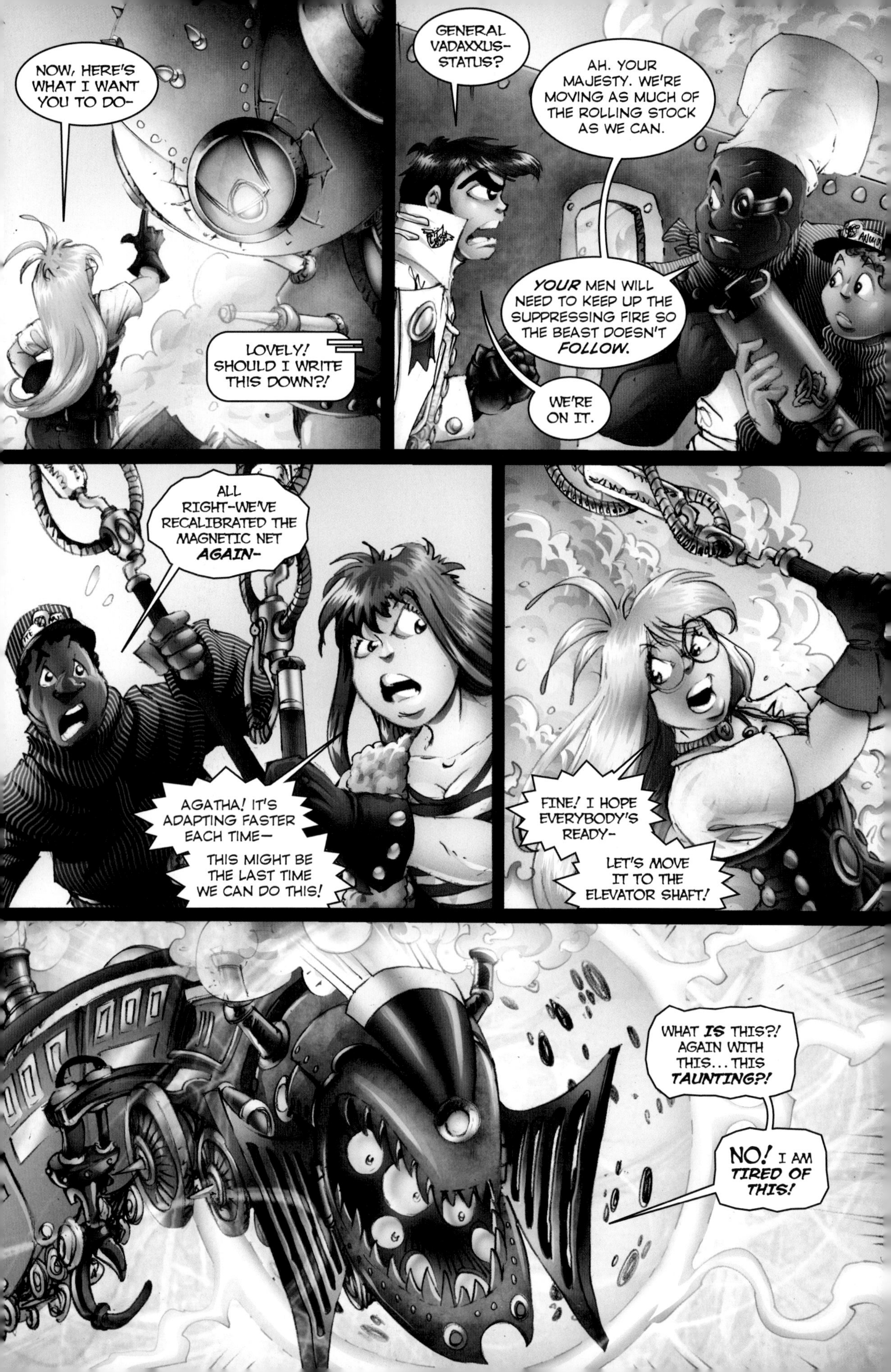
NOW, HERE'S WHAT I WANT YOU TO DO-
LOVELY! SHOULD I WRITE THIS DOWN?!
GENERAL VADAXXUS-STATUS?
AH. YOUR MAJESTY. WE'RE MOVING AS MUCH OF THE ROLLING STOCK AS WE CAN.
YOUR MEN WILL NEED TO KEEP UP THE SUPPRESSING FIRE SO THE BEAST DOESN'T FOLLOW.
WE'RE ON IT.
ALL RIGHT-WE'VE RECALIBRATED THE MAGNETIC NET AGAIN-
AGATHA! IT'S ADAPTING FASTER EACH TIME—
THIS MIGHT BE THE LAST TIME WE CAN DO THIS!
FINE! I HOPE EVERYBODY'S READY-
LET'S MOVE IT TO THE ELEVATOR SHAFT!
WHAT IS THIS?! AGAIN WITH THIS... THIS TAUNTING?!
NO! I AM TIRED OF THIS!

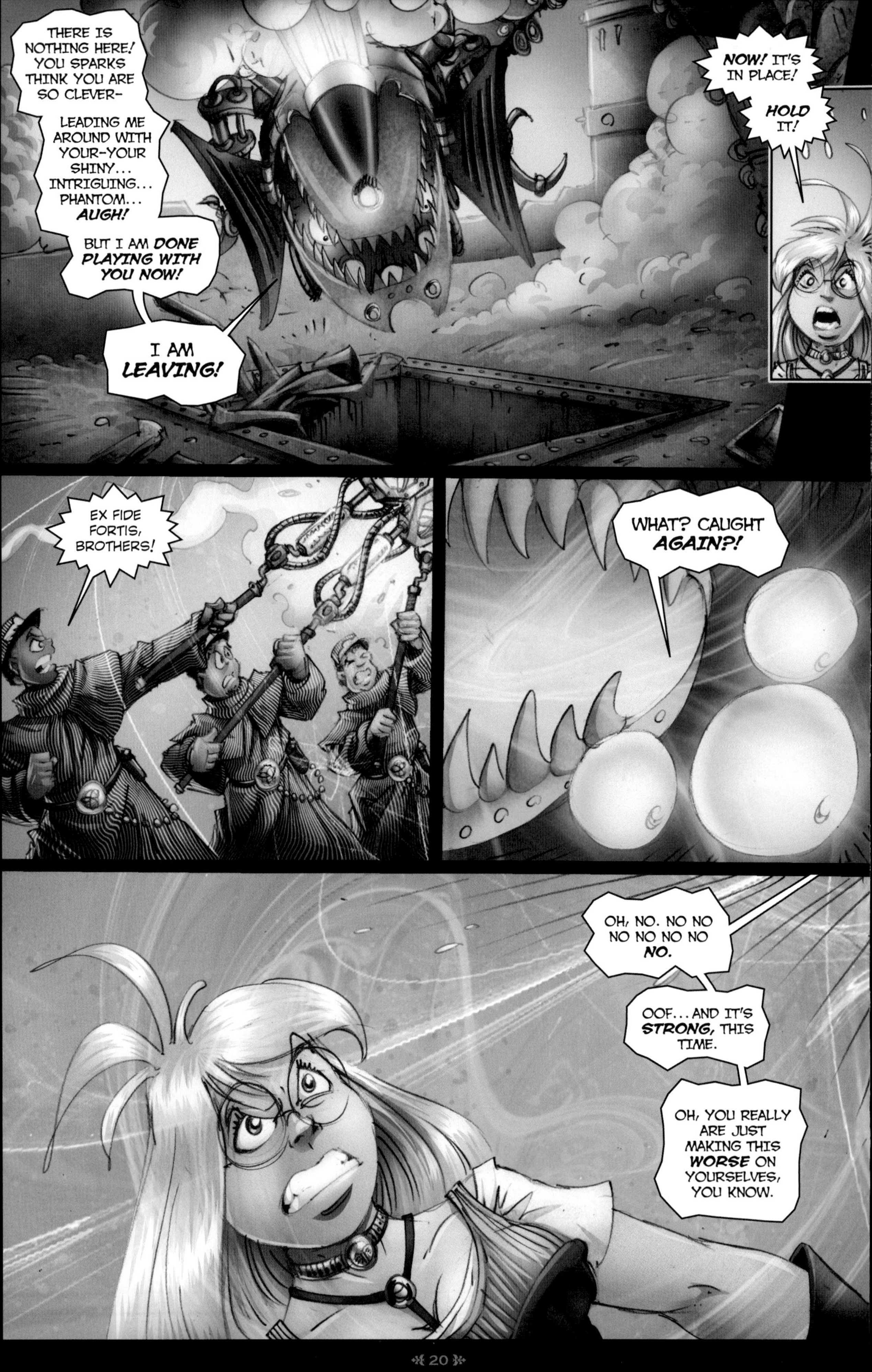
THERE IS NOTHING HERE! YOU SPARKS THINK YOU ARE SO CLEVER-
LEADING ME AROUND WITH YOUR-YOUR SHINY... INTRIGUING... PHANTOM... AUGH!
BUT I AM DONE PLAYING WITH YOU NOW!
I AM LEAVING!
NOW! IT'S IN PLACE!
HOLD IT!
EX FIDE FORTIS, BROTHERS!
WHAT? CAUGHT AGAIN?!
OH, NO. NO NO NO NO NO NO NO.
OOF... AND IT'S STRONG, THIS TIME.
OH, YOU REALLY ARE JUST MAKING THIS WORSE ON YOURSELVES, YOU KNOW.

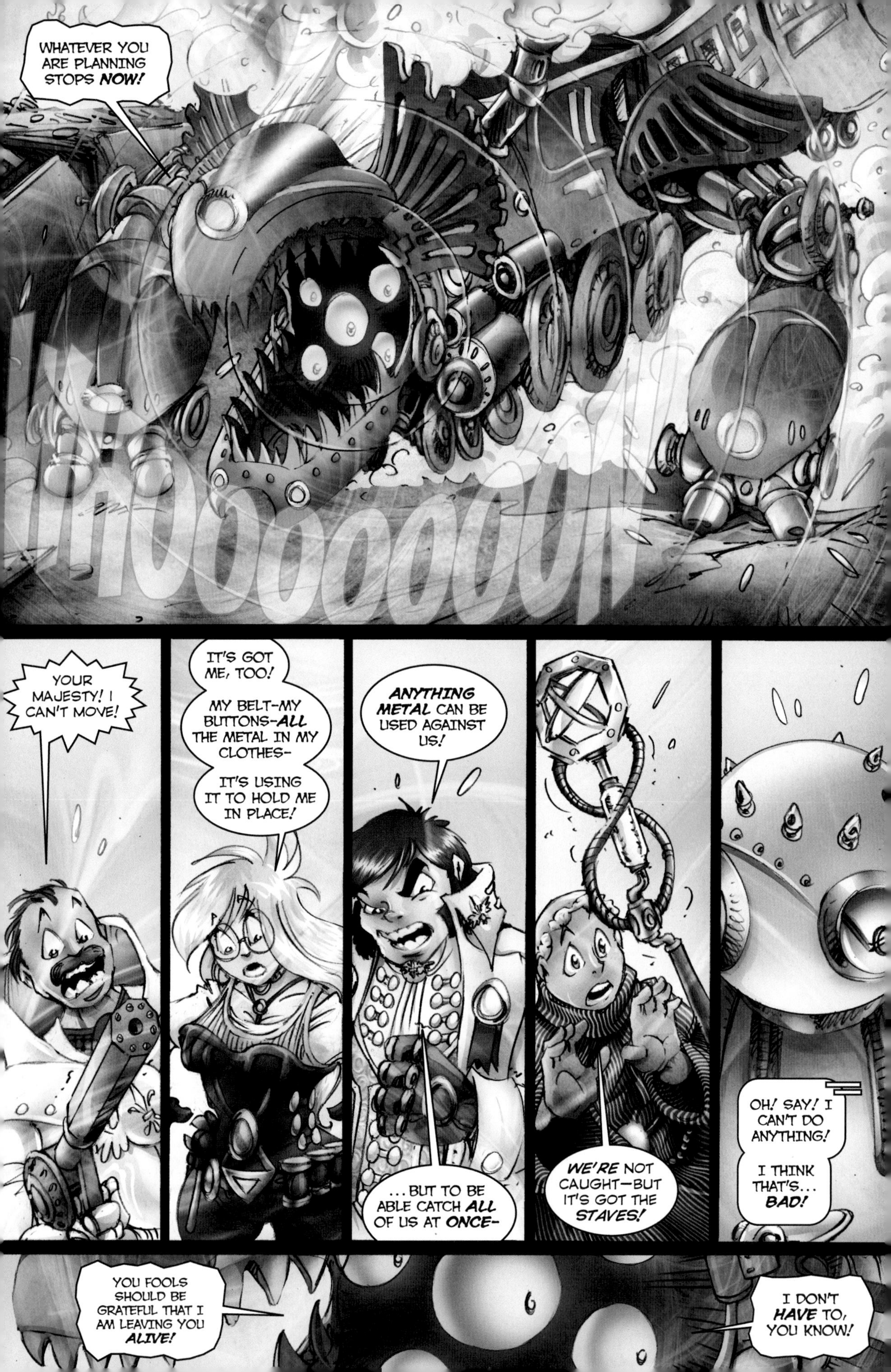
WHATEVER YOU ARE PLANNING STOPS NOW!
YOUR MAJESTY! I CAN'T MOVE!
IT'S GOT ME, TOO!
MY BELT–MY BUTTONS–ALL THE METAL IN MY CLOTHES–
IT'S USING IT TO HOLD ME IN PLACE!
ANYTHING METAL CAN BE USED AGAINST US!
...BUT TO BE ABLE CATCH ALL OF US AT ONCE-
WE'RE NOT CAUGHT—BUT IT'S GOT THE STAVES!
OH! SAY! I CAN'T DO ANYTHING!
I THINK THAT'S... BAD!
YOU FOOLS SHOULD BE GRATEFUL THAT I AM LEAVING YOU ALIVE!
I DON'T HAVE TO, YOU KNOW!

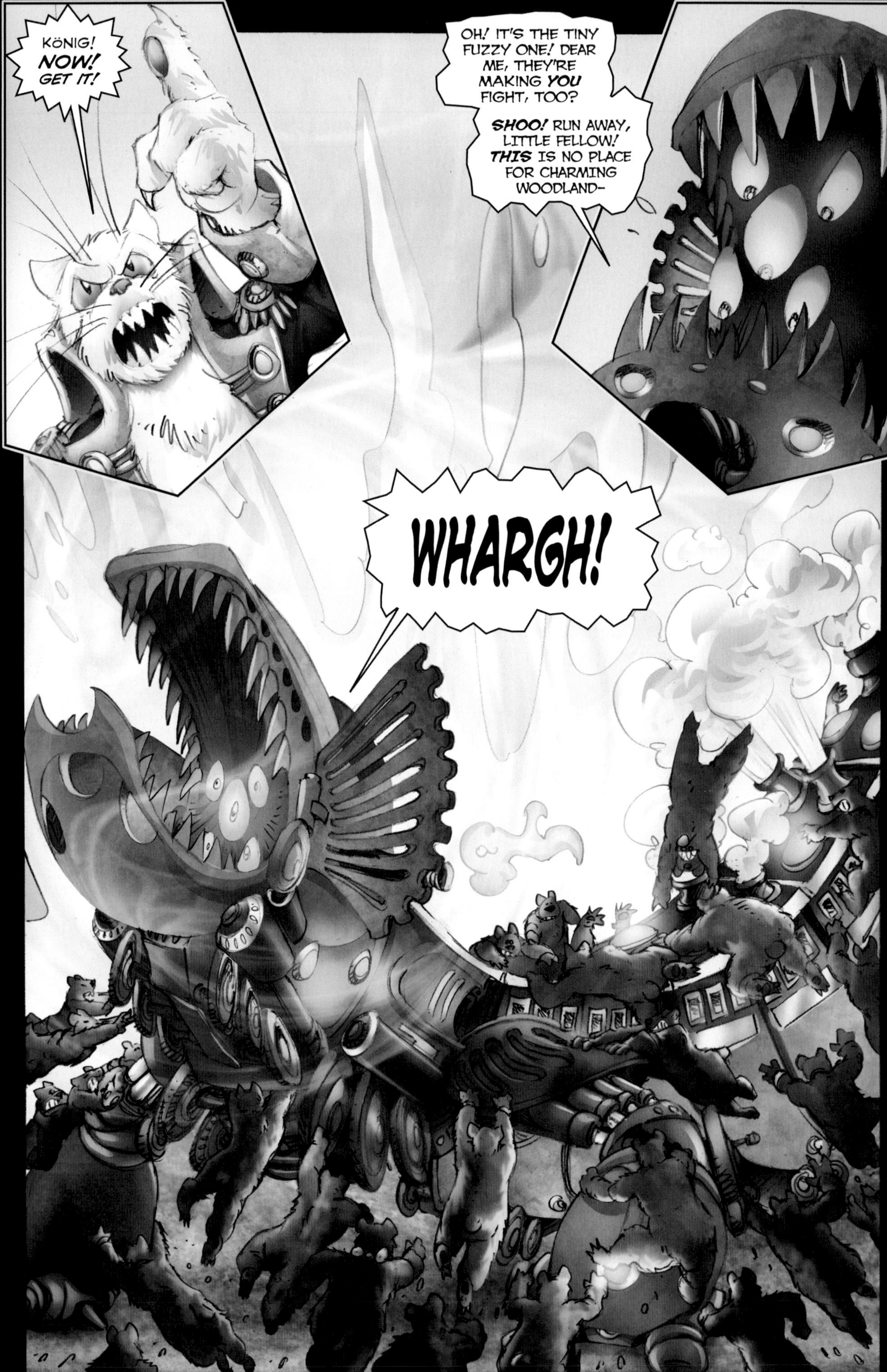
KÖNIG! NOW! GET IT!
OH! IT'S THE TINY FUZZY ONE! DEAR ME, THEY'RE MAKING YOU FIGHT, TOO?
SHOO! RUN AWAY, LITTLE FELLOW! THIS IS NO PLACE FOR CHARMING WOODLAND-
WHARGH!

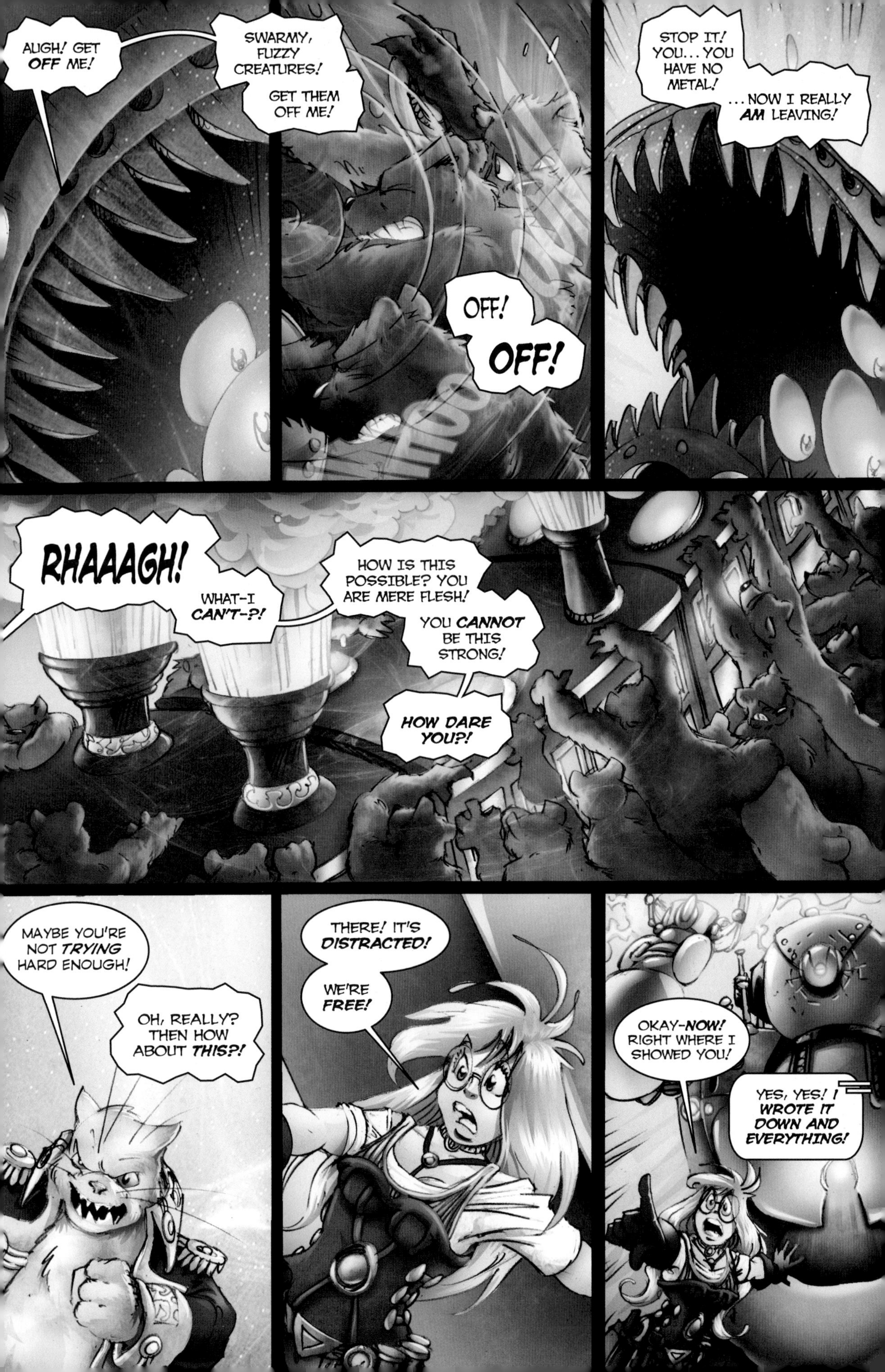

AUGH! GET OFF ME!
SWARMY, FUZZY CREATURES!
GET THEM OFF ME!
OFF!
OFF!
STOP IT! YOU... YOU HAVE NO METAL!
...NOW I REALLY AM LEAVING!
RHAAAGH!
WHAT-I CAN'T-?!
HOW IS THIS POSSIBLE? YOU ARE MERE FLESH!
YOU CANNOT BE THIS STRONG!
HOW DARE YOU?!
MAYBE YOU'RE NOT TRYING HARD ENOUGH!
OH, REALLY? THEN HOW ABOUT THIS?!
THERE! IT'S DISTRACTED!
WE'RE FREE!
OKAY-NOW! RIGHT WHERE I SHOWED YOU!
YES, YES! I WROTE IT DOWN AND EVERYTHING!

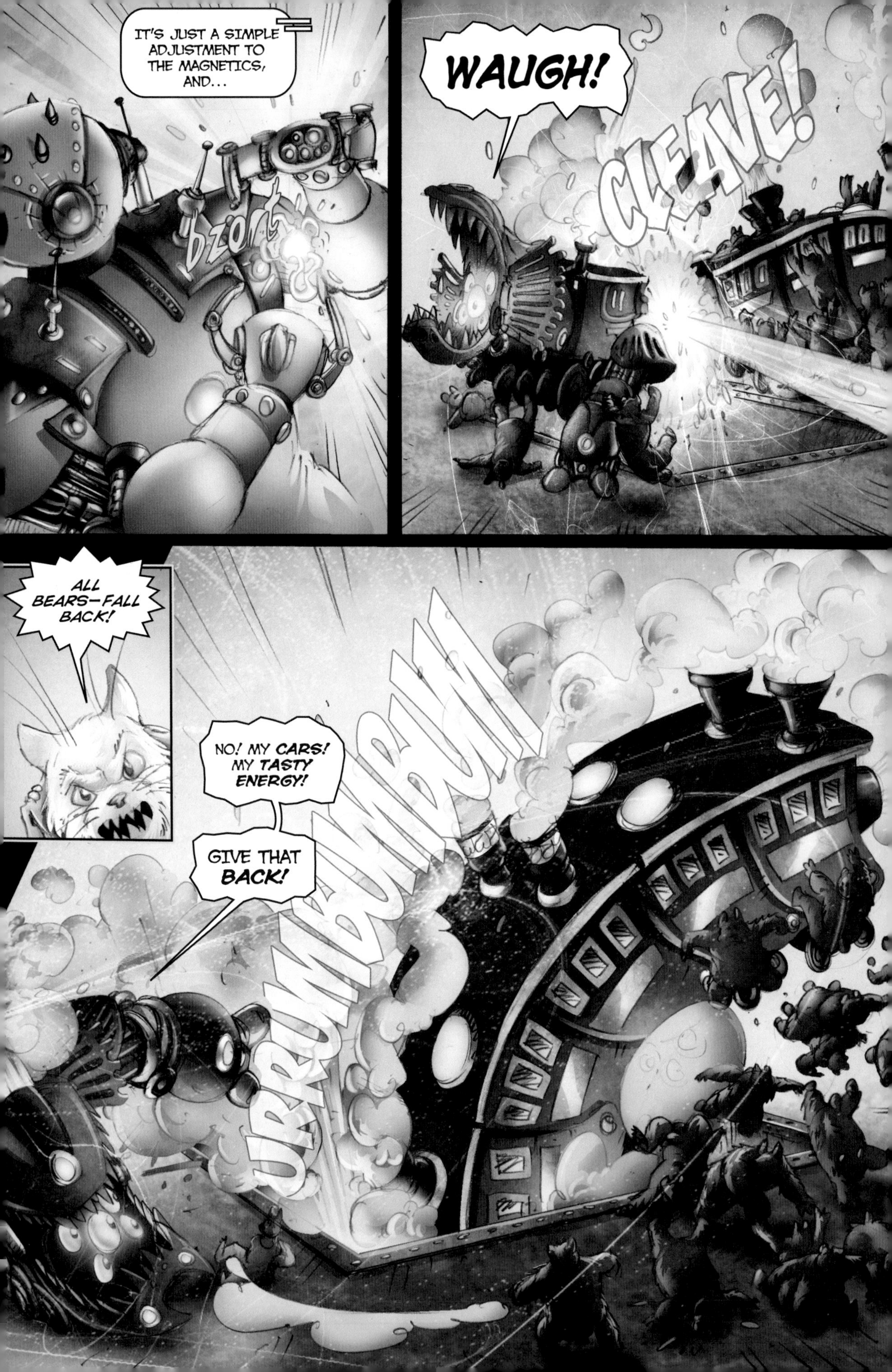
IT'S JUST A SIMPLE ADJUSTMENT TO THE MAGNETICS, AND...
bzort
WAUGH!
CLEAVE!
ALL BEARS—FALL BACK!
NO! MY CARS! MY TASTY ENERGY!
GIVE THAT BACK!
URRUMBRUMBRUM

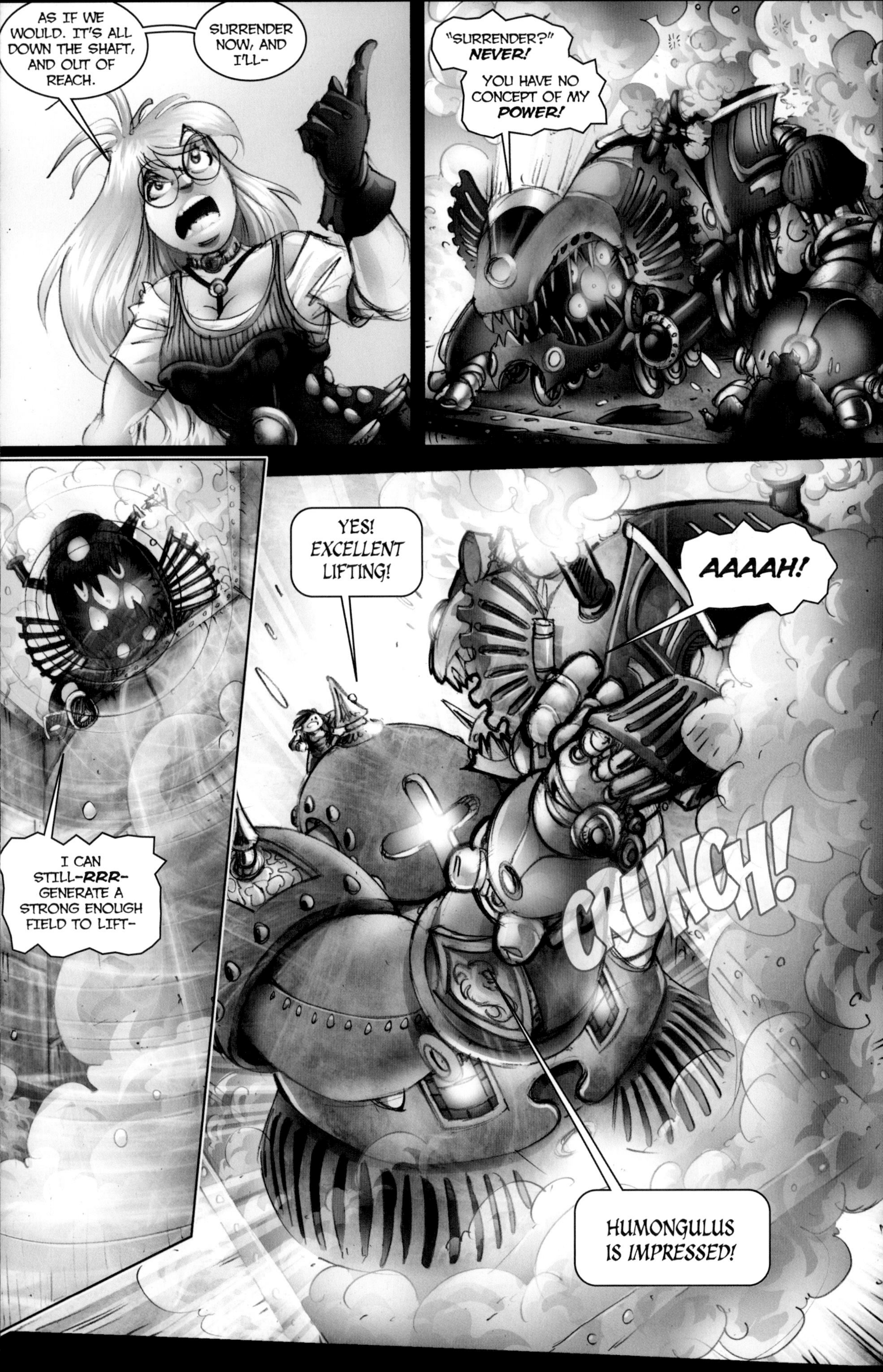
SURRENDER NOW, AND I'LL-
AS IF WE WOULD. IT'S ALL DOWN THE SHAFT, AND OUT OF REACH.
"SURRENDER?" NEVER!
YOU HAVE NO CONCEPT OF MY POWER!
I CAN STILL-RRR- GENERATE A STRONG ENOUGH FIELD TO LIFT-
YES! EXCELLENT LIFTING!
AAAAH!
CRUNCH!
HUMONGULUS IS IMPRESSED!

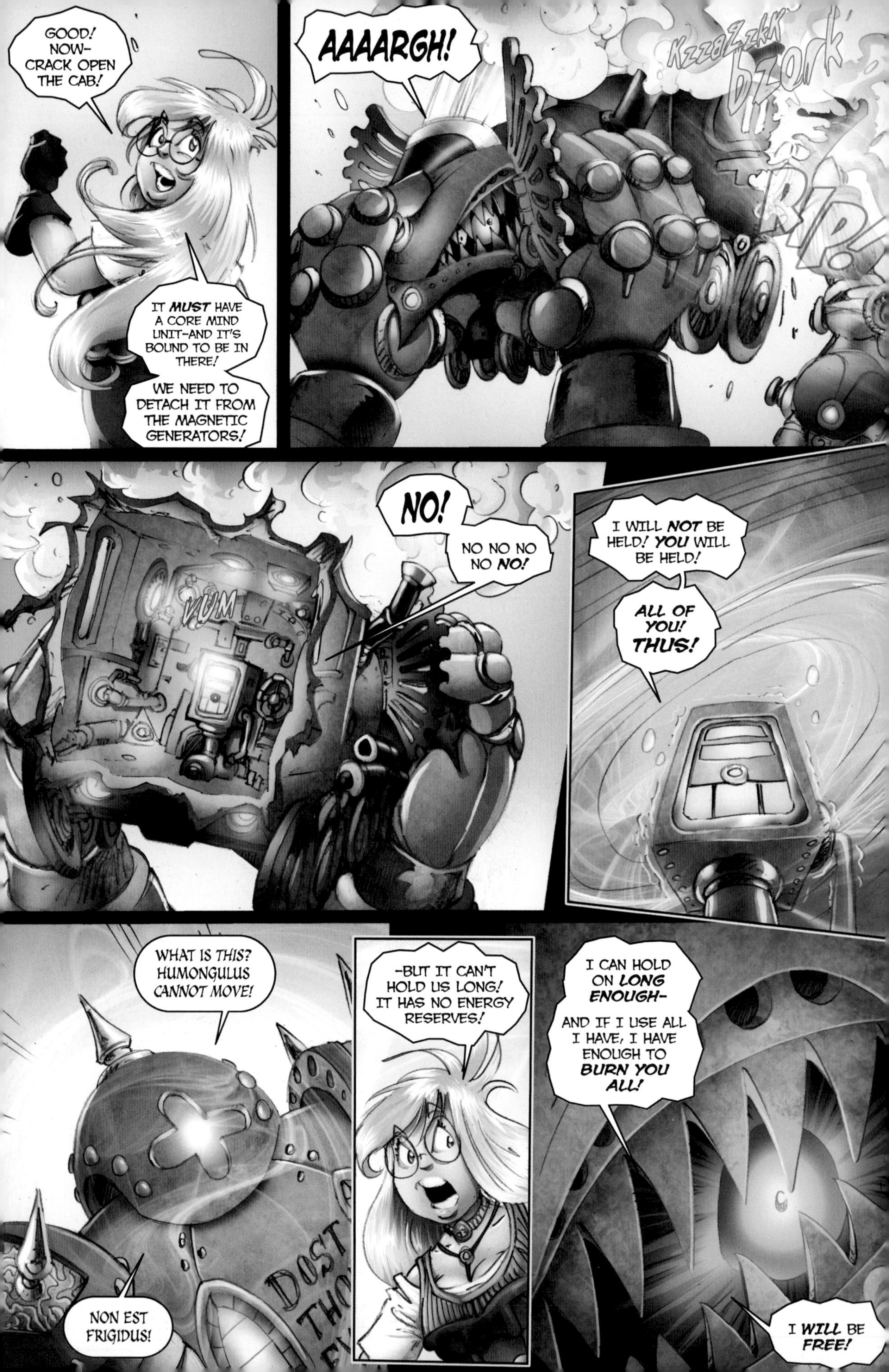
GOOD! NOW— CRACK OPEN THE CAB!
IT **MUST** HAVE A CORE MIND UNIT—AND IT'S BOUND TO BE IN THERE!
WE NEED TO DETACH IT FROM THE MAGNETIC GENERATORS!
AAAARGH!
bzork
RIP!
VUM
NO!
NO NO NO NO **NO!**
I WILL **NOT** BE HELD! **YOU** WILL BE HELD!
ALL OF YOU! THUS!
WHAT IS *THIS?* HUMONGULUS CANNOT MOVE!
NON EST FRIGIDUS!
—BUT IT CAN'T HOLD US LONG! IT HAS NO ENERGY RESERVES!
I CAN HOLD ON **LONG ENOUGH—**
AND IF I USE ALL I HAVE, I HAVE ENOUGH TO **BURN YOU ALL!**
I **WILL** BE **FREE!**

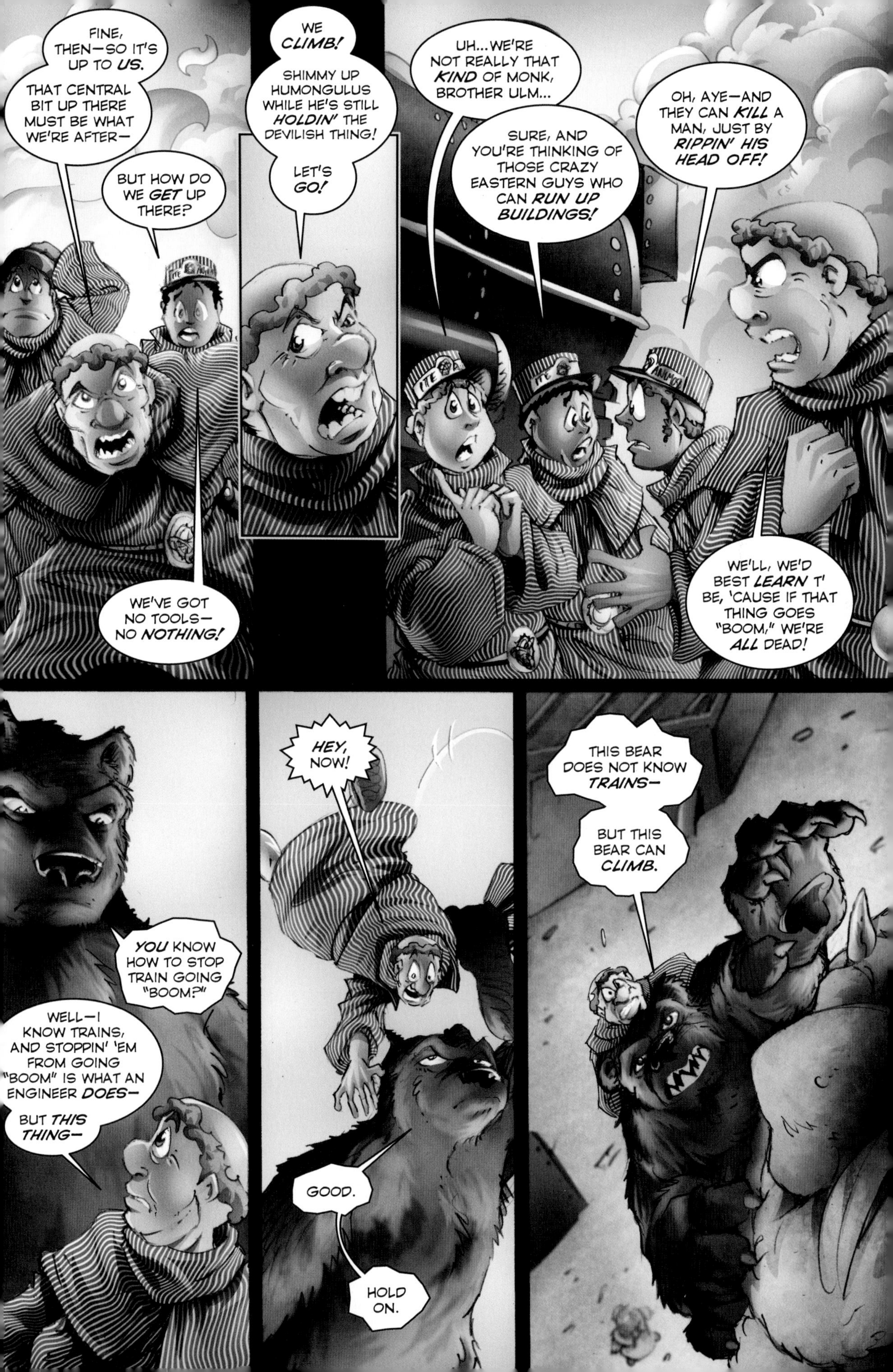
FINE, THEN—SO IT'S UP TO US.
THAT CENTRAL BIT UP THERE MUST BE WHAT WE'RE AFTER—
BUT HOW DO WE GET UP THERE?
WE'VE GOT NO TOOLS— NO NOTHING!
WE CLIMB!
SHIMMY UP HUMONGULUS WHILE HE'S STILL HOLDIN' THE DEVILISH THING!
LET'S GO!
UH...WE'RE NOT REALLY THAT KIND OF MONK, BROTHER ULM...
SURE, AND YOU'RE THINKING OF THOSE CRAZY EASTERN GUYS WHO CAN RUN UP BUILDINGS!
OH, AYE—AND THEY CAN KILL A MAN, JUST BY RIPPIN' HIS HEAD OFF!
WE'LL, WE'D BEST LEARN T' BE, 'CAUSE IF THAT THING GOES "BOOM," WE'RE ALL DEAD!
YOU KNOW HOW TO STOP TRAIN GOING "BOOM?"
WELL—I KNOW TRAINS, AND STOPPIN' 'EM FROM GOING "BOOM" IS WHAT AN ENGINEER DOES—
BUT THIS THING—
HEY, NOW!
GOOD.
HOLD ON.
THIS BEAR DOES NOT KNOW TRAINS—
BUT THIS BEAR CAN CLIMB.

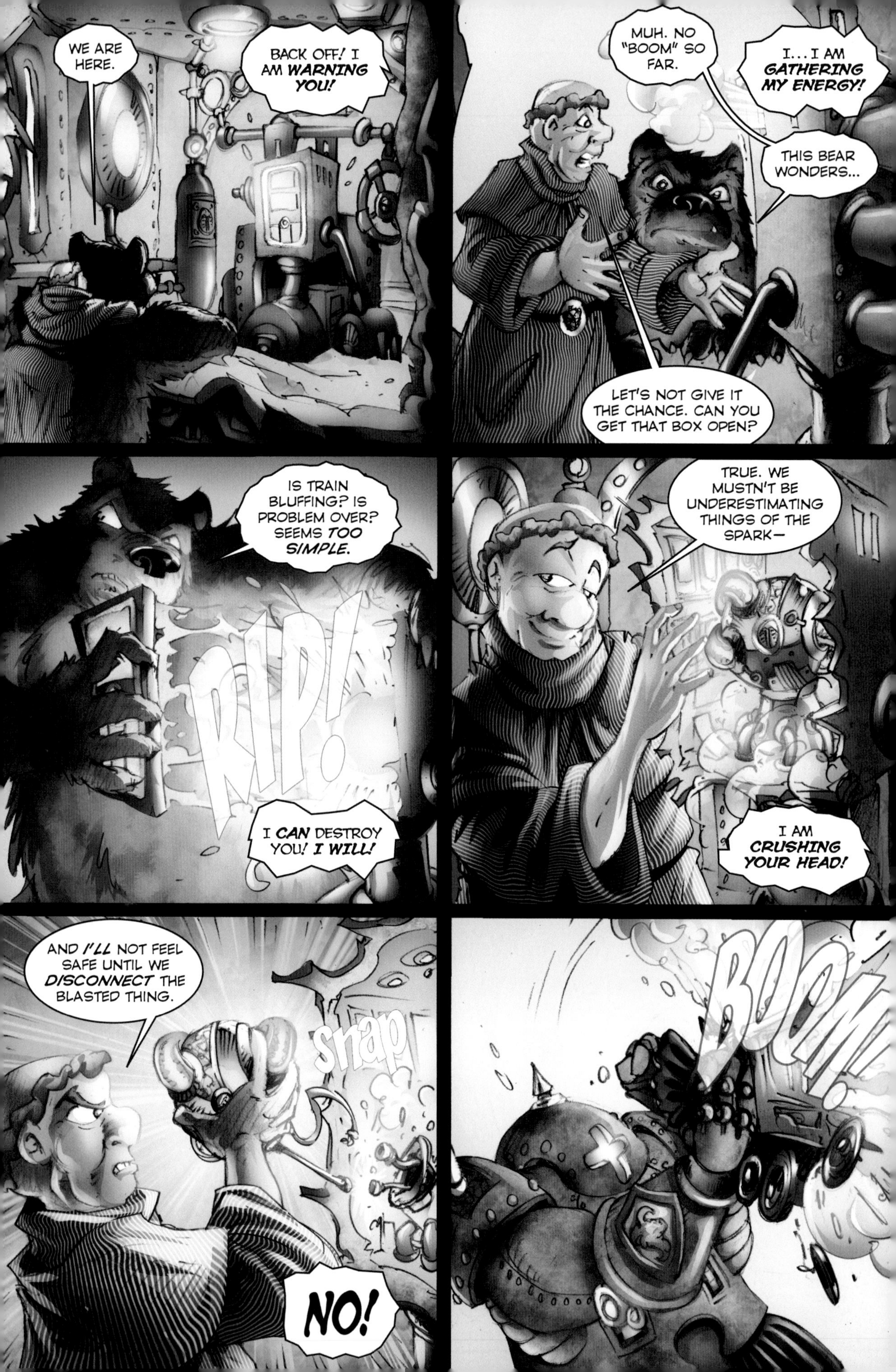
WE ARE HERE.
BACK OFF! I AM WARNING YOU!
MUH. NO "BOOM" SO FAR.
I... I AM GATHERING MY ENERGY!
THIS BEAR WONDERS...
LET'S NOT GIVE IT THE CHANCE. CAN YOU GET THAT BOX OPEN?
IS TRAIN BLUFFING? IS PROBLEM OVER? SEEMS TOO SIMPLE.
RIP!
I CAN DESTROY YOU! I WILL!
TRUE. WE MUSTN'T BE UNDERESTIMATING THINGS OF THE SPARK—
I AM CRUSHING YOUR HEAD!
AND I'LL NOT FEEL SAFE UNTIL WE DISCONNECT THE BLASTED THING.
snap
NO!
BOOM!

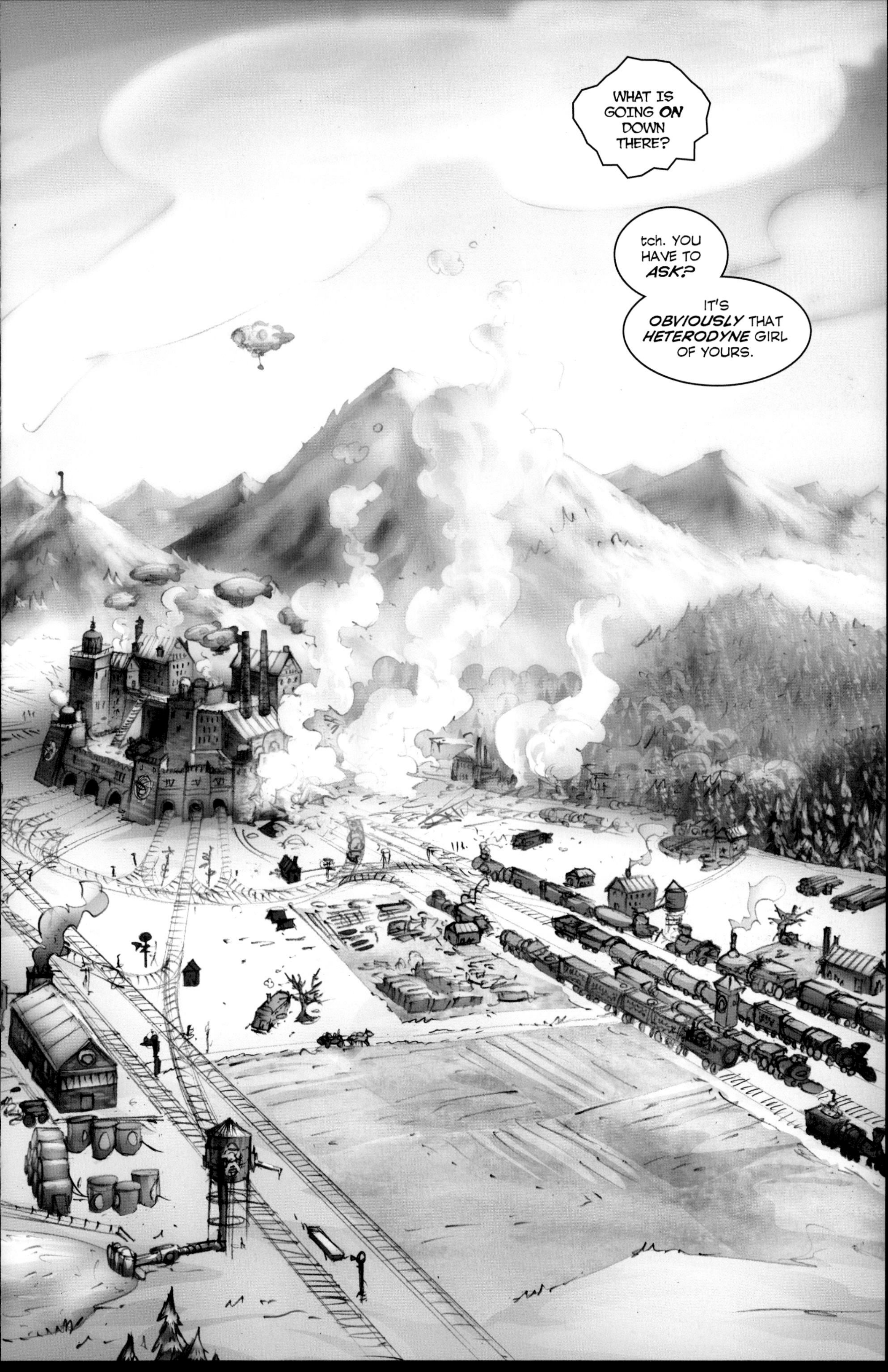
WHAT IS GOING ON DOWN THERE?
tch. YOU HAVE TO ASK?
IT'S OBVIOUSLY THAT HETERODYNE GIRL OF YOURS.

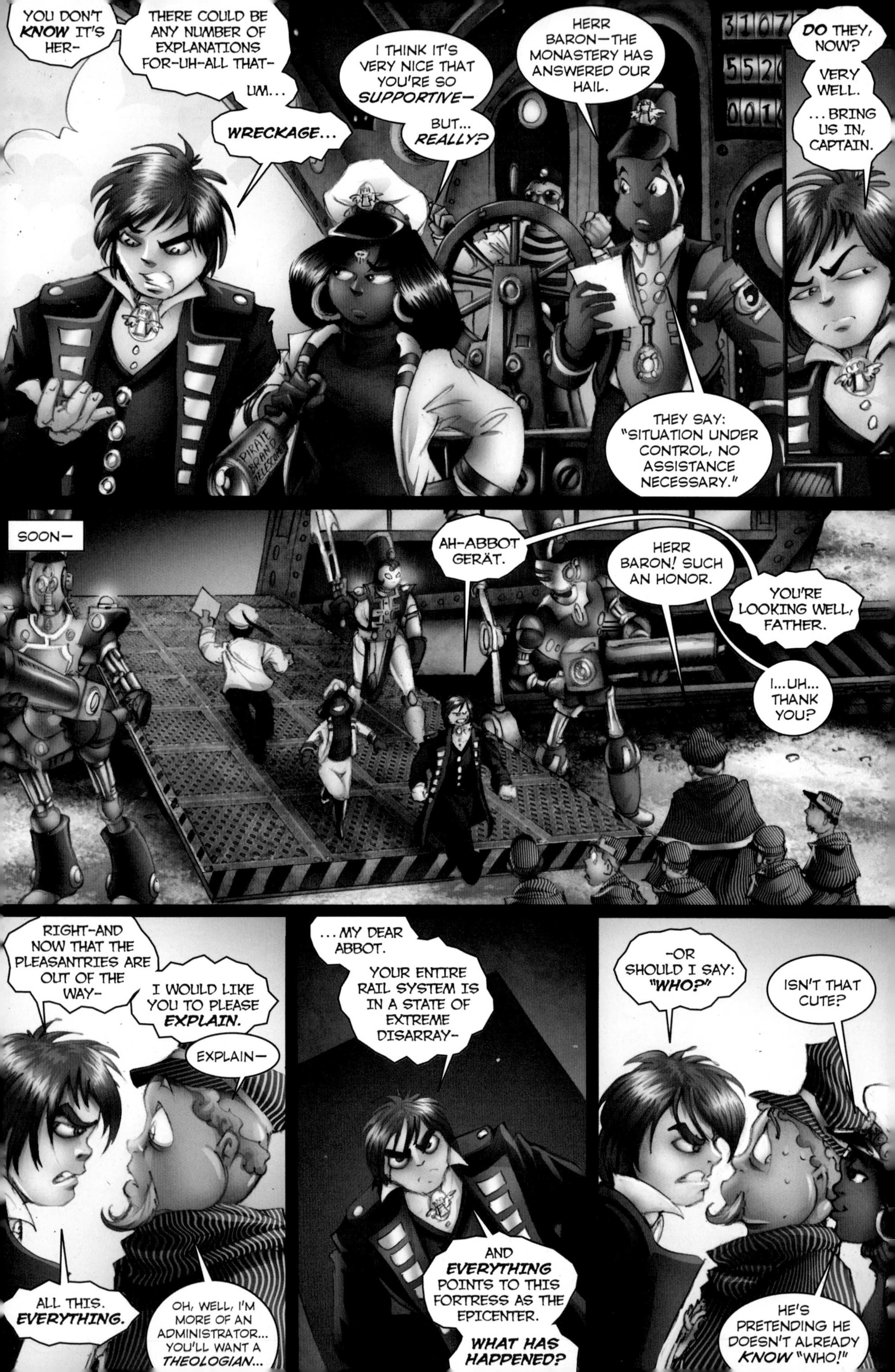
YOU DON'T *KNOW* IT'S HER-
THERE COULD BE ANY NUMBER OF EXPLANATIONS FOR-UH-ALL THAT-
UM...
WRECKAGE...
I THINK IT'S VERY NICE THAT YOU'RE SO *SUPPORTIVE*—
BUT... *REALLY?*
HERR BARON—THE MONASTERY HAS ANSWERED OUR HAIL.
THEY SAY: "SITUATION UNDER CONTROL, NO ASSISTANCE NECESSARY."
DO THEY, NOW?
VERY WELL.
...BRING US IN, CAPTAIN.
PIRATE BRAND TELESCOPE
SOON—
AH-ABBOT GERÄT.
HERR BARON! SUCH AN HONOR.
YOU'RE LOOKING WELL, FATHER.
I...UH... THANK YOU?
RIGHT-AND NOW THAT THE PLEASANTRIES ARE OUT OF THE WAY-
I WOULD LIKE YOU TO PLEASE *EXPLAIN.*
EXPLAIN—
ALL THIS. *EVERYTHING.*
OH, WELL, I'M MORE OF AN ADMINISTRATOR... YOU'LL WANT A *THEOLOGIAN...*
...MY DEAR ABBOT.
YOUR ENTIRE RAIL SYSTEM IS IN A STATE OF EXTREME DISARRAY-
AND *EVERYTHING* POINTS TO THIS FORTRESS AS THE EPICENTER.
WHAT HAS HAPPENED?
-OR SHOULD I SAY: *"WHO?"*
ISN'T THAT CUTE?
HE'S PRETENDING HE DOESN'T ALREADY *KNOW* "WHO!"

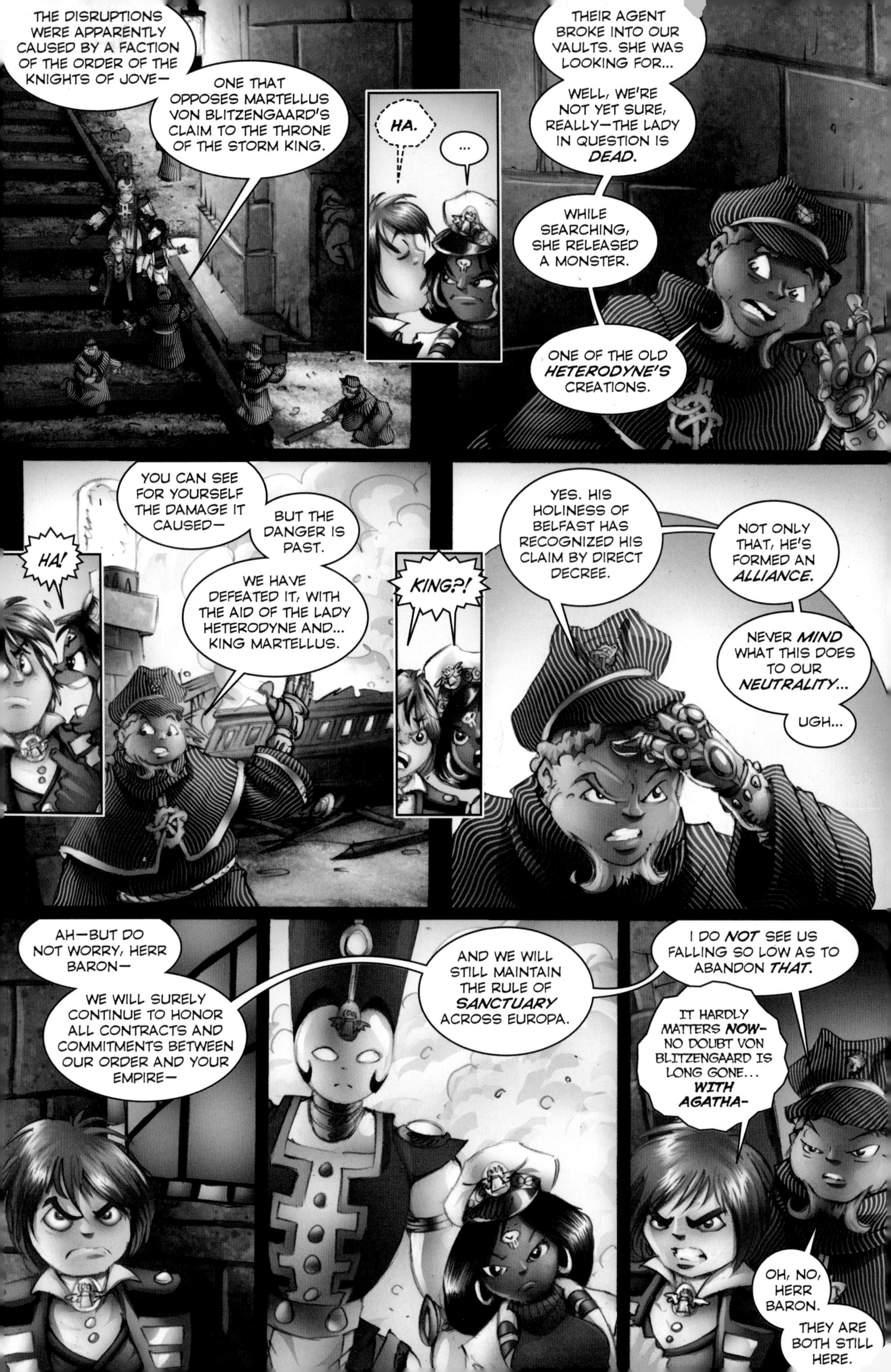
THE DISRUPTIONS WERE APPARENTLY CAUSED BY A FACTION OF THE ORDER OF THE KNIGHTS OF JOVE—
ONE THAT OPPOSES MARTELLUS VON BLITZENGAARD'S CLAIM TO THE THRONE OF THE STORM KING.
HA.
...
THEIR AGENT BROKE INTO OUR VAULTS. SHE WAS LOOKING FOR...
WELL, WE'RE NOT YET SURE, REALLY—THE LADY IN QUESTION IS DEAD.
WHILE SEARCHING, SHE RELEASED A MONSTER.
ONE OF THE OLD HETERODYNE'S CREATIONS.
YOU CAN SEE FOR YOURSELF THE DAMAGE IT CAUSED—
BUT THE DANGER IS PAST.
WE HAVE DEFEATED IT, WITH THE AID OF THE LADY HETERODYNE AND... KING MARTELLUS.
HA!
KING?!
YES. HIS HOLINESS OF BELFAST HAS RECOGNIZED HIS CLAIM BY DIRECT DECREE.
NOT ONLY THAT, HE'S FORMED AN ALLIANCE.
NEVER MIND WHAT THIS DOES TO OUR NEUTRALITY...
UGH...
AH—BUT DO NOT WORRY, HERR BARON—
WE WILL SURELY CONTINUE TO HONOR ALL CONTRACTS AND COMMITMENTS BETWEEN OUR ORDER AND YOUR EMPIRE—
AND WE WILL STILL MAINTAIN THE RULE OF SANCTUARY ACROSS EUROPA.
I DO NOT SEE US FALLING SO LOW AS TO ABANDON THAT.
IT HARDLY MATTERS NOW- NO DOUBT VON BLITZENGAARD IS LONG GONE... WITH AGATHA-
OH, NO, HERR BARON.
THEY ARE BOTH STILL HERE.

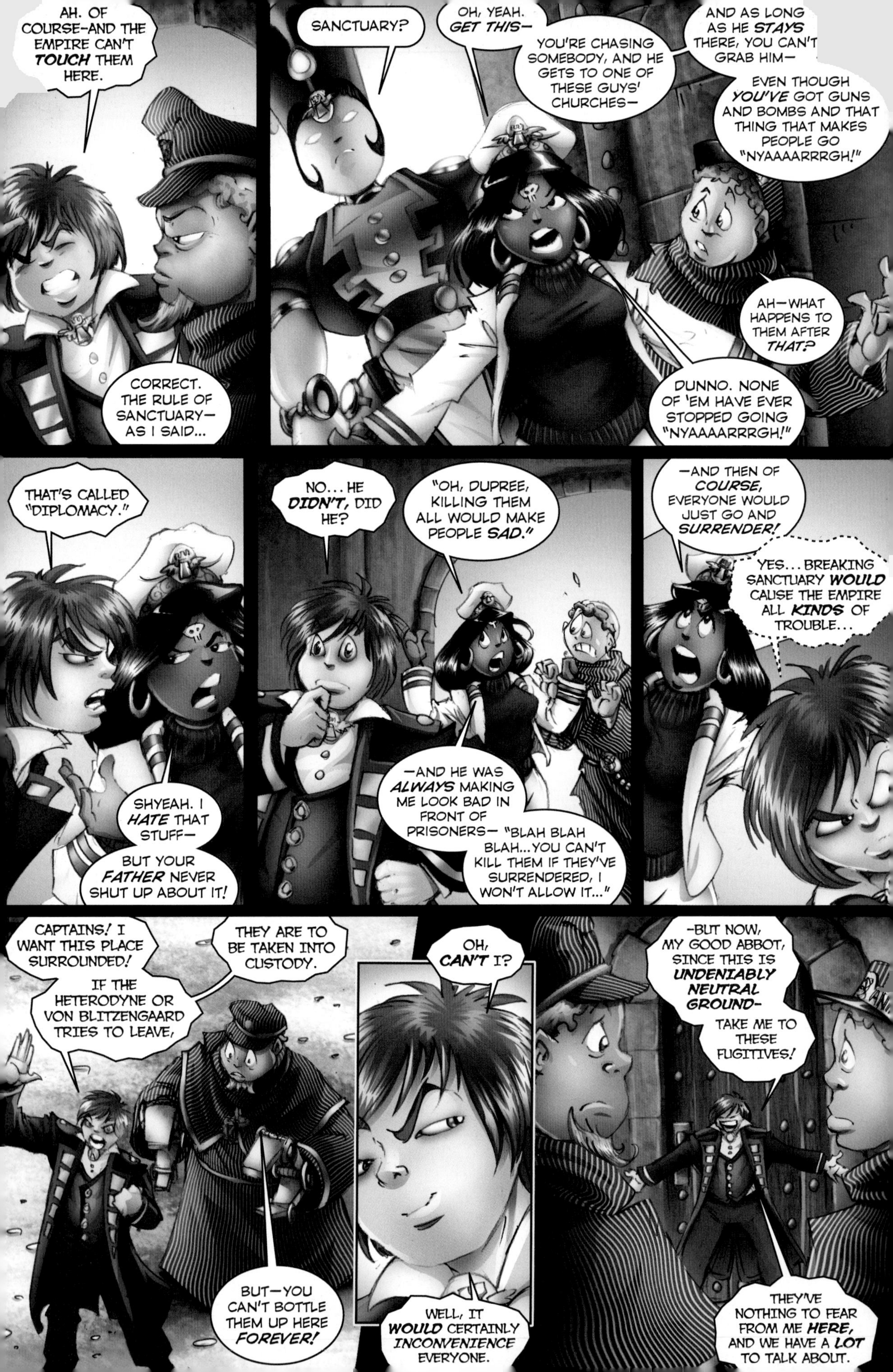
AH. OF COURSE—AND THE EMPIRE CAN'T TOUCH THEM HERE.
CORRECT. THE RULE OF SANCTUARY—AS I SAID...
SANCTUARY?
OH, YEAH. GET THIS—
YOU'RE CHASING SOMEBODY, AND HE GETS TO ONE OF THESE GUYS' CHURCHES—
AND AS LONG AS HE STAYS THERE, YOU CAN'T GRAB HIM—
EVEN THOUGH YOU'VE GOT GUNS AND BOMBS AND THAT THING THAT MAKES PEOPLE GO "NYAAAARRRGH!"
AH—WHAT HAPPENS TO THEM AFTER THAT?
DUNNO. NONE OF 'EM HAVE EVER STOPPED GOING "NYAAAARRRGH!"
THAT'S CALLED "DIPLOMACY."
SHYEAH. I HATE THAT STUFF—
BUT YOUR FATHER NEVER SHUT UP ABOUT IT!
NO... HE DIDN'T, DID HE?
"OH, DUPREE, KILLING THEM ALL WOULD MAKE PEOPLE SAD."
—AND HE WAS ALWAYS MAKING ME LOOK BAD IN FRONT OF PRISONERS—
"BLAH BLAH BLAH...YOU CAN'T KILL THEM IF THEY'VE SURRENDERED, I WON'T ALLOW IT..."
—AND THEN OF COURSE, EVERYONE WOULD JUST GO AND SURRENDER!
YES... BREAKING SANCTUARY WOULD CAUSE THE EMPIRE ALL KINDS OF TROUBLE...
CAPTAINS! I WANT THIS PLACE SURROUNDED!
IF THE HETERODYNE OR VON BLITZENGAARD TRIES TO LEAVE,
THEY ARE TO BE TAKEN INTO CUSTODY.
BUT—YOU CAN'T BOTTLE THEM UP HERE FOREVER!
OH, CAN'T I?
WELL, IT WOULD CERTAINLY INCONVENIENCE EVERYONE.
-BUT NOW, MY GOOD ABBOT, SINCE THIS IS UNDENIABLY NEUTRAL GROUND-
TAKE ME TO THESE FUGITIVES!
THEY'VE NOTHING TO FEAR FROM ME HERE, AND WE HAVE A LOT TO TALK ABOUT.

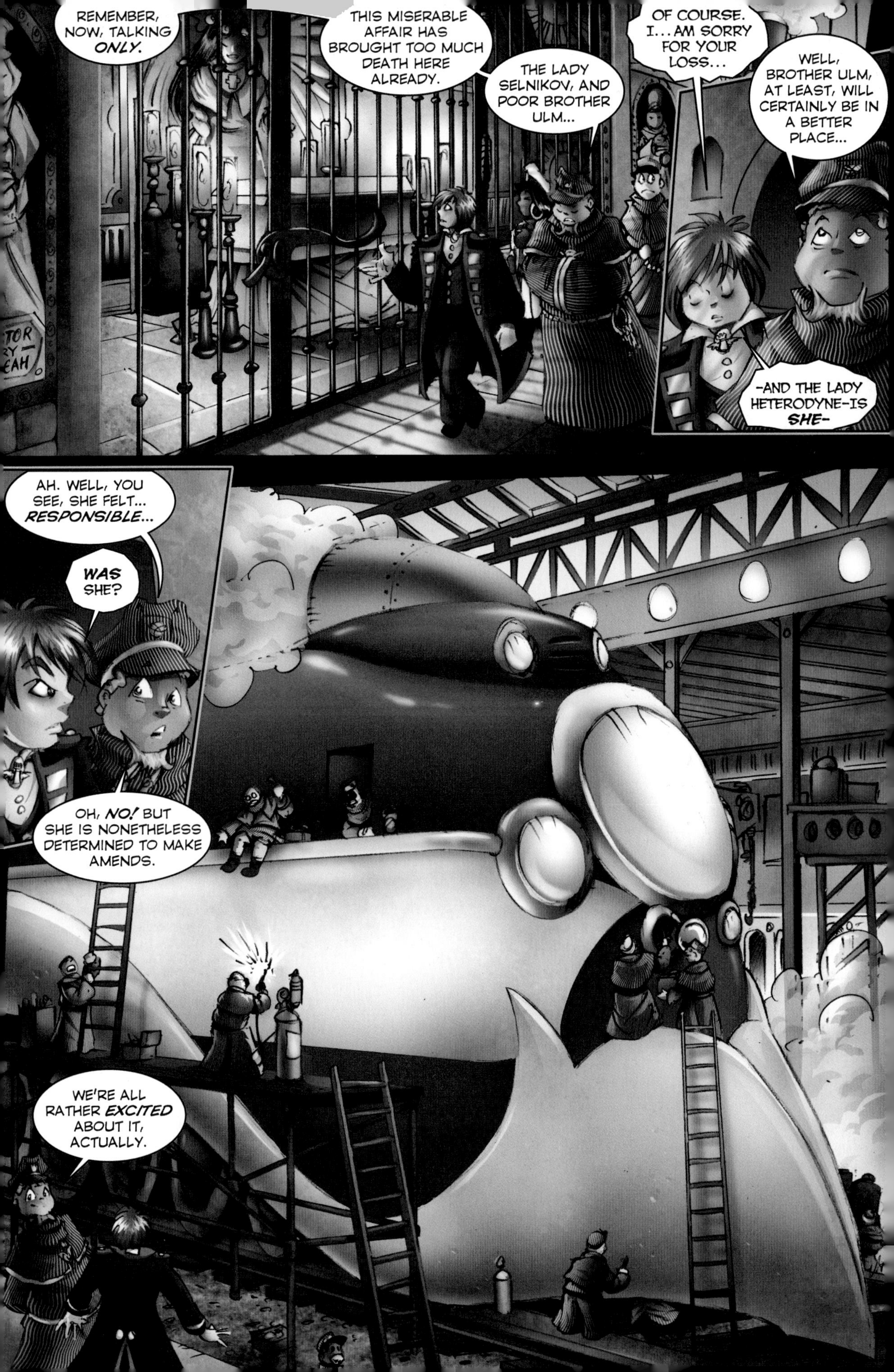

REMEMBER, NOW, TALKING *ONLY.*
THIS MISERABLE AFFAIR HAS BROUGHT TOO MUCH DEATH HERE ALREADY.
THE LADY SELNIKOV, AND POOR BROTHER ULM...
OF COURSE. I...AM SORRY FOR YOUR LOSS...
WELL, BROTHER ULM, AT LEAST, WILL CERTAINLY BE IN A BETTER PLACE...
-AND THE LADY HETERODYNE-IS *SHE-*
AH. WELL, YOU SEE, SHE FELT... *RESPONSIBLE...*
WAS SHE?
OH, *NO!* BUT SHE IS NONETHELESS DETERMINED TO MAKE AMENDS.
WE'RE ALL RATHER *EXCITED* ABOUT IT, ACTUALLY.

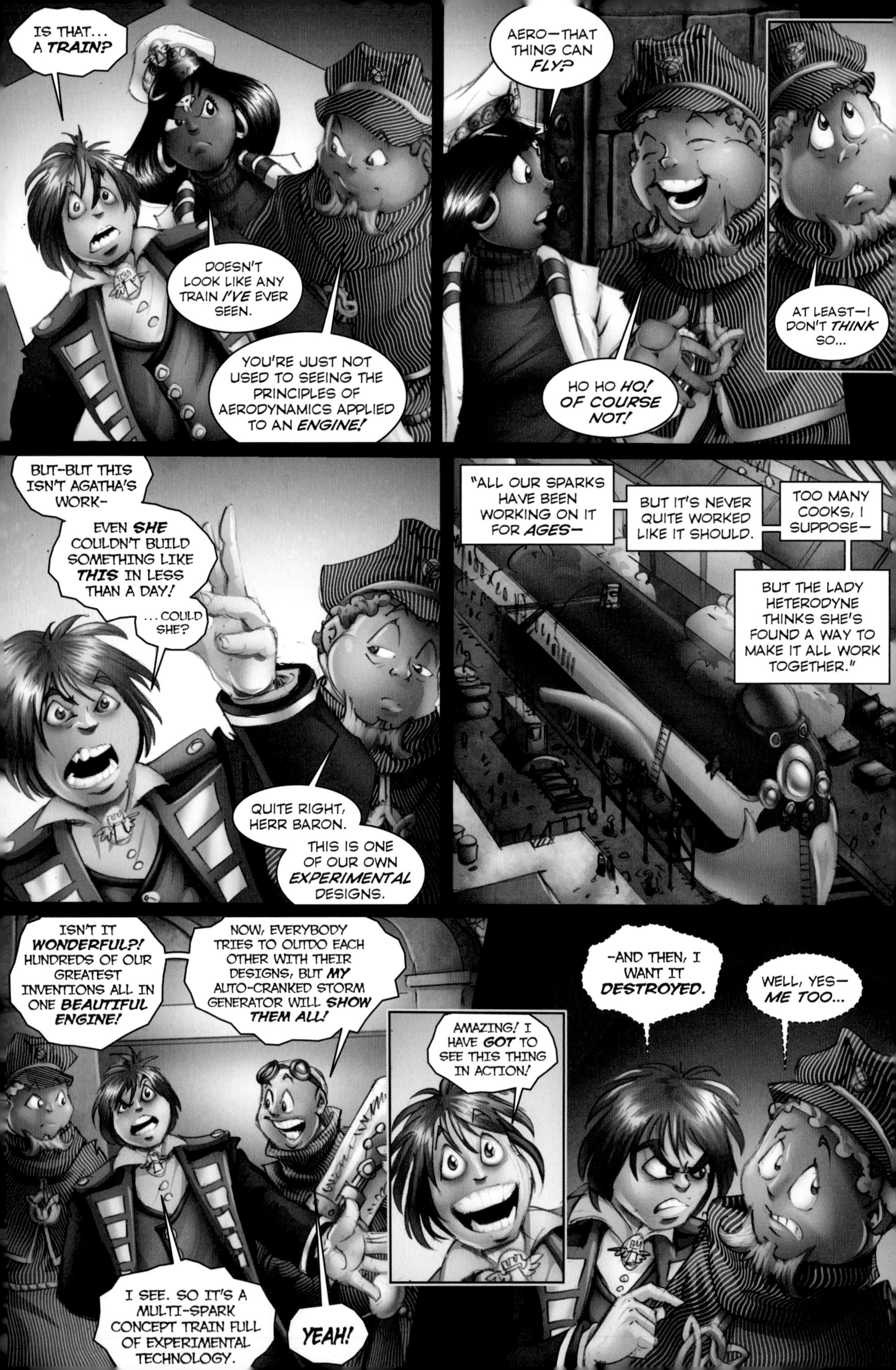

IS THAT... A *TRAIN?*
DOESN'T LOOK LIKE ANY TRAIN *I'VE* EVER SEEN.
YOU'RE JUST NOT USED TO SEEING THE PRINCIPLES OF AERODYNAMICS APPLIED TO AN *ENGINE!*
AERO—THAT THING CAN *FLY?*
HO HO *HO! OF COURSE NOT!*
AT LEAST—I DON'T *THINK* SO...
BUT-BUT THIS ISN'T AGATHA'S WORK-
EVEN **SHE** COULDN'T BUILD SOMETHING LIKE **THIS** IN LESS THAN A DAY!
...COULD SHE?
QUITE RIGHT, HERR BARON.
THIS IS ONE OF OUR OWN *EXPERIMENTAL* DESIGNS.
"ALL OUR SPARKS HAVE BEEN WORKING ON IT FOR *AGES*—
BUT IT'S NEVER QUITE WORKED LIKE IT SHOULD.
TOO MANY COOKS, I SUPPOSE—
BUT THE LADY HETERODYNE THINKS SHE'S FOUND A WAY TO MAKE IT ALL WORK TOGETHER."
ISN'T IT ***WONDERFUL?!*** HUNDREDS OF OUR GREATEST INVENTIONS ALL IN ONE ***BEAUTIFUL ENGINE!***
NOW, EVERYBODY TRIES TO OUTDO EACH OTHER WITH THEIR DESIGNS, BUT ***MY*** AUTO-CRANKED STORM GENERATOR WILL ***SHOW THEM ALL!***
I SEE. SO IT'S A MULTI-SPARK CONCEPT TRAIN FULL OF EXPERIMENTAL TECHNOLOGY.
YEAH!
AMAZING! I HAVE **GOT** TO SEE THIS THING IN ACTION!
-AND THEN, I WANT IT ***DESTROYED.***
WELL, YES— *ME TOO...*

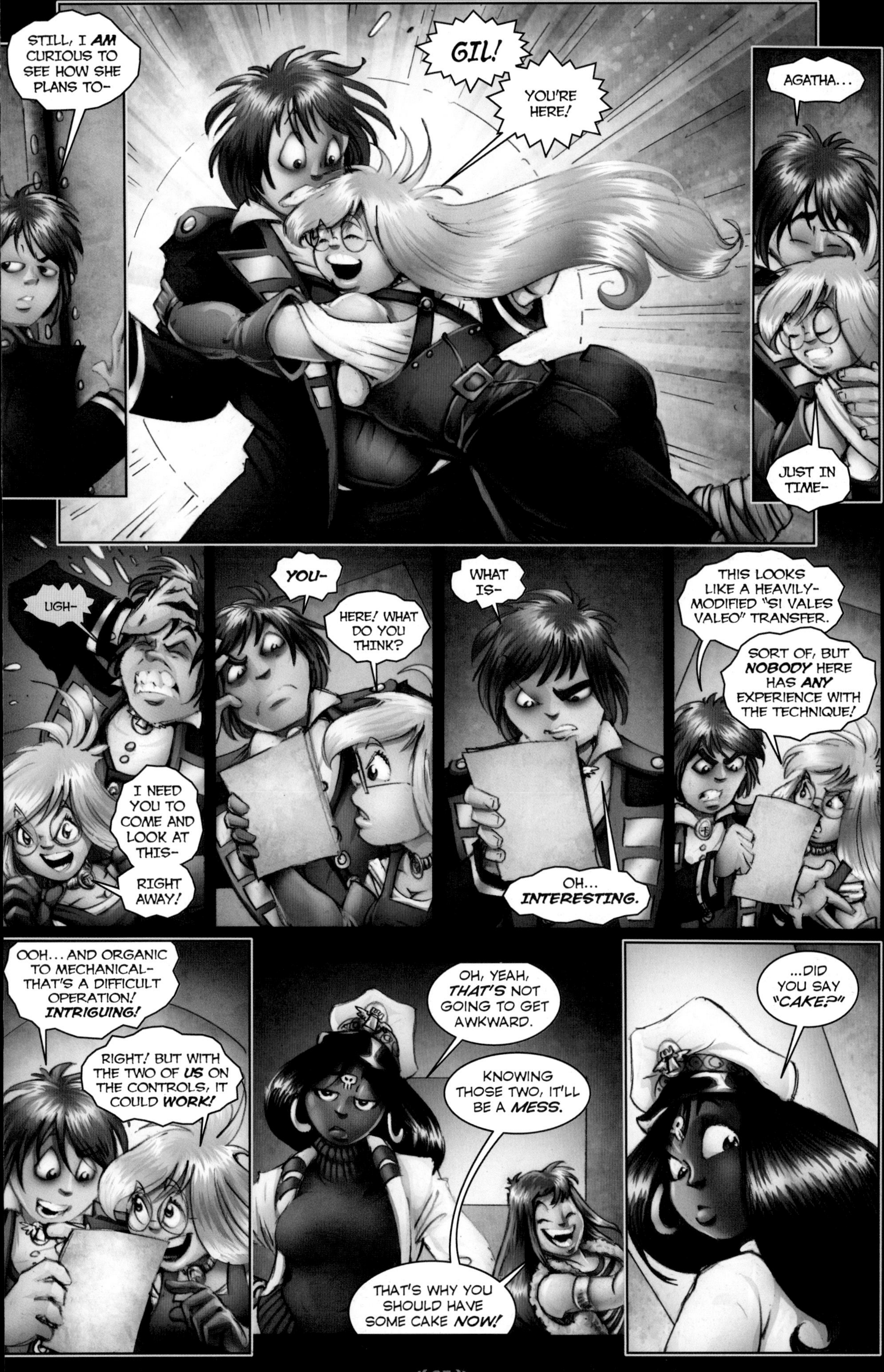
STILL, I AM CURIOUS TO SEE HOW SHE PLANS TO-
GIL!
YOU'RE HERE!
AGATHA...
JUST IN TIME-
UGH-
I NEED YOU TO COME AND LOOK AT THIS-
RIGHT AWAY!
YOU-
HERE! WHAT DO YOU THINK?
WHAT IS-
OH... INTERESTING.
THIS LOOKS LIKE A HEAVILY-MODIFIED "SI VALES VALEO" TRANSFER.
SORT OF, BUT NOBODY HERE HAS ANY EXPERIENCE WITH THE TECHNIQUE!
OOH... AND ORGANIC TO MECHANICAL-THAT'S A DIFFICULT OPERATION! INTRIGUING!
RIGHT! BUT WITH THE TWO OF US ON THE CONTROLS, IT COULD WORK!
OH, YEAH, THAT'S NOT GOING TO GET AWKWARD.
KNOWING THOSE TWO, IT'LL BE A MESS.
THAT'S WHY YOU SHOULD HAVE SOME CAKE NOW!
...DID YOU SAY "CAKE?"

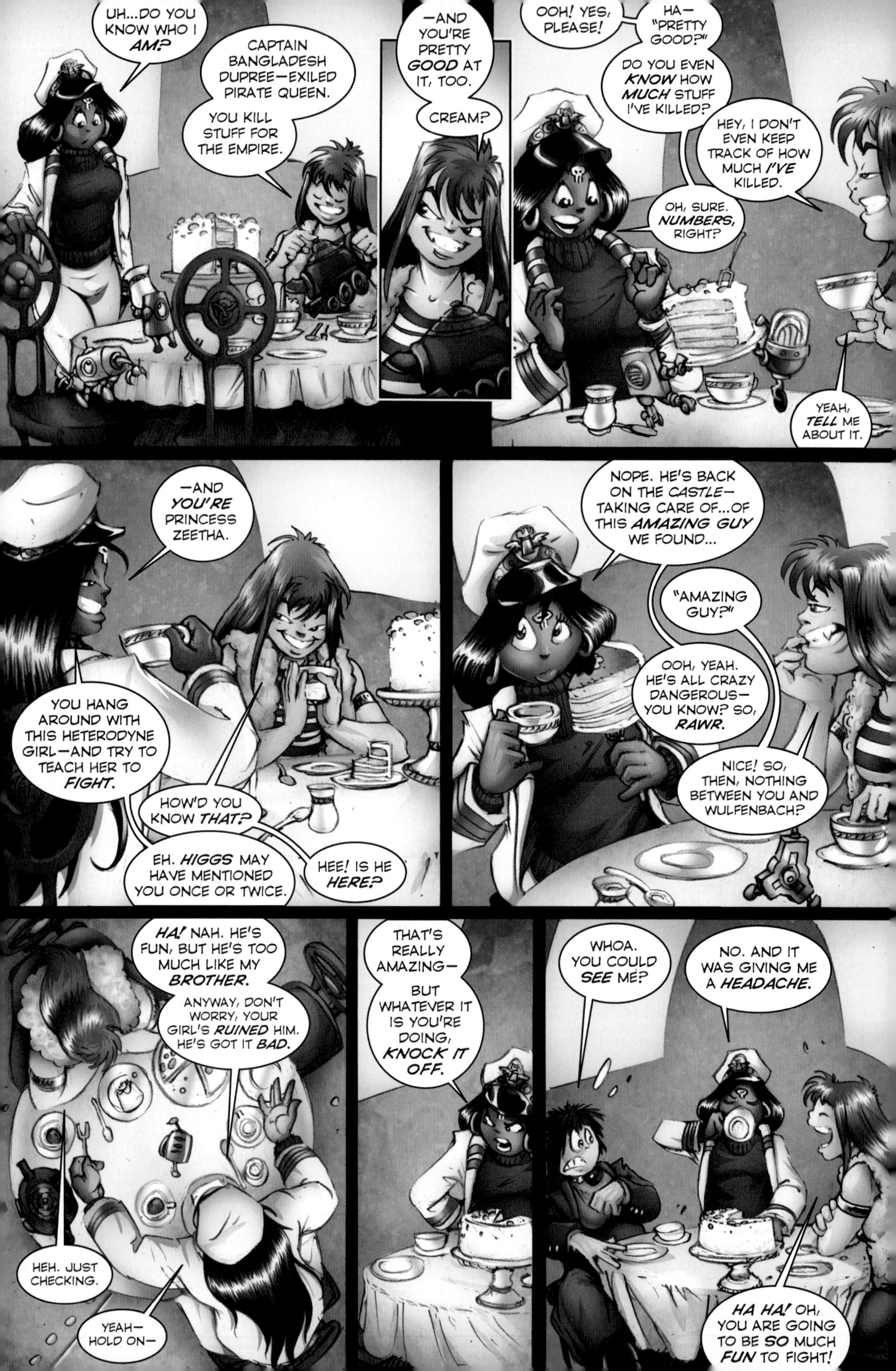
UH...DO YOU KNOW WHO I *AM?*
CAPTAIN BANGLADESH DUPREE—EXILED PIRATE QUEEN.
YOU KILL STUFF FOR THE EMPIRE.
—AND YOU'RE PRETTY *GOOD* AT IT, TOO.
CREAM?
OOH! YES, PLEASE!
HA— "PRETTY GOOD?"
DO YOU EVEN *KNOW* HOW *MUCH* STUFF I'VE KILLED?
HEY, I DON'T EVEN KEEP TRACK OF HOW MUCH *I'VE* KILLED.
OH, SURE. *NUMBERS,* RIGHT?
YEAH, *TELL* ME ABOUT IT.
—AND *YOU'RE* PRINCESS ZEETHA.
YOU HANG AROUND WITH THIS HETERODYNE GIRL—AND TRY TO TEACH HER TO *FIGHT*.
HOW'D YOU KNOW *THAT?*
EH. *HIGGS* MAY HAVE MENTIONED YOU ONCE OR TWICE.
HEE! IS HE *HERE?*
NOPE. HE'S BACK ON THE *CASTLE*—TAKING CARE OF...OF THIS *AMAZING GUY* WE FOUND...
"AMAZING GUY?"
OOH, YEAH. HE'S ALL CRAZY DANGEROUS—YOU KNOW? SO, *RAWR.*
NICE! SO, THEN, NOTHING BETWEEN YOU AND WULFENBACH?
HA! NAH. HE'S FUN, BUT HE'S TOO MUCH LIKE MY *BROTHER*.
ANYWAY, DON'T WORRY, YOUR GIRL'S *RUINED* HIM. HE'S GOT IT *BAD*.
HEH. JUST CHECKING.
YEAH—HOLD ON—
THAT'S REALLY AMAZING—
BUT WHATEVER IT IS YOU'RE DOING, *KNOCK IT OFF*.
WHOA. YOU COULD *SEE* ME?
NO. AND IT WAS GIVING ME A *HEADACHE.*
HA HA! OH, YOU ARE GOING TO BE *SO* MUCH *FUN* TO FIGHT!

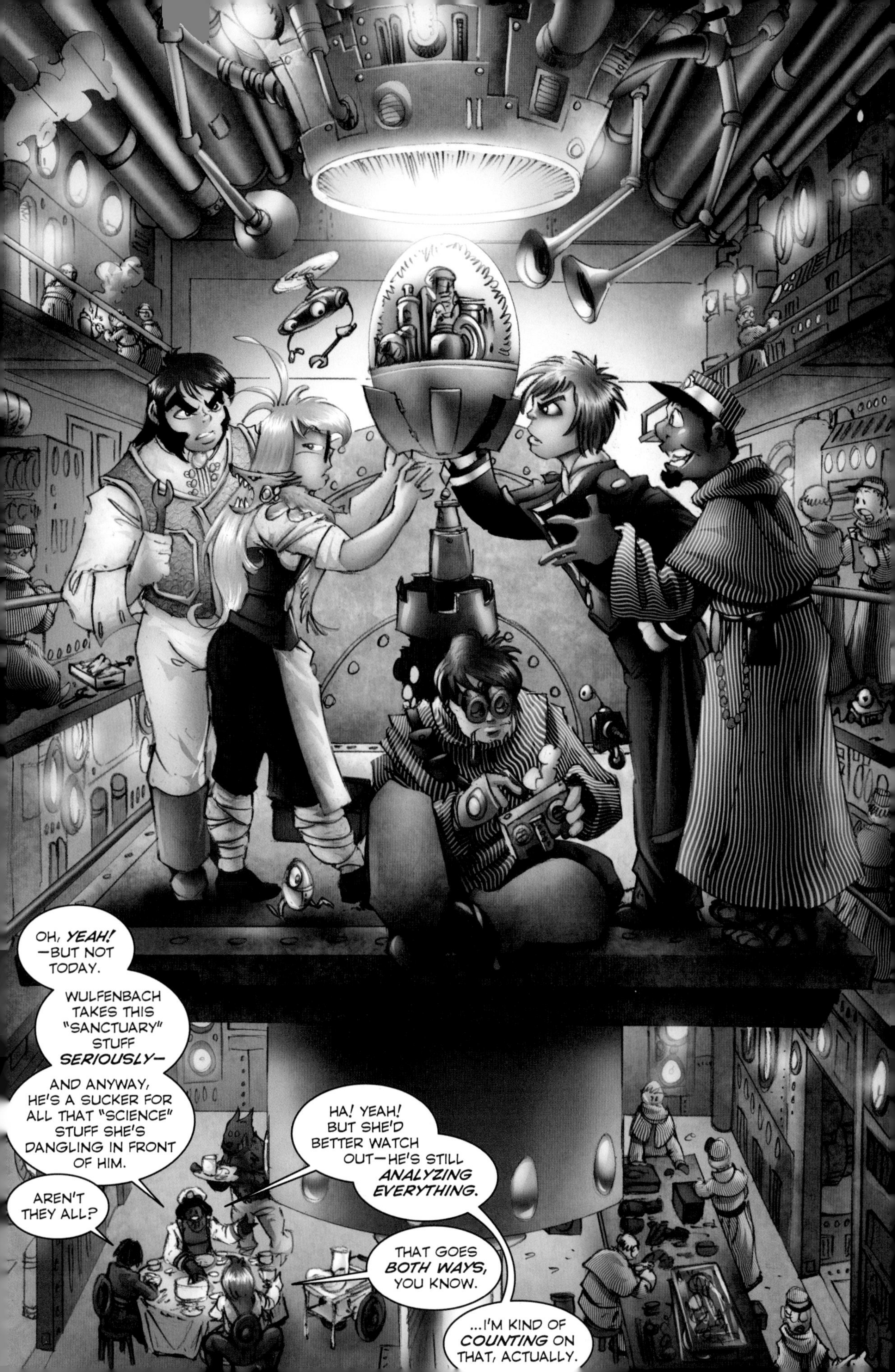

OH, *YEAH!* —BUT NOT TODAY.
WULFENBACH TAKES THIS "SANCTUARY" STUFF *SERIOUSLY—*
AND ANYWAY, HE'S A SUCKER FOR ALL THAT "SCIENCE" STUFF SHE'S DANGLING IN FRONT OF HIM.
AREN'T THEY ALL?
HA! YEAH! BUT SHE'D BETTER WATCH OUT—HE'S STILL *ANALYZING EVERYTHING.*
THAT GOES *BOTH WAYS,* YOU KNOW.
...I'M KIND OF *COUNTING* ON THAT, ACTUALLY.

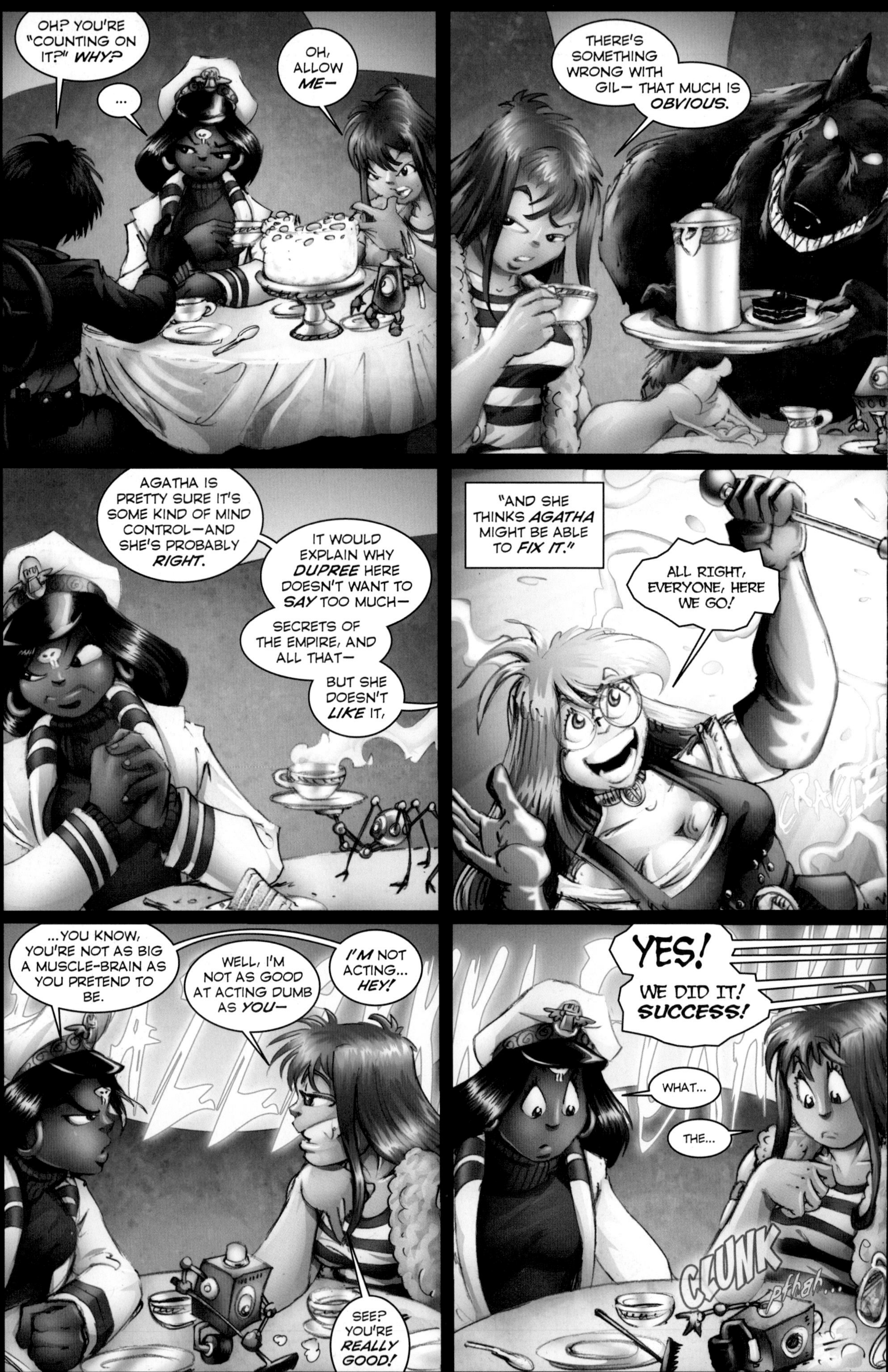
OH? YOU'RE "COUNTING ON IT?" WHY?
...
OH, ALLOW ME—
THERE'S SOMETHING WRONG WITH GIL— THAT MUCH IS OBVIOUS.
AGATHA IS PRETTY SURE IT'S SOME KIND OF MIND CONTROL—AND SHE'S PROBABLY RIGHT.
IT WOULD EXPLAIN WHY DUPREE HERE DOESN'T WANT TO SAY TOO MUCH—
SECRETS OF THE EMPIRE, AND ALL THAT—
BUT SHE DOESN'T LIKE IT,
"AND SHE THINKS AGATHA MIGHT BE ABLE TO FIX IT."
ALL RIGHT, EVERYONE, HERE WE GO!
...YOU KNOW, YOU'RE NOT AS BIG A MUSCLE-BRAIN AS YOU PRETEND TO BE.
WELL, I'M NOT AS GOOD AT ACTING DUMB AS YOU—
I'M NOT ACTING... HEY!
SEE? YOU'RE REALLY GOOD!
YES!
WE DID IT! SUCCESS!
WHAT...
THE...
CLUNK
pfhat...

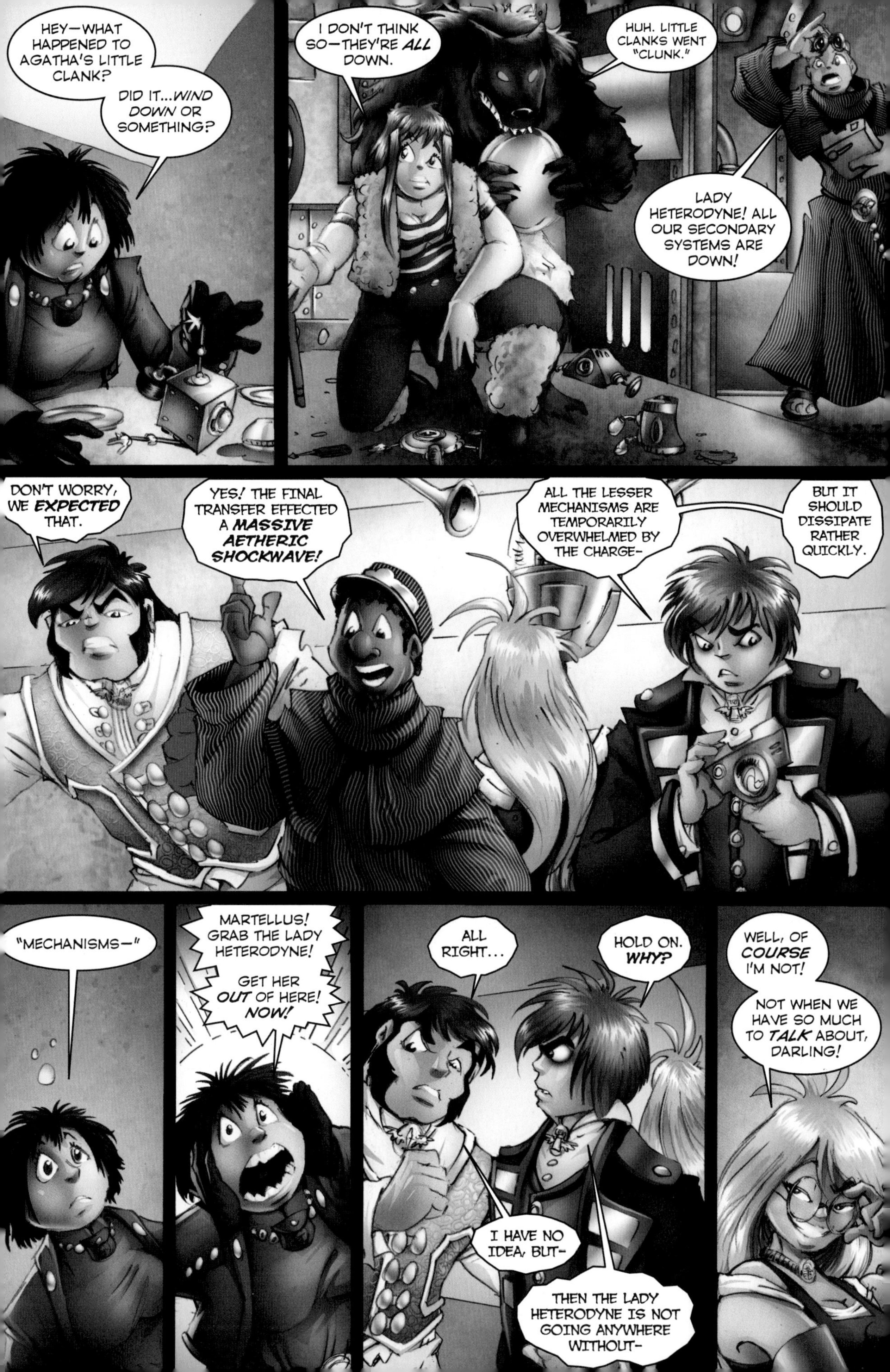
HEY—WHAT HAPPENED TO AGATHA'S LITTLE CLANK?
DID IT...*WIND DOWN* OR SOMETHING?
I DON'T THINK SO—THEY'RE *ALL* DOWN.
HUH. LITTLE CLANKS WENT "CLUNK."
LADY HETERODYNE! ALL OUR SECONDARY SYSTEMS ARE DOWN!
DON'T WORRY, WE **EXPECTED** THAT.
YES! THE FINAL TRANSFER EFFECTED A ***MASSIVE AETHERIC SHOCKWAVE!***
ALL THE LESSER MECHANISMS ARE TEMPORARILY OVERWHELMED BY THE CHARGE-
BUT IT SHOULD DISSIPATE RATHER QUICKLY.
"MECHANISMS—"
MARTELLUS! GRAB THE LADY HETERODYNE!
GET HER *OUT* OF HERE! ***NOW!***
ALL RIGHT...
HOLD ON. ***WHY?***
I HAVE NO IDEA, BUT-
THEN THE LADY HETERODYNE IS NOT GOING ANYWHERE WITHOUT-
WELL, OF *COURSE* I'M NOT!
NOT WHEN WE HAVE SO MUCH TO *TALK* ABOUT, DARLING!

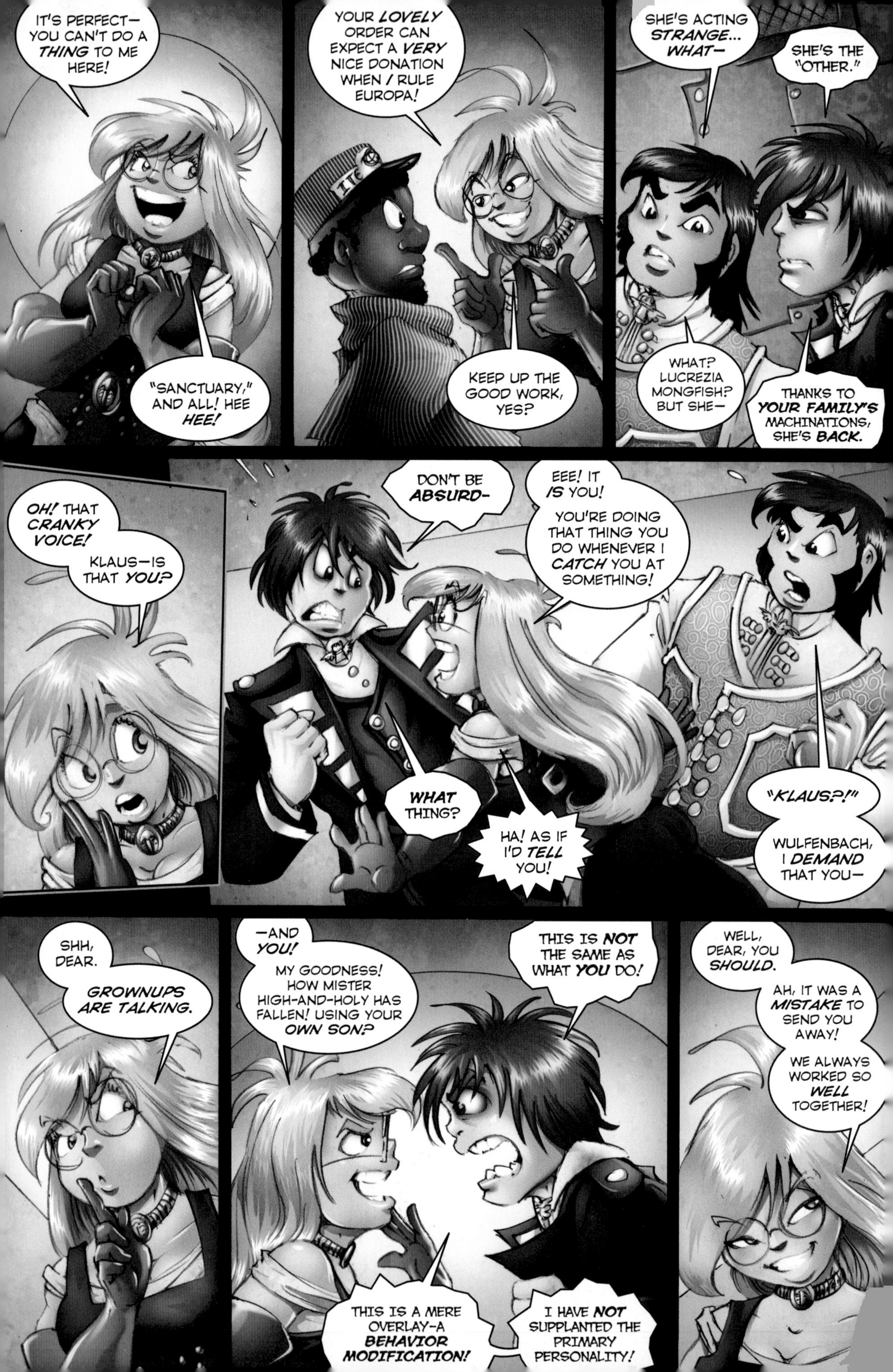
IT'S PERFECT—YOU CAN'T DO A THING TO ME HERE!
"SANCTUARY," AND ALL! HEE HEE!
YOUR LOVELY ORDER CAN EXPECT A VERY NICE DONATION WHEN I RULE EUROPA!
KEEP UP THE GOOD WORK, YES?
ITC
SHE'S ACTING STRANGE... WHAT—
SHE'S THE "OTHER."
WHAT? LUCREZIA MONGFISH? BUT SHE—
THANKS TO YOUR FAMILY'S MACHINATIONS, SHE'S BACK.
OH! THAT CRANKY VOICE!
KLAUS—IS THAT YOU?
DON'T BE ABSURD-
EEE! IT IS YOU!
YOU'RE DOING THAT THING YOU DO WHENEVER I CATCH YOU AT SOMETHING!
WHAT THING?
HA! AS IF I'D TELL YOU!
"KLAUS?!"
WULFENBACH, I DEMAND THAT YOU—
SHH, DEAR.
GROWNUPS ARE TALKING.
—AND YOU!
MY GOODNESS! HOW MISTER HIGH-AND-HOLY HAS FALLEN! USING YOUR OWN SON?
THIS IS NOT THE SAME AS WHAT YOU DO!
THIS IS A MERE OVERLAY—A BEHAVIOR MODIFICATION!
I HAVE NOT SUPPLANTED THE PRIMARY PERSONALITY!
WELL, DEAR, YOU SHOULD.
AH, IT WAS A MISTAKE TO SEND YOU AWAY!
WE ALWAYS WORKED SO WELL TOGETHER!

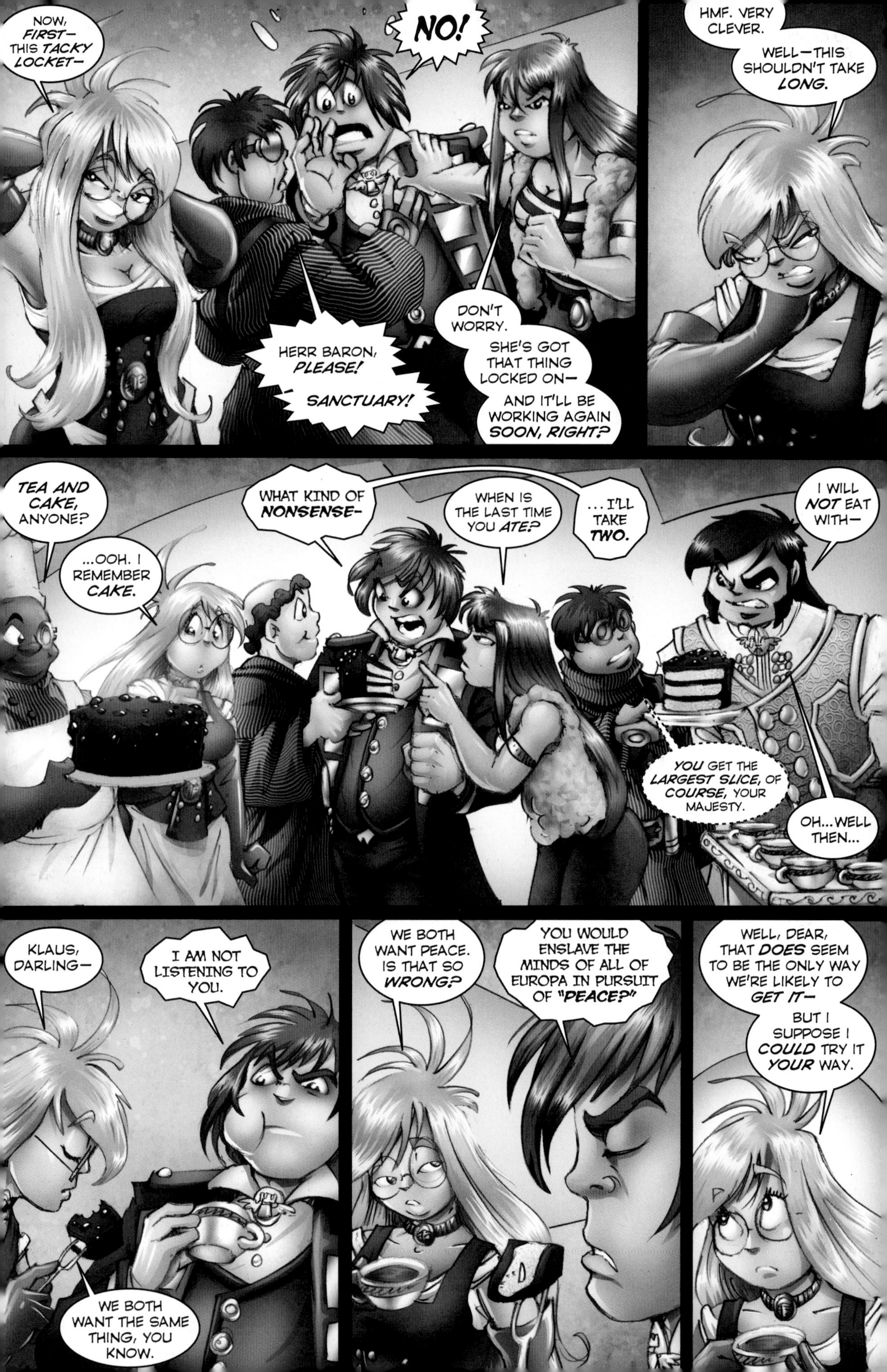
NOW, FIRST— THIS TACKY LOCKET—
NO!
HERR BARON, PLEASE!
SANCTUARY!
DON'T WORRY.
SHE'S GOT THAT THING LOCKED ON—
AND IT'LL BE WORKING AGAIN SOON, RIGHT?
HMF. VERY CLEVER.
WELL—THIS SHOULDN'T TAKE LONG.
TEA AND CAKE, ANYONE?
...OOH. I REMEMBER CAKE.
WHAT KIND OF NONSENSE-
WHEN IS THE LAST TIME YOU ATE?
...I'LL TAKE TWO.
I WILL NOT EAT WITH—
YOU GET THE LARGEST SLICE, OF COURSE, YOUR MAJESTY.
OH...WELL THEN...
KLAUS, DARLING—
I AM NOT LISTENING TO YOU.
WE BOTH WANT THE SAME THING, YOU KNOW.
WE BOTH WANT PEACE. IS THAT SO WRONG?
YOU WOULD ENSLAVE THE MINDS OF ALL OF EUROPA IN PURSUIT OF "PEACE?"
WELL, DEAR, THAT DOES SEEM TO BE THE ONLY WAY WE'RE LIKELY TO GET IT—
BUT I SUPPOSE I COULD TRY IT YOUR WAY.

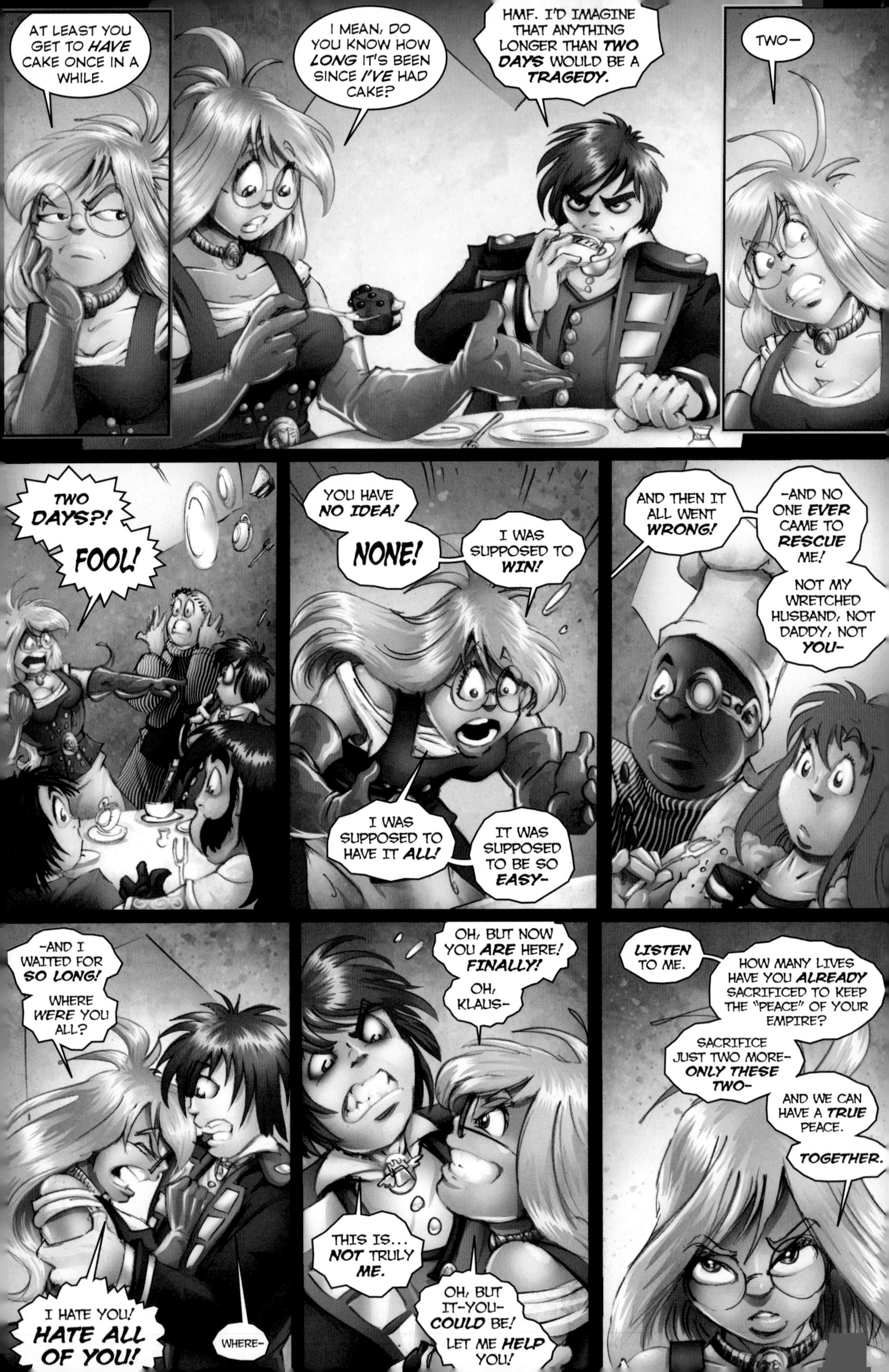
AT LEAST YOU GET TO HAVE CAKE ONCE IN A WHILE.
I MEAN, DO YOU KNOW HOW LONG IT'S BEEN SINCE I'VE HAD CAKE?
HMF. I'D IMAGINE THAT ANYTHING LONGER THAN TWO DAYS WOULD BE A TRAGEDY.
TWO-
TWO DAYS?!
FOOL!
YOU HAVE NO IDEA!
NONE!
I WAS SUPPOSED TO WIN!
I WAS SUPPOSED TO HAVE IT ALL!
IT WAS SUPPOSED TO BE SO EASY-
AND THEN IT ALL WENT WRONG!
-AND NO ONE EVER CAME TO RESCUE ME!
NOT MY WRETCHED HUSBAND, NOT DADDY, NOT YOU-
-AND I WAITED FOR SO LONG!
WHERE WERE YOU ALL?
I HATE YOU! HATE ALL OF YOU!
WHERE-
OH, BUT NOW YOU ARE HERE! FINALLY!
OH, KLAUS-
THIS IS... NOT TRULY ME.
OH, BUT IT-YOU-COULD BE!
LET ME HELP YOU!
LISTEN TO ME.
HOW MANY LIVES HAVE YOU ALREADY SACRIFICED TO KEEP THE "PEACE" OF YOUR EMPIRE?
SACRIFICE JUST TWO MORE-ONLY THESE TWO-
AND WE CAN HAVE A TRUE PEACE.
TOGETHER.

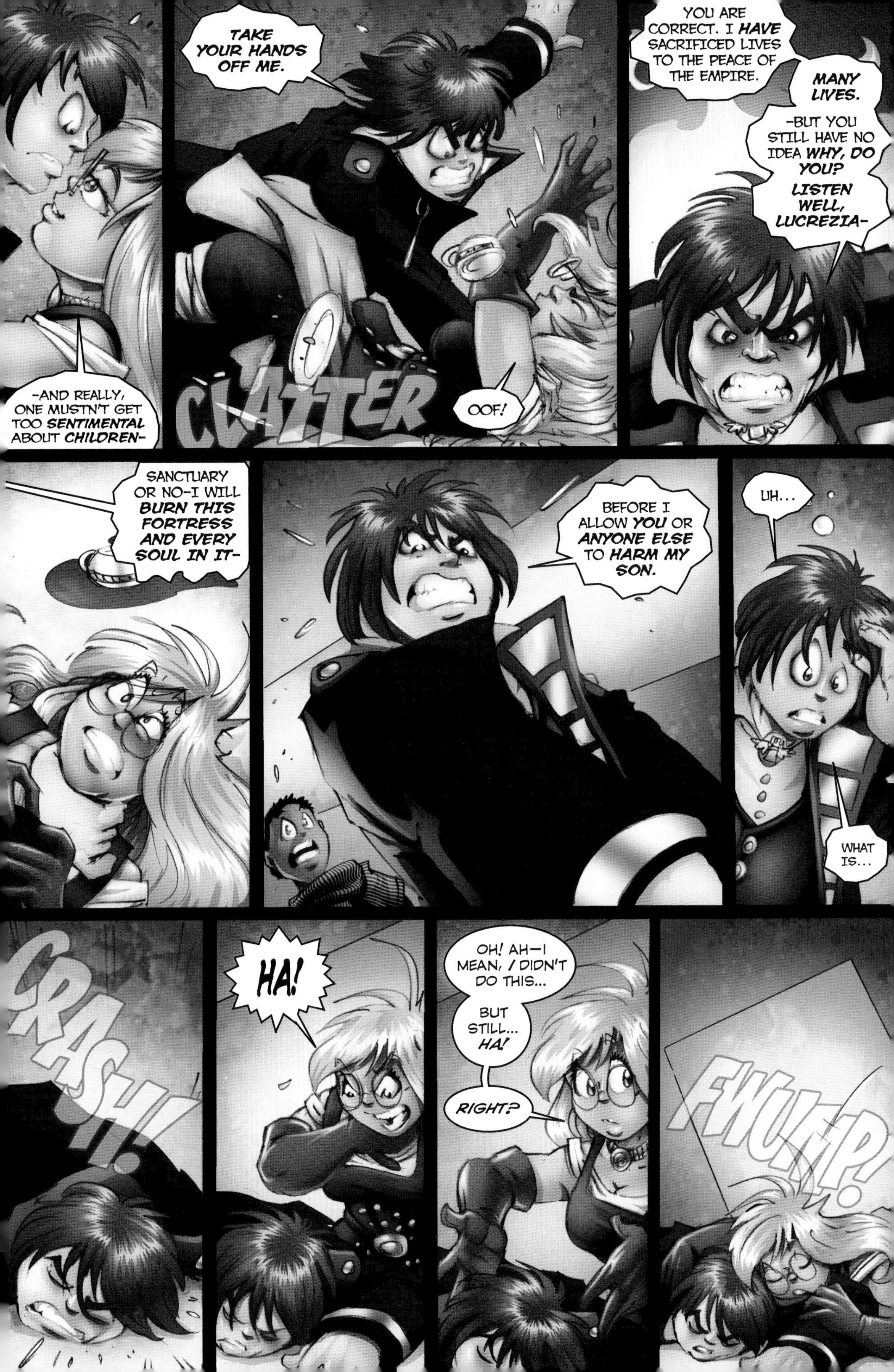
-AND REALLY, ONE MUSTN'T GET TOO SENTIMENTAL ABOUT CHILDREN-
TAKE YOUR HANDS OFF ME.
CLATTER
OOF!
YOU ARE CORRECT. I HAVE SACRIFICED LIVES TO THE PEACE OF THE EMPIRE.
MANY LIVES.
-BUT YOU STILL HAVE NO IDEA WHY, DO YOU?
LISTEN WELL, LUCREZIA-
SANCTUARY OR NO-I WILL BURN THIS FORTRESS AND EVERY SOUL IN IT-
BEFORE I ALLOW YOU OR ANYONE ELSE TO HARM MY SON.
UH...
WHAT IS...
CRASH!
HA!
OH! AH-I MEAN, I DIDN'T DO THIS...
BUT STILL... HA!
RIGHT?
FWUMP!

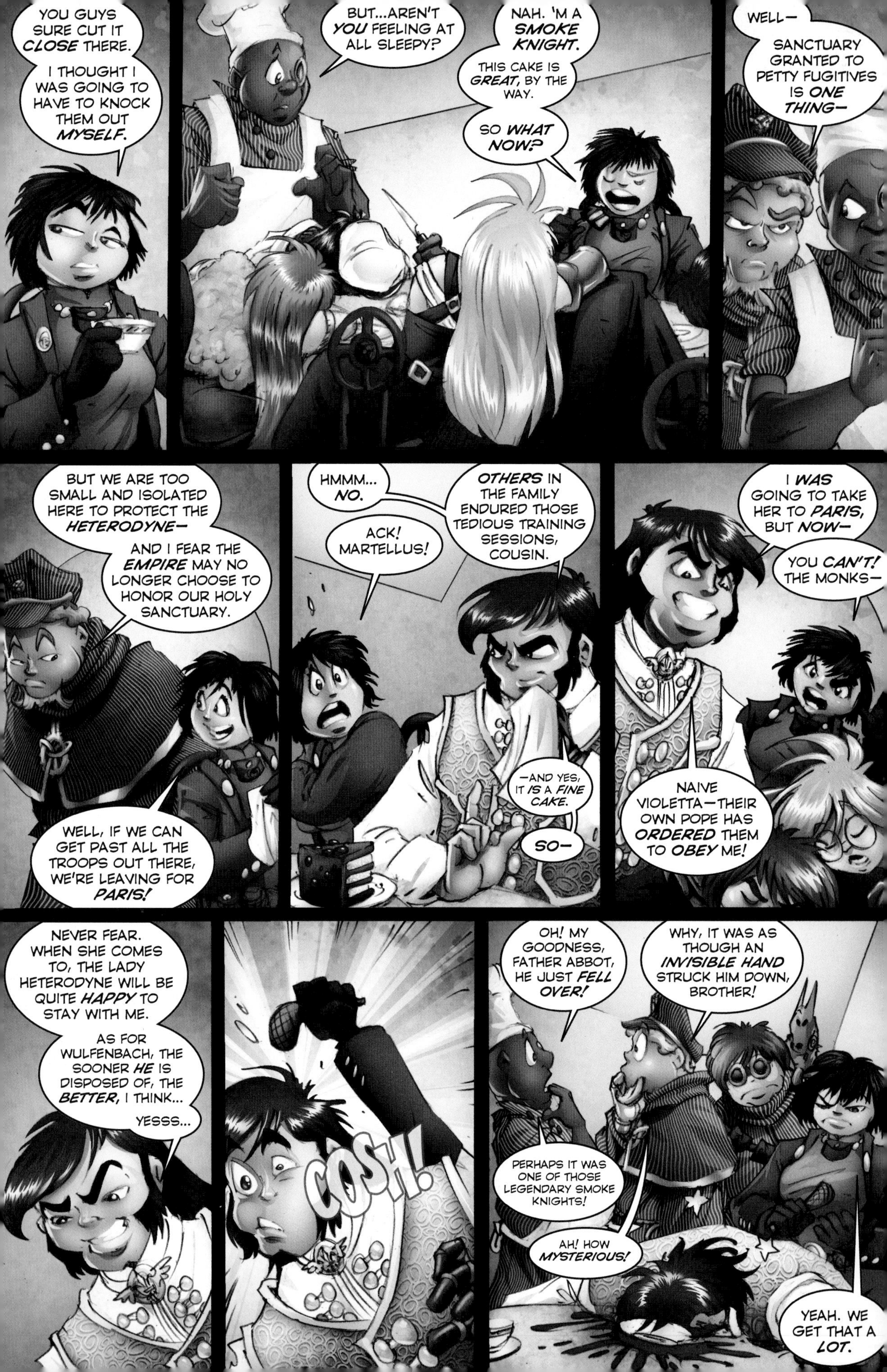
YOU GUYS SURE CUT IT CLOSE THERE.
I THOUGHT I WAS GOING TO HAVE TO KNOCK THEM OUT MYSELF.
BUT...AREN'T YOU FEELING AT ALL SLEEPY?
NAH. 'M A SMOKE KNIGHT.
THIS CAKE IS GREAT, BY THE WAY.
SO WHAT NOW?
WELL—
SANCTUARY GRANTED TO PETTY FUGITIVES IS ONE THING—
BUT WE ARE TOO SMALL AND ISOLATED HERE TO PROTECT THE HETERODYNE—
AND I FEAR THE EMPIRE MAY NO LONGER CHOOSE TO HONOR OUR HOLY SANCTUARY.
WELL, IF WE CAN GET PAST ALL THE TROOPS OUT THERE, WE'RE LEAVING FOR PARIS!
HMMM... NO.
ACK! MARTELLUS!
OTHERS IN THE FAMILY ENDURED THOSE TEDIOUS TRAINING SESSIONS, COUSIN.
—AND YES, IT IS A FINE CAKE.
SO—
I WAS GOING TO TAKE HER TO PARIS, BUT NOW—
YOU CAN'T! THE MONKS—
NAIVE VIOLETTA—THEIR OWN POPE HAS ORDERED THEM TO OBEY ME!
NEVER FEAR. WHEN SHE COMES TO, THE LADY HETERODYNE WILL BE QUITE HAPPY TO STAY WITH ME.
AS FOR WULFENBACH, THE SOONER HE IS DISPOSED OF, THE BETTER, I THINK...
YESSS...
COSH!
OH! MY GOODNESS, FATHER ABBOT, HE JUST FELL OVER!
WHY, IT WAS AS THOUGH AN INVISIBLE HAND STRUCK HIM DOWN, BROTHER!
PERHAPS IT WAS ONE OF THOSE LEGENDARY SMOKE KNIGHTS!
AH! HOW MYSTERIOUS!
YEAH. WE GET THAT A LOT.

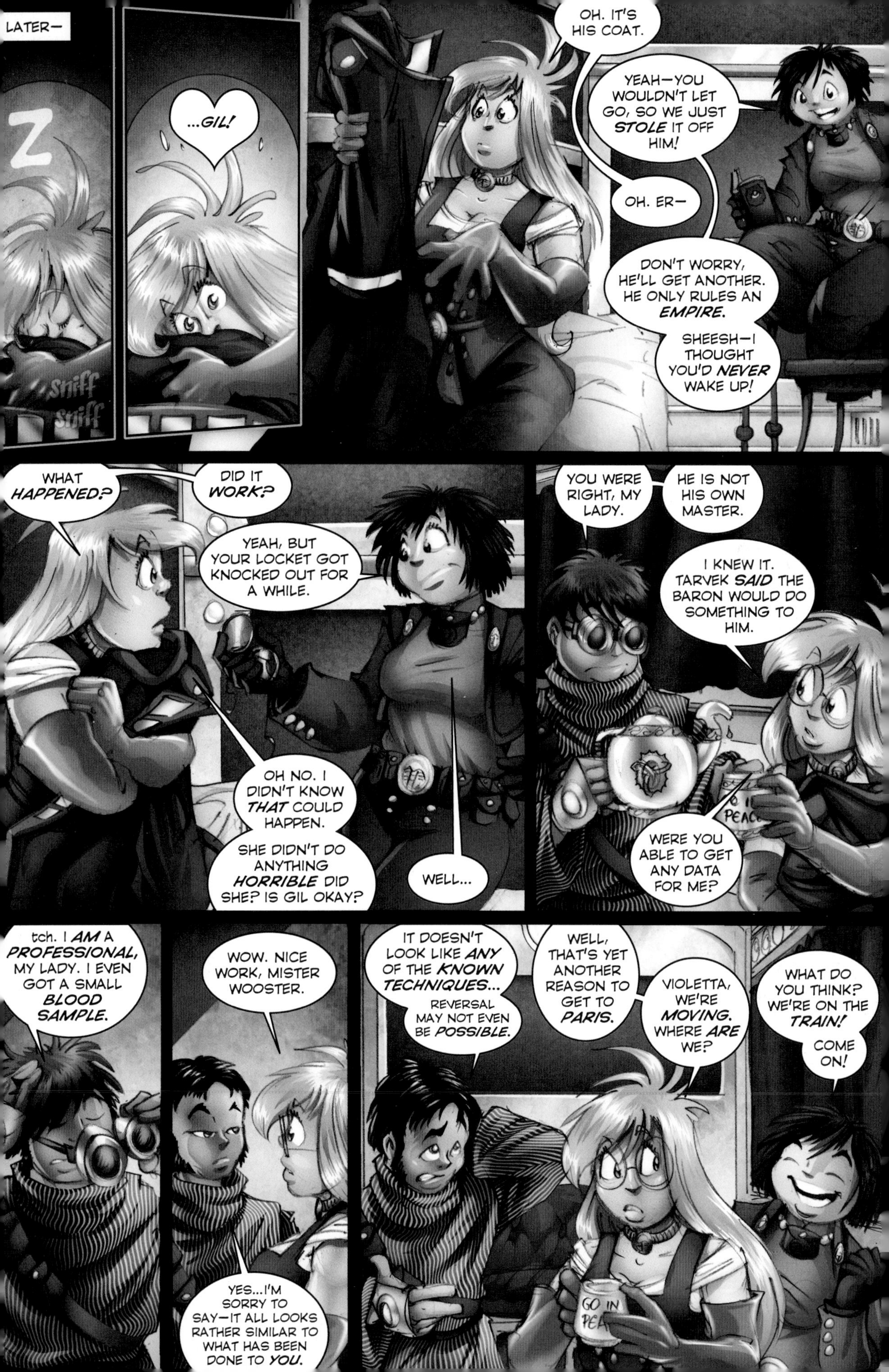
LATER—
Z
Sniff Sniff
...GIL!
OH. IT'S HIS COAT.
YEAH—YOU WOULDN'T LET GO, SO WE JUST STOLE IT OFF HIM!
OH. ER—
DON'T WORRY, HE'LL GET ANOTHER. HE ONLY RULES AN EMPIRE.
SHEESH—I THOUGHT YOU'D NEVER WAKE UP!
WHAT HAPPENED?
DID IT WORK?
YEAH, BUT YOUR LOCKET GOT KNOCKED OUT FOR A WHILE.
OH NO. I DIDN'T KNOW THAT COULD HAPPEN.
SHE DIDN'T DO ANYTHING HORRIBLE DID SHE? IS GIL OKAY?
WELL...
YOU WERE RIGHT, MY LADY.
HE IS NOT HIS OWN MASTER.
I KNEW IT. TARVEK SAID THE BARON WOULD DO SOMETHING TO HIM.
WERE YOU ABLE TO GET ANY DATA FOR ME?
tch. I AM A PROFESSIONAL, MY LADY. I EVEN GOT A SMALL BLOOD SAMPLE.
WOW. NICE WORK, MISTER WOOSTER.
YES...I'M SORRY TO SAY—IT ALL LOOKS RATHER SIMILAR TO WHAT HAS BEEN DONE TO YOU.
IT DOESN'T LOOK LIKE ANY OF THE KNOWN TECHNIQUES...
REVERSAL MAY NOT EVEN BE POSSIBLE.
WELL, THAT'S YET ANOTHER REASON TO GET TO PARIS.
VIOLETTA, WE'RE MOVING. WHERE ARE WE?
WHAT DO YOU THINK? WE'RE ON THE TRAIN!
COME ON!
GO IN PEA

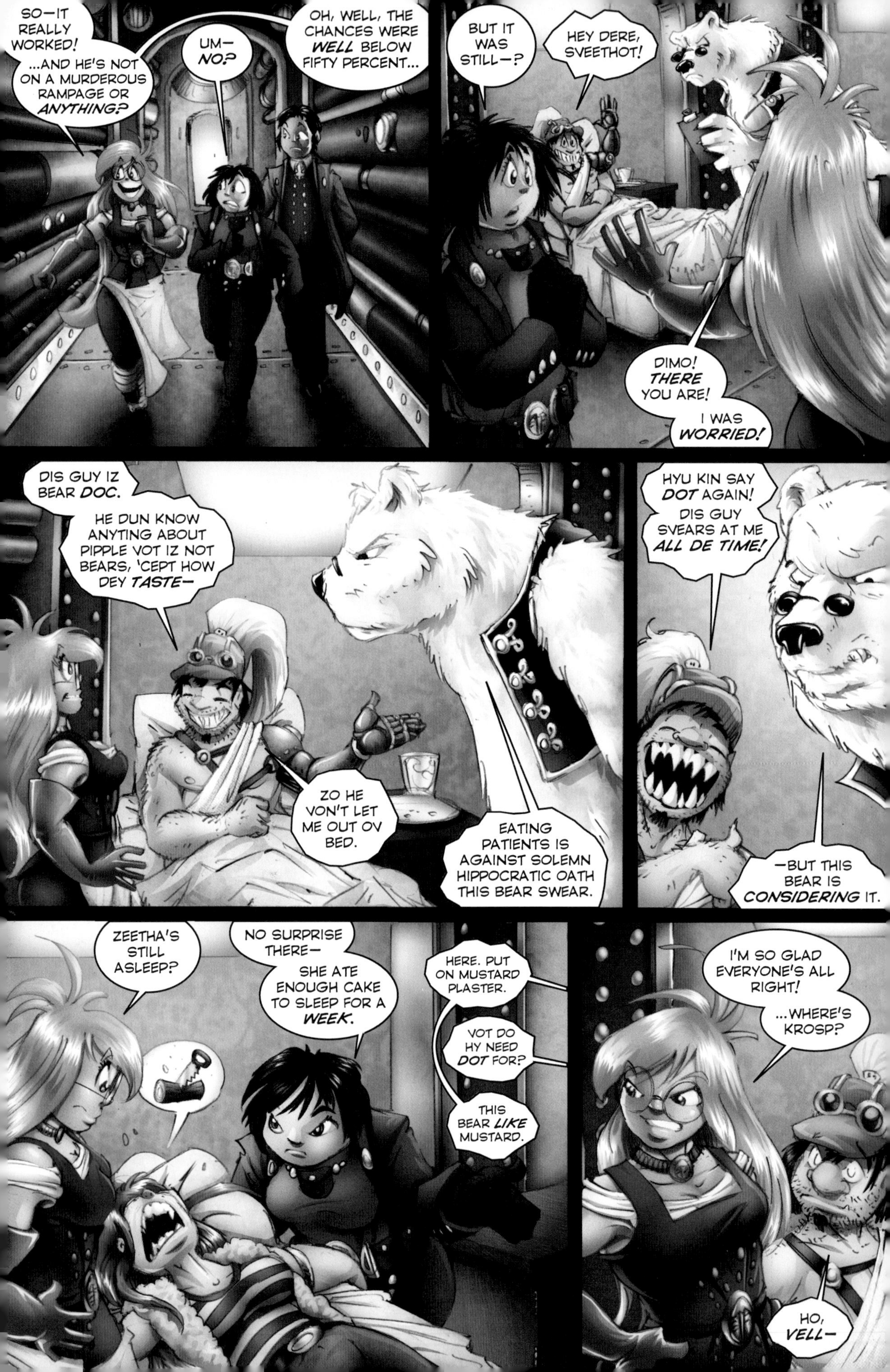
SO—IT REALLY WORKED!
...AND HE'S NOT ON A MURDEROUS RAMPAGE OR ANYTHING?
UM—NO?
OH, WELL, THE CHANCES WERE WELL BELOW FIFTY PERCENT...
BUT IT WAS STILL—?
HEY DERE, SVEETHOT!
DIMO! THERE YOU ARE!
I WAS WORRIED!
DIS GUY IZ BEAR DOC.
HE DUN KNOW ANYTING ABOUT PIPPLE VOT IZ NOT BEARS, 'CEPT HOW DEY TASTE—
ZO HE VON'T LET ME OUT OV BED.
EATING PATIENTS IS AGAINST SOLEMN HIPPOCRATIC OATH THIS BEAR SWEAR.
HYU KIN SAY DOT AGAIN!
DIS GUY SVEARS AT ME ALL DE TIME!
—BUT THIS BEAR IS CONSIDERING IT.
ZEETHA'S STILL ASLEEP?
NO SURPRISE THERE—
SHE ATE ENOUGH CAKE TO SLEEP FOR A WEEK.
HERE. PUT ON MUSTARD PLASTER.
VOT DO HY NEED DOT FOR?
THIS BEAR LIKE MUSTARD.
I'M SO GLAD EVERYONE'S ALL RIGHT!
...WHERE'S KROSP?
HO, VELL—

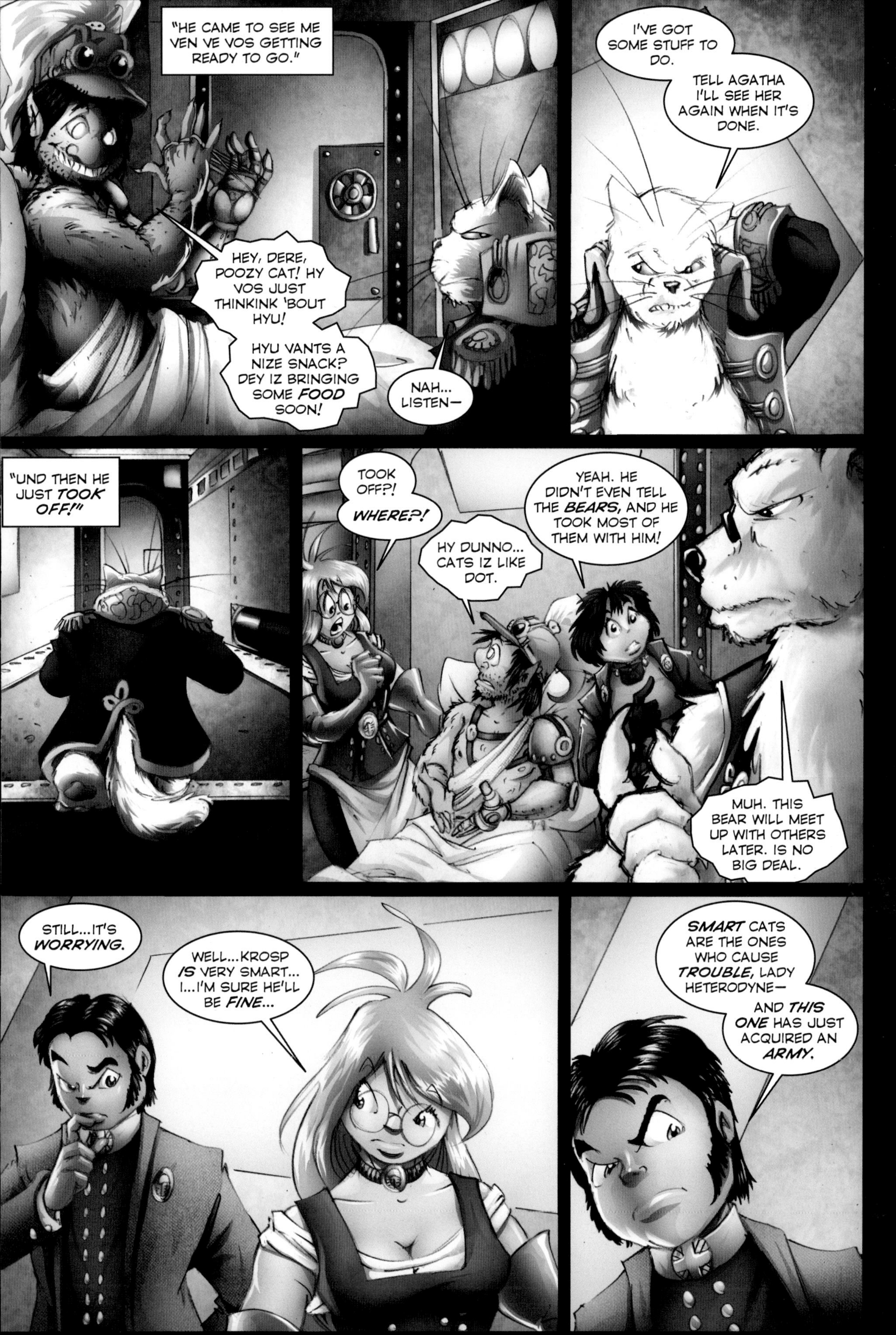
"HE CAME TO SEE ME VEN VE VOS GETTING READY TO GO."
HEY, DERE, POOZY CAT! HY VOS JUST THINKINK 'BOUT HYU!
HYU VANTS A NIZE SNACK? DEY IZ BRINGING SOME FOOD SOON!
NAH... LISTEN—
I'VE GOT SOME STUFF TO DO.
TELL AGATHA I'LL SEE HER AGAIN WHEN IT'S DONE.
"UND THEN HE JUST TOOK OFF!"
TOOK OFF?!
WHERE?!
HY DUNNO... CATS IZ LIKE DOT.
YEAH. HE DIDN'T EVEN TELL THE BEARS, AND HE TOOK MOST OF THEM WITH HIM!
MUH. THIS BEAR WILL MEET UP WITH OTHERS LATER. IS NO BIG DEAL.
STILL...IT'S WORRYING.
WELL...KROSP IS VERY SMART... I...I'M SURE HE'LL BE FINE...
SMART CATS ARE THE ONES WHO CAUSE TROUBLE, LADY HETERODYNE—
AND THIS ONE HAS JUST ACQUIRED AN ARMY.

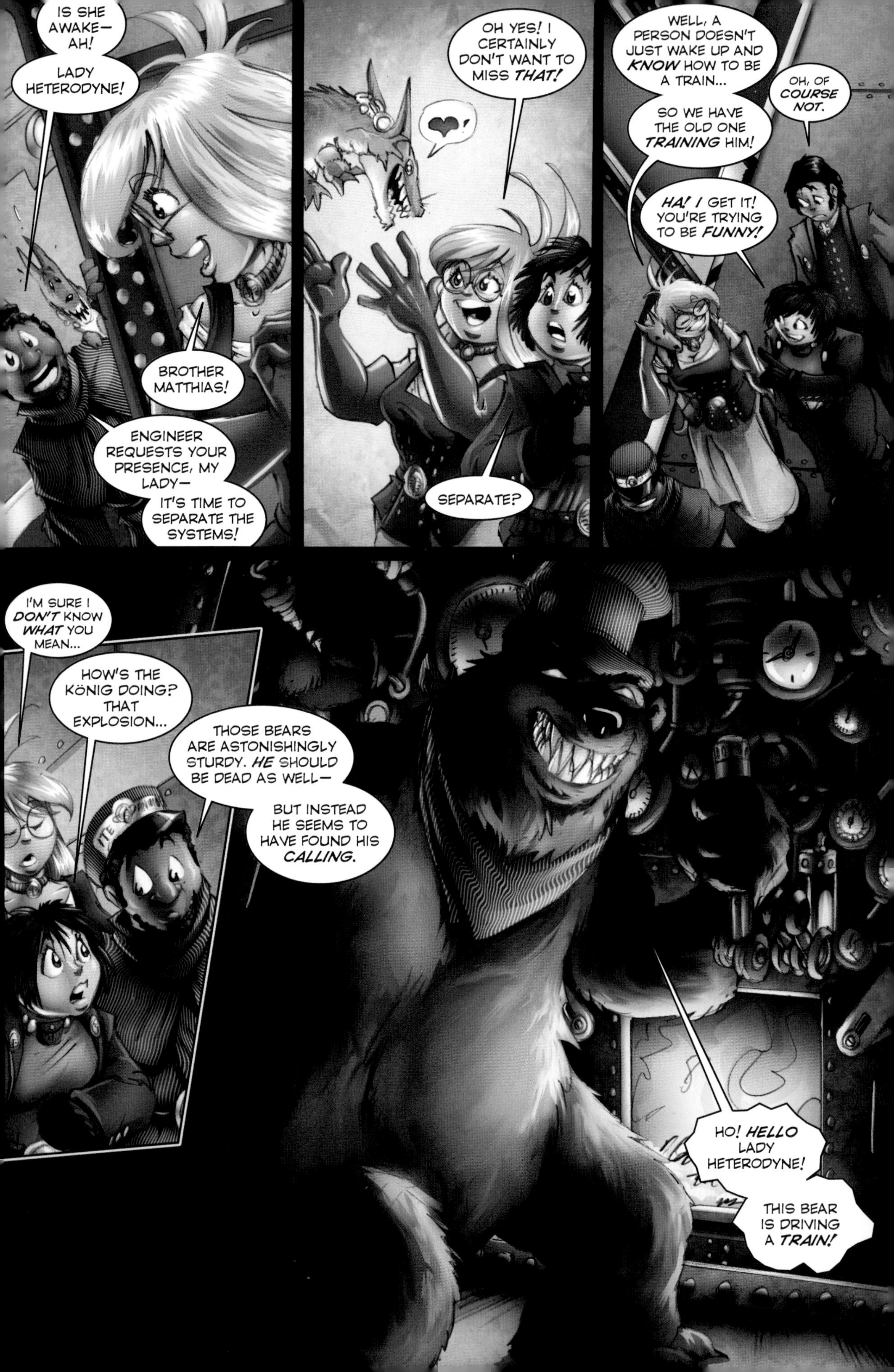

IS SHE AWAKE—AH!
LADY HETERODYNE!
BROTHER MATTHIAS!
ENGINEER REQUESTS YOUR PRESENCE, MY LADY—
IT'S TIME TO SEPARATE THE SYSTEMS!
OH YES! I CERTAINLY DON'T WANT TO MISS THAT!
SEPARATE?
WELL, A PERSON DOESN'T JUST WAKE UP AND KNOW HOW TO BE A TRAIN...
SO WE HAVE THE OLD ONE TRAINING HIM!
OH, OF COURSE NOT.
HA! I GET IT! YOU'RE TRYING TO BE FUNNY!
I'M SURE I DON'T KNOW WHAT YOU MEAN...
HOW'S THE KÖNIG DOING? THAT EXPLOSION...
THOSE BEARS ARE ASTONISHINGLY STURDY. HE SHOULD BE DEAD AS WELL—
BUT INSTEAD HE SEEMS TO HAVE FOUND HIS CALLING.
HO! HELLO LADY HETERODYNE!
THIS BEAR IS DRIVING A TRAIN!

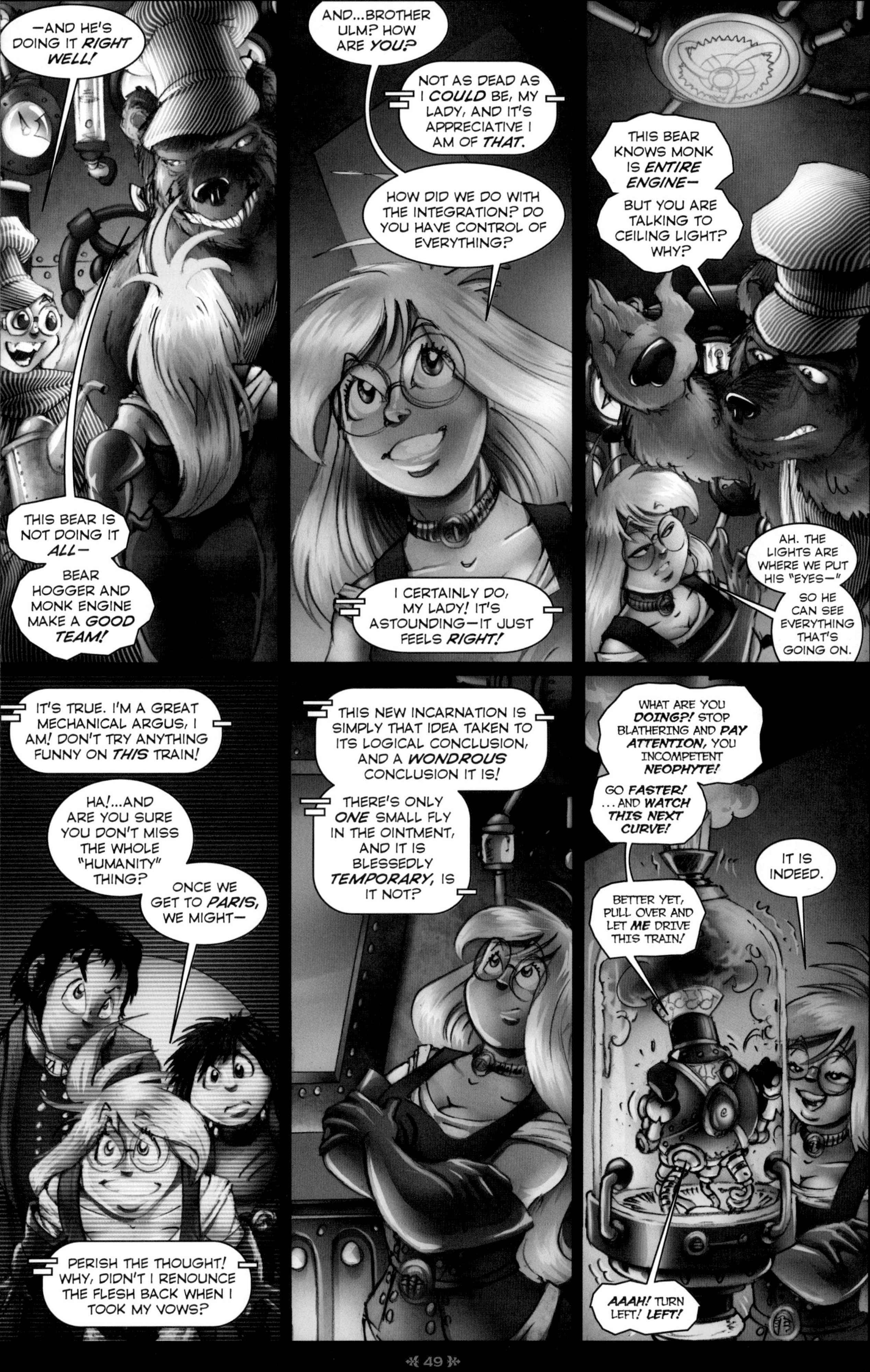
—AND HE'S DOING IT RIGHT WELL!
THIS BEAR IS NOT DOING IT ALL—
BEAR HOGGER AND MONK ENGINE MAKE A GOOD TEAM!
AND...BROTHER ULM? HOW ARE YOU?
NOT AS DEAD AS I COULD BE, MY LADY, AND IT'S APPRECIATIVE I AM OF THAT.
HOW DID WE DO WITH THE INTEGRATION? DO YOU HAVE CONTROL OF EVERYTHING?
I CERTAINLY DO, MY LADY! IT'S ASTOUNDING—IT JUST FEELS RIGHT!
THIS BEAR KNOWS MONK IS ENTIRE ENGINE—
BUT YOU ARE TALKING TO CEILING LIGHT? WHY?
AH. THE LIGHTS ARE WHERE WE PUT HIS "EYES—"
SO HE CAN SEE EVERYTHING THAT'S GOING ON.
IT'S TRUE. I'M A GREAT MECHANICAL ARGUS, I AM! DON'T TRY ANYTHING FUNNY ON THIS TRAIN!
HA!...AND ARE YOU SURE YOU DON'T MISS THE WHOLE "HUMANITY" THING?
ONCE WE GET TO PARIS, WE MIGHT—
PERISH THE THOUGHT! WHY, DIDN'T I RENOUNCE THE FLESH BACK WHEN I TOOK MY VOWS?
THIS NEW INCARNATION IS SIMPLY THAT IDEA TAKEN TO ITS LOGICAL CONCLUSION, AND A WONDROUS CONCLUSION IT IS!
THERE'S ONLY ONE SMALL FLY IN THE OINTMENT, AND IT IS BLESSEDLY TEMPORARY, IS IT NOT?
WHAT ARE YOU DOING?! STOP BLATHERING AND PAY ATTENTION, YOU INCOMPETENT NEOPHYTE!
GO FASTER! ...AND WATCH THIS NEXT CURVE!
IT IS INDEED.
BETTER YET, PULL OVER AND LET ME DRIVE THIS TRAIN!
AAAH! TURN LEFT! LEFT!

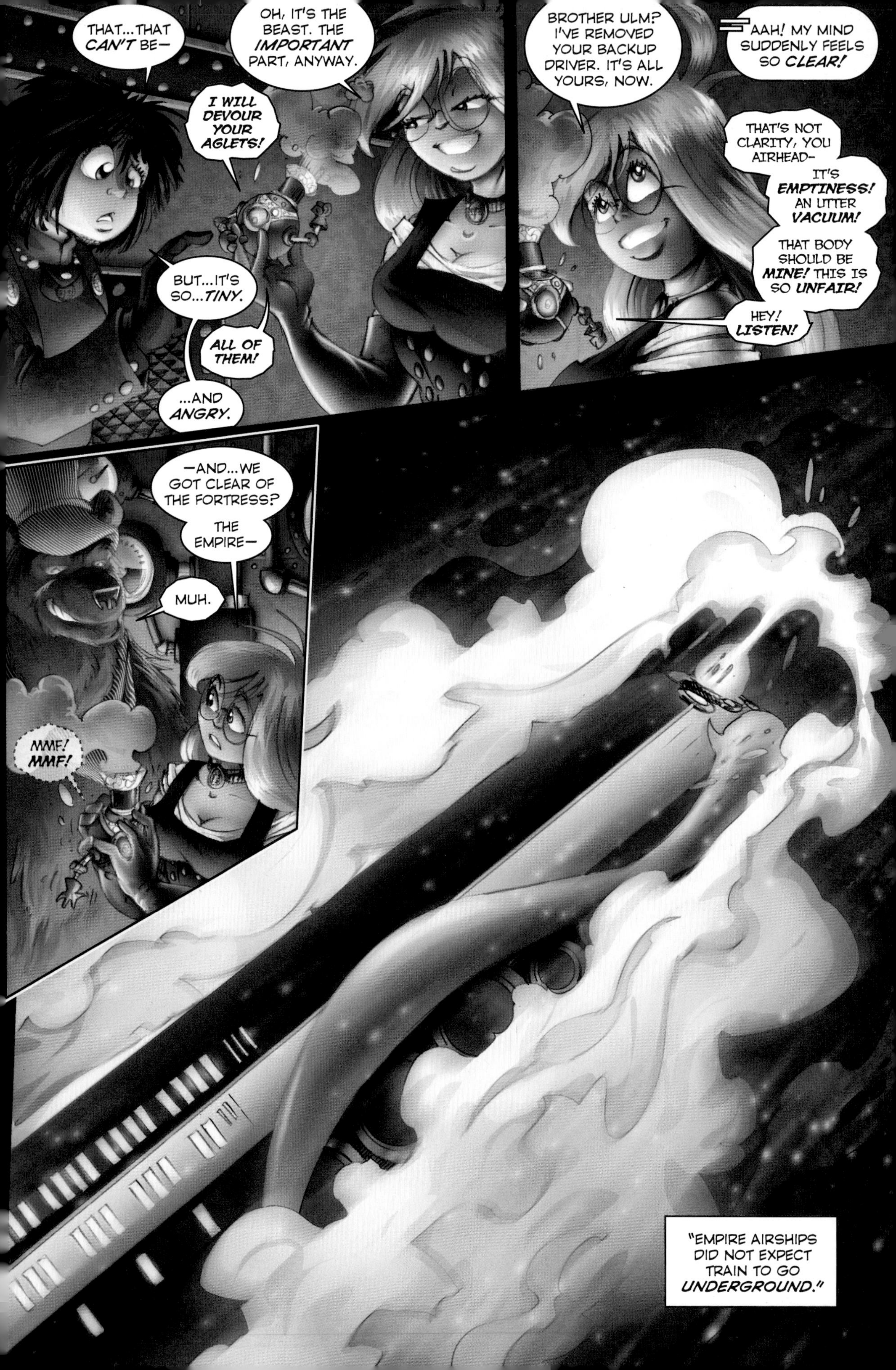
THAT...THAT CAN'T BE—
OH, IT'S THE BEAST. THE IMPORTANT PART, ANYWAY.
I WILL DEVOUR YOUR AGLETS!
BUT...IT'S SO...TINY.
ALL OF THEM!
...AND ANGRY.
BROTHER ULM? I'VE REMOVED YOUR BACKUP DRIVER. IT'S ALL YOURS, NOW.
AAH! MY MIND SUDDENLY FEELS SO CLEAR!
THAT'S NOT CLARITY, YOU AIRHEAD—
IT'S EMPTINESS! AN UTTER VACUUM!
THAT BODY SHOULD BE MINE! THIS IS SO UNFAIR!
HEY! LISTEN!
—AND...WE GOT CLEAR OF THE FORTRESS?
THE EMPIRE—
MUH.
MMF! MMF!
"EMPIRE AIRSHIPS DID NOT EXPECT TRAIN TO GO UNDERGROUND."

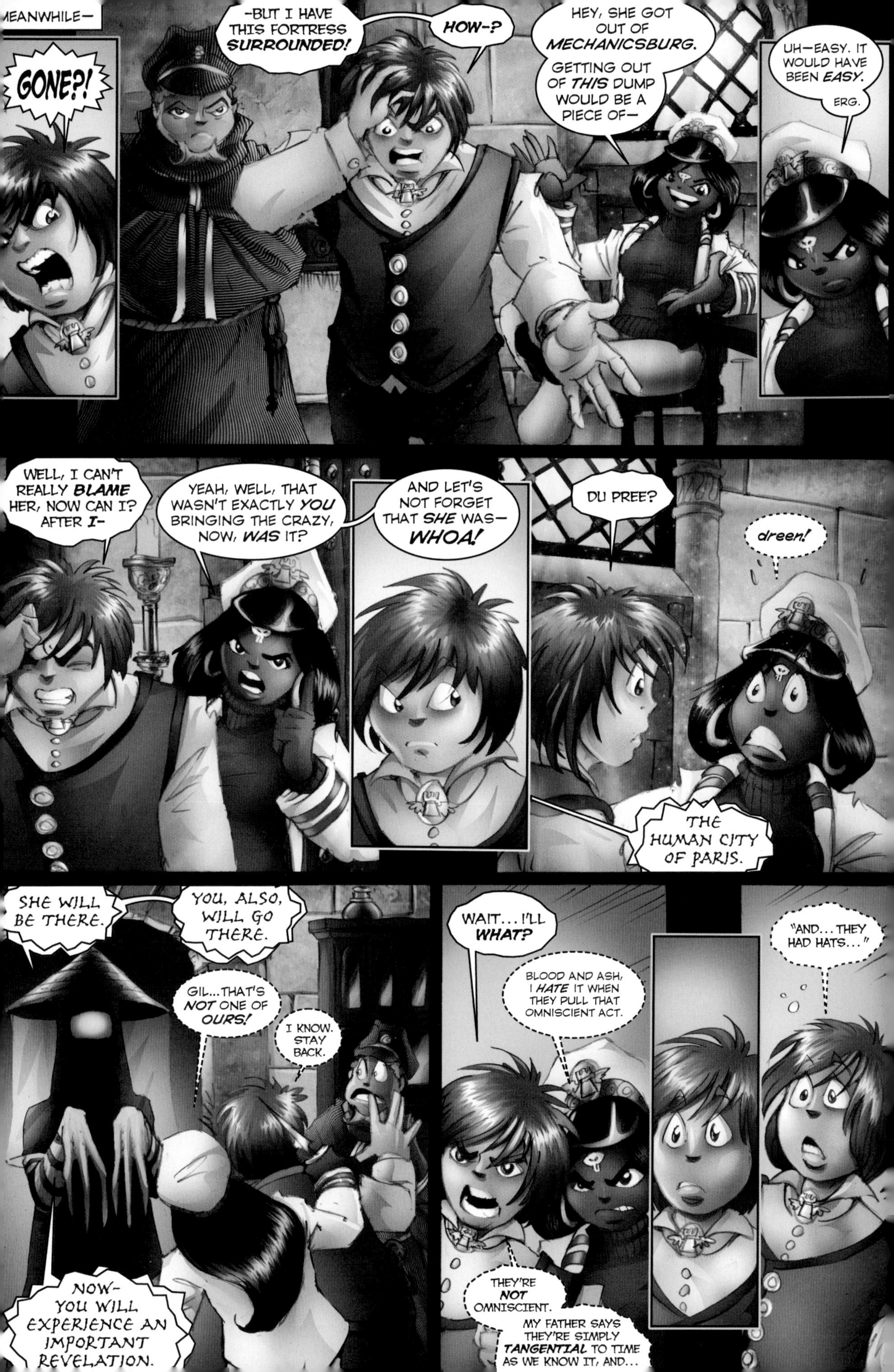

MEANWHILE—
GONE?!
—BUT I HAVE THIS FORTRESS SURROUNDED!
HOW—?
HEY, SHE GOT OUT OF MECHANICSBURG.
GETTING OUT OF THIS DUMP WOULD BE A PIECE OF—
UH—EASY. IT WOULD HAVE BEEN EASY.
ERG.
WELL, I CAN'T REALLY BLAME HER, NOW CAN I? AFTER I—
YEAH, WELL, THAT WASN'T EXACTLY YOU BRINGING THE CRAZY, NOW, WAS IT?
AND LET'S NOT FORGET THAT SHE WAS— WHOA!
DU PREE?
dreen!
THE HUMAN CITY OF PARIS.
SHE WILL BE THERE.
YOU, ALSO, WILL GO THERE.
GIL...THAT'S NOT ONE OF OURS!
I KNOW. STAY BACK.
NOW— YOU WILL EXPERIENCE AN IMPORTANT REVELATION.
WAIT...I'LL WHAT?
BLOOD AND ASH, I HATE IT WHEN THEY PULL THAT OMNISCIENT ACT.
THEY'RE NOT OMNISCIENT.
MY FATHER SAYS THEY'RE SIMPLY TANGENTIAL TO TIME AS WE KNOW IT, AND...
"AND...THEY HAD HATS..."

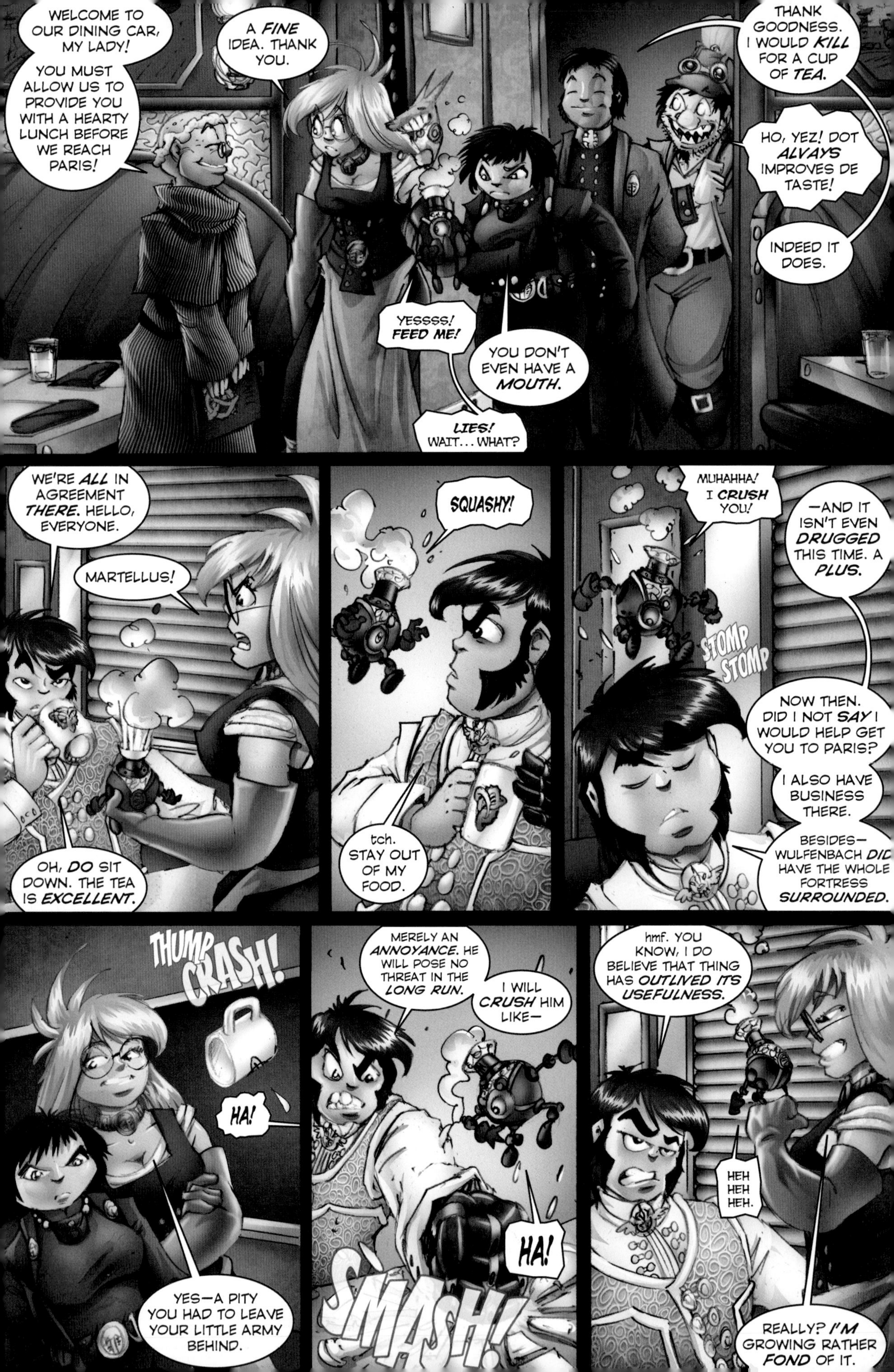
WELCOME TO OUR DINING CAR, MY LADY!
YOU MUST ALLOW US TO PROVIDE YOU WITH A HEARTY LUNCH BEFORE WE REACH PARIS!
A FINE IDEA. THANK YOU.
THANK GOODNESS. I WOULD KILL FOR A CUP OF TEA.
HO, YEZ! DOT ALVAYS IMPROVES DE TASTE!
INDEED IT DOES.
YESSSS! FEED ME!
YOU DON'T EVEN HAVE A MOUTH.
LIES! WAIT... WHAT?
WE'RE ALL IN AGREEMENT THERE. HELLO, EVERYONE.
MARTELLUS!
OH, DO SIT DOWN. THE TEA IS EXCELLENT.
SQUASHY!
tch. STAY OUT OF MY FOOD.
MUHAHHA! I CRUSH YOU!
STOMP STOMP
—AND IT ISN'T EVEN DRUGGED THIS TIME. A PLUS.
NOW THEN. DID I NOT SAY I WOULD HELP GET YOU TO PARIS?
I ALSO HAVE BUSINESS THERE.
BESIDES— WULFENBACH DID HAVE THE WHOLE FORTRESS SURROUNDED.
THUMP CRASH!
HA!
YES—A PITY YOU HAD TO LEAVE YOUR LITTLE ARMY BEHIND.
MERELY AN ANNOYANCE. HE WILL POSE NO THREAT IN THE LONG RUN.
I WILL CRUSH HIM LIKE—
HA!
SMASH!
hmf. YOU KNOW, I DO BELIEVE THAT THING HAS OUTLIVED ITS USEFULNESS.
HEH HEH HEH.
REALLY? I'M GROWING RATHER FOND OF IT.

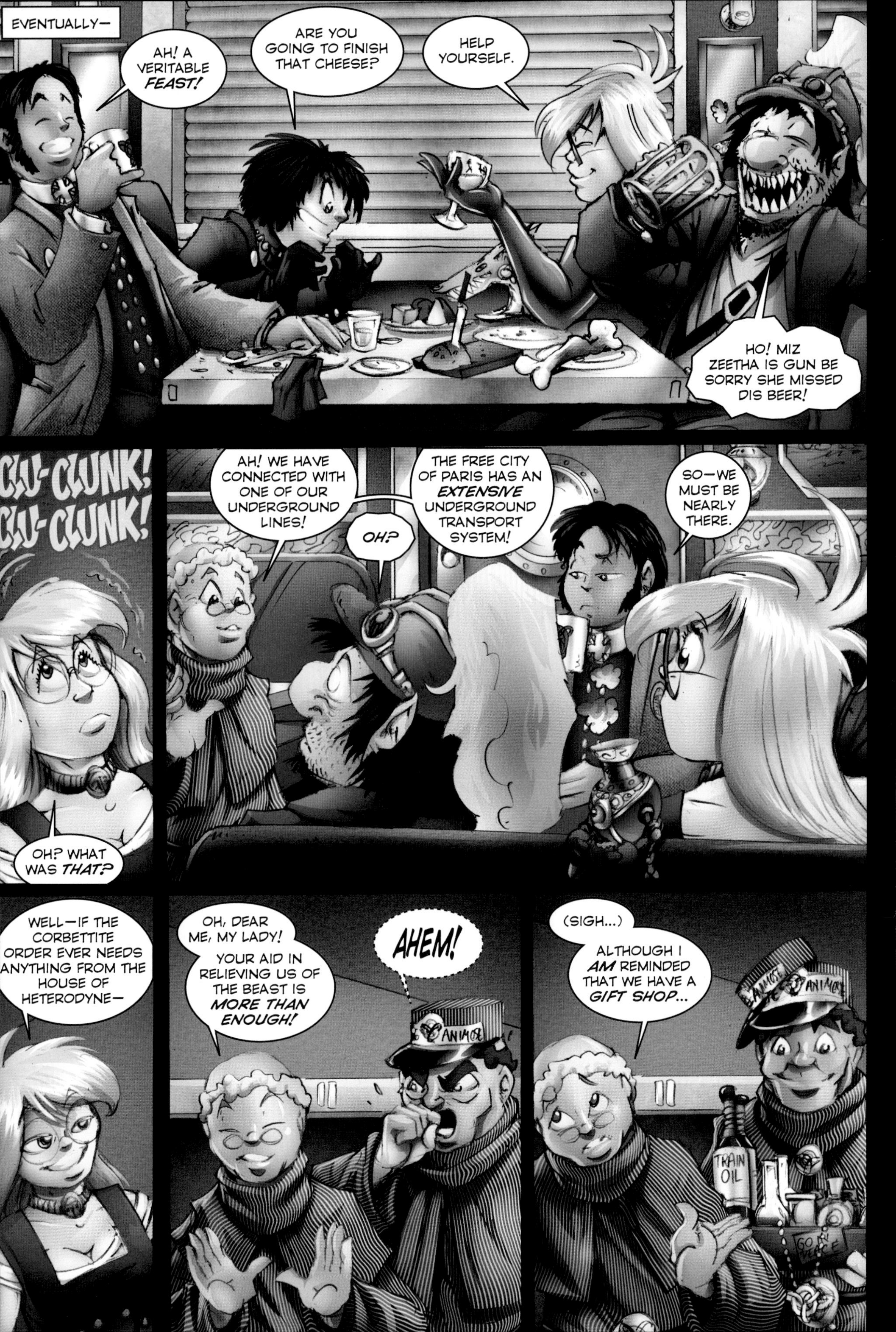
EVENTUALLY—
AH! A VERITABLE *FEAST!*
ARE YOU GOING TO FINISH THAT CHEESE?
HELP YOURSELF.
HO! MIZ ZEETHA IS GUN BE SORRY SHE MISSED DIS BEER!
CLU-CLUNK! CLU-CLUNK!
OH? WHAT WAS *THAT?*
AH! WE HAVE CONNECTED WITH ONE OF OUR UNDERGROUND LINES!
OH?
THE FREE CITY OF PARIS HAS AN *EXTENSIVE* UNDERGROUND TRANSPORT SYSTEM!
SO—WE MUST BE NEARLY THERE.
WELL—IF THE CORBETTITE ORDER EVER NEEDS ANYTHING FROM THE HOUSE OF HETERODYNE—
OH, DEAR ME, MY LADY!
YOUR AID IN RELIEVING US OF THE BEAST IS ***MORE THAN ENOUGH!***
AHEM!
(SIGH...)
ALTHOUGH I ***AM*** REMINDED THAT WE HAVE A ***GIFT SHOP...***
TRAIN OIL
GO IN PEACE

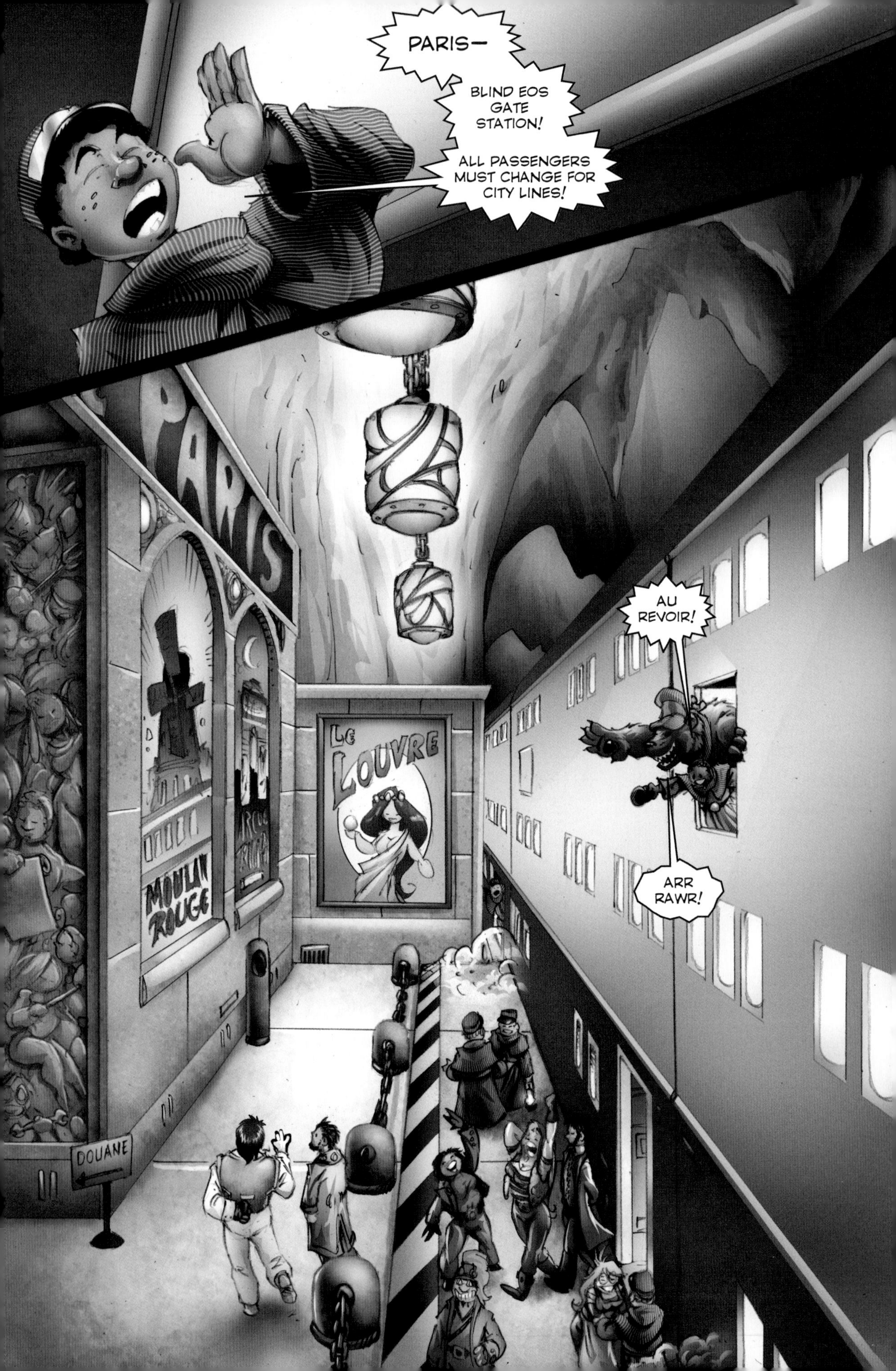
PARIS—
BLIND EOS GATE STATION!
ALL PASSENGERS MUST CHANGE FOR CITY LINES!
PARIS
MOULIN ROUGE
LE LOUVRE
AU REVOIR!
ARR RAWR!
DOUANE

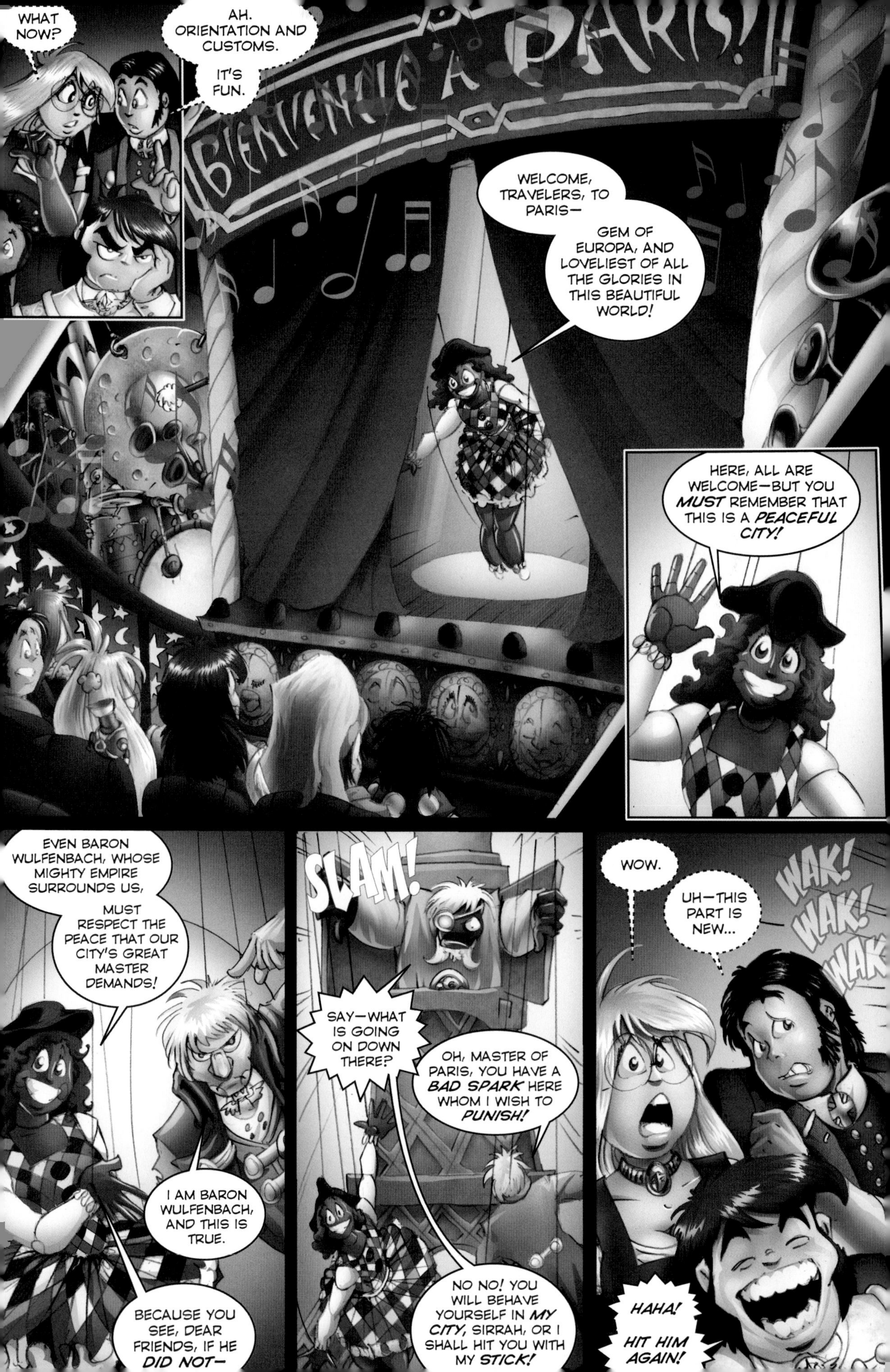
WHAT NOW?
AH. ORIENTATION AND CUSTOMS.
IT'S FUN.
BIENVENUE A PARIS!
WELCOME, TRAVELERS, TO PARIS—
GEM OF EUROPA, AND LOVELIEST OF ALL THE GLORIES IN THIS BEAUTIFUL WORLD!
HERE, ALL ARE WELCOME—BUT YOU *MUST* REMEMBER THAT THIS IS A *PEACEFUL CITY!*
EVEN BARON WULFENBACH, WHOSE MIGHTY EMPIRE SURROUNDS US,
MUST RESPECT THE PEACE THAT OUR CITY'S GREAT MASTER DEMANDS!
I AM BARON WULFENBACH, AND THIS IS TRUE.
BECAUSE YOU SEE, DEAR FRIENDS, IF HE *DID NOT—*
SLAM!
SAY—WHAT IS GOING ON DOWN THERE?
OH, MASTER OF PARIS, YOU HAVE A *BAD SPARK* HERE WHOM I WISH TO *PUNISH!*
NO NO! YOU WILL BEHAVE YOURSELF IN *MY CITY,* SIRRAH, OR I SHALL HIT YOU WITH MY *STICK!*
WOW.
UH—THIS PART IS NEW...
WAK! WAK! WAK
HAHA!
HIT HIM AGAIN!

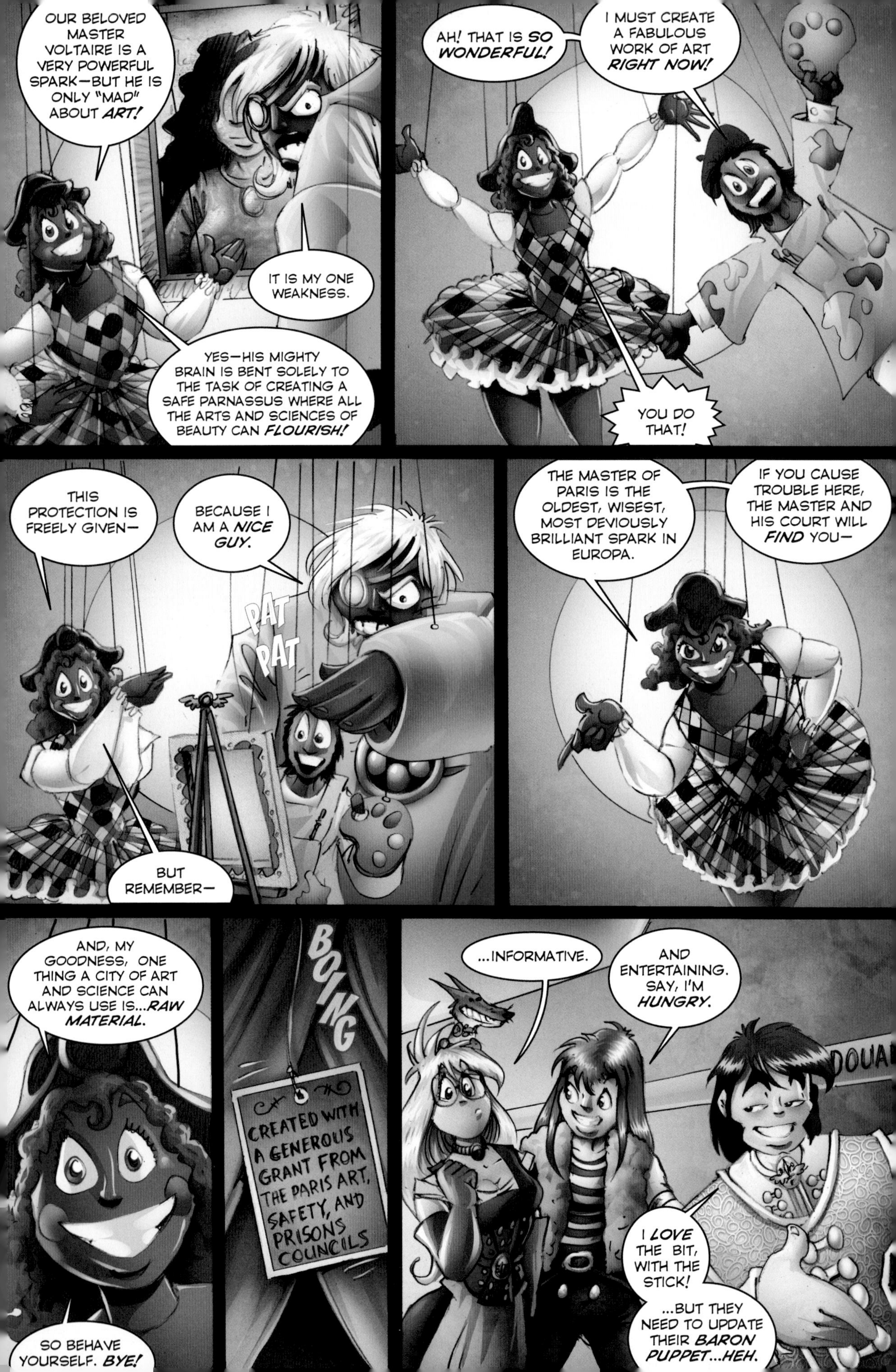
OUR BELOVED MASTER VOLTAIRE IS A VERY POWERFUL SPARK—BUT HE IS ONLY "MAD" ABOUT *ART!*
IT IS MY ONE WEAKNESS.
YES—HIS MIGHTY BRAIN IS BENT SOLELY TO THE TASK OF CREATING A SAFE PARNASSUS WHERE ALL THE ARTS AND SCIENCES OF BEAUTY CAN *FLOURISH!*
AH! THAT IS **SO WONDERFUL!**
I MUST CREATE A FABULOUS WORK OF ART ***RIGHT NOW!***
YOU DO THAT!
THIS PROTECTION IS FREELY GIVEN—
BECAUSE I AM A ***NICE GUY.***
PAT PAT
BUT REMEMBER—
THE MASTER OF PARIS IS THE OLDEST, WISEST, MOST DEVIOUSLY BRILLIANT SPARK IN EUROPA.
IF YOU CAUSE TROUBLE HERE, THE MASTER AND HIS COURT WILL *FIND* YOU—
AND, MY GOODNESS, ONE THING A CITY OF ART AND SCIENCE CAN ALWAYS USE IS...***RAW MATERIAL.***
SO BEHAVE YOURSELF. ***BYE!***
BOING
CREATED WITH A GENEROUS GRANT FROM THE PARIS ART, SAFETY, AND PRISONS COUNCILS
...INFORMATIVE.
AND ENTERTAINING. SAY, I'M ***HUNGRY.***
I ***LOVE*** THE BIT, WITH THE STICK!
...BUT THEY NEED TO UPDATE THEIR ***BARON PUPPET***...***HEH.***

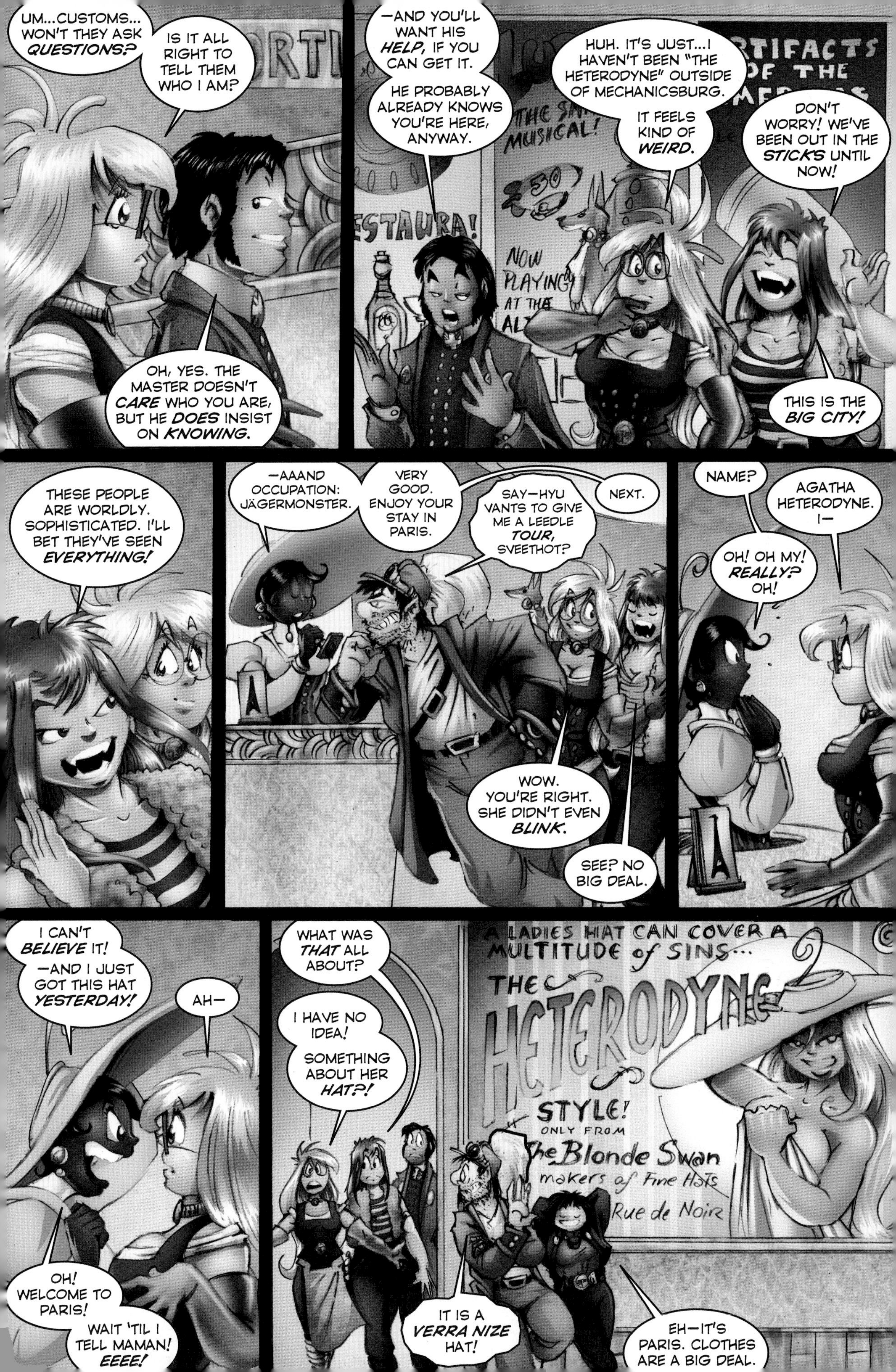
UM...CUSTOMS... WON'T THEY ASK QUESTIONS?
IS IT ALL RIGHT TO TELL THEM WHO I AM?
OH, YES. THE MASTER DOESN'T CARE WHO YOU ARE, BUT HE DOES INSIST ON KNOWING.
—AND YOU'LL WANT HIS HELP, IF YOU CAN GET IT.
HE PROBABLY ALREADY KNOWS YOU'RE HERE, ANYWAY.
NOW PLAYING AT THE
HUH. IT'S JUST...I HAVEN'T BEEN "THE HETERODYNE" OUTSIDE OF MECHANICSBURG.
IT FEELS KIND OF WEIRD.
DON'T WORRY! WE'VE BEEN OUT IN THE STICKS UNTIL NOW!
THIS IS THE BIG CITY!
THESE PEOPLE ARE WORLDLY. SOPHISTICATED. I'LL BET THEY'VE SEEN EVERYTHING!
—AAAND OCCUPATION: JÄGERMONSTER.
VERY GOOD. ENJOY YOUR STAY IN PARIS.
SAY—HYU VANTS TO GIVE ME A LEEDLE TOUR, SVEETHOT?
NEXT.
WOW. YOU'RE RIGHT. SHE DIDN'T EVEN BLINK.
SEE? NO BIG DEAL.
NAME?
AGATHA HETERODYNE. I—
OH! OH MY! REALLY? OH!
I CAN'T BELIEVE IT! —AND I JUST GOT THIS HAT YESTERDAY!
AH—
OH! WELCOME TO PARIS!
WAIT 'TIL I TELL MAMAN! EEEE!
WHAT WAS THAT ALL ABOUT?
I HAVE NO IDEA!
SOMETHING ABOUT HER HAT?!
A LADIES HAT CAN COVER A MULTITUDE of SINS...
THE HETERODYNE STYLE!
ONLY FROM The Blonde Swan
makers of Fine Hats
Rue de Noir
IT IS A VERRA NIZE HAT!
EH—IT'S PARIS. CLOTHES ARE A BIG DEAL.

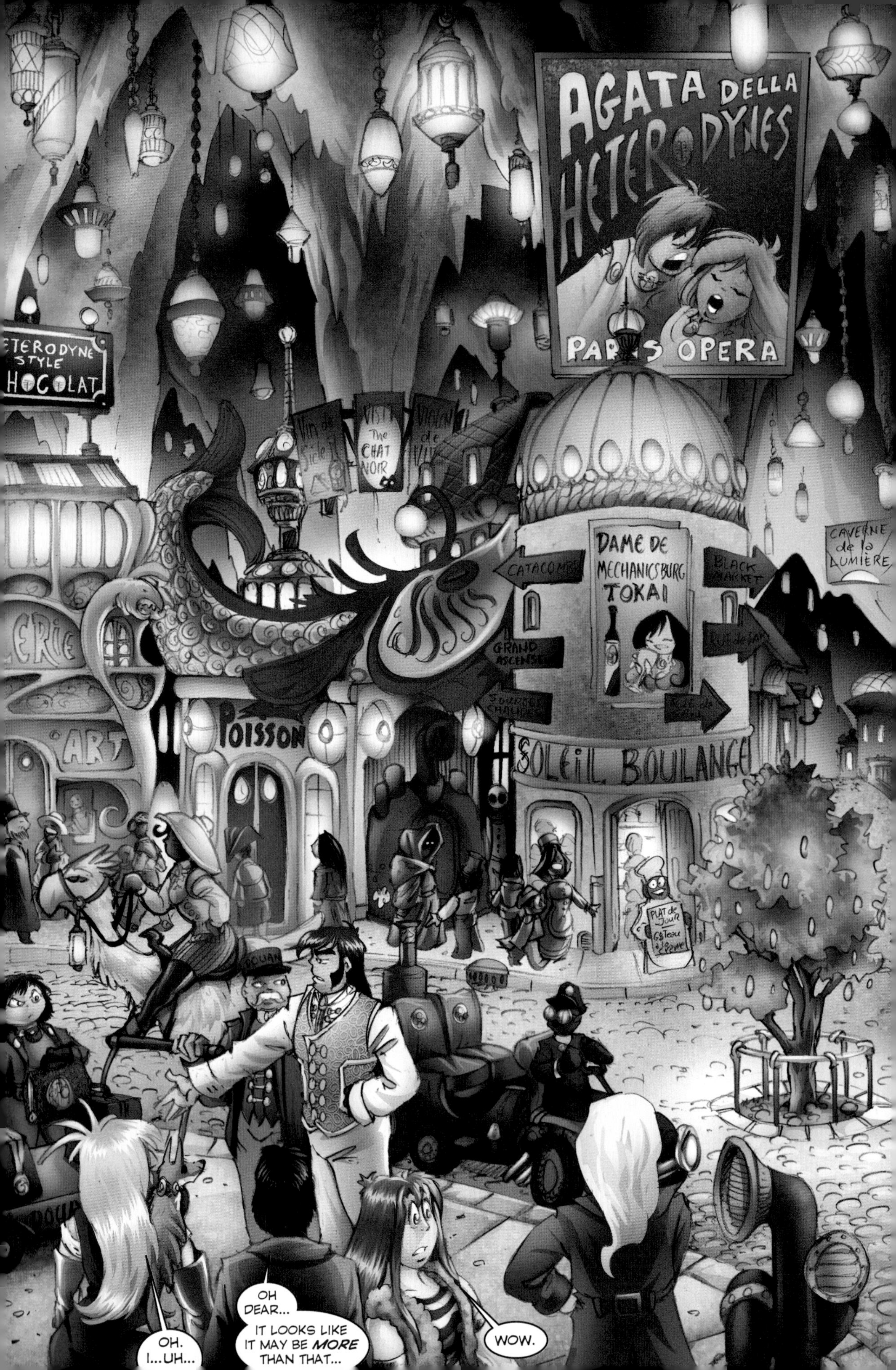
AGATA DELLA HETERODYNES
PAR S OPERA
ETERODYNE STYLE
HOCOLAT
The CHAT NOIR
DAME DE MECHANICSBURG TOKAI
CATACOMBE
BLACK MARKET
CAVERNE de la LUMIERE
POISSON
ART
SOLEIL BOULANGE
OH. I...UH...
OH DEAR... IT LOOKS LIKE IT MAY BE *MORE* THAN THAT...
WOW.

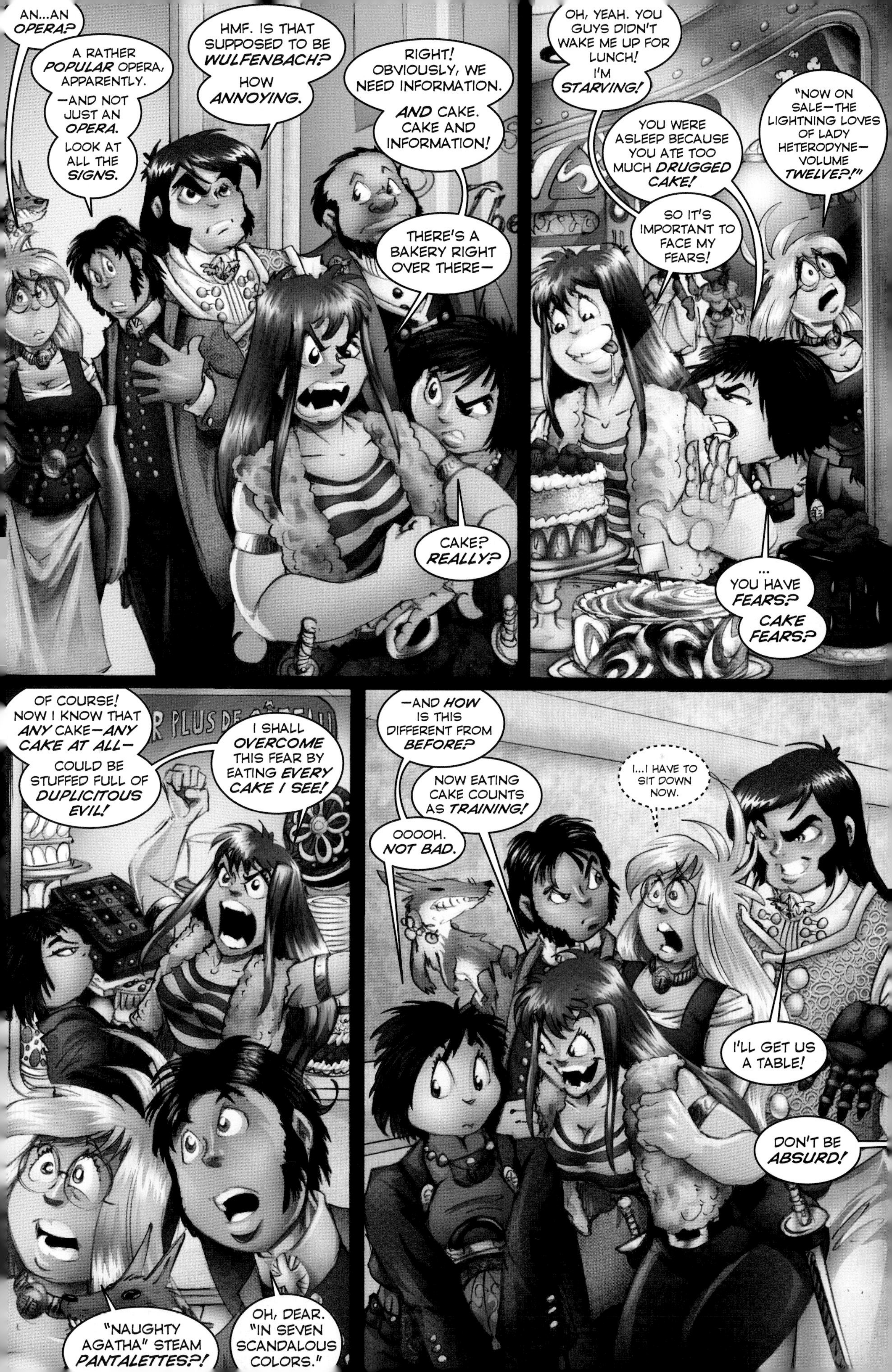
AN...AN OPERA?
A RATHER POPULAR OPERA, APPARENTLY.
—AND NOT JUST AN OPERA. LOOK AT ALL THE SIGNS.
HMF. IS THAT SUPPOSED TO BE WULFENBACH? HOW ANNOYING.
RIGHT! OBVIOUSLY, WE NEED INFORMATION.
AND CAKE. CAKE AND INFORMATION!
THERE'S A BAKERY RIGHT OVER THERE—
CAKE? REALLY?
OH, YEAH. YOU GUYS DIDN'T WAKE ME UP FOR LUNCH! I'M STARVING!
YOU WERE ASLEEP BECAUSE YOU ATE TOO MUCH DRUGGED CAKE!
SO IT'S IMPORTANT TO FACE MY FEARS!
"NOW ON SALE—THE LIGHTNING LOVES OF LADY HETERODYNE—VOLUME TWELVE?!"
... YOU HAVE FEARS? CAKE FEARS?
OF COURSE! NOW I KNOW THAT ANY CAKE—ANY CAKE AT ALL—COULD BE STUFFED FULL OF DUPLICITOUS EVIL!
I SHALL OVERCOME THIS FEAR BY EATING EVERY CAKE I SEE!
"NAUGHTY AGATHA" STEAM PANTALETTES?!
OH, DEAR. "IN SEVEN SCANDALOUS COLORS."
—AND HOW IS THIS DIFFERENT FROM BEFORE?
NOW EATING CAKE COUNTS AS TRAINING!
OOOOH. NOT BAD.
I...I HAVE TO SIT DOWN NOW.
I'LL GET US A TABLE!
DON'T BE ABSURD!

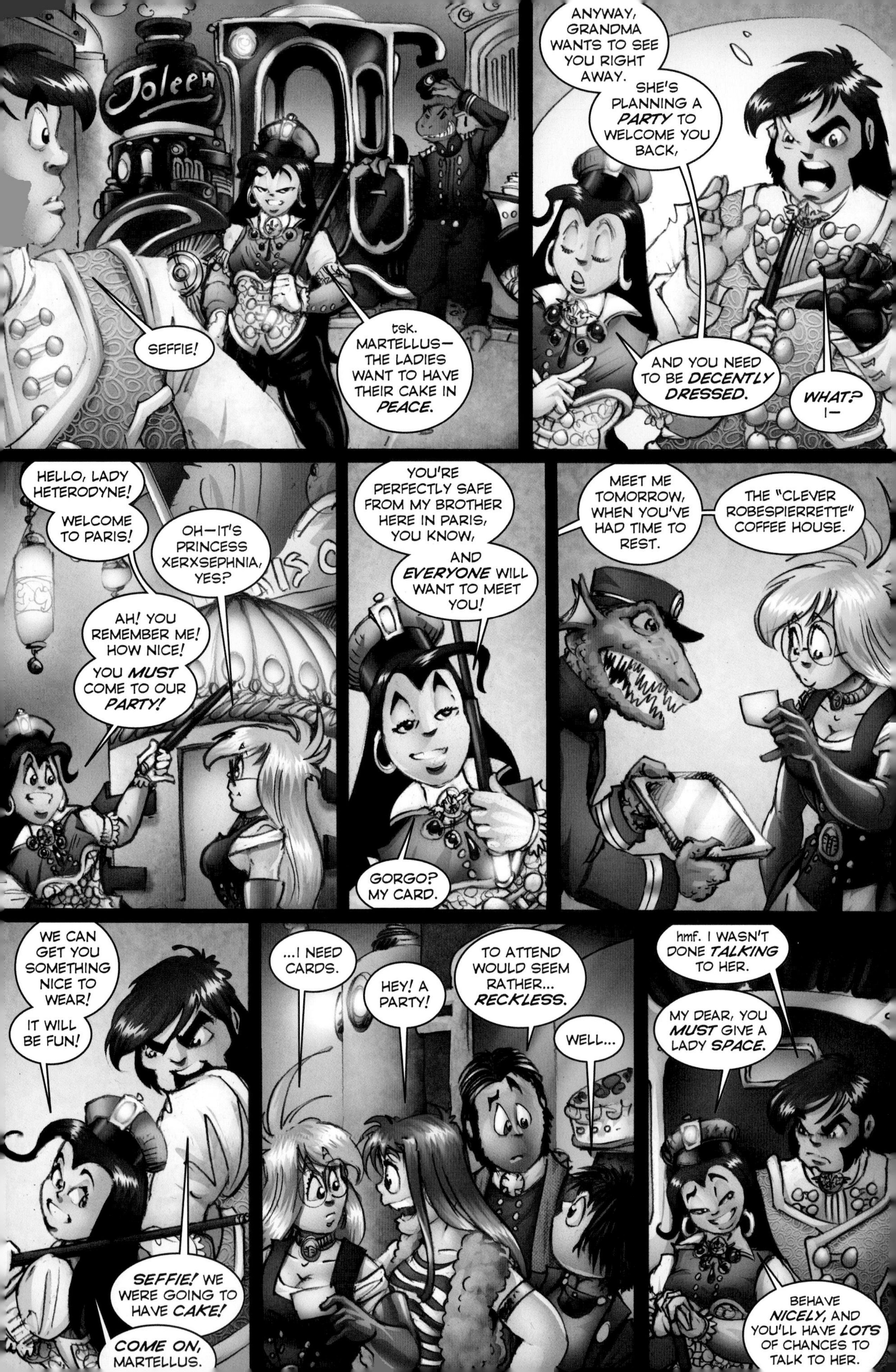
Joleen
SEFFIE!
tsk. MARTELLUS— THE LADIES WANT TO HAVE THEIR CAKE IN *PEACE*.
ANYWAY, GRANDMA WANTS TO SEE YOU RIGHT AWAY.
SHE'S PLANNING A *PARTY* TO WELCOME YOU BACK,
AND YOU NEED TO BE ***DECENTLY DRESSED.***
WHAT? I—
HELLO, LADY HETERODYNE!
WELCOME TO PARIS!
OH—IT'S PRINCESS XERXSEPHNIA, YES?
AH! YOU REMEMBER ME! HOW NICE!
YOU ***MUST*** COME TO OUR ***PARTY!***
YOU'RE PERFECTLY SAFE FROM MY BROTHER HERE IN PARIS, YOU KNOW,
AND ***EVERYONE*** WILL WANT TO MEET YOU!
GORGO? MY CARD.
MEET ME TOMORROW, WHEN YOU'VE HAD TIME TO REST.
THE "CLEVER ROBESPIERRETTE" COFFEE HOUSE.
WE CAN GET YOU SOMETHING NICE TO WEAR!
IT WILL BE FUN!
SEFFIE! WE WERE GOING TO HAVE ***CAKE!***
COME ON, MARTELLUS.
...I NEED CARDS.
HEY! A PARTY!
TO ATTEND WOULD SEEM RATHER... ***RECKLESS.***
WELL...
hmf. I WASN'T DONE ***TALKING*** TO HER.
MY DEAR, YOU ***MUST*** GIVE A LADY ***SPACE.***
BEHAVE ***NICELY,*** AND YOU'LL HAVE ***LOTS*** OF CHANCES TO TALK TO HER.

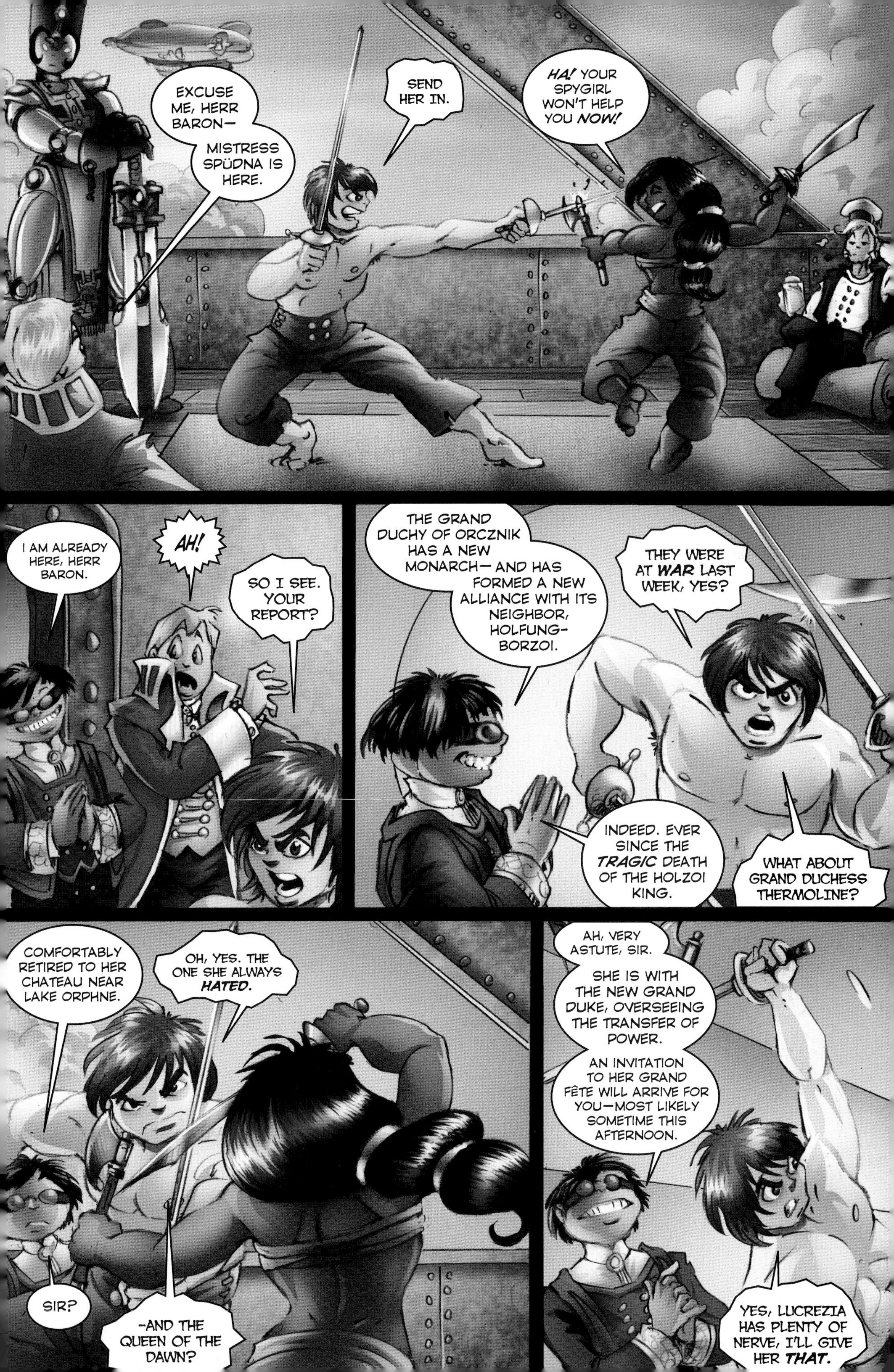

EXCUSE ME, HERR BARON—
MISTRESS SPÜDNA IS HERE.
SEND HER IN.
HA! YOUR SPYGIRL WON'T HELP YOU NOW!
I AM ALREADY HERE, HERR BARON.
AH!
SO I SEE. YOUR REPORT?
THE GRAND DUCHY OF ORCZNIK HAS A NEW MONARCH— AND HAS FORMED A NEW ALLIANCE WITH ITS NEIGHBOR, HOLFUNG-BORZOI.
THEY WERE AT WAR LAST WEEK, YES?
INDEED. EVER SINCE THE TRAGIC DEATH OF THE HOLZOI KING.
WHAT ABOUT GRAND DUCHESS THERMOLINE?
COMFORTABLY RETIRED TO HER CHATEAU NEAR LAKE ORPHNE.
OH, YES. THE ONE SHE ALWAYS HATED.
SIR?
-AND THE QUEEN OF THE DAWN?
AH, VERY ASTUTE, SIR.
SHE IS WITH THE NEW GRAND DUKE, OVERSEEING THE TRANSFER OF POWER.
AN INVITATION TO HER GRAND FÊTE WILL ARRIVE FOR YOU—MOST LIKELY SOMETIME THIS AFTERNOON.
YES, LUCREZIA HAS PLENTY OF NERVE, I'LL GIVE HER THAT.

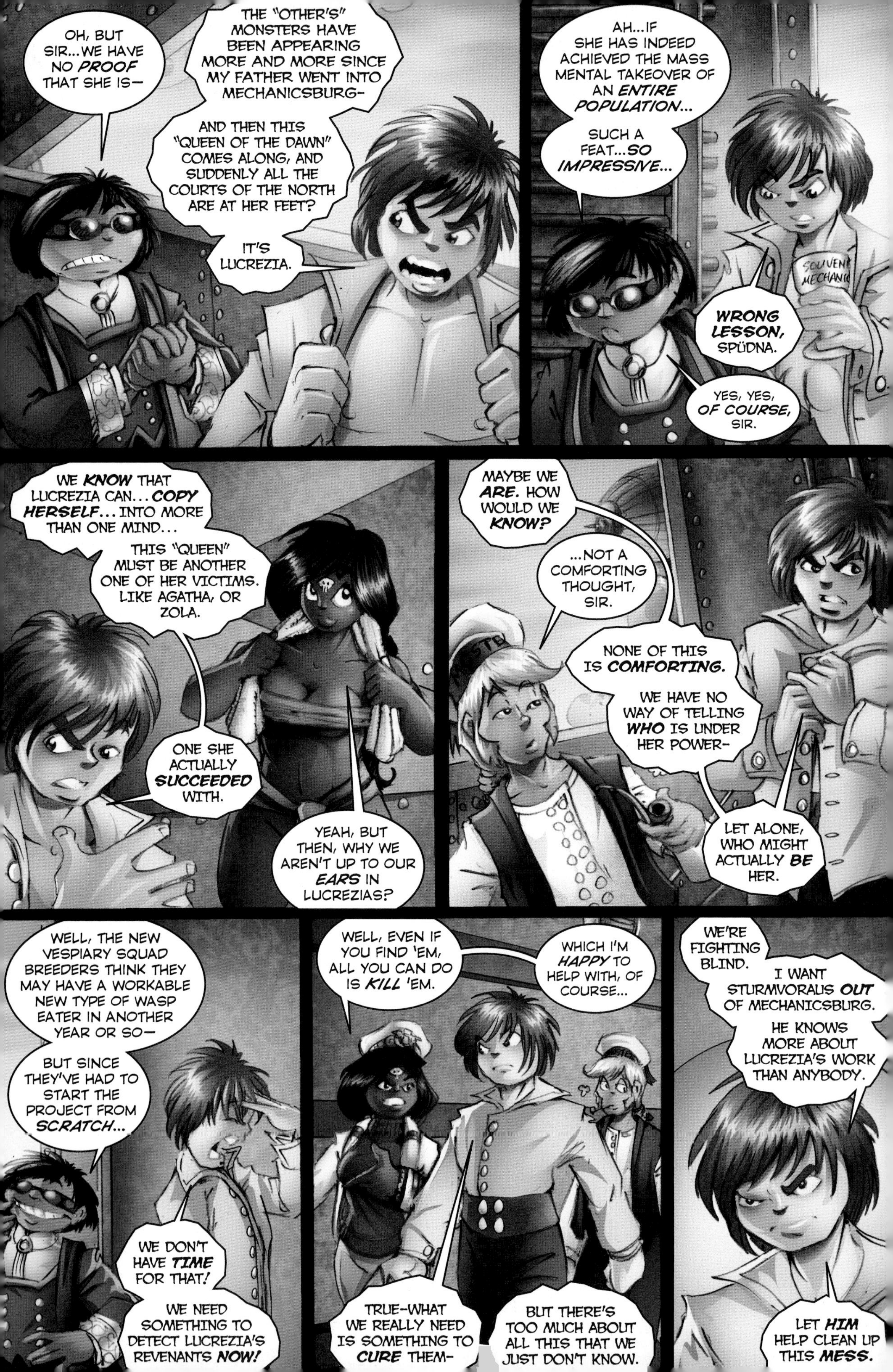

OH, BUT SIR...WE HAVE NO *PROOF* THAT SHE IS—
THE "OTHER'S" MONSTERS HAVE BEEN APPEARING MORE AND MORE SINCE MY FATHER WENT INTO MECHANICSBURG-
AND THEN THIS "QUEEN OF THE DAWN" COMES ALONG, AND SUDDENLY ALL THE COURTS OF THE NORTH ARE AT HER FEET?
IT'S LUCREZIA.
AH...IF SHE HAS INDEED ACHIEVED THE MASS MENTAL TAKEOVER OF AN *ENTIRE POPULATION*...
SUCH A FEAT...*SO IMPRESSIVE*...
WRONG LESSON, SPÜDNA.
YES, YES, *OF COURSE,* SIR.
WE *KNOW* THAT LUCREZIA CAN... *COPY HERSELF*... INTO MORE THAN ONE MIND...
THIS "QUEEN" MUST BE ANOTHER ONE OF HER VICTIMS. LIKE AGATHA, OR ZOLA.
ONE SHE ACTUALLY *SUCCEEDED* WITH.
YEAH, BUT THEN, WHY WE AREN'T UP TO OUR *EARS* IN LUCREZIAS?
MAYBE WE *ARE.* HOW WOULD WE *KNOW?*
...NOT A COMFORTING THOUGHT, SIR.
NONE OF THIS IS *COMFORTING.*
WE HAVE NO WAY OF TELLING *WHO* IS UNDER HER POWER-
LET ALONE, WHO MIGHT ACTUALLY *BE* HER.
WELL, THE NEW VESPIARY SQUAD BREEDERS THINK THEY MAY HAVE A WORKABLE NEW TYPE OF WASP EATER IN ANOTHER YEAR OR SO—
BUT SINCE THEY'VE HAD TO START THE PROJECT FROM *SCRATCH*...
WE DON'T HAVE *TIME* FOR THAT!
WE NEED SOMETHING TO DETECT LUCREZIA'S REVENANTS *NOW!*
WELL, EVEN IF YOU FIND 'EM, ALL YOU CAN DO IS *KILL* 'EM.
WHICH I'M *HAPPY* TO HELP WITH, OF COURSE...
TRUE-WHAT WE REALLY NEED IS SOMETHING TO *CURE* THEM-
BUT THERE'S TOO MUCH ABOUT ALL THIS THAT WE JUST DON'T KNOW.
WE'RE FIGHTING BLIND.
I WANT STURMVORAUS *OUT* OF MECHANICSBURG.
HE KNOWS MORE ABOUT LUCREZIA'S WORK THAN ANYBODY.
LET *HIM* HELP CLEAN UP THIS *MESS.*

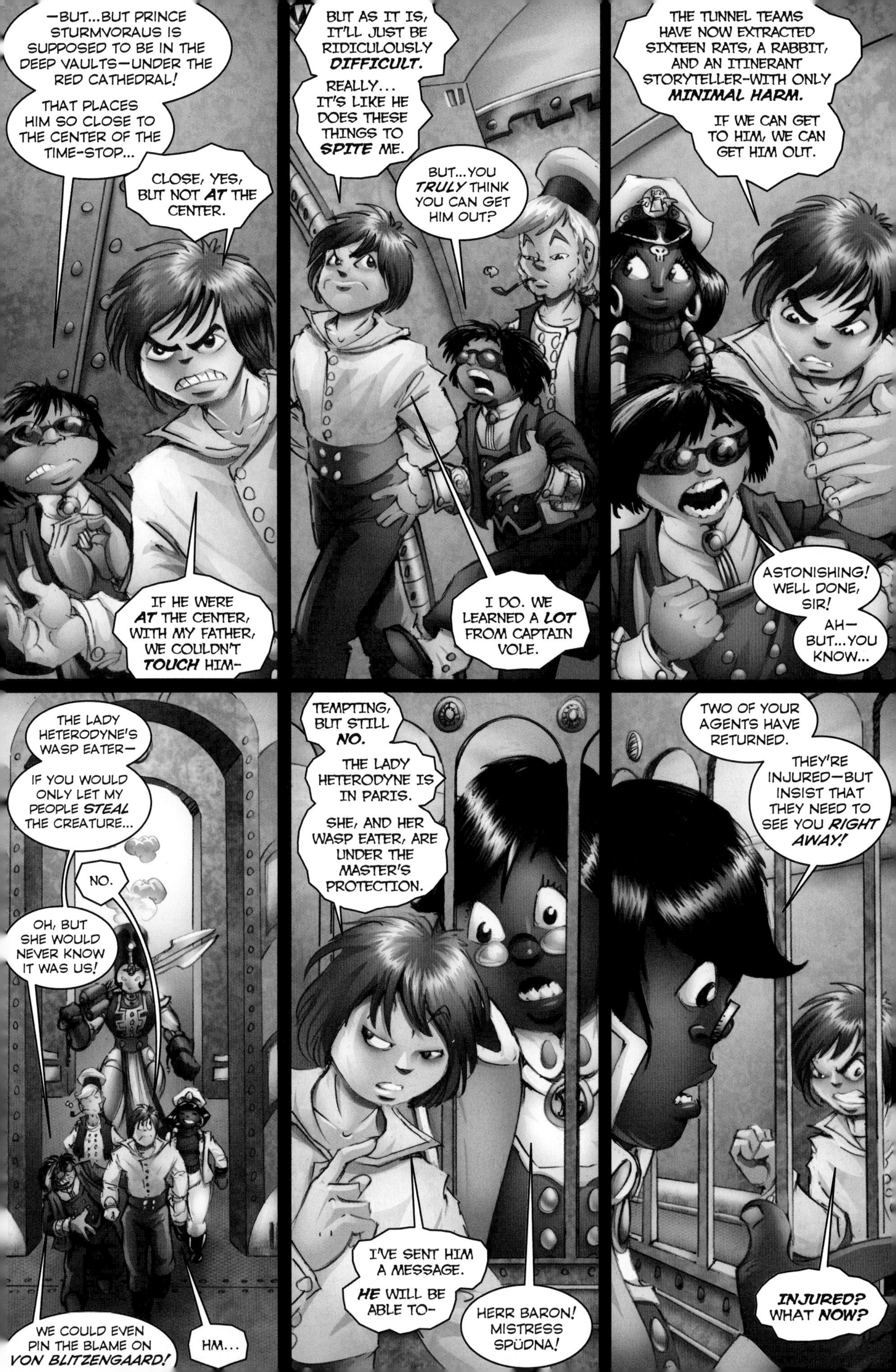
—BUT...BUT PRINCE STURMVORAUS IS SUPPOSED TO BE IN THE DEEP VAULTS—UNDER THE RED CATHEDRAL!
THAT PLACES HIM SO CLOSE TO THE CENTER OF THE TIME-STOP...
CLOSE, YES, BUT NOT AT THE CENTER.
IF HE WERE AT THE CENTER, WITH MY FATHER, WE COULDN'T TOUCH HIM-
BUT AS IT IS, IT'LL JUST BE RIDICULOUSLY DIFFICULT.
REALLY... IT'S LIKE HE DOES THESE THINGS TO SPITE ME.
BUT...YOU TRULY THINK YOU CAN GET HIM OUT?
I DO. WE LEARNED A LOT FROM CAPTAIN VOLE.
THE TUNNEL TEAMS HAVE NOW EXTRACTED SIXTEEN RATS, A RABBIT, AND AN ITINERANT STORYTELLER-WITH ONLY MINIMAL HARM.
IF WE CAN GET TO HIM, WE CAN GET HIM OUT.
ASTONISHING! WELL DONE, SIR!
AH— BUT...YOU KNOW...
THE LADY HETERODYNE'S WASP EATER—
IF YOU WOULD ONLY LET MY PEOPLE STEAL THE CREATURE...
NO.
OH, BUT SHE WOULD NEVER KNOW IT WAS US!
WE COULD EVEN PIN THE BLAME ON VON BLITZENGAARD!
HM...
TEMPTING, BUT STILL NO.
THE LADY HETERODYNE IS IN PARIS.
SHE, AND HER WASP EATER, ARE UNDER THE MASTER'S PROTECTION.
I'VE SENT HIM A MESSAGE.
HE WILL BE ABLE TO-
HERR BARON! MISTRESS SPÜDNA!
TWO OF YOUR AGENTS HAVE RETURNED.
THEY'RE INJURED—BUT INSIST THAT THEY NEED TO SEE YOU RIGHT AWAY!
INJURED? WHAT NOW?

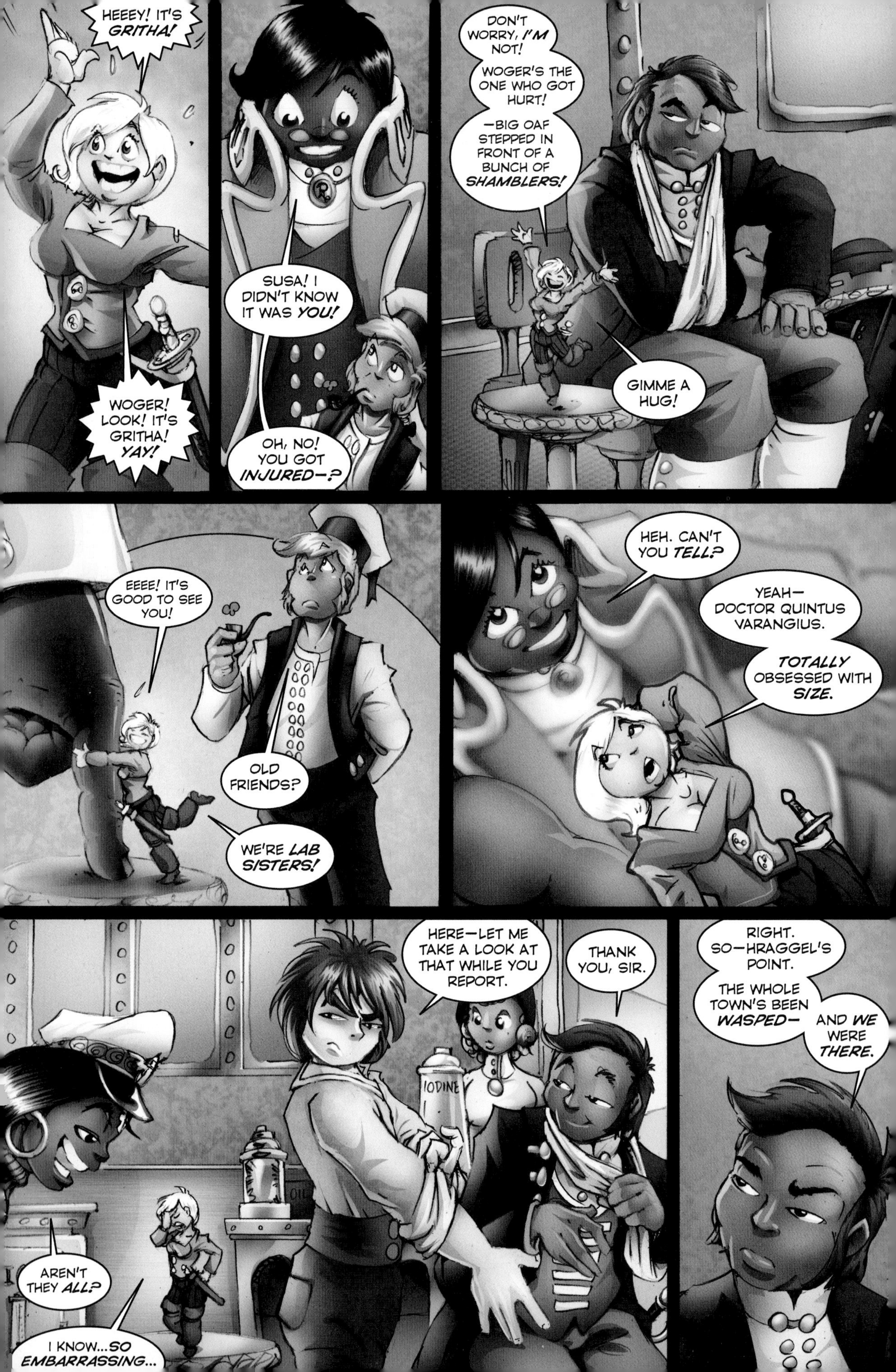
HEEEY! IT'S GRITHA!
WOGER! LOOK! IT'S GRITHA! YAY!
SUSA! I DIDN'T KNOW IT WAS YOU!
OH, NO! YOU GOT INJURED—?
DON'T WORRY, I'M NOT!
WOGER'S THE ONE WHO GOT HURT!
—BIG OAF STEPPED IN FRONT OF A BUNCH OF SHAMBLERS!
GIMME A HUG!
EEEE! IT'S GOOD TO SEE YOU!
OLD FRIENDS?
WE'RE LAB SISTERS!
HEH. CAN'T YOU TELL?
YEAH— DOCTOR QUINTUS VARANGIUS.
TOTALLY OBSESSED WITH SIZE.
HERE—LET ME TAKE A LOOK AT THAT WHILE YOU REPORT.
THANK YOU, SIR.
IODINE
OIL
AREN'T THEY ALL?
I KNOW...SO EMBARRASSING...
RIGHT. SO—HRAGGEL'S POINT.
THE WHOLE TOWN'S BEEN WASPED—
AND WE WERE THERE.

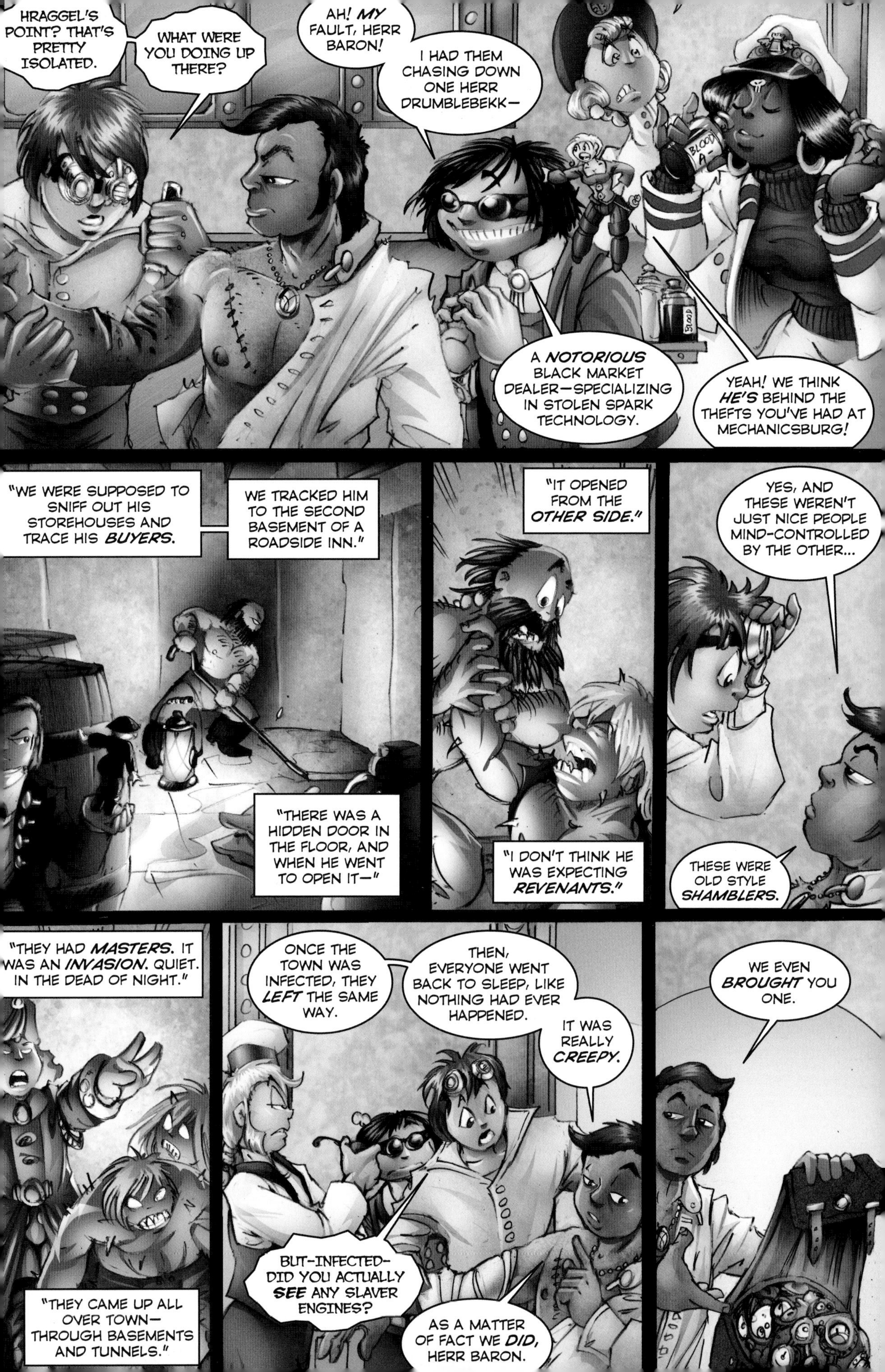

HRAGGEL'S POINT? THAT'S PRETTY ISOLATED.
WHAT WERE YOU DOING UP THERE?
AH! MY FAULT, HERR BARON!
I HAD THEM CHASING DOWN ONE HERR DRUMBLEBEKK—
A NOTORIOUS BLACK MARKET DEALER—SPECIALIZING IN STOLEN SPARK TECHNOLOGY.
YEAH! WE THINK HE'S BEHIND THE THEFTS YOU'VE HAD AT MECHANICSBURG!
BLOOD A-
BLOOD
"WE WERE SUPPOSED TO SNIFF OUT HIS STOREHOUSES AND TRACE HIS BUYERS.
WE TRACKED HIM TO THE SECOND BASEMENT OF A ROADSIDE INN."
"THERE WAS A HIDDEN DOOR IN THE FLOOR, AND WHEN HE WENT TO OPEN IT—"
"IT OPENED FROM THE OTHER SIDE."
"I DON'T THINK HE WAS EXPECTING REVENANTS."
YES, AND THESE WEREN'T JUST NICE PEOPLE MIND-CONTROLLED BY THE OTHER...
THESE WERE OLD STYLE SHAMBLERS.
"THEY HAD MASTERS. IT WAS AN INVASION. QUIET. IN THE DEAD OF NIGHT."
"THEY CAME UP ALL OVER TOWN—THROUGH BASEMENTS AND TUNNELS."
ONCE THE TOWN WAS INFECTED, THEY LEFT THE SAME WAY.
THEN, EVERYONE WENT BACK TO SLEEP, LIKE NOTHING HAD EVER HAPPENED.
IT WAS REALLY CREEPY.
BUT-INFECTED-DID YOU ACTUALLY SEE ANY SLAVER ENGINES?
AS A MATTER OF FACT WE DID, HERR BARON.
WE EVEN BROUGHT YOU ONE.

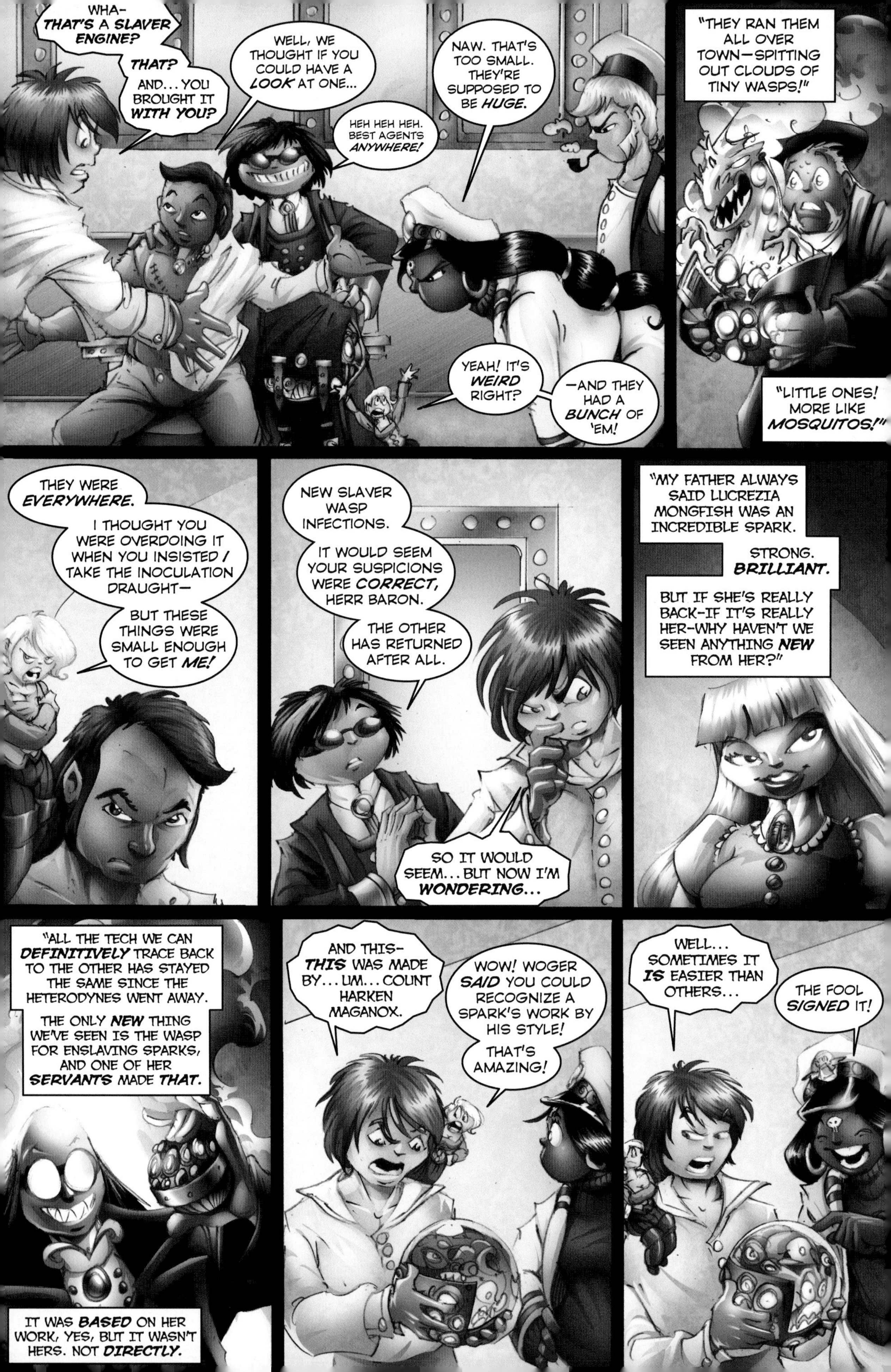
WHA- THAT'S A SLAVER ENGINE?
THAT?
AND... YOU BROUGHT IT WITH YOU?
WELL, WE THOUGHT IF YOU COULD HAVE A LOOK AT ONE...
HEH HEH HEH. BEST AGENTS ANYWHERE!
NAW. THAT'S TOO SMALL. THEY'RE SUPPOSED TO BE HUGE.
YEAH! IT'S WEIRD RIGHT?
—AND THEY HAD A BUNCH OF 'EM!
"THEY RAN THEM ALL OVER TOWN—SPITTING OUT CLOUDS OF TINY WASPS!"
"LITTLE ONES! MORE LIKE MOSQUITOS!"
THEY WERE EVERYWHERE.
I THOUGHT YOU WERE OVERDOING IT WHEN YOU INSISTED I TAKE THE INOCULATION DRAUGHT—
BUT THESE THINGS WERE SMALL ENOUGH TO GET ME!
NEW SLAVER WASP INFECTIONS.
IT WOULD SEEM YOUR SUSPICIONS WERE CORRECT, HERR BARON.
THE OTHER HAS RETURNED AFTER ALL.
SO IT WOULD SEEM... BUT NOW I'M WONDERING...
"MY FATHER ALWAYS SAID LUCREZIA MONGFISH WAS AN INCREDIBLE SPARK.
STRONG. BRILLIANT.
BUT IF SHE'S REALLY BACK-IF IT'S REALLY HER-WHY HAVEN'T WE SEEN ANYTHING NEW FROM HER?"
"ALL THE TECH WE CAN DEFINITIVELY TRACE BACK TO THE OTHER HAS STAYED THE SAME SINCE THE HETERODYNES WENT AWAY.
THE ONLY NEW THING WE'VE SEEN IS THE WASP FOR ENSLAVING SPARKS, AND ONE OF HER SERVANTS MADE THAT.
IT WAS BASED ON HER WORK, YES, BUT IT WASN'T HERS. NOT DIRECTLY.
AND THIS- THIS WAS MADE BY... UM... COUNT HARKEN MAGANOX.
WOW! WOGER SAID YOU COULD RECOGNIZE A SPARK'S WORK BY HIS STYLE!
THAT'S AMAZING!
WELL... SOMETIMES IT IS EASIER THAN OTHERS...
THE FOOL SIGNED IT!

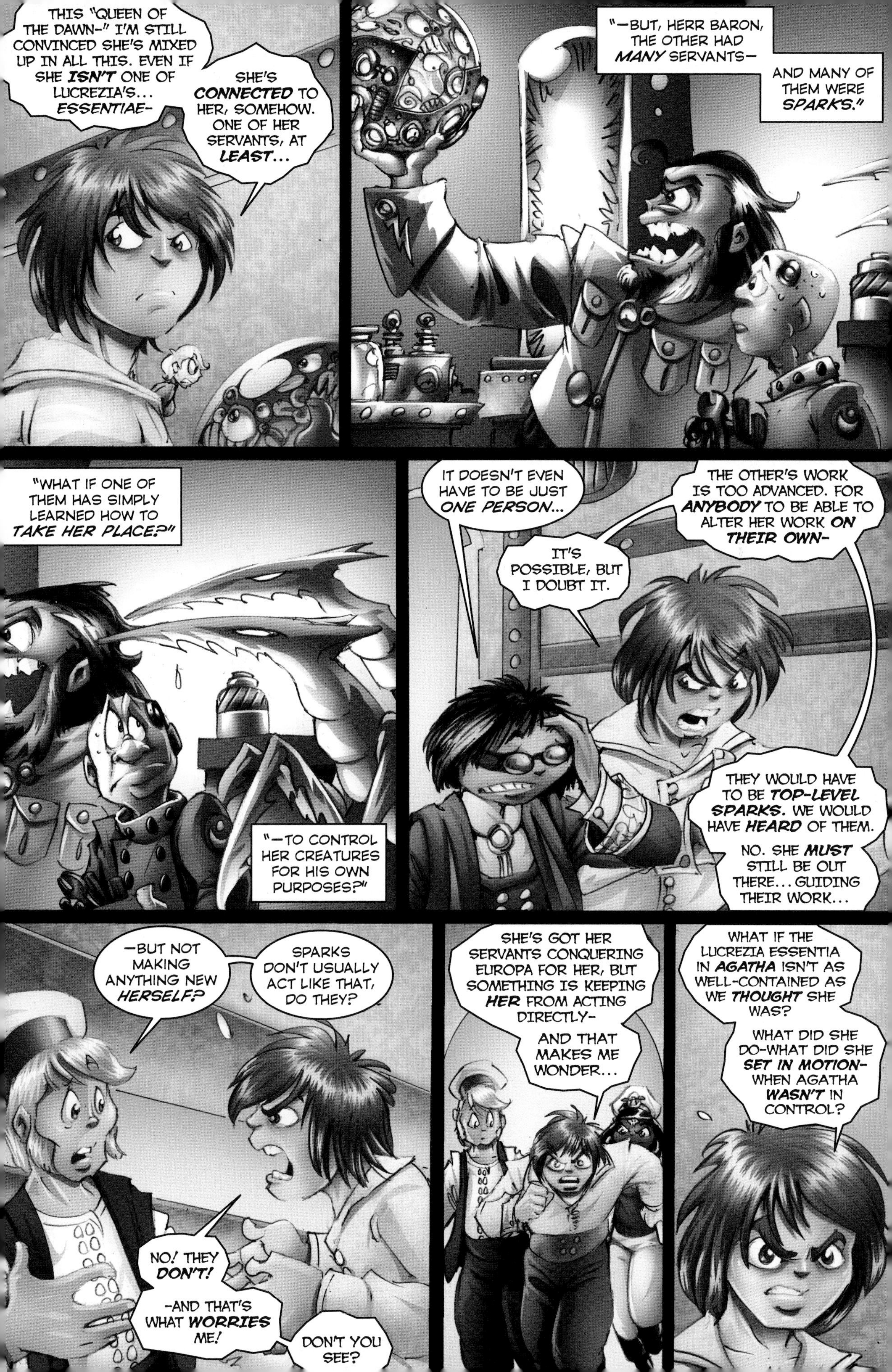
THIS "QUEEN OF THE DAWN-" I'M STILL CONVINCED SHE'S MIXED UP IN ALL THIS. EVEN IF SHE *ISN'T* ONE OF LUCREZIA'S... *ESSENTIAE*-
SHE'S *CONNECTED* TO HER, SOMEHOW. ONE OF HER SERVANTS, AT *LEAST*...
"—BUT, HERR BARON, THE OTHER HAD *MANY* SERVANTS—
AND MANY OF THEM WERE *SPARKS*."
"WHAT IF ONE OF THEM HAS SIMPLY LEARNED HOW TO *TAKE HER PLACE?*"
"—TO CONTROL HER CREATURES FOR HIS OWN PURPOSES?"
IT DOESN'T EVEN HAVE TO BE JUST *ONE PERSON*...
IT'S POSSIBLE, BUT I DOUBT IT.
THE OTHER'S WORK IS TOO ADVANCED. FOR *ANYBODY* TO BE ABLE TO ALTER HER WORK *ON THEIR OWN*-
THEY WOULD HAVE TO BE *TOP-LEVEL SPARKS*. WE WOULD HAVE *HEARD* OF THEM.
NO. SHE *MUST* STILL BE OUT THERE... GUIDING THEIR WORK...
—BUT NOT MAKING ANYTHING NEW *HERSELF?*
SPARKS DON'T USUALLY ACT LIKE THAT, DO THEY?
NO! THEY *DON'T!*
-AND THAT'S WHAT *WORRIES* ME!
DON'T YOU SEE?
SHE'S GOT HER SERVANTS CONQUERING EUROPA FOR HER, BUT SOMETHING IS KEEPING *HER* FROM ACTING DIRECTLY-
AND THAT MAKES ME WONDER...
WHAT IF THE LUCREZIA ESSENTIA IN *AGATHA* ISN'T AS WELL-CONTAINED AS WE *THOUGHT* SHE WAS?
WHAT DID SHE DO-WHAT DID SHE *SET IN MOTION*- WHEN AGATHA *WASN'T* IN CONTROL?

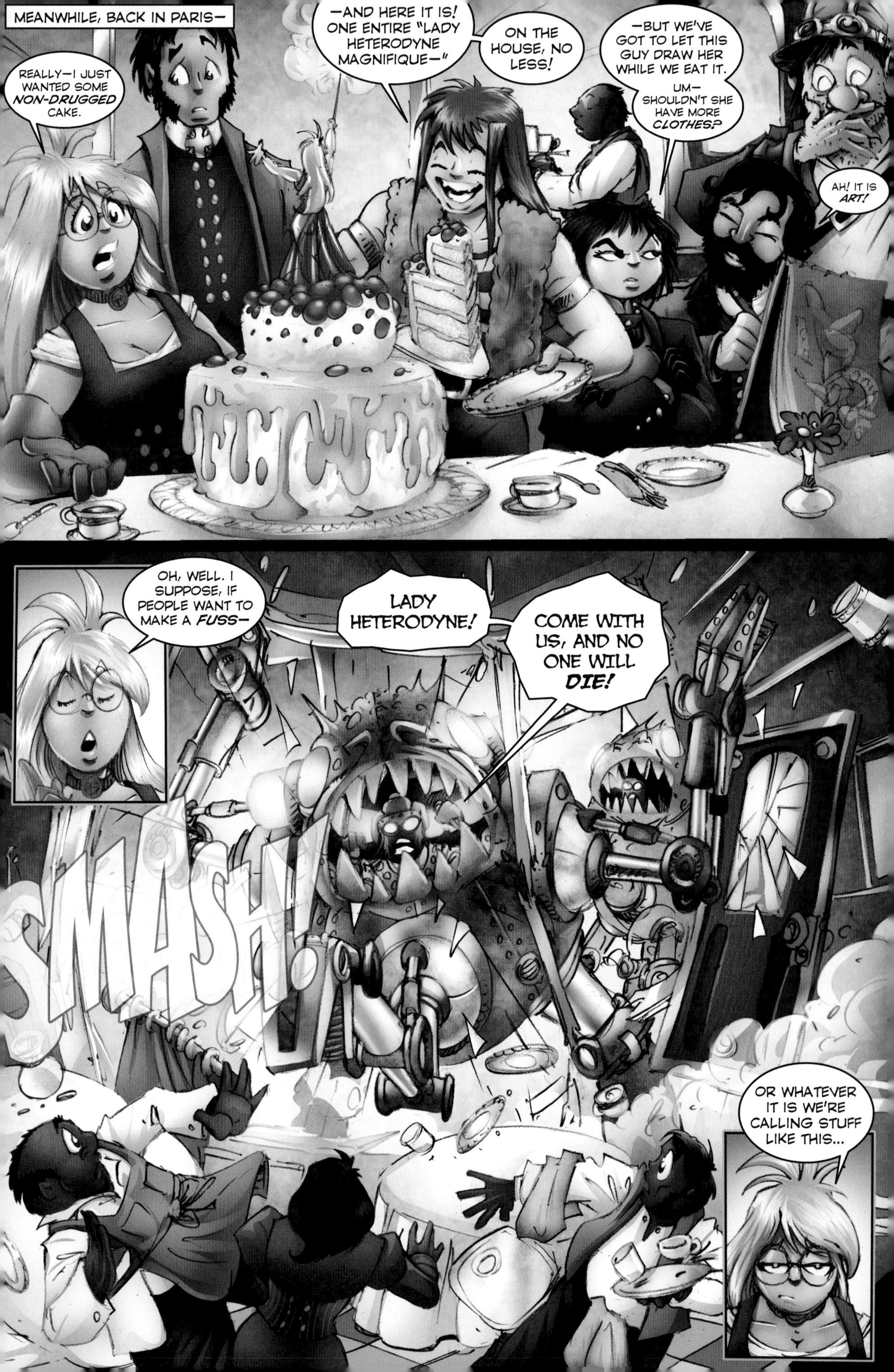
MEANWHILE, BACK IN PARIS—
REALLY—I JUST WANTED SOME NON-DRUGGED CAKE.
—AND HERE IT IS! ONE ENTIRE "LADY HETERODYNE MAGNIFIQUE—"
ON THE HOUSE, NO LESS!
—BUT WE'VE GOT TO LET THIS GUY DRAW HER WHILE WE EAT IT.
UM— SHOULDN'T SHE HAVE MORE CLOTHES?
AH! IT IS ART!
OH, WELL. I SUPPOSE, IF PEOPLE WANT TO MAKE A FUSS—
LADY HETERODYNE!
COME WITH US, AND NO ONE WILL DIE!
SMASH!
OR WHATEVER IT IS WE'RE CALLING STUFF LIKE THIS...

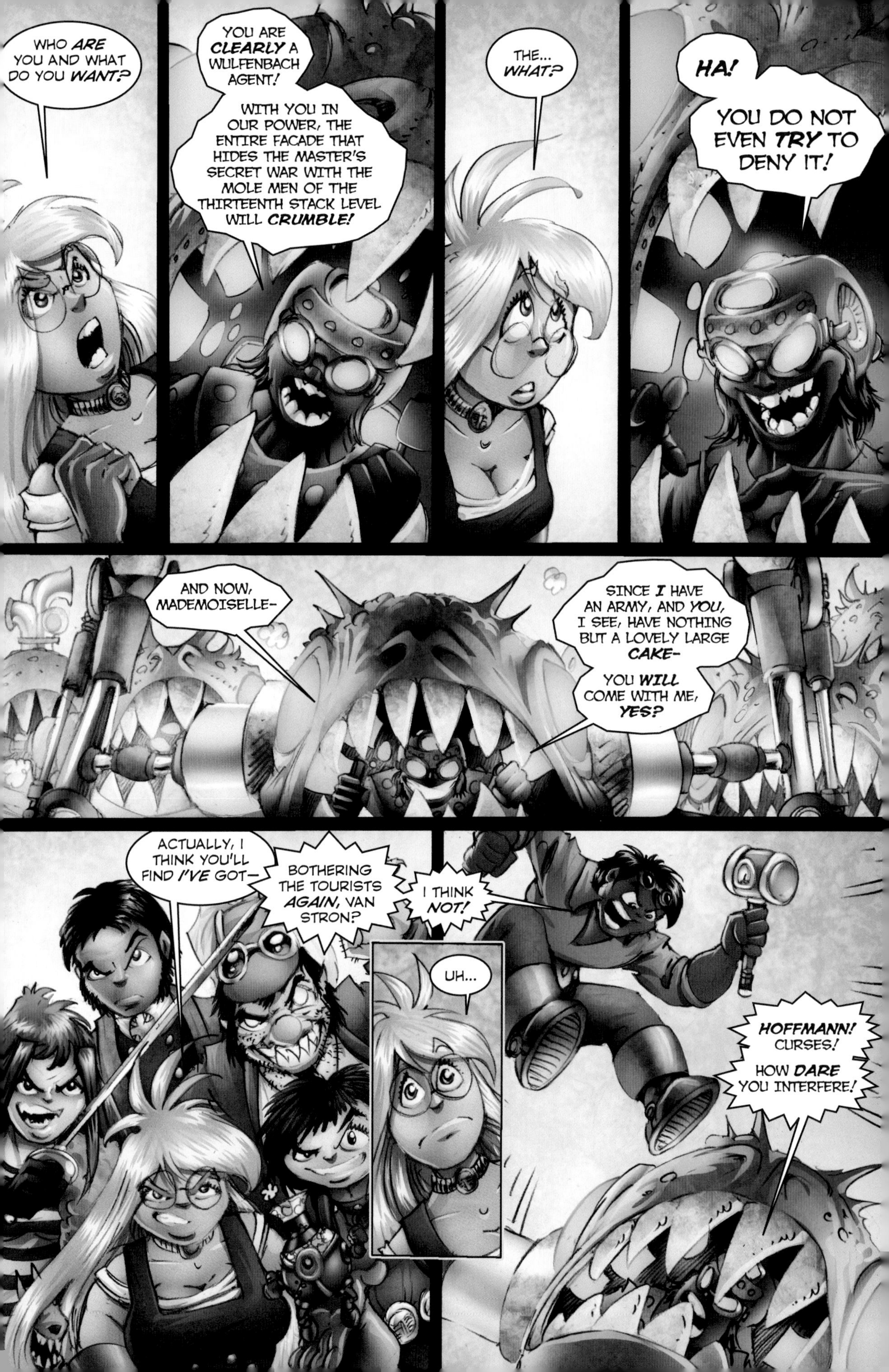
WHO ARE YOU AND WHAT DO YOU WANT?
YOU ARE CLEARLY A WULFENBACH AGENT!
WITH YOU IN OUR POWER, THE ENTIRE FACADE THAT HIDES THE MASTER'S SECRET WAR WITH THE MOLE MEN OF THE THIRTEENTH STACK LEVEL WILL CRUMBLE!
THE... WHAT?
HA!
YOU DO NOT EVEN TRY TO DENY IT!
AND NOW, MADEMOISELLE-
SINCE I HAVE AN ARMY, AND YOU, I SEE, HAVE NOTHING BUT A LOVELY LARGE CAKE-
YOU WILL COME WITH ME, YES?
ACTUALLY, I THINK YOU'LL FIND I'VE GOT—
BOTHERING THE TOURISTS AGAIN, VAN STRON?
I THINK NOT!
UH...
HOFFMANN! CURSES!
HOW DARE YOU INTERFERE!

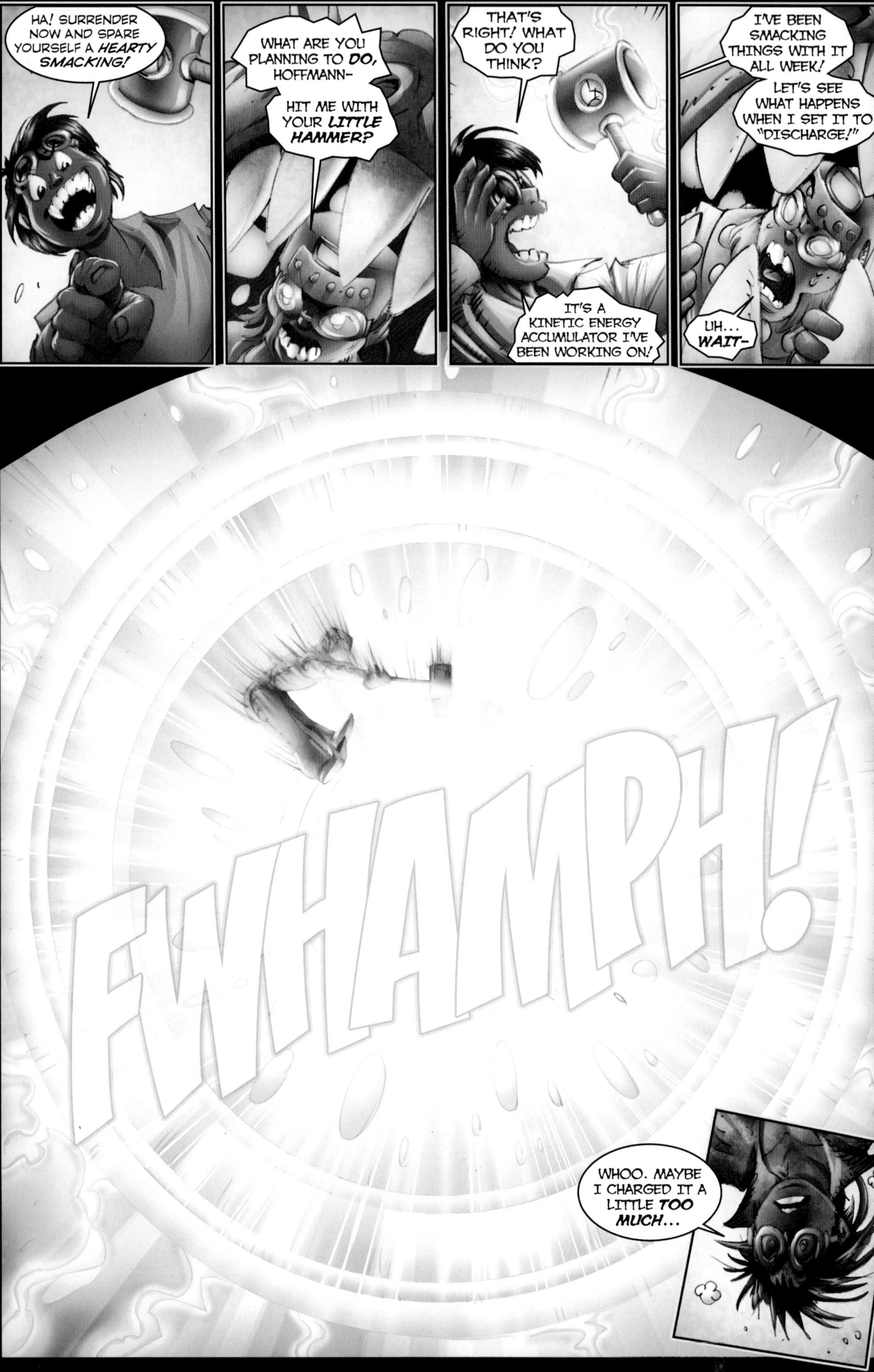
HA! SURRENDER NOW AND SPARE YOURSELF A *HEARTY SMACKING!*
WHAT ARE YOU PLANNING TO *DO,* HOFFMANN-
HIT ME WITH YOUR *LITTLE HAMMER?*
THAT'S RIGHT! WHAT DO YOU THINK?
IT'S A KINETIC ENERGY ACCUMULATOR I'VE BEEN WORKING ON!
I'VE BEEN SMACKING THINGS WITH IT ALL WEEK!
LET'S SEE WHAT HAPPENS WHEN I SET IT TO "DISCHARGE!"
UH... *WAIT-*
FWHAMPH!
WHOO. MAYBE I CHARGED IT A LITTLE *TOO MUCH...*

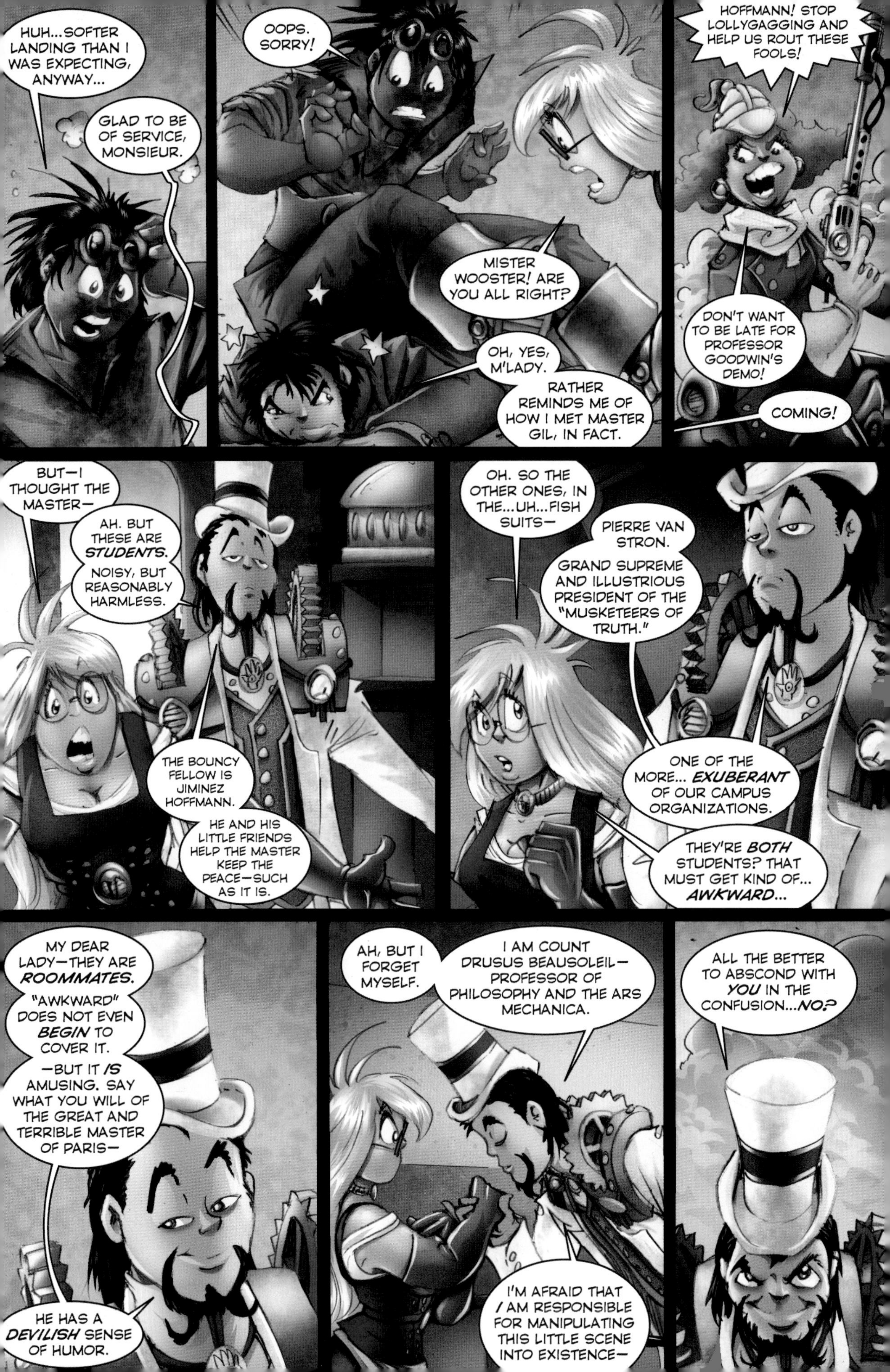
HUH...SOFTER LANDING THAN I WAS EXPECTING, ANYWAY...
GLAD TO BE OF SERVICE, MONSIEUR.
OOPS. SORRY!
MISTER WOOSTER! ARE YOU ALL RIGHT?
OH, YES, M'LADY.
RATHER REMINDS ME OF HOW I MET MASTER GIL, IN FACT.
HOFFMANN! STOP LOLLYGAGGING AND HELP US ROUT THESE FOOLS!
DON'T WANT TO BE LATE FOR PROFESSOR GOODWIN'S DEMO!
COMING!
BUT—I THOUGHT THE MASTER—
AH. BUT THESE ARE *STUDENTS*.
NOISY, BUT REASONABLY HARMLESS.
THE BOUNCY FELLOW IS JIMINEZ HOFFMANN.
HE AND HIS LITTLE FRIENDS HELP THE MASTER KEEP THE PEACE—SUCH AS IT IS.
OH. SO THE OTHER ONES, IN THE...UH...FISH SUITS—
PIERRE VAN STRON.
GRAND SUPREME AND ILLUSTRIOUS PRESIDENT OF THE "MUSKETEERS OF TRUTH."
ONE OF THE MORE... *EXUBERANT* OF OUR CAMPUS ORGANIZATIONS.
THEY'RE *BOTH* STUDENTS? THAT MUST GET KIND OF... *AWKWARD*...
MY DEAR LADY—THEY ARE *ROOMMATES*.
"AWKWARD" DOES NOT EVEN *BEGIN* TO COVER IT.
—BUT IT *IS* AMUSING. SAY WHAT YOU WILL OF THE GREAT AND TERRIBLE MASTER OF PARIS—
HE HAS A *DEVILISH* SENSE OF HUMOR.
AH, BUT I FORGET MYSELF.
I AM COUNT DRUSUS BEAUSOLEIL—PROFESSOR OF PHILOSOPHY AND THE ARS MECHANICA.
I'M AFRAID THAT *I* AM RESPONSIBLE FOR MANIPULATING THIS LITTLE SCENE INTO EXISTENCE—
ALL THE BETTER TO ABSCOND WITH *YOU* IN THE CONFUSION...*NO?*

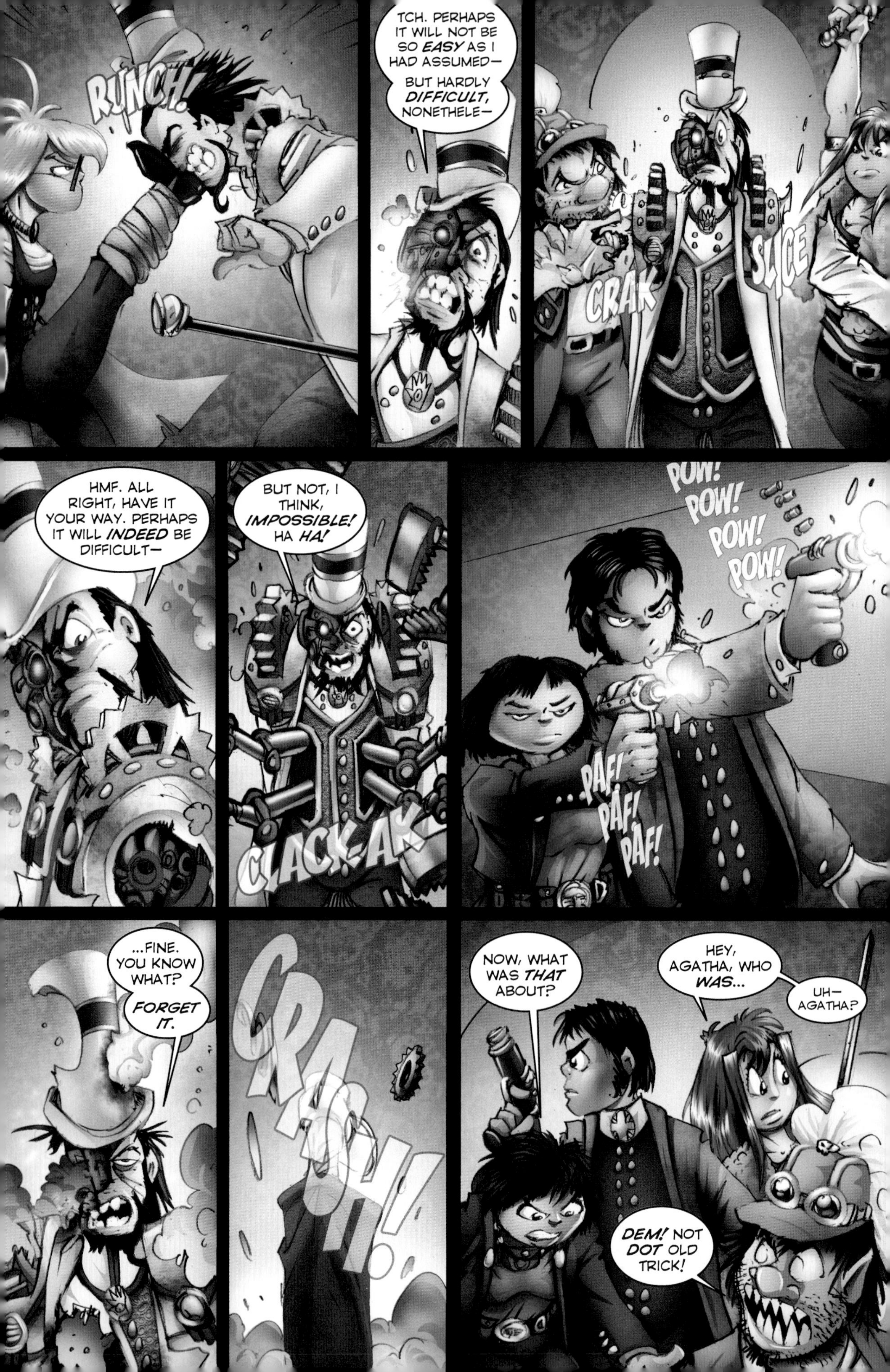
RUNCH!
TCH. PERHAPS IT WILL NOT BE SO EASY AS I HAD ASSUMED—
BUT HARDLY DIFFICULT, NONETHELE—
CRAK
SLICE
HMF. ALL RIGHT, HAVE IT YOUR WAY. PERHAPS IT WILL INDEED BE DIFFICULT—
BUT NOT, I THINK, IMPOSSIBLE! HA HA!
CLACK-AK
POW! POW! POW! POW!
PAF! PAF! PAF!
...FINE. YOU KNOW WHAT?
FORGET IT.
CRASH!
NOW, WHAT WAS THAT ABOUT?
HEY, AGATHA, WHO WAS...
UH— AGATHA?
DEM! NOT DOT OLD TRICK!

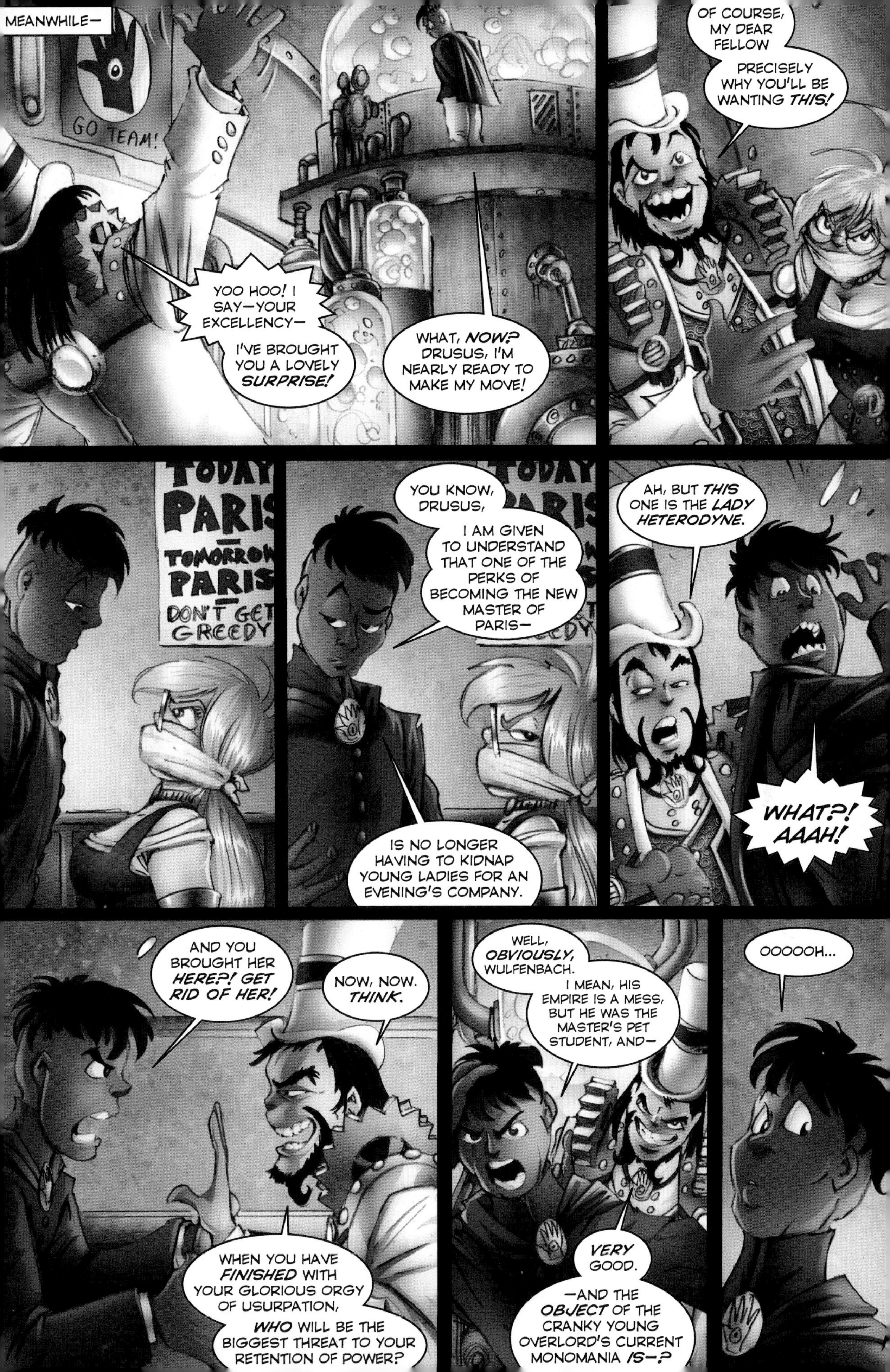
MEANWHILE—
GO TEAM!
YOO HOO! I SAY—YOUR EXCELLENCY—
I'VE BROUGHT YOU A LOVELY SURPRISE!
WHAT, NOW? DRUSUS, I'M NEARLY READY TO MAKE MY MOVE!
OF COURSE, MY DEAR FELLOW
PRECISELY WHY YOU'LL BE WANTING THIS!
TODAY PARIS — TOMORROW PARIS — DON'T GET GREEDY
YOU KNOW, DRUSUS,
I AM GIVEN TO UNDERSTAND THAT ONE OF THE PERKS OF BECOMING THE NEW MASTER OF PARIS—
IS NO LONGER HAVING TO KIDNAP YOUNG LADIES FOR AN EVENING'S COMPANY.
AH, BUT THIS ONE IS THE LADY HETERODYNE.
WHAT?! AAAH!
AND YOU BROUGHT HER HERE?! GET RID OF HER!
NOW, NOW. THINK.
WHEN YOU HAVE FINISHED WITH YOUR GLORIOUS ORGY OF USURPATION,
WHO WILL BE THE BIGGEST THREAT TO YOUR RETENTION OF POWER?
WELL, OBVIOUSLY, WULFENBACH.
I MEAN, HIS EMPIRE IS A MESS, BUT HE WAS THE MASTER'S PET STUDENT, AND—
VERY GOOD.
—AND THE OBJECT OF THE CRANKY YOUNG OVERLORD'S CURRENT MONOMANIA IS—?
OOOOOH...

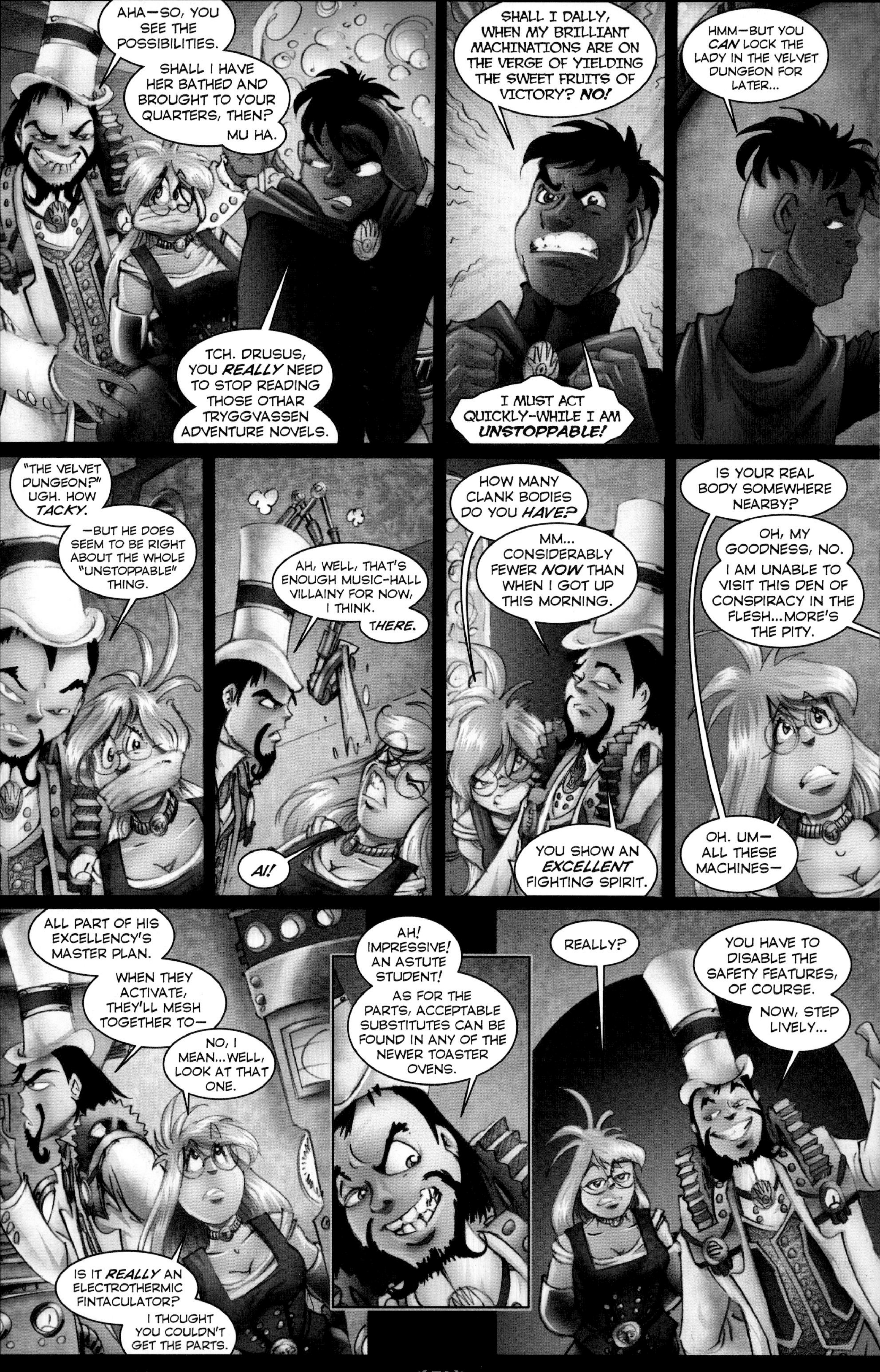
AHA—SO, YOU SEE THE POSSIBILITIES.
SHALL I HAVE HER BATHED AND BROUGHT TO YOUR QUARTERS, THEN? MU HA.
TCH. DRUSUS, YOU *REALLY* NEED TO STOP READING THOSE OTHAR TRYGGVASSEN ADVENTURE NOVELS.
SHALL I DALLY, WHEN MY BRILLIANT MACHINATIONS ARE ON THE VERGE OF YIELDING THE SWEET FRUITS OF VICTORY? *NO!*
I MUST ACT QUICKLY-WHILE I AM *UNSTOPPABLE!*
HMM—BUT YOU *CAN* LOCK THE LADY IN THE VELVET DUNGEON FOR LATER...
"THE VELVET DUNGEON?" UGH. HOW *TACKY*.
—BUT HE DOES SEEM TO BE RIGHT ABOUT THE WHOLE "UNSTOPPABLE" THING.
AH, WELL, THAT'S ENOUGH MUSIC-HALL VILLAINY FOR NOW, I THINK.
T*HERE*.
AI!
HOW MANY CLANK BODIES DO YOU *HAVE?*
MM... CONSIDERABLY FEWER *NOW* THAN WHEN I GOT UP THIS MORNING.
YOU SHOW AN *EXCELLENT* FIGHTING SPIRIT.
IS YOUR REAL BODY SOMEWHERE NEARBY?
OH, MY GOODNESS, NO.
I AM UNABLE TO VISIT THIS DEN OF CONSPIRACY IN THE FLESH...MORE'S THE PITY.
OH. UM— ALL THESE MACHINES—
ALL PART OF HIS EXCELLENCY'S MASTER PLAN.
WHEN THEY ACTIVATE, THEY'LL MESH TOGETHER TO—
NO, I MEAN...WELL, LOOK AT THAT ONE.
IS IT *REALLY* AN ELECTROTHERMIC FINTACULATOR?
I THOUGHT YOU COULDN'T GET THE PARTS.
AH! IMPRESSIVE! AN ASTUTE STUDENT!
AS FOR THE PARTS, ACCEPTABLE SUBSTITUTES CAN BE FOUND IN ANY OF THE NEWER TOASTER OVENS.
REALLY?
YOU HAVE TO DISABLE THE SAFETY FEATURES, OF COURSE.
NOW, STEP LIVELY...

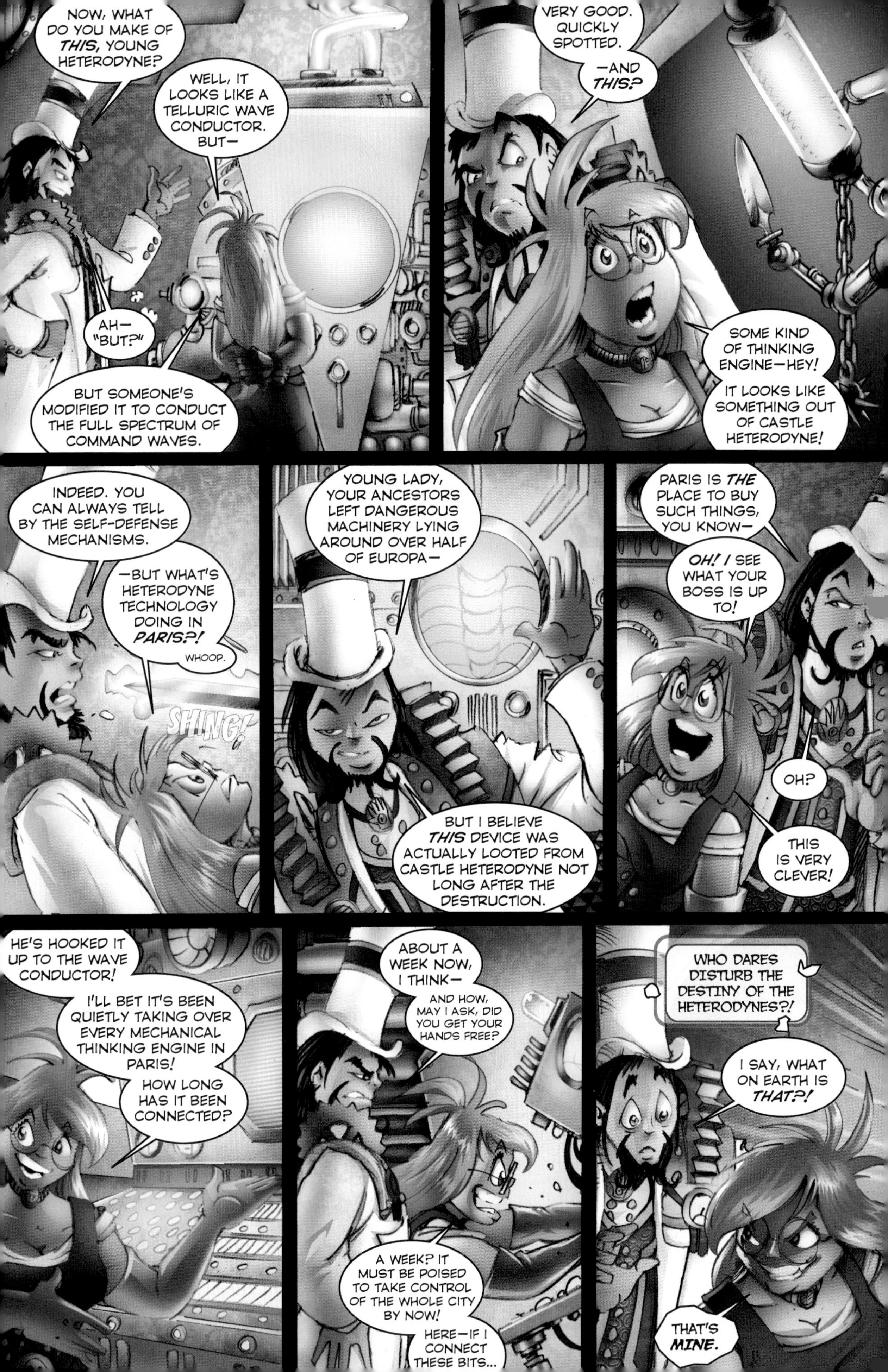

NOW, WHAT DO YOU MAKE OF *THIS,* YOUNG HETERODYNE?
WELL, IT LOOKS LIKE A TELLURIC WAVE CONDUCTOR. BUT—
AH— "BUT?"
BUT SOMEONE'S MODIFIED IT TO CONDUCT THE FULL SPECTRUM OF COMMAND WAVES.
VERY GOOD. QUICKLY SPOTTED.
—AND *THIS?*
SOME KIND OF THINKING ENGINE—HEY!
IT LOOKS LIKE SOMETHING OUT OF CASTLE HETERODYNE!
INDEED. YOU CAN ALWAYS TELL BY THE SELF-DEFENSE MECHANISMS.
—BUT WHAT'S HETERODYNE TECHNOLOGY DOING IN *PARIS?!*
WHOOP.
SHING!
YOUNG LADY, YOUR ANCESTORS LEFT DANGEROUS MACHINERY LYING AROUND OVER HALF OF EUROPA—
BUT I BELIEVE *THIS* DEVICE WAS ACTUALLY LOOTED FROM CASTLE HETERODYNE NOT LONG AFTER THE DESTRUCTION.
PARIS IS *THE* PLACE TO BUY SUCH THINGS, YOU KNOW—
OH! I SEE WHAT YOUR BOSS IS UP TO!
OH?
THIS IS VERY CLEVER!
HE'S HOOKED IT UP TO THE WAVE CONDUCTOR!
I'LL BET IT'S BEEN QUIETLY TAKING OVER EVERY MECHANICAL THINKING ENGINE IN PARIS!
HOW LONG HAS IT BEEN CONNECTED?
ABOUT A WEEK NOW, I THINK—
AND HOW, MAY I ASK, DID YOU GET YOUR HANDS FREE?
A WEEK? IT MUST BE POISED TO TAKE CONTROL OF THE WHOLE CITY BY NOW!
HERE—IF I CONNECT THESE BITS...
WHO DARES DISTURB THE DESTINY OF THE HETERODYNES?!
I SAY, WHAT ON EARTH IS *THAT?!*
THAT'S **MINE.**

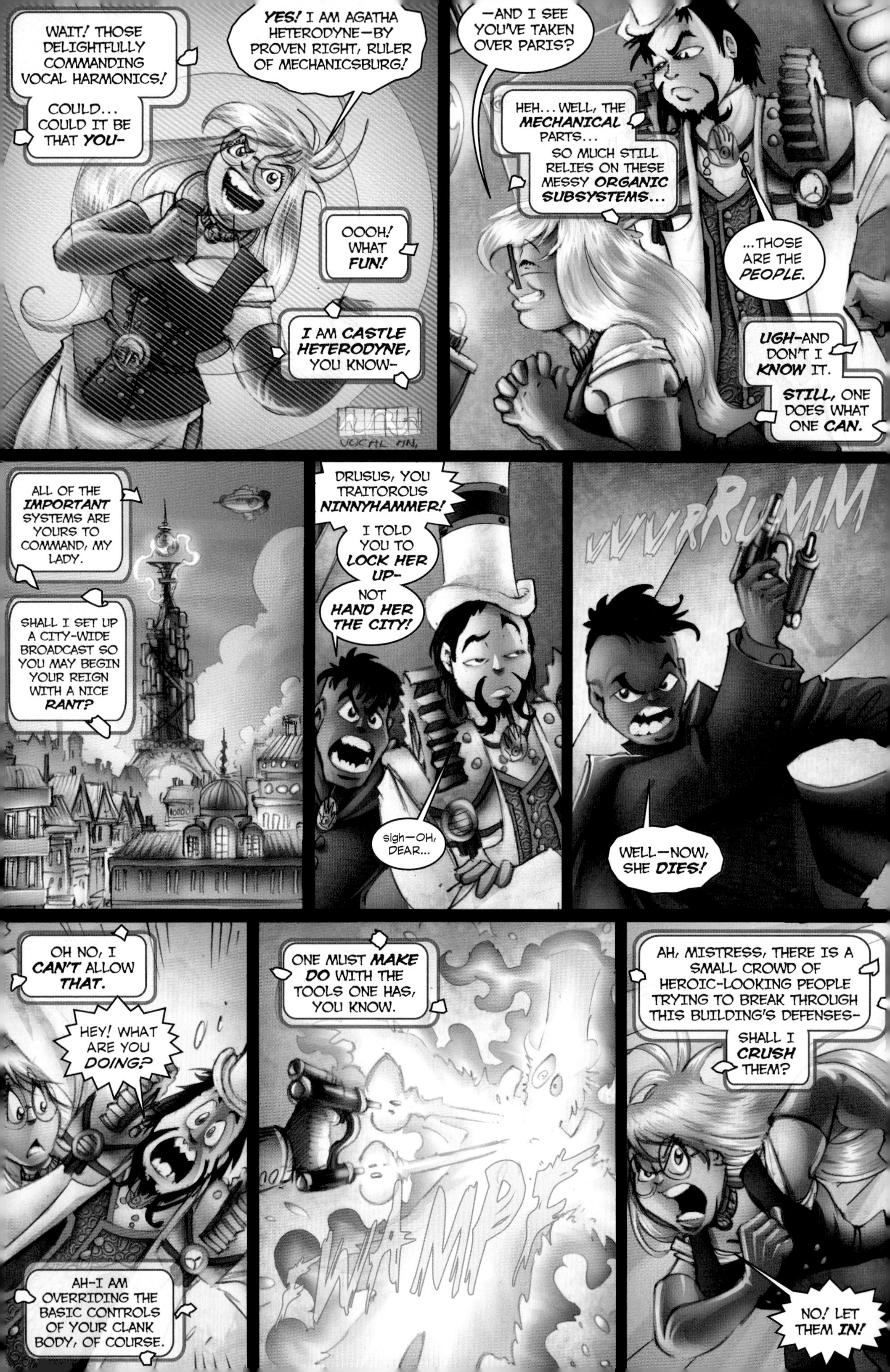
WAIT! THOSE DELIGHTFULLY COMMANDING VOCAL HARMONICS!
COULD... COULD IT BE THAT YOU-
YES! I AM AGATHA HETERODYNE—BY PROVEN RIGHT, RULER OF MECHANICSBURG!
OOOH! WHAT FUN!
I AM CASTLE HETERODYNE, YOU KNOW-
—AND I SEE YOU'VE TAKEN OVER PARIS?
HEH... WELL, THE MECHANICAL PARTS...
SO MUCH STILL RELIES ON THESE MESSY ORGANIC SUBSYSTEMS...
...THOSE ARE THE PEOPLE.
UGH-AND DON'T I KNOW IT.
STILL, ONE DOES WHAT ONE CAN.
ALL OF THE IMPORTANT SYSTEMS ARE YOURS TO COMMAND, MY LADY.
SHALL I SET UP A CITY-WIDE BROADCAST SO YOU MAY BEGIN YOUR REIGN WITH A NICE RANT?
DRUSUS, YOU TRAITOROUS NINNYHAMMER!
I TOLD YOU TO LOCK HER UP-
NOT HAND HER THE CITY!
sigh—OH, DEAR...
VVVVRRUMM
WELL—NOW, SHE DIES!
OH NO, I CAN'T ALLOW THAT.
HEY! WHAT ARE YOU DOING?
AH-I AM OVERRIDING THE BASIC CONTROLS OF YOUR CLANK BODY, OF COURSE.
ONE MUST MAKE DO WITH THE TOOLS ONE HAS, YOU KNOW.
FWAMPF
AH, MISTRESS, THERE IS A SMALL CROWD OF HEROIC-LOOKING PEOPLE TRYING TO BREAK THROUGH THIS BUILDING'S DEFENSES-
SHALL I CRUSH THEM?
NO! LET THEM IN!

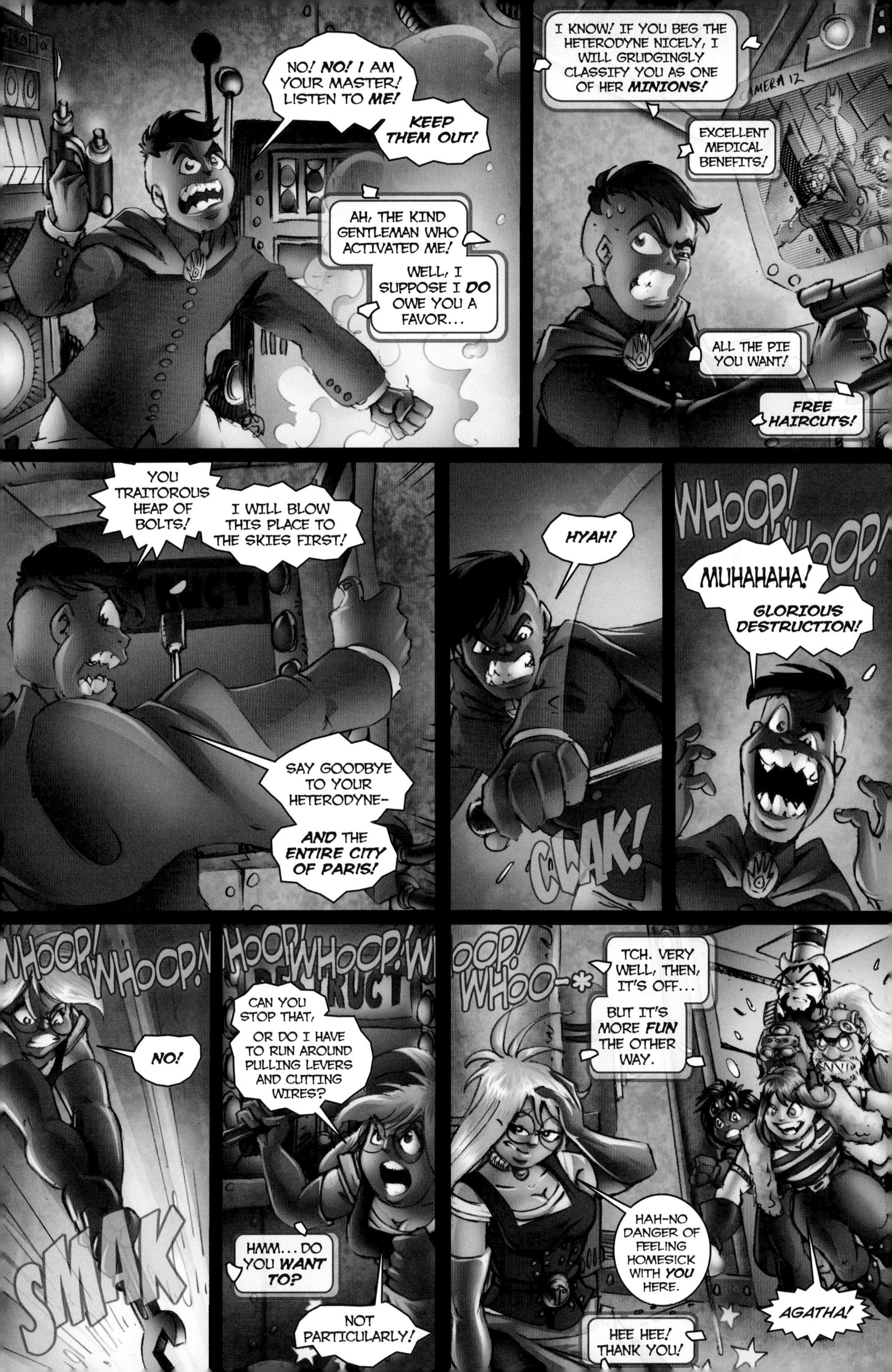
NO! NO! I AM YOUR MASTER! LISTEN TO ME!
KEEP THEM OUT!
AH, THE KIND GENTLEMAN WHO ACTIVATED ME!
WELL, I SUPPOSE I DO OWE YOU A FAVOR...
I KNOW! IF YOU BEG THE HETERODYNE NICELY, I WILL GRUDGINGLY CLASSIFY YOU AS ONE OF HER MINIONS!
CAMERA 12
EXCELLENT MEDICAL BENEFITS!
ALL THE PIE YOU WANT!
FREE HAIRCUTS!
YOU TRAITOROUS HEAP OF BOLTS!
I WILL BLOW THIS PLACE TO THE SKIES FIRST!
SAY GOODBYE TO YOUR HETERODYNE-
AND THE ENTIRE CITY OF PARIS!
HYAH!
CLAK!
WHOOP! WHOOP!
MUHAHAHA!
GLORIOUS DESTRUCTION!
WHOOP! WHOOP!
NO!
SMAK
WHOOP! WHOOP!
CAN YOU STOP THAT,
OR DO I HAVE TO RUN AROUND PULLING LEVERS AND CUTTING WIRES?
HMM... DO YOU WANT TO?
NOT PARTICULARLY!
OOP! WHOO-*
TCH. VERY WELL, THEN, IT'S OFF...
BUT IT'S MORE FUN THE OTHER WAY.
HAH-NO DANGER OF FEELING HOMESICK WITH YOU HERE.
HEE HEE! THANK YOU!
AGATHA!

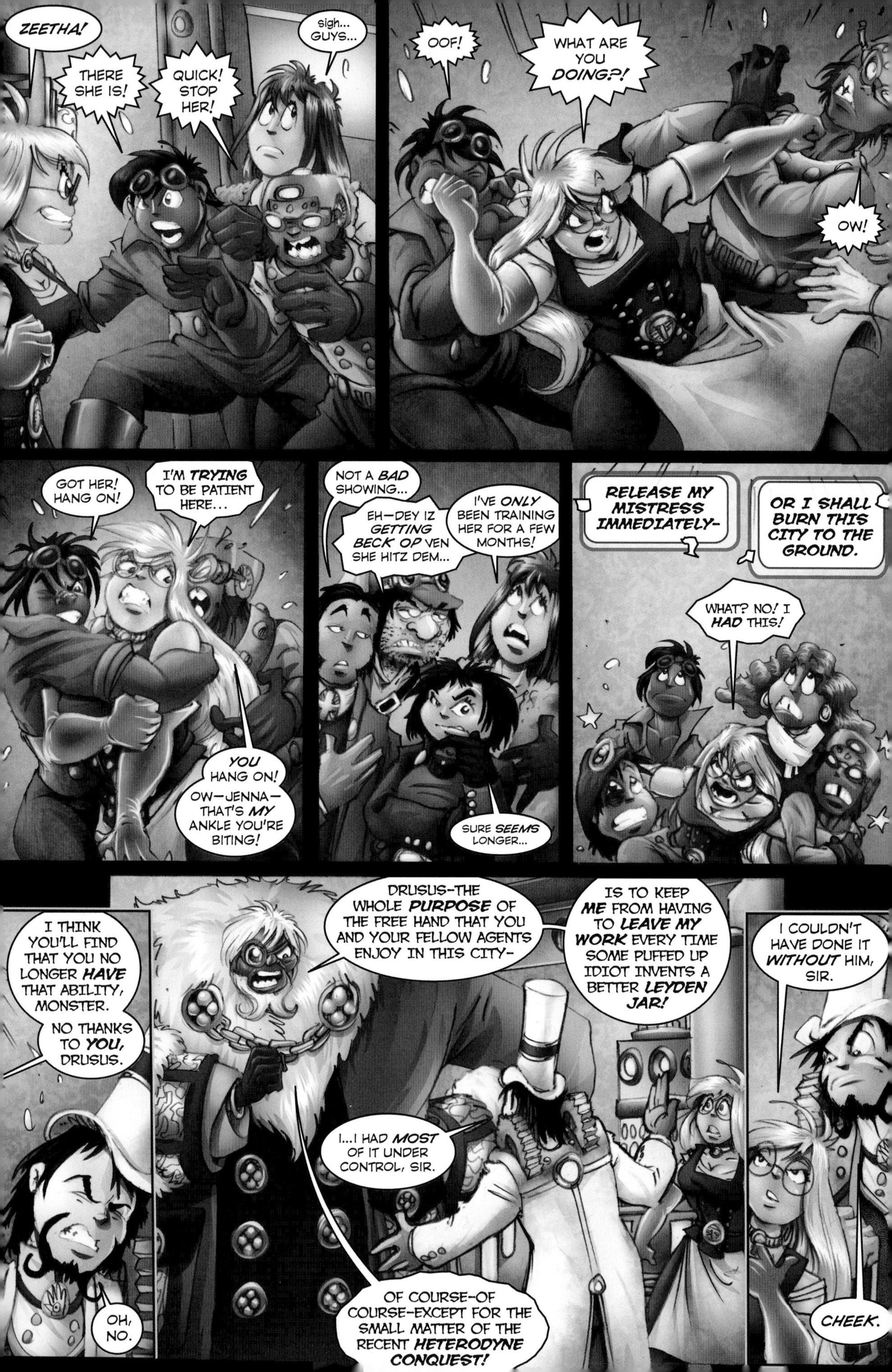
ZEETHA!
THERE SHE IS!
QUICK! STOP HER!
sigh... GUYS...
OOF!
WHAT ARE YOU DOING?!
OW!
GOT HER! HANG ON!
I'M TRYING TO BE PATIENT HERE...
YOU HANG ON!
OW—JENNA—THAT'S MY ANKLE YOU'RE BITING!
NOT A BAD SHOWING...
EH—DEY IZ GETTING BECK OP VEN SHE HITZ DEM...
I'VE ONLY BEEN TRAINING HER FOR A FEW MONTHS!
SURE SEEMS LONGER...
RELEASE MY MISTRESS IMMEDIATELY-
OR I SHALL BURN THIS CITY TO THE GROUND.
WHAT? NO! I HAD THIS!
I THINK YOU'LL FIND THAT YOU NO LONGER HAVE THAT ABILITY, MONSTER.
NO THANKS TO YOU, DRUSUS.
OH, NO.
DRUSUS-THE WHOLE PURPOSE OF THE FREE HAND THAT YOU AND YOUR FELLOW AGENTS ENJOY IN THIS CITY-
IS TO KEEP ME FROM HAVING TO LEAVE MY WORK EVERY TIME SOME PUFFED UP IDIOT INVENTS A BETTER LEYDEN JAR!
I...I HAD MOST OF IT UNDER CONTROL, SIR.
OF COURSE-OF COURSE-EXCEPT FOR THE SMALL MATTER OF THE RECENT HETERODYNE CONQUEST!
I COULDN'T HAVE DONE IT WITHOUT HIM, SIR.
CHEEK.

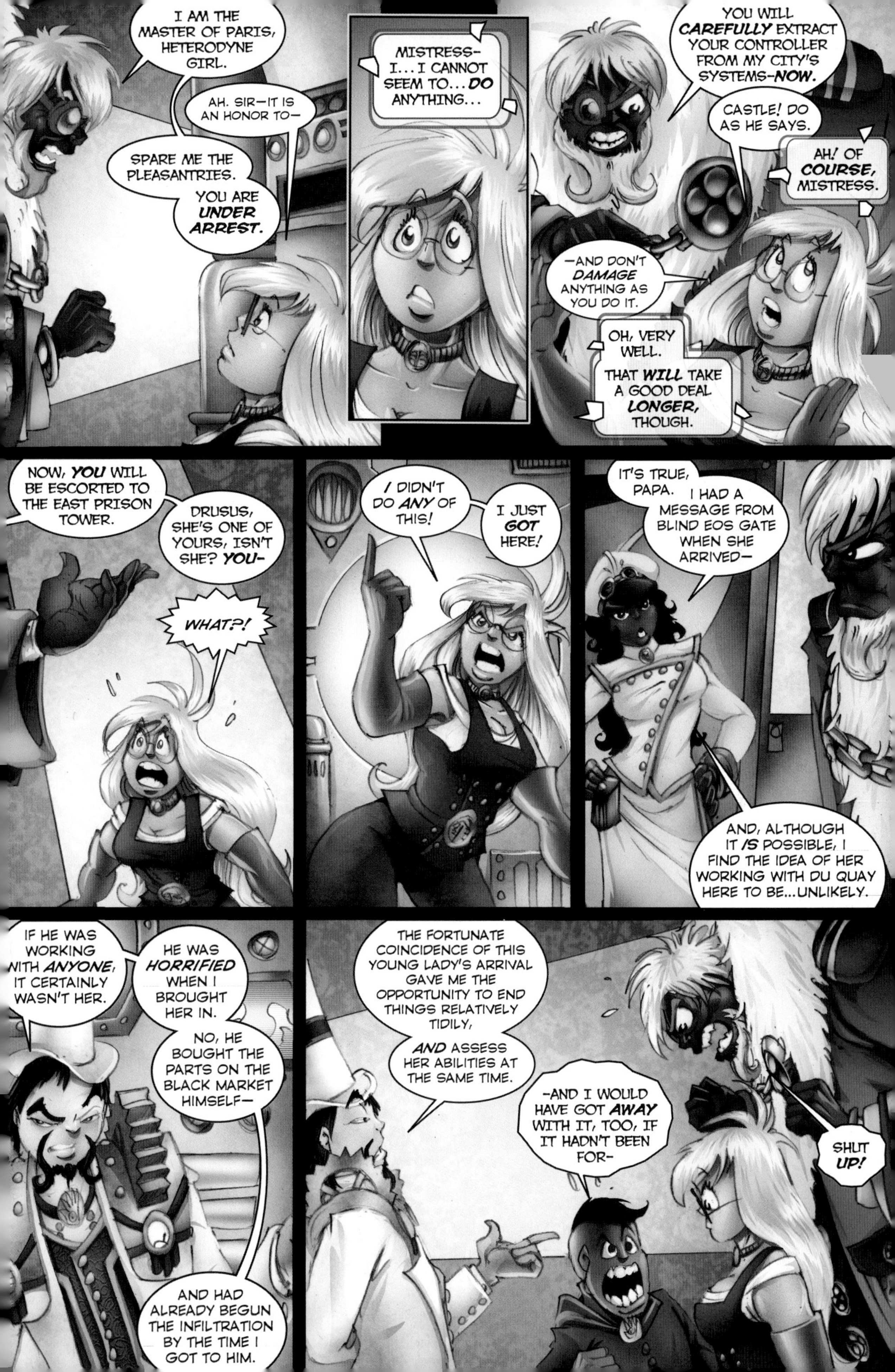
I AM THE MASTER OF PARIS, HETERODYNE GIRL.
AH. SIR—IT IS AN HONOR TO—
SPARE ME THE PLEASANTRIES.
YOU ARE UNDER ARREST.
MISTRESS-I... I CANNOT SEEM TO... DO ANYTHING...
YOU WILL CAREFULLY EXTRACT YOUR CONTROLLER FROM MY CITY'S SYSTEMS-NOW.
CASTLE! DO AS HE SAYS.
AH! OF COURSE, MISTRESS.
—AND DON'T DAMAGE ANYTHING AS YOU DO IT.
OH, VERY WELL.
THAT WILL TAKE A GOOD DEAL LONGER, THOUGH.
NOW, YOU WILL BE ESCORTED TO THE EAST PRISON TOWER.
DRUSUS, SHE'S ONE OF YOURS, ISN'T SHE? YOU-
WHAT?!
I DIDN'T DO ANY OF THIS!
I JUST GOT HERE!
IT'S TRUE, PAPA.
I HAD A MESSAGE FROM BLIND EOS GATE WHEN SHE ARRIVED—
AND, ALTHOUGH IT IS POSSIBLE, I FIND THE IDEA OF HER WORKING WITH DU QUAY HERE TO BE...UNLIKELY.
IF HE WAS WORKING WITH ANYONE, IT CERTAINLY WASN'T HER.
HE WAS HORRIFIED WHEN I BROUGHT HER IN.
NO, HE BOUGHT THE PARTS ON THE BLACK MARKET HIMSELF—
AND HAD ALREADY BEGUN THE INFILTRATION BY THE TIME I GOT TO HIM.
THE FORTUNATE COINCIDENCE OF THIS YOUNG LADY'S ARRIVAL GAVE ME THE OPPORTUNITY TO END THINGS RELATIVELY TIDILY,
AND ASSESS HER ABILITIES AT THE SAME TIME.
-AND I WOULD HAVE GOT AWAY WITH IT, TOO, IF IT HADN'T BEEN FOR-
SHUT UP!

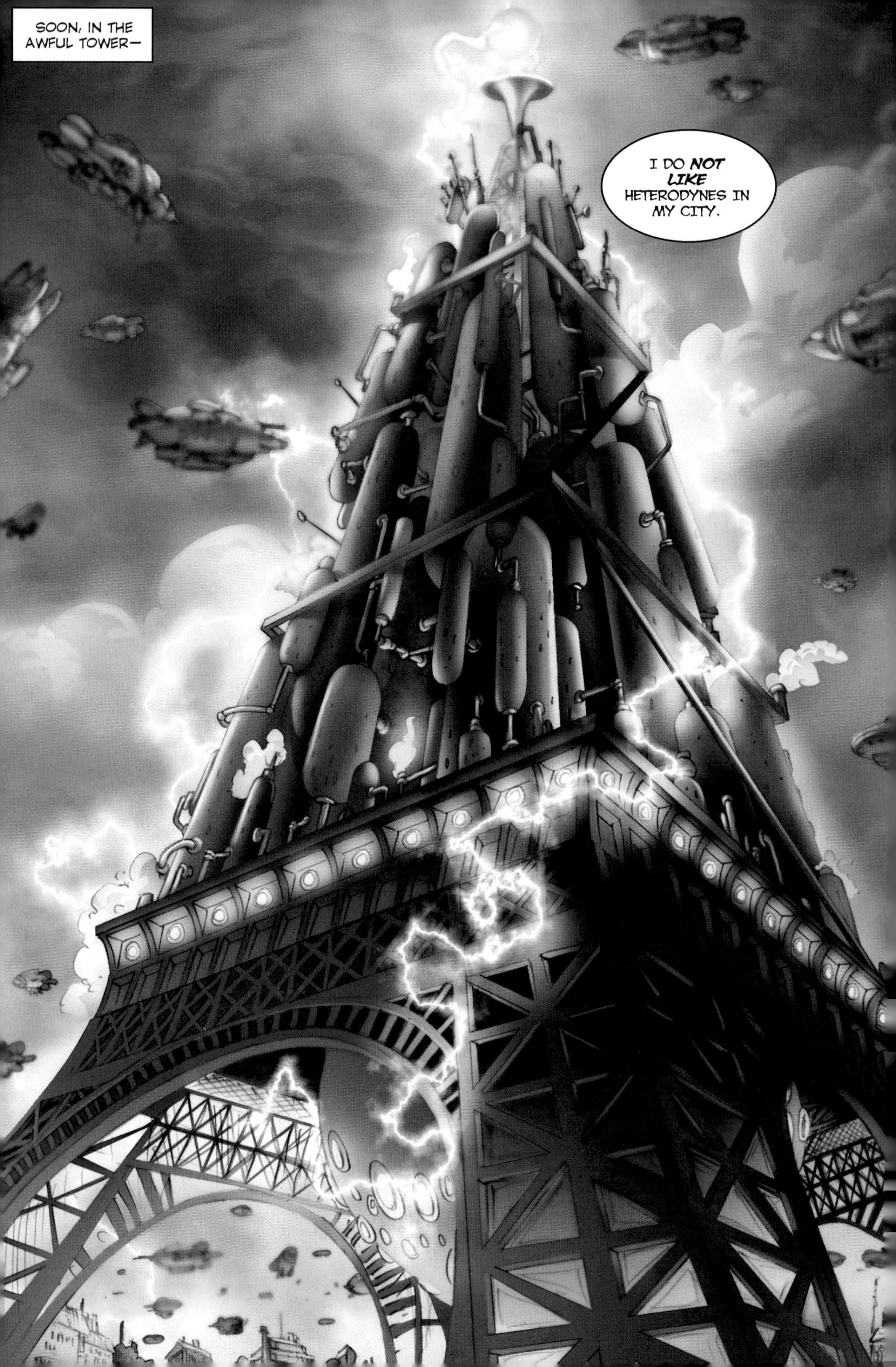
SOON, IN THE AWFUL TOWER—
I DO **NOT LIKE** HETERODYNES IN MY CITY.

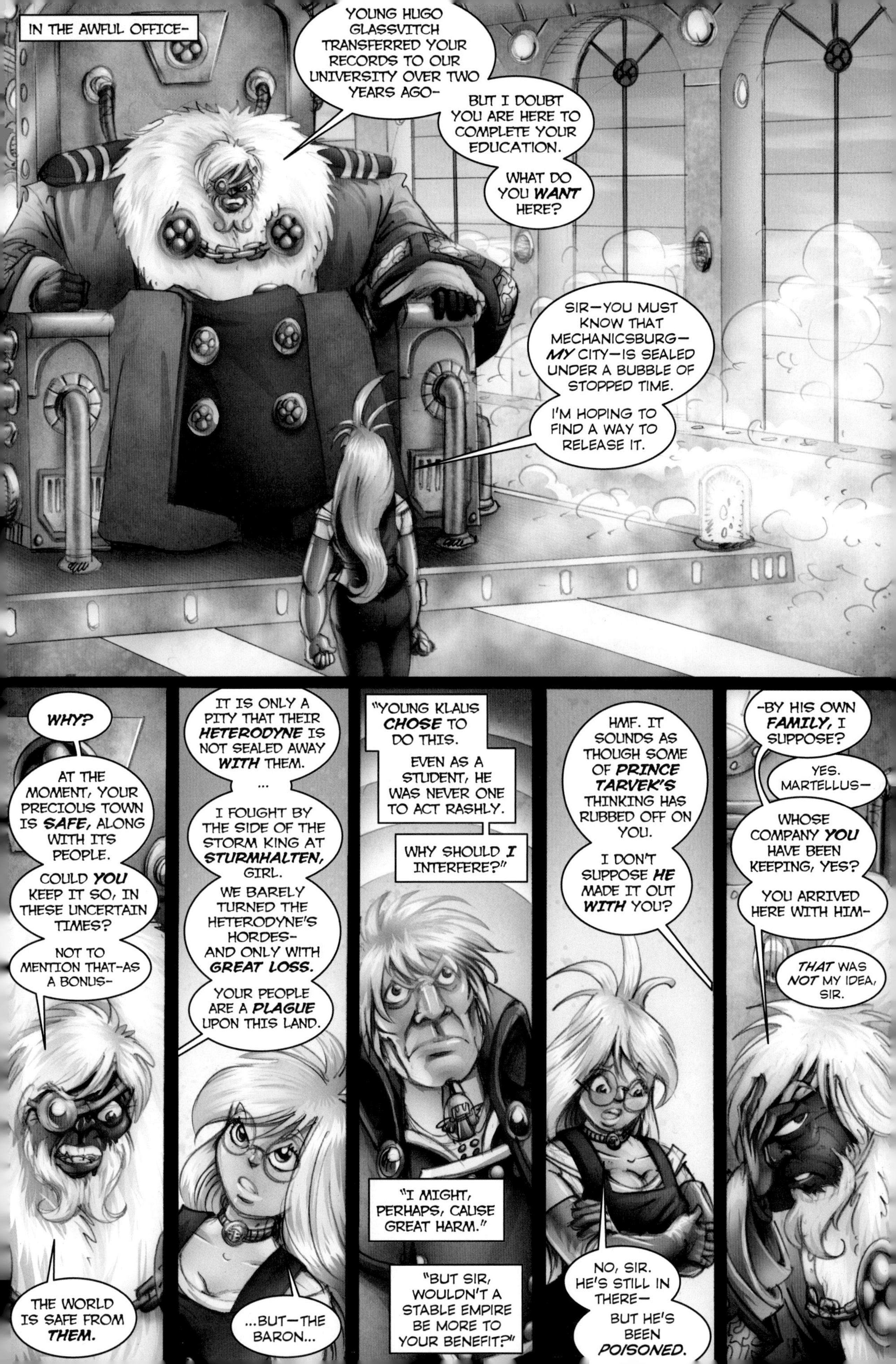
IN THE AWFUL OFFICE-
YOUNG HUGO GLASSVITCH TRANSFERRED YOUR RECORDS TO OUR UNIVERSITY OVER TWO YEARS AGO-
BUT I DOUBT YOU ARE HERE TO COMPLETE YOUR EDUCATION.
WHAT DO YOU **WANT** HERE?
SIR—YOU MUST KNOW THAT MECHANICSBURG—**MY** CITY—IS SEALED UNDER A BUBBLE OF STOPPED TIME.
I'M HOPING TO FIND A WAY TO RELEASE IT.
WHY?
AT THE MOMENT, YOUR PRECIOUS TOWN IS **SAFE,** ALONG WITH ITS PEOPLE.
COULD **YOU** KEEP IT SO, IN THESE UNCERTAIN TIMES?
NOT TO MENTION THAT-AS A BONUS-
THE WORLD IS SAFE FROM **THEM.**
IT IS ONLY A PITY THAT THEIR **HETERODYNE** IS NOT SEALED AWAY **WITH** THEM.
...
I FOUGHT BY THE SIDE OF THE STORM KING AT **STURMHALTEN,** GIRL.
WE BARELY TURNED THE HETERODYNE'S HORDES-
AND ONLY WITH **GREAT LOSS.**
YOUR PEOPLE ARE A **PLAGUE** UPON THIS LAND.
...BUT—THE BARON...
"YOUNG KLAUS **CHOSE** TO DO THIS.
EVEN AS A STUDENT, HE WAS NEVER ONE TO ACT RASHLY.
WHY SHOULD ***I*** INTERFERE?"
"I MIGHT, PERHAPS, CAUSE GREAT HARM."
"BUT SIR, WOULDN'T A STABLE EMPIRE BE MORE TO YOUR BENEFIT?"
HMF. IT SOUNDS AS THOUGH SOME OF **PRINCE TARVEK'S** THINKING HAS RUBBED OFF ON YOU.
I DON'T SUPPOSE **HE** MADE IT OUT **WITH** YOU?
NO, SIR. HE'S STILL IN THERE—
BUT HE'S BEEN **POISONED.**
-BY HIS OWN **FAMILY,** I SUPPOSE?
YES. MARTELLUS—
WHOSE COMPANY **YOU** HAVE BEEN KEEPING, YES?
YOU ARRIVED HERE WITH HIM-
THAT WAS **NOT** MY IDEA, SIR.

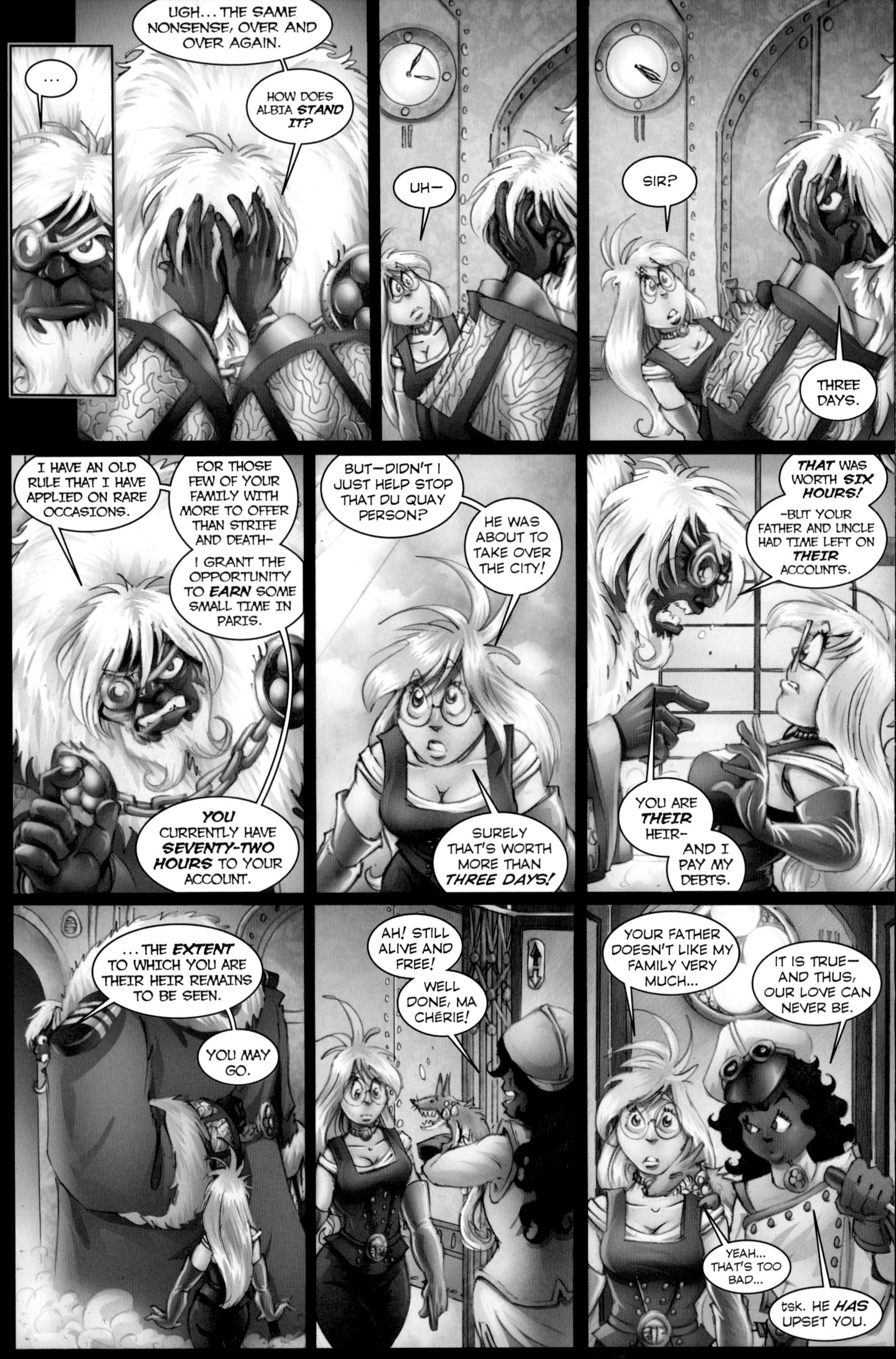
...
UGH... THE SAME NONSENSE, OVER AND OVER AGAIN.
HOW DOES ALBIA STAND IT?
UH—
SIR?
THREE DAYS.
I HAVE AN OLD RULE THAT I HAVE APPLIED ON RARE OCCASIONS.
FOR THOSE FEW OF YOUR FAMILY WITH MORE TO OFFER THAN STRIFE AND DEATH—
I GRANT THE OPPORTUNITY TO EARN SOME SMALL TIME IN PARIS.
YOU CURRENTLY HAVE SEVENTY-TWO HOURS TO YOUR ACCOUNT.
BUT—DIDN'T I JUST HELP STOP THAT DU QUAY PERSON?
HE WAS ABOUT TO TAKE OVER THE CITY!
SURELY THAT'S WORTH MORE THAN THREE DAYS!
THAT WAS WORTH SIX HOURS!
-BUT YOUR FATHER AND UNCLE HAD TIME LEFT ON THEIR ACCOUNTS.
YOU ARE THEIR HEIR-
AND I PAY MY DEBTS.
...THE EXTENT TO WHICH YOU ARE THEIR HEIR REMAINS TO BE SEEN.
YOU MAY GO.
AH! STILL ALIVE AND FREE!
WELL DONE, MA CHÉRIE!
YOUR FATHER DOESN'T LIKE MY FAMILY VERY MUCH...
IT IS TRUE—AND THUS, OUR LOVE CAN NEVER BE.
YEAH... THAT'S TOO BAD...
tsk. HE HAS UPSET YOU.

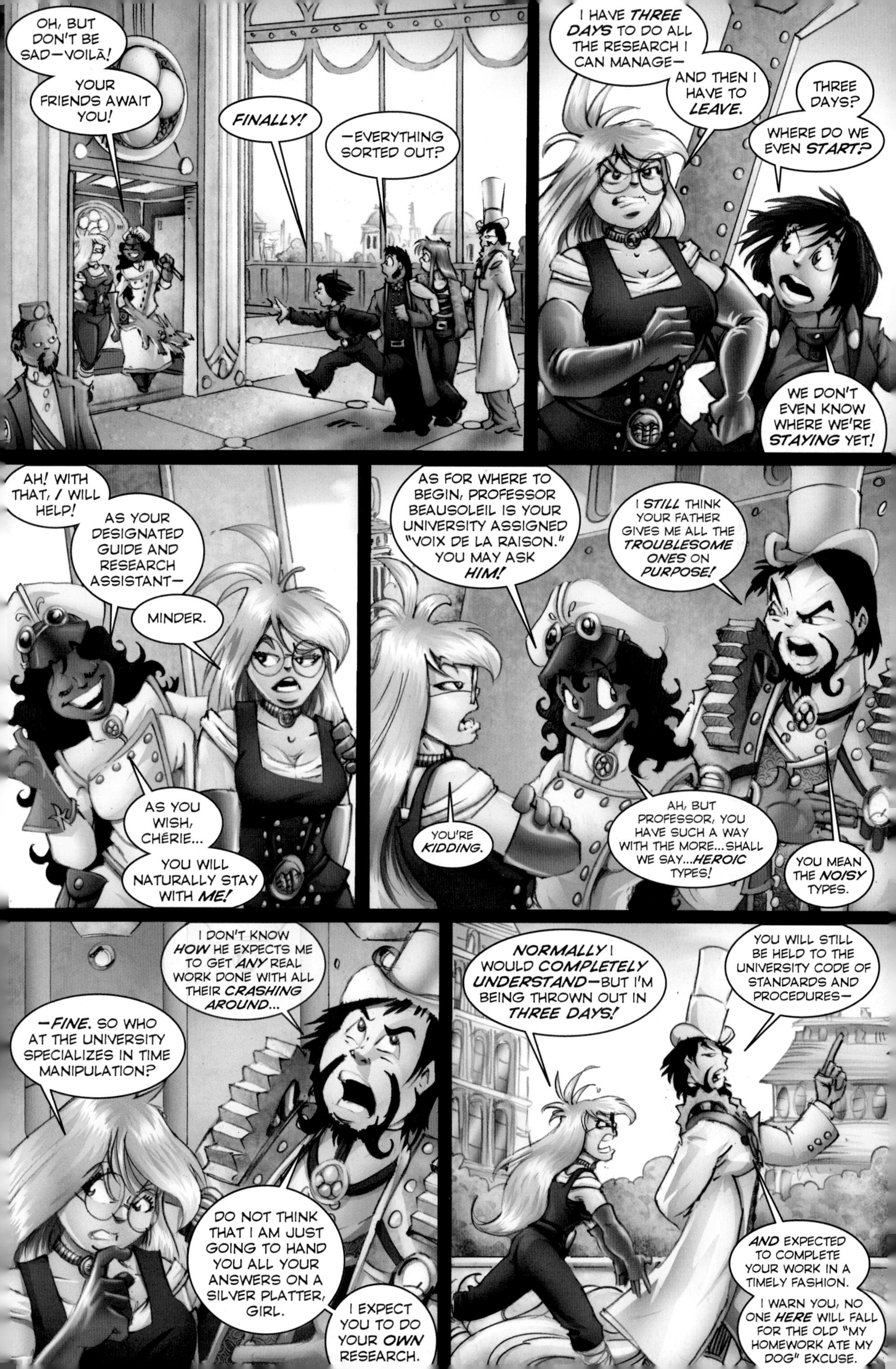
OH, BUT DON'T BE SAD—VOILÀ!
YOUR FRIENDS AWAIT YOU!
FINALLY!
—EVERYTHING SORTED OUT?
I HAVE THREE DAYS TO DO ALL THE RESEARCH I CAN MANAGE—
AND THEN I HAVE TO LEAVE.
THREE DAYS?
WHERE DO WE EVEN START?
WE DON'T EVEN KNOW WHERE WE'RE STAYING YET!
AH! WITH THAT, I WILL HELP!
AS YOUR DESIGNATED GUIDE AND RESEARCH ASSISTANT—
MINDER.
AS YOU WISH, CHÉRIE...
YOU WILL NATURALLY STAY WITH ME!
AS FOR WHERE TO BEGIN, PROFESSOR BEAUSOLEIL IS YOUR UNIVERSITY ASSIGNED "VOIX DE LA RAISON." YOU MAY ASK HIM!
I STILL THINK YOUR FATHER GIVES ME ALL THE TROUBLESOME ONES ON PURPOSE!
YOU'RE KIDDING.
AH, BUT PROFESSOR, YOU HAVE SUCH A WAY WITH THE MORE...SHALL WE SAY...HEROIC TYPES!
YOU MEAN THE NOISY TYPES.
I DON'T KNOW HOW HE EXPECTS ME TO GET ANY REAL WORK DONE WITH ALL THEIR CRASHING AROUND...
—FINE. SO WHO AT THE UNIVERSITY SPECIALIZES IN TIME MANIPULATION?
DO NOT THINK THAT I AM JUST GOING TO HAND YOU ALL YOUR ANSWERS ON A SILVER PLATTER, GIRL.
I EXPECT YOU TO DO YOUR OWN RESEARCH.
NORMALLY I WOULD COMPLETELY UNDERSTAND—BUT I'M BEING THROWN OUT IN THREE DAYS!
YOU WILL STILL BE HELD TO THE UNIVERSITY CODE OF STANDARDS AND PROCEDURES—
AND EXPECTED TO COMPLETE YOUR WORK IN A TIMELY FASHION.
I WARN YOU, NO ONE HERE WILL FALL FOR THE OLD "MY HOMEWORK ATE MY DOG" EXCUSE.

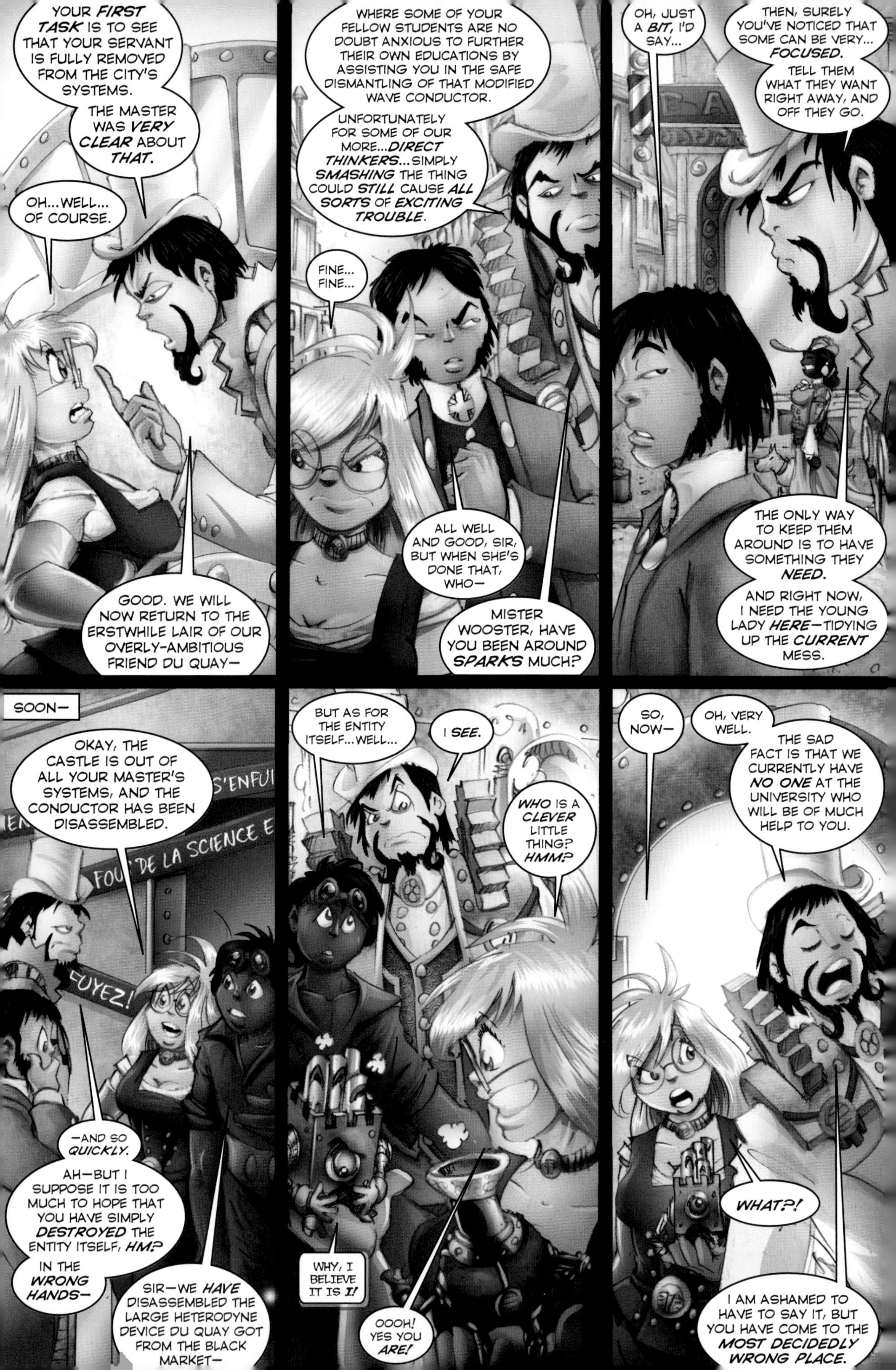
YOUR ***FIRST TASK*** IS TO SEE THAT YOUR SERVANT IS FULLY REMOVED FROM THE CITY'S SYSTEMS.
THE MASTER WAS ***VERY CLEAR*** ABOUT ***THAT***.
OH...WELL... OF COURSE.
GOOD. WE WILL NOW RETURN TO THE ERSTWHILE LAIR OF OUR OVERLY-AMBITIOUS FRIEND DU QUAY—
WHERE SOME OF YOUR FELLOW STUDENTS ARE NO DOUBT ANXIOUS TO FURTHER THEIR OWN EDUCATIONS BY ASSISTING YOU IN THE SAFE DISMANTLING OF THAT MODIFIED WAVE CONDUCTOR.
UNFORTUNATELY FOR SOME OF OUR MORE...***DIRECT THINKERS***...SIMPLY ***SMASHING*** THE THING COULD ***STILL*** CAUSE ***ALL SORTS*** OF ***EXCITING TROUBLE***.
FINE... FINE...
ALL WELL AND GOOD, SIR, BUT WHEN SHE'S DONE THAT, WHO—
MISTER WOOSTER, HAVE YOU BEEN AROUND ***SPARKS*** MUCH?
OH, JUST A ***BIT***, I'D SAY...
THEN, SURELY YOU'VE NOTICED THAT SOME CAN BE VERY... ***FOCUSED***.
TELL THEM WHAT THEY WANT RIGHT AWAY, AND OFF THEY GO.
THE ONLY WAY TO KEEP THEM AROUND IS TO HAVE SOMETHING THEY ***NEED***.
AND RIGHT NOW, I NEED THE YOUNG LADY ***HERE***—TIDYING UP THE ***CURRENT*** MESS.
SOON—
OKAY, THE CASTLE IS OUT OF ALL YOUR MASTER'S SYSTEMS, AND THE CONDUCTOR HAS BEEN DISASSEMBLED.
FOU DE LA SCIENCE
FUYEZ!
—AND SO ***QUICKLY***.
AH—BUT I SUPPOSE IT IS TOO MUCH TO HOPE THAT YOU HAVE SIMPLY ***DESTROYED*** THE ENTITY ITSELF, ***HM?***
IN THE ***WRONG HANDS***—
SIR—WE ***HAVE*** DISASSEMBLED THE LARGE HETERODYNE DEVICE DU QUAY GOT FROM THE BLACK MARKET—
BUT AS FOR THE ENTITY ITSELF...WELL...
I ***SEE***.
WHO IS A ***CLEVER*** LITTLE THING? ***HMM?***
WHY, I BELIEVE IT IS ***I!***
OOOH! YES YOU ***ARE!***
SO, NOW—
OH, VERY WELL.
THE SAD FACT IS THAT WE CURRENTLY HAVE ***NO ONE*** AT THE UNIVERSITY WHO WILL BE OF MUCH HELP TO YOU.
WHAT?!
I AM ASHAMED TO HAVE TO SAY IT, BUT YOU HAVE COME TO THE ***MOST DECIDEDLY WRONG PLACE***.

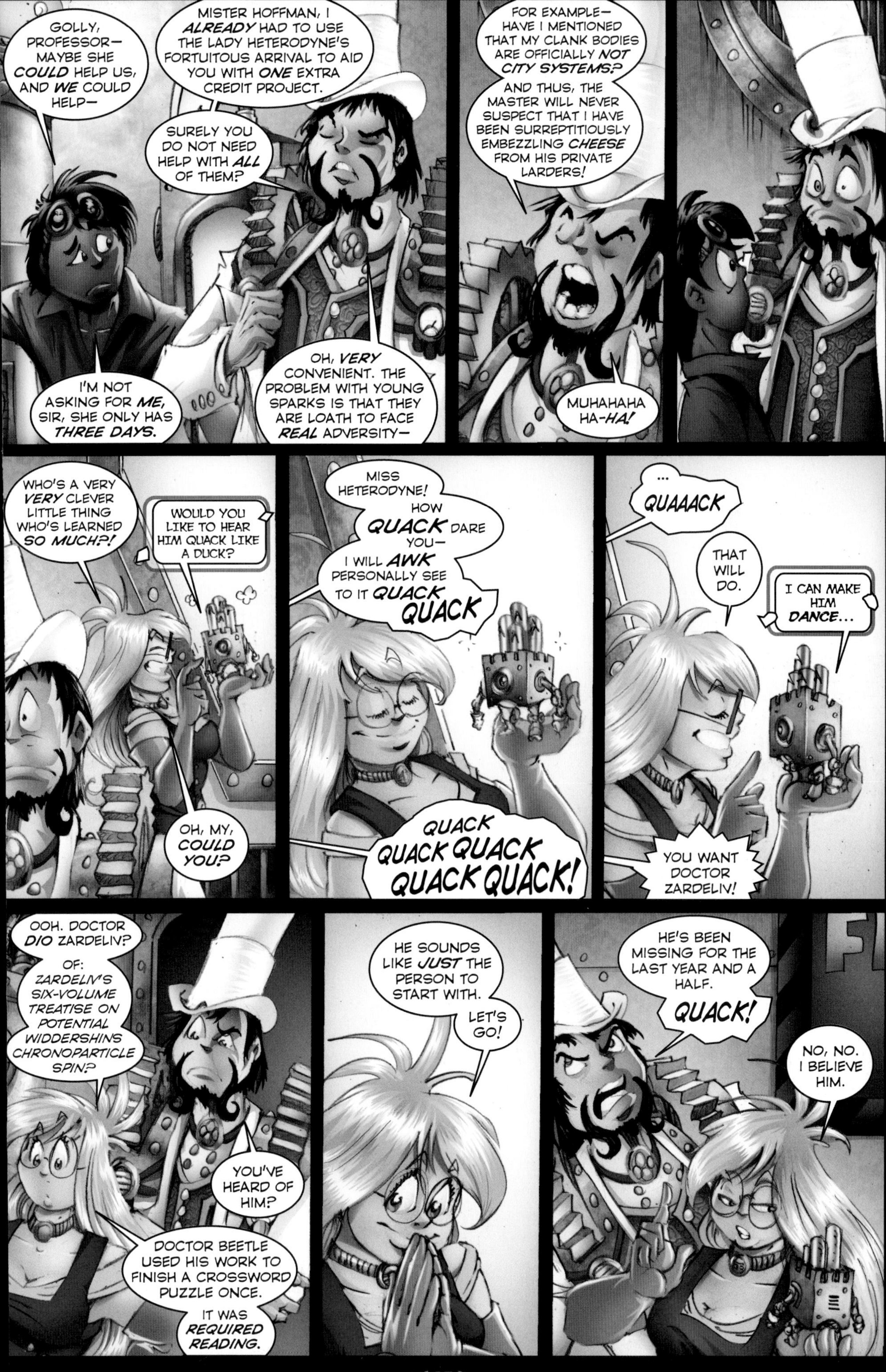

GOLLY, PROFESSOR— MAYBE SHE *COULD* HELP US, AND *WE* COULD HELP—
MISTER HOFFMAN, I *ALREADY* HAD TO USE THE LADY HETERODYNE'S FORTUITOUS ARRIVAL TO AID YOU WITH *ONE* EXTRA CREDIT PROJECT.
SURELY YOU DO NOT NEED HELP WITH *ALL* OF THEM?
I'M NOT ASKING FOR *ME*, SIR, SHE ONLY HAS *THREE DAYS.*
OH, *VERY* CONVENIENT. THE PROBLEM WITH YOUNG SPARKS IS THAT THEY ARE LOATH TO FACE *REAL* ADVERSITY—
FOR EXAMPLE— HAVE I MENTIONED THAT MY CLANK BODIES ARE OFFICIALLY *NOT CITY SYSTEMS?*
AND THUS, THE MASTER WILL NEVER SUSPECT THAT I HAVE BEEN SURREPTITIOUSLY EMBEZZLING *CHEESE* FROM HIS PRIVATE LARDERS!
MUHAHAHA HA-*HA!*
WHO'S A VERY *VERY* CLEVER LITTLE THING WHO'S LEARNED *SO MUCH?!*
WOULD YOU LIKE TO HEAR HIM QUACK LIKE A DUCK?
OH, MY, *COULD YOU?*
MISS HETERODYNE! HOW *QUACK* DARE YOU— I WILL *AWK* PERSONALLY SEE TO IT *QUACK QUACK*
QUACK QUACK QUACK QUACK QUACK!
... QUAAACK
THAT WILL DO.
I CAN MAKE HIM *DANCE...*
YOU WANT DOCTOR ZARDELIV!
OOH. DOCTOR *DIO* ZARDELIV?
OF: *ZARDELIV'S SIX-VOLUME TREATISE ON POTENTIAL WIDDERSHINS CHRONOPARTICLE SPIN?*
YOU'VE HEARD OF HIM?
DOCTOR BEETLE USED HIS WORK TO FINISH A CROSSWORD PUZZLE ONCE.
IT WAS *REQUIRED READING.*
HE SOUNDS LIKE *JUST* THE PERSON TO START WITH.
LET'S GO!
HE'S BEEN MISSING FOR THE LAST YEAR AND A HALF.
QUACK!
NO, NO. I BELIEVE HIM.

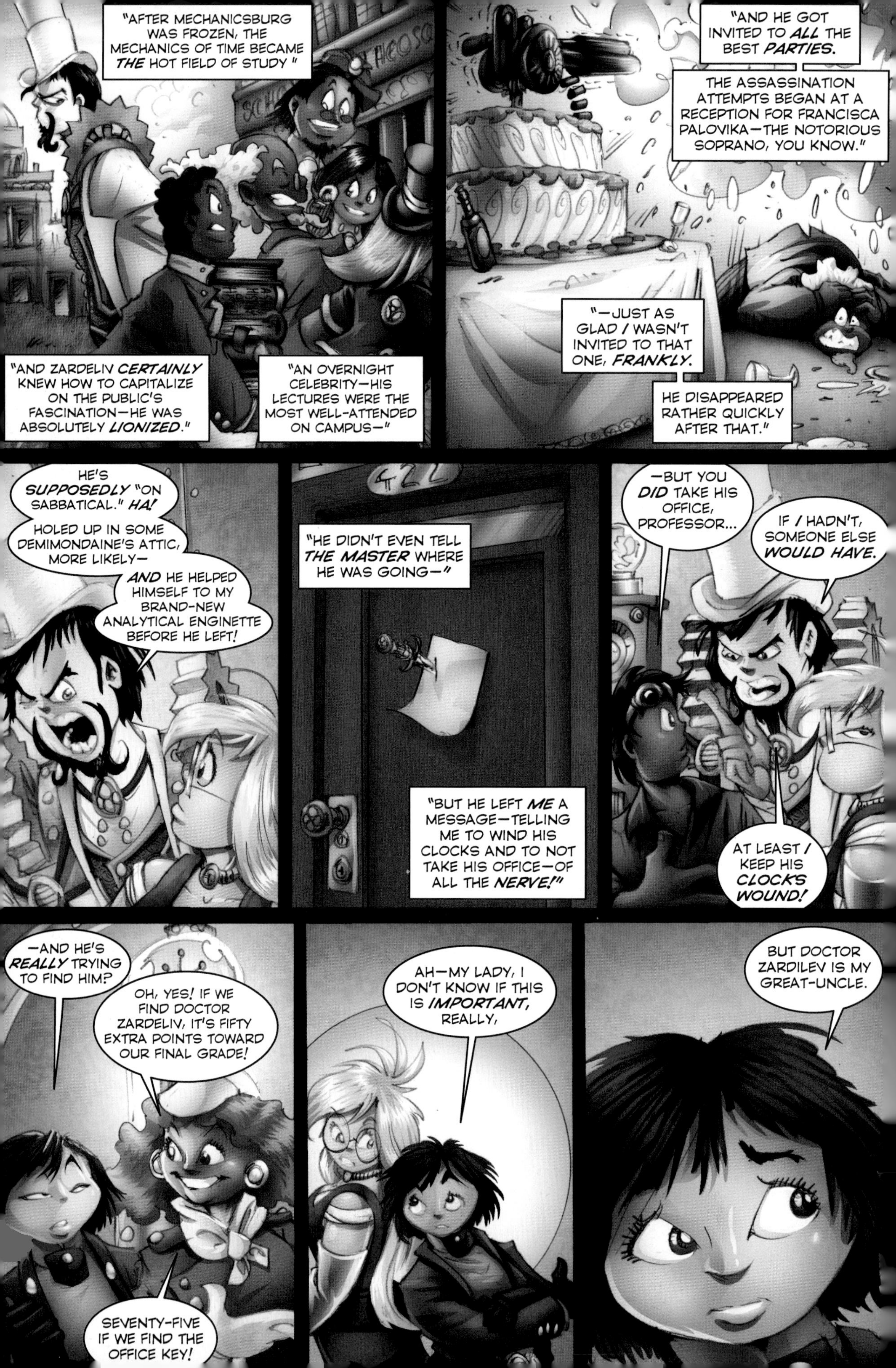

"AFTER MECHANICSBURG WAS FROZEN, THE MECHANICS OF TIME BECAME *THE* HOT FIELD OF STUDY "
"AND ZARDELIV *CERTAINLY* KNEW HOW TO CAPITALIZE ON THE PUBLIC'S FASCINATION—HE WAS ABSOLUTELY *LIONIZED*."
"AN OVERNIGHT CELEBRITY—HIS LECTURES WERE THE MOST WELL-ATTENDED ON CAMPUS—"
"AND HE GOT INVITED TO *ALL* THE BEST *PARTIES*.
THE ASSASSINATION ATTEMPTS BEGAN AT A RECEPTION FOR FRANCISCA PALOVIKA—THE NOTORIOUS SOPRANO, YOU KNOW."
"—JUST AS GLAD *I* WASN'T INVITED TO THAT ONE, *FRANKLY*.
HE DISAPPEARED RATHER QUICKLY AFTER THAT."
HE'S *SUPPOSEDLY* "ON SABBATICAL." *HA!*
HOLED UP IN SOME DEMIMONDAINE'S ATTIC, MORE LIKELY—
AND HE HELPED HIMSELF TO MY BRAND-NEW ANALYTICAL ENGINETTE BEFORE HE LEFT!
"HE DIDN'T EVEN TELL *THE MASTER* WHERE HE WAS GOING—"
"BUT HE LEFT *ME* A MESSAGE—TELLING ME TO WIND HIS CLOCKS AND TO NOT TAKE HIS OFFICE—OF ALL THE *NERVE!*"
—BUT YOU *DID* TAKE HIS OFFICE, PROFESSOR...
IF *I* HADN'T, SOMEONE ELSE *WOULD HAVE*.
AT LEAST *I* KEEP HIS *CLOCKS WOUND!*
—AND HE'S *REALLY* TRYING TO FIND HIM?
OH, YES! IF WE FIND DOCTOR ZARDELIV, IT'S FIFTY EXTRA POINTS TOWARD OUR FINAL GRADE!
SEVENTY-FIVE IF WE FIND THE OFFICE KEY!
AH—MY LADY, I DON'T KNOW IF THIS IS *IMPORTANT*, REALLY,
BUT DOCTOR ZARDILEV IS MY GREAT-UNCLE.

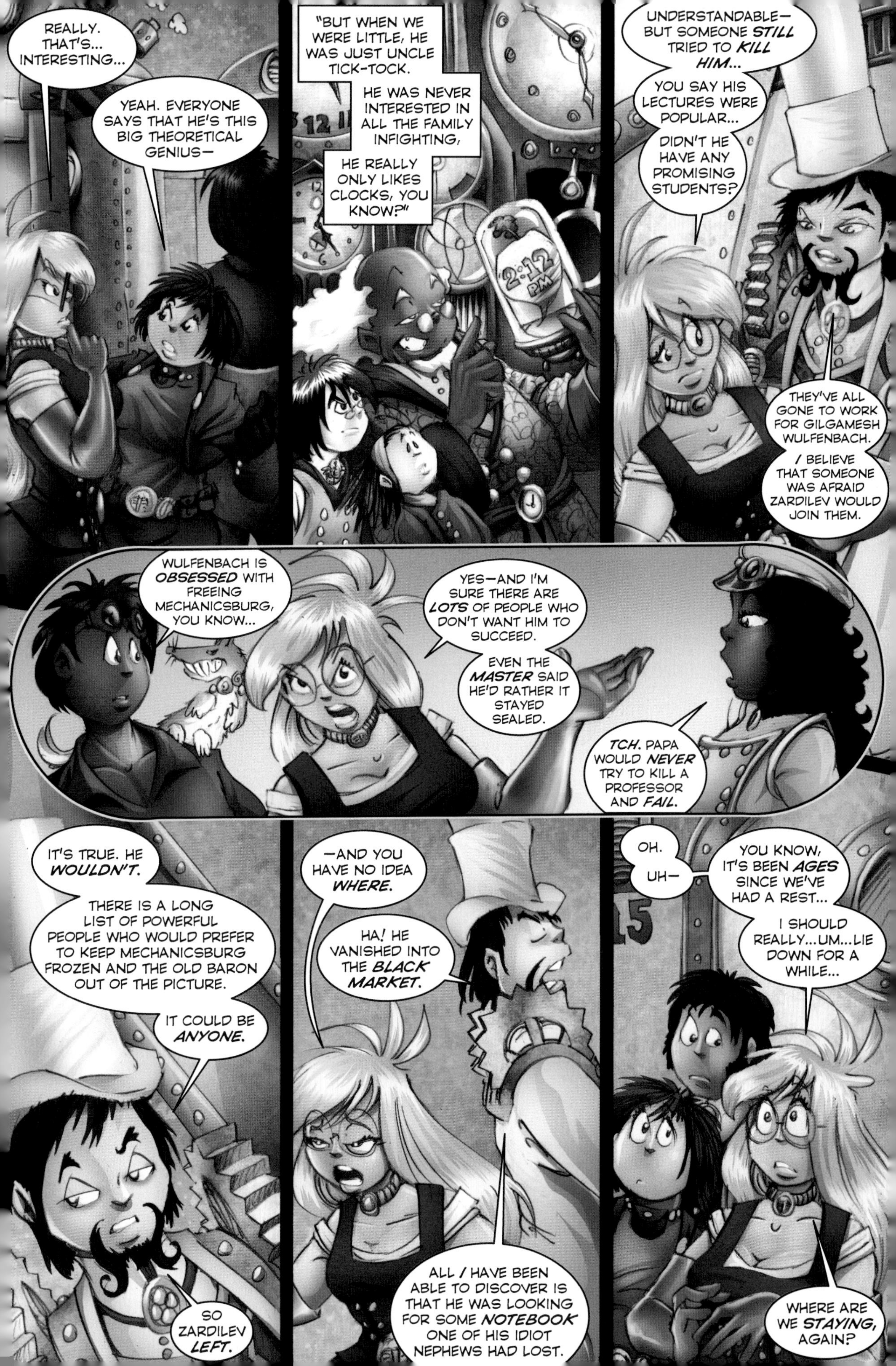

REALLY. THAT'S... INTERESTING...
YEAH. EVERYONE SAYS THAT HE'S THIS BIG THEORETICAL GENIUS—
"BUT WHEN WE WERE LITTLE, HE WAS JUST UNCLE TICK-TOCK.
HE WAS NEVER INTERESTED IN ALL THE FAMILY INFIGHTING,
HE REALLY ONLY LIKES CLOCKS, YOU KNOW?"
2:12 PM
UNDERSTANDABLE—BUT SOMEONE STILL TRIED TO KILL HIM...
YOU SAY HIS LECTURES WERE POPULAR...
DIDN'T HE HAVE ANY PROMISING STUDENTS?
THEY'VE ALL GONE TO WORK FOR GILGAMESH WULFENBACH.
I BELIEVE THAT SOMEONE WAS AFRAID ZARDILEV WOULD JOIN THEM.
WULFENBACH IS OBSESSED WITH FREEING MECHANICSBURG, YOU KNOW...
YES—AND I'M SURE THERE ARE LOTS OF PEOPLE WHO DON'T WANT HIM TO SUCCEED.
EVEN THE MASTER SAID HE'D RATHER IT STAYED SEALED.
TCH. PAPA WOULD NEVER TRY TO KILL A PROFESSOR AND FAIL.
IT'S TRUE. HE WOULDN'T.
THERE IS A LONG LIST OF POWERFUL PEOPLE WHO WOULD PREFER TO KEEP MECHANICSBURG FROZEN AND THE OLD BARON OUT OF THE PICTURE.
IT COULD BE ANYONE.
SO ZARDILEV LEFT.
—AND YOU HAVE NO IDEA WHERE.
HA! HE VANISHED INTO THE BLACK MARKET.
ALL I HAVE BEEN ABLE TO DISCOVER IS THAT HE WAS LOOKING FOR SOME NOTEBOOK ONE OF HIS IDIOT NEPHEWS HAD LOST.
OH.
UH—
YOU KNOW, IT'S BEEN AGES SINCE WE'VE HAD A REST...
I SHOULD REALLY...UM...LIE DOWN FOR A WHILE...
WHERE ARE WE STAYING, AGAIN?

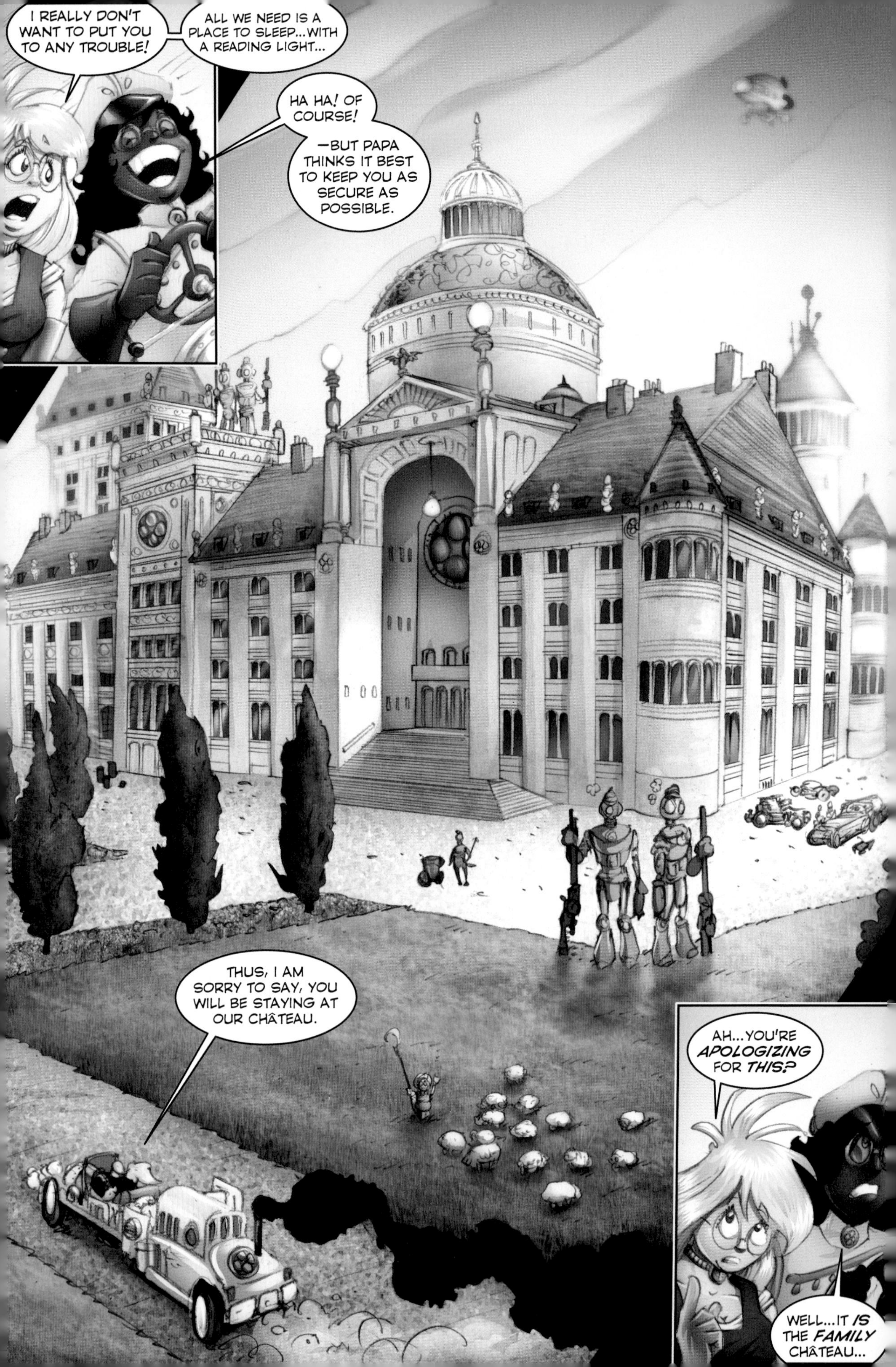
I REALLY DON'T WANT TO PUT YOU TO ANY TROUBLE!
ALL WE NEED IS A PLACE TO SLEEP...WITH A READING LIGHT...
HA HA! OF COURSE!
—BUT PAPA THINKS IT BEST TO KEEP YOU AS SECURE AS POSSIBLE.
THUS, I AM SORRY TO SAY, YOU WILL BE STAYING AT OUR CHÂTEAU.
AH...YOU'RE *APOLOGIZING* FOR *THIS?*
WELL...IT *IS* THE *FAMILY* CHÂTEAU...

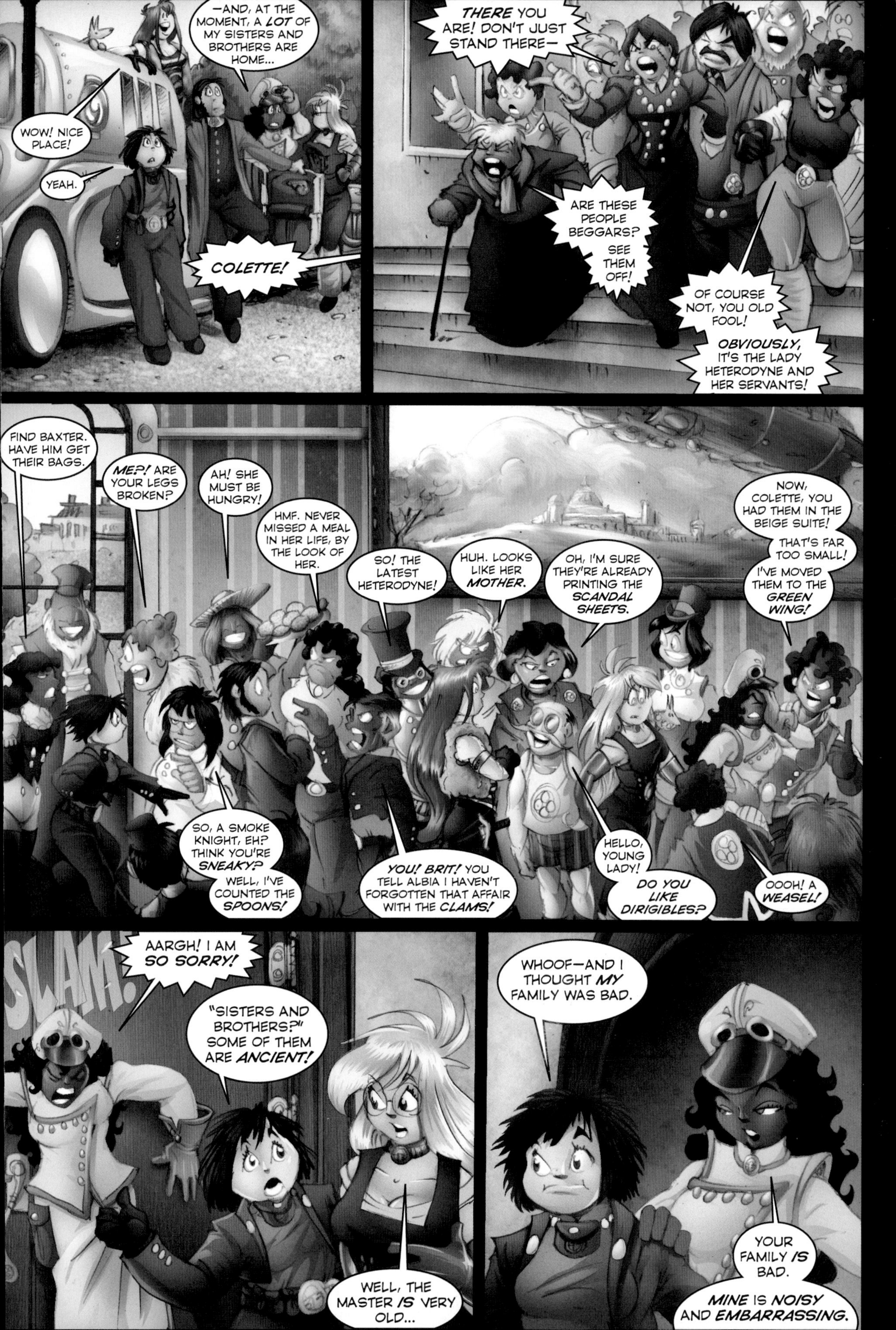

—AND, AT THE MOMENT, A LOT OF MY SISTERS AND BROTHERS ARE HOME...
WOW! NICE PLACE!
YEAH.
COLETTE!
THERE YOU ARE! DON'T JUST STAND THERE—
ARE THESE PEOPLE BEGGARS? SEE THEM OFF!
OF COURSE NOT, YOU OLD FOOL!
OBVIOUSLY, IT'S THE LADY HETERODYNE AND HER SERVANTS!
FIND BAXTER. HAVE HIM GET THEIR BAGS.
ME?! ARE YOUR LEGS BROKEN?
AH! SHE MUST BE HUNGRY!
HMF. NEVER MISSED A MEAL IN HER LIFE, BY THE LOOK OF HER.
SO! THE LATEST HETERODYNE!
HUH. LOOKS LIKE HER MOTHER.
OH, I'M SURE THEY'RE ALREADY PRINTING THE SCANDAL SHEETS.
NOW, COLETTE, YOU HAD THEM IN THE BEIGE SUITE!
THAT'S FAR TOO SMALL!
I'VE MOVED THEM TO THE GREEN WING!
SO, A SMOKE KNIGHT, EH? THINK YOU'RE SNEAKY?
WELL, I'VE COUNTED THE SPOONS!
YOU! BRIT! YOU TELL ALBIA I HAVEN'T FORGOTTEN THAT AFFAIR WITH THE CLAMS!
HELLO, YOUNG LADY!
DO YOU LIKE DIRIGIBLES?
OOOH! A WEASEL!
SLAM!
AARGH! I AM SO SORRY!
"SISTERS AND BROTHERS?" SOME OF THEM ARE ANCIENT!
WELL, THE MASTER IS VERY OLD...
WHOOF—AND I THOUGHT MY FAMILY WAS BAD.
YOUR FAMILY IS BAD.
MINE IS NOISY AND EMBARRASSING.

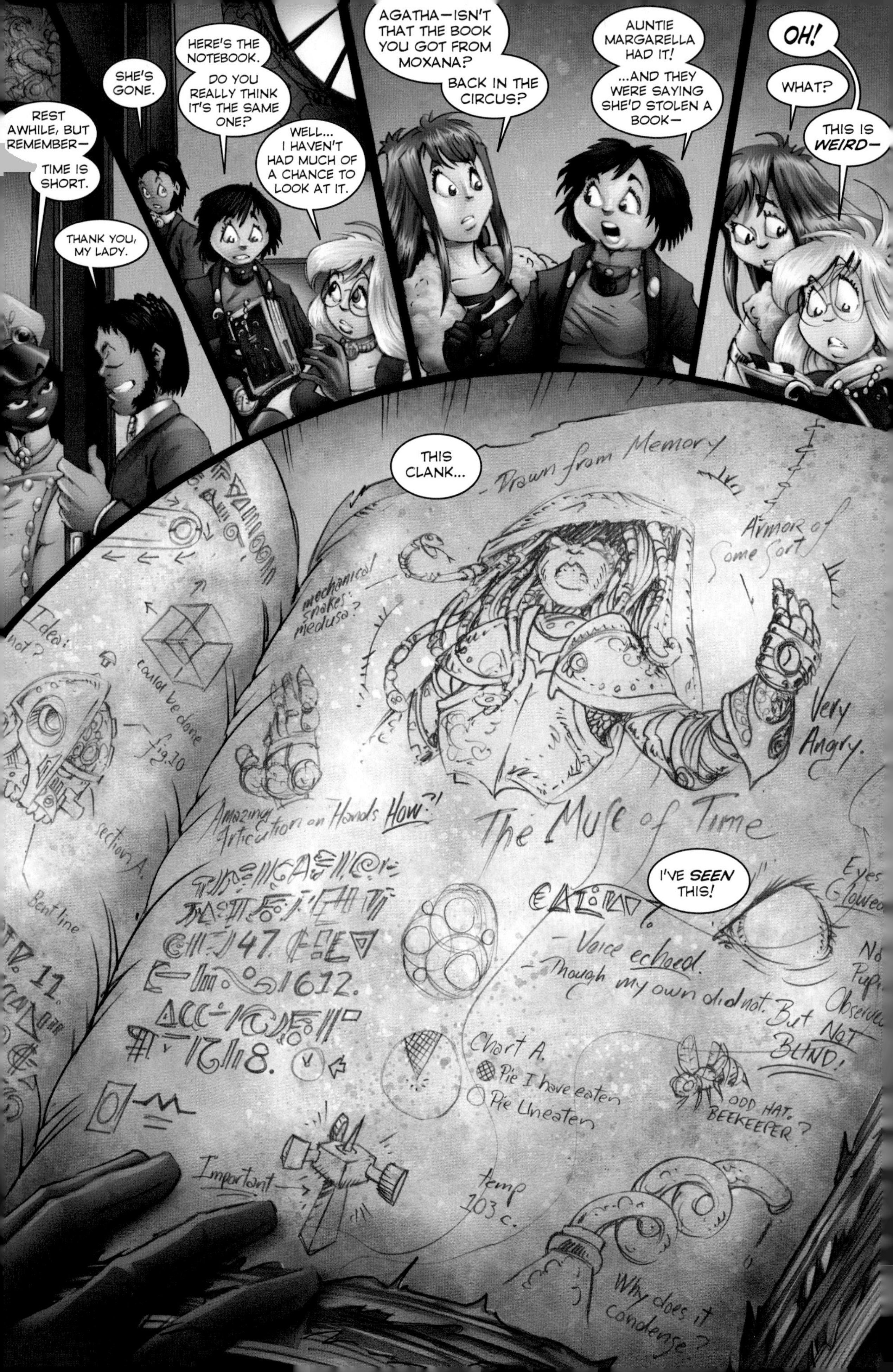
REST AWHILE, BUT REMEMBER—
TIME IS SHORT.
THANK YOU, MY LADY.
SHE'S GONE.
HERE'S THE NOTEBOOK.
DO YOU REALLY THINK IT'S THE SAME ONE?
WELL... I HAVEN'T HAD MUCH OF A CHANCE TO LOOK AT IT.
AGATHA—ISN'T THAT THE BOOK YOU GOT FROM MOXANA?
BACK IN THE CIRCUS?
AUNTIE MARGARELLA HAD IT!
...AND THEY WERE SAYING SHE'D STOLEN A BOOK—
OH!
WHAT?
THIS IS WEIRD—
THIS CLANK...
I'VE SEEN THIS!
Drawn from Memory
Armor of Some Sort
mechanical snakes: medusa?
Very Angry.
Amazing Articulation on Hands How?!
The Muse of Time
could be done
fig.10
section A.
Bent line
Voice echoed.
Though my own did not.
But NOT BLIND!
Chart A.
Pie I have eaten
Pie Uneaten
ODD HAT. BEEKEEPER?
Important
temp 103 c.
Why does it condense?

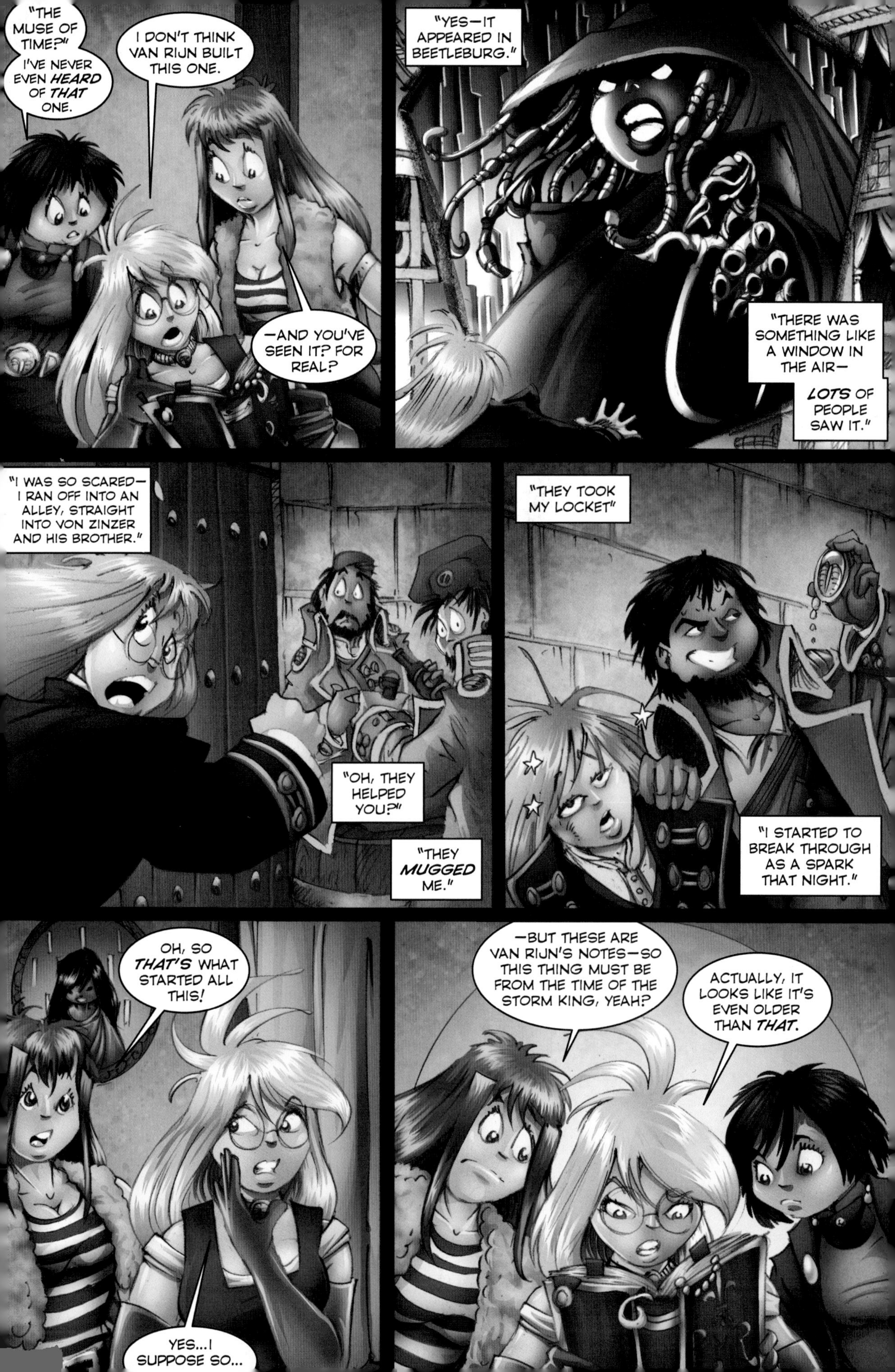
"THE MUSE OF TIME?"
I'VE NEVER EVEN HEARD OF THAT ONE.
I DON'T THINK VAN RIJN BUILT THIS ONE.
—AND YOU'VE SEEN IT? FOR REAL?
"YES—IT APPEARED IN BEETLEBURG."
"THERE WAS SOMETHING LIKE A WINDOW IN THE AIR—
LOTS OF PEOPLE SAW IT."
"I WAS SO SCARED—I RAN OFF INTO AN ALLEY, STRAIGHT INTO VON ZINZER AND HIS BROTHER."
"OH, THEY HELPED YOU?"
"THEY MUGGED ME."
"THEY TOOK MY LOCKET"
"I STARTED TO BREAK THROUGH AS A SPARK THAT NIGHT."
OH, SO THAT'S WHAT STARTED ALL THIS!
YES...I SUPPOSE SO...
—BUT THESE ARE VAN RIJN'S NOTES—SO THIS THING MUST BE FROM THE TIME OF THE STORM KING, YEAH?
ACTUALLY, IT LOOKS LIKE IT'S EVEN OLDER THAN THAT.

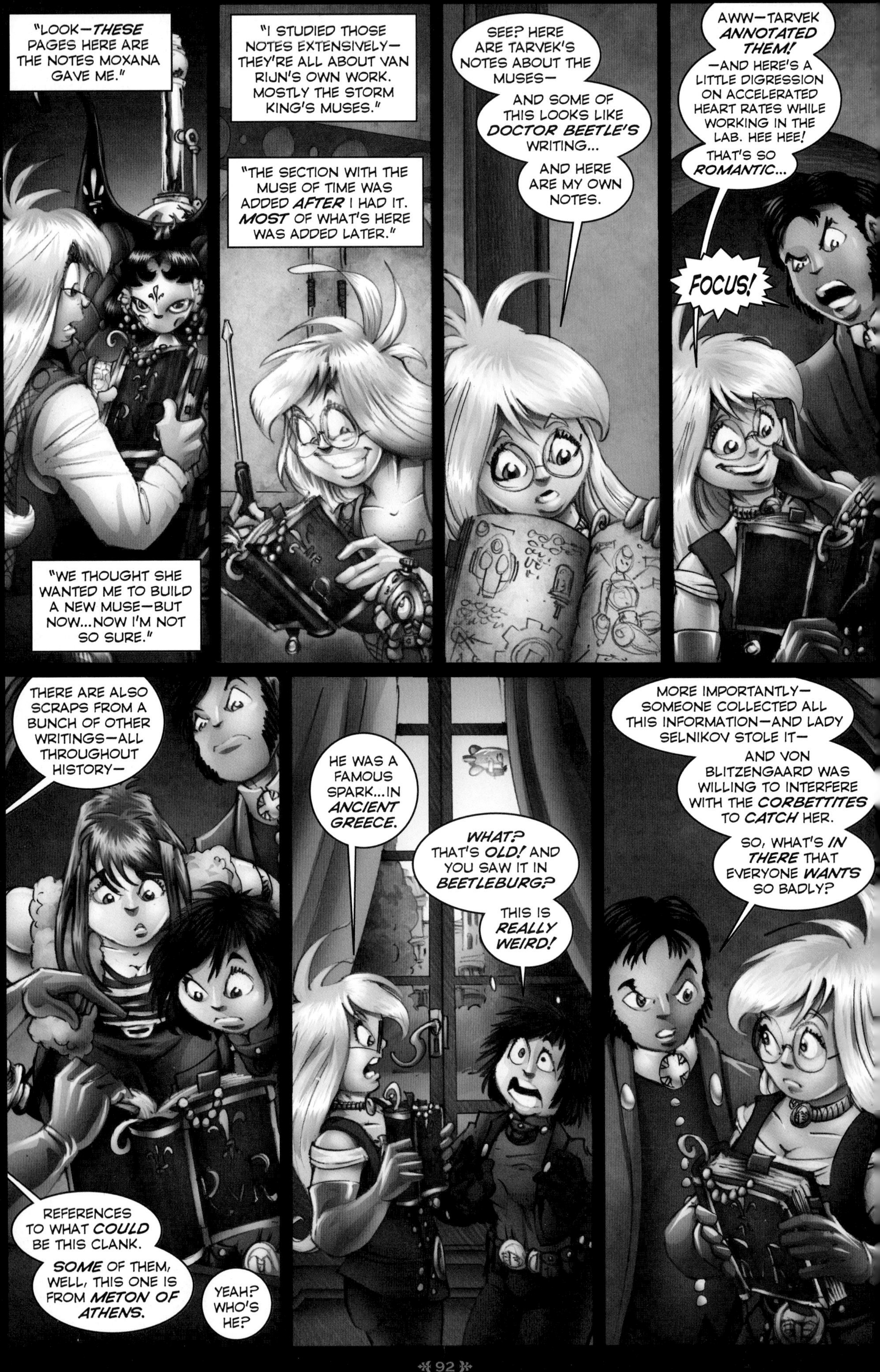
"LOOK—THESE PAGES HERE ARE THE NOTES MOXANA GAVE ME."
"WE THOUGHT SHE WANTED ME TO BUILD A NEW MUSE—BUT NOW...NOW I'M NOT SO SURE."
"I STUDIED THOSE NOTES EXTENSIVELY—THEY'RE ALL ABOUT VAN RIJN'S OWN WORK. MOSTLY THE STORM KING'S MUSES."
"THE SECTION WITH THE MUSE OF TIME WAS ADDED AFTER I HAD IT. MOST OF WHAT'S HERE WAS ADDED LATER."
SEE? HERE ARE TARVEK'S NOTES ABOUT THE MUSES—
AND SOME OF THIS LOOKS LIKE DOCTOR BEETLE'S WRITING...
AND HERE ARE MY OWN NOTES.
AWW—TARVEK ANNOTATED THEM!
—AND HERE'S A LITTLE DIGRESSION ON ACCELERATED HEART RATES WHILE WORKING IN THE LAB. HEE HEE!
THAT'S SO ROMANTIC...
FOCUS!
THERE ARE ALSO SCRAPS FROM A BUNCH OF OTHER WRITINGS—ALL THROUGHOUT HISTORY—
REFERENCES TO WHAT COULD BE THIS CLANK.
SOME OF THEM, WELL, THIS ONE IS FROM METON OF ATHENS.
YEAH? WHO'S HE?
HE WAS A FAMOUS SPARK...IN ANCIENT GREECE.
WHAT? THAT'S OLD! AND YOU SAW IT IN BEETLEBURG?
THIS IS REALLY WEIRD!
MORE IMPORTANTLY—SOMEONE COLLECTED ALL THIS INFORMATION—AND LADY SELNIKOV STOLE IT—
AND VON BLITZENGAARD WAS WILLING TO INTERFERE WITH THE CORBETTITES TO CATCH HER.
SO, WHAT'S IN THERE THAT EVERYONE WANTS SO BADLY?

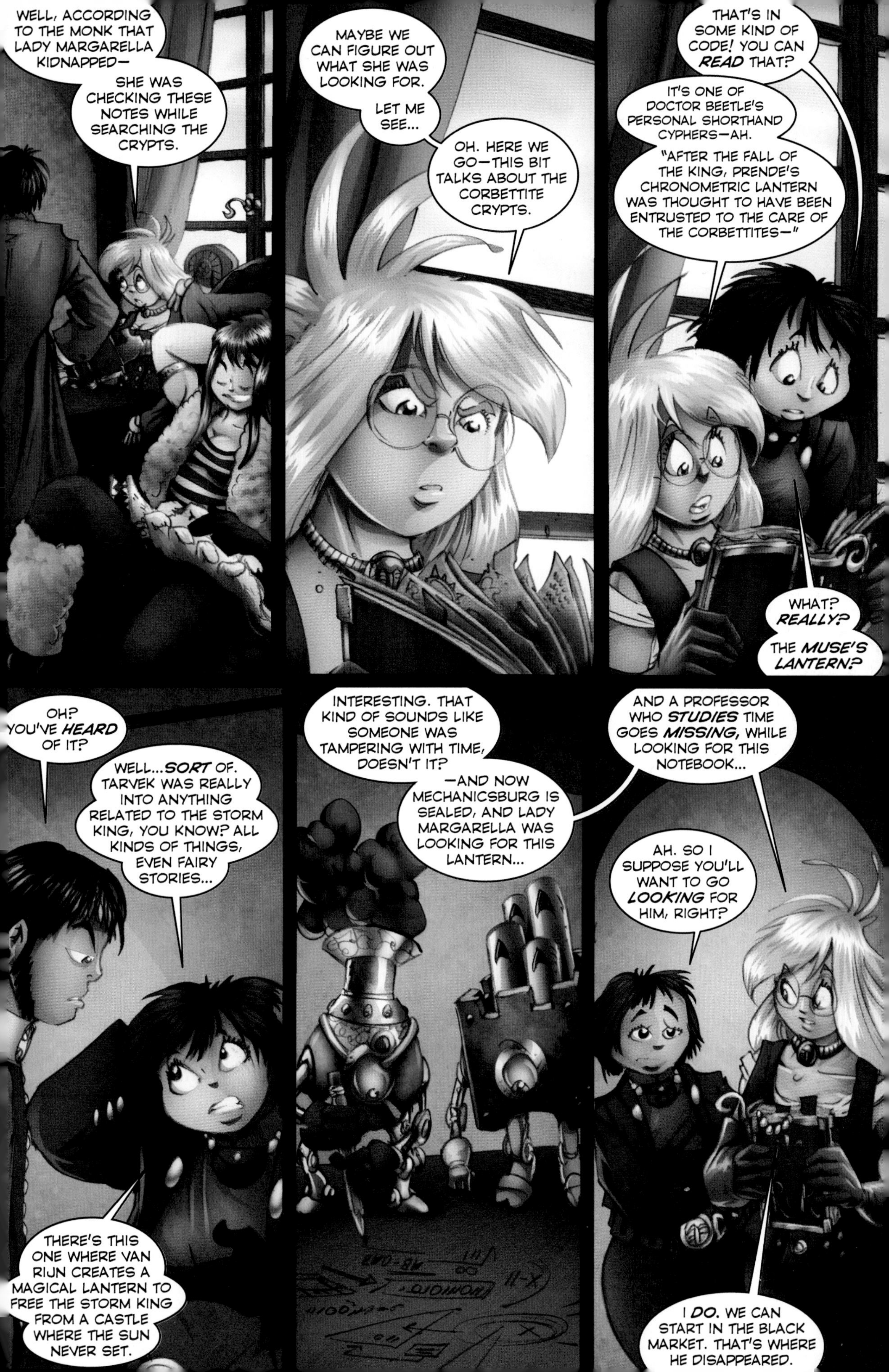

WELL, ACCORDING TO THE MONK THAT LADY MARGARELLA KIDNAPPED—
SHE WAS CHECKING THESE NOTES WHILE SEARCHING THE CRYPTS.
MAYBE WE CAN FIGURE OUT WHAT SHE WAS LOOKING FOR.
LET ME SEE...
OH. HERE WE GO—THIS BIT TALKS ABOUT THE CORBETTITE CRYPTS.
THAT'S IN SOME KIND OF CODE! YOU CAN *READ* THAT?
IT'S ONE OF DOCTOR BEETLE'S PERSONAL SHORTHAND CYPHERS—AH.
"AFTER THE FALL OF THE KING, PRENDE'S CHRONOMETRIC LANTERN WAS THOUGHT TO HAVE BEEN ENTRUSTED TO THE CARE OF THE CORBETTITES—"
WHAT? *REALLY?*
THE *MUSE'S LANTERN?*
OH? YOU'VE *HEARD* OF IT?
WELL...*SORT* OF. TARVEK WAS REALLY INTO ANYTHING RELATED TO THE STORM KING, YOU KNOW? ALL KINDS OF THINGS, EVEN FAIRY STORIES...
THERE'S THIS ONE WHERE VAN RIJN CREATES A MAGICAL LANTERN TO FREE THE STORM KING FROM A CASTLE WHERE THE SUN NEVER SET.
INTERESTING. THAT KIND OF SOUNDS LIKE SOMEONE WAS TAMPERING WITH TIME, DOESN'T IT?
—AND NOW MECHANICSBURG IS SEALED, AND LADY MARGARELLA WAS LOOKING FOR THIS LANTERN...
AND A PROFESSOR WHO *STUDIES* TIME GOES *MISSING,* WHILE LOOKING FOR THIS NOTEBOOK...
AH. SO I SUPPOSE YOU'LL WANT TO GO *LOOKING* FOR HIM, RIGHT?
I *DO.* WE CAN START IN THE BLACK MARKET. THAT'S WHERE HE DISAPPEARED.

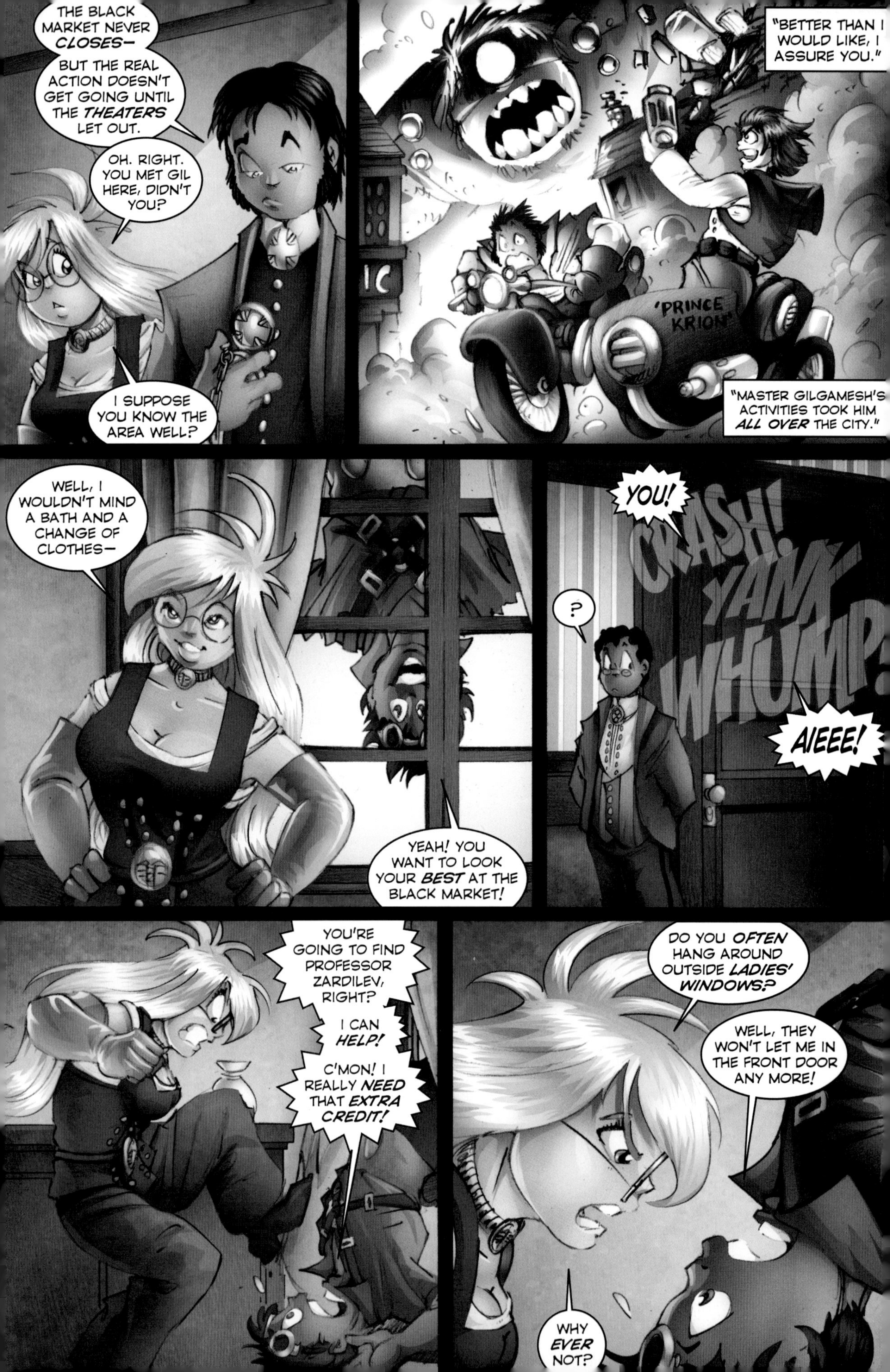
THE BLACK MARKET NEVER *CLOSES*—
BUT THE REAL ACTION DOESN'T GET GOING UNTIL THE *THEATERS* LET OUT.
OH. RIGHT. YOU MET GIL HERE, DIDN'T YOU?
I SUPPOSE YOU KNOW THE AREA WELL?
"BETTER THAN I WOULD LIKE, I ASSURE YOU."
'PRINCE KRION'
"MASTER GILGAMESH'S ACTIVITIES TOOK HIM *ALL OVER* THE CITY."
WELL, I WOULDN'T MIND A BATH AND A CHANGE OF CLOTHES—
YEAH! YOU WANT TO LOOK YOUR *BEST* AT THE BLACK MARKET!
YOU!
CRASH!
YANK
WHUMP!
?
AIEEE!
YOU'RE GOING TO FIND PROFESSOR ZARDILEV, RIGHT?
I CAN *HELP!*
C'MON! I REALLY *NEED* THAT *EXTRA CREDIT!*
DO YOU *OFTEN* HANG AROUND OUTSIDE *LADIES' WINDOWS?*
WELL, THEY WON'T LET ME IN THE FRONT DOOR ANY MORE!
WHY *EVER* NOT?

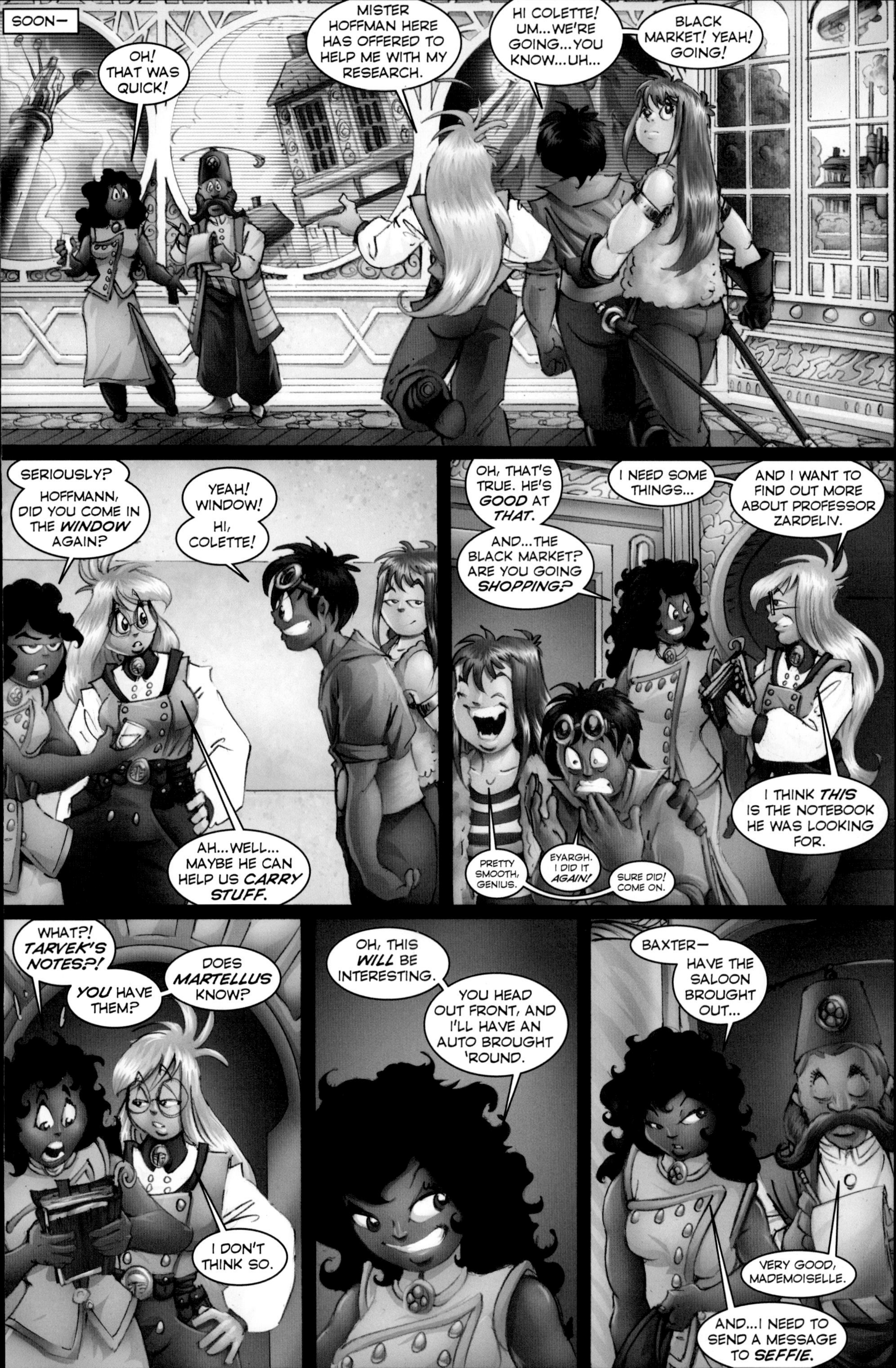
SOON—
OH! THAT WAS QUICK!
MISTER HOFFMAN HERE HAS OFFERED TO HELP ME WITH MY RESEARCH.
HI COLETTE! UM...WE'RE GOING...YOU KNOW...UH...
BLACK MARKET! YEAH! GOING!
SERIOUSLY? HOFFMANN, DID YOU COME IN THE WINDOW AGAIN?
YEAH! WINDOW! HI, COLETTE!
AH...WELL... MAYBE HE CAN HELP US CARRY STUFF.
OH, THAT'S TRUE. HE'S GOOD AT THAT.
AND...THE BLACK MARKET? ARE YOU GOING SHOPPING?
I NEED SOME THINGS...
AND I WANT TO FIND OUT MORE ABOUT PROFESSOR ZARDELIV.
I THINK THIS IS THE NOTEBOOK HE WAS LOOKING FOR.
PRETTY SMOOTH, GENIUS.
EYARGH. I DID IT AGAIN!
SURE DID! COME ON.
WHAT?! TARVEK'S NOTES?!
YOU HAVE THEM?
DOES MARTELLUS KNOW?
I DON'T THINK SO.
OH, THIS WILL BE INTERESTING.
YOU HEAD OUT FRONT, AND I'LL HAVE AN AUTO BROUGHT 'ROUND.
BAXTER—
HAVE THE SALOON BROUGHT OUT...
VERY GOOD, MADEMOISELLE.
AND...I NEED TO SEND A MESSAGE TO SEFFIE.

SO, YOU LIKE COLETTE, EH?

AW—DOES IT *SHOW?*

MAYBE A LITTLE.

—MAYBE A WHOLE LOT.

OH. HANG ON, I'LL BE RIGHT THERE.

HM? IS IT TIME FOR—?

YEAH.

AH. WE'LL BE OUTSIDE.

THANKS.

...

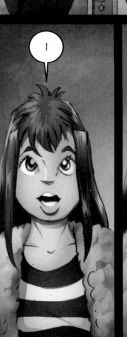

I

LOVE

YOU

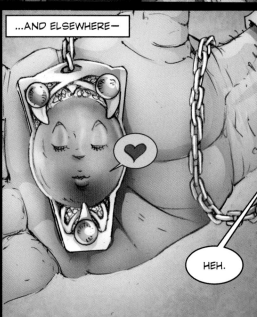

...AND ELSEWHERE—

♥

HEH.

AND I, YOU.

HUH. IS THAT THE THING OFF PRINCESS ZEETHA'S CIRCLET? I ALWAYS WANTED TO *EXAMINE* THAT...

NOPE. SOME THINGS, YOU EXAMINE 'EM TOO CLOSE AND THEY *BREAK,* SIR.

...I *PROBABLY* WOULDN'T BREAK IT *MUCH...*

sigh... EVEN SO, SIR.

⊰ 96 ⊱

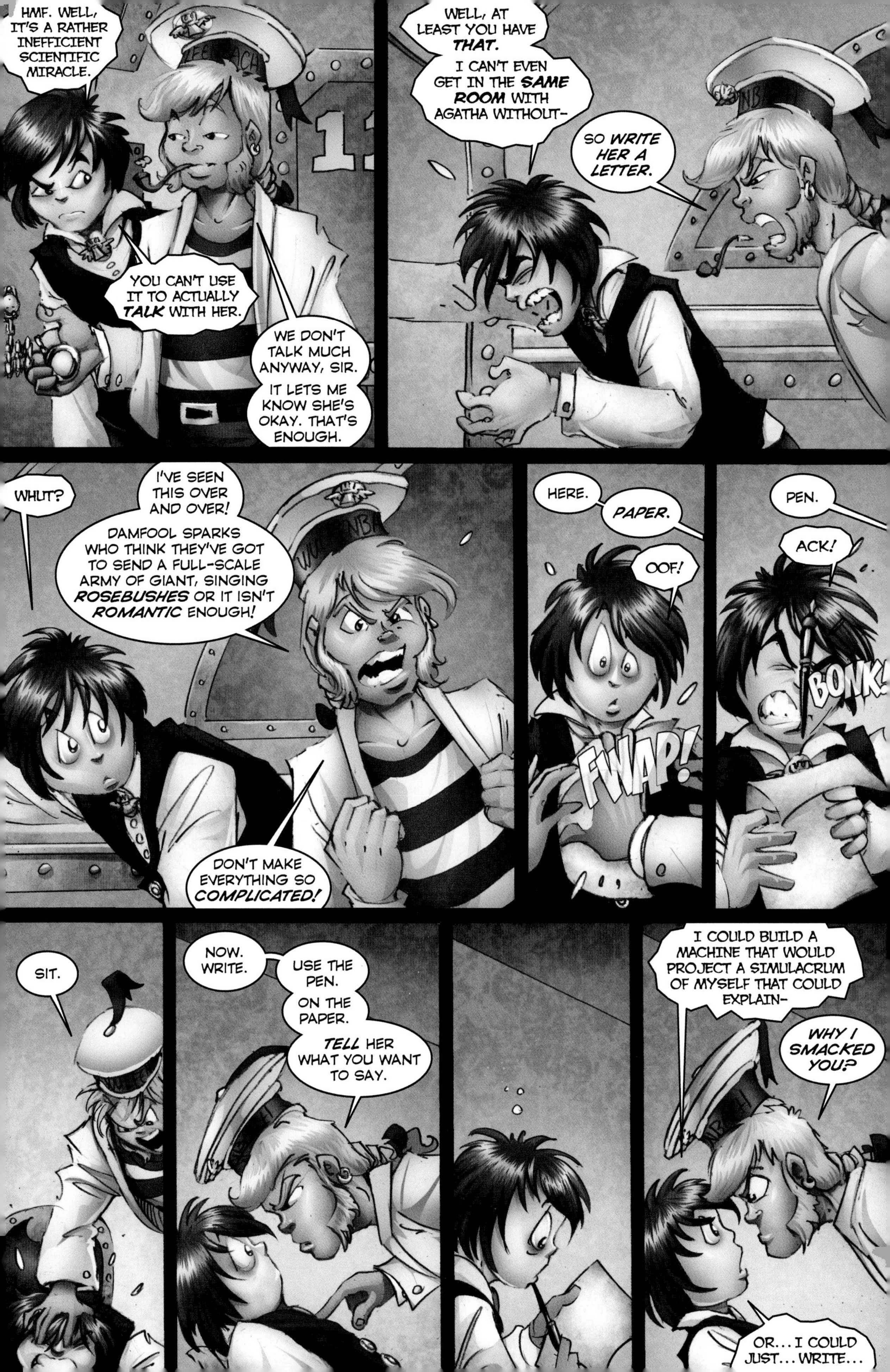
HMF. WELL, IT'S A RATHER INEFFICIENT SCIENTIFIC MIRACLE.
YOU CAN'T USE IT TO ACTUALLY TALK WITH HER.
WE DON'T TALK MUCH ANYWAY, SIR.
IT LETS ME KNOW SHE'S OKAY. THAT'S ENOUGH.
WELL, AT LEAST YOU HAVE THAT.
I CAN'T EVEN GET IN THE SAME ROOM WITH AGATHA WITHOUT-
SO WRITE HER A LETTER.
WHUT?
I'VE SEEN THIS OVER AND OVER!
DAMFOOL SPARKS WHO THINK THEY'VE GOT TO SEND A FULL-SCALE ARMY OF GIANT, SINGING ROSEBUSHES OR IT ISN'T ROMANTIC ENOUGH!
DON'T MAKE EVERYTHING SO COMPLICATED!
HERE.
PAPER.
OOF!
FWAP!
PEN.
ACK!
BONK!
SIT.
NOW. WRITE.
USE THE PEN.
ON THE PAPER.
TELL HER WHAT YOU WANT TO SAY.
I COULD BUILD A MACHINE THAT WOULD PROJECT A SIMULACRUM OF MYSELF THAT COULD EXPLAIN-
WHY I SMACKED YOU?
OR... I COULD JUST... WRITE...

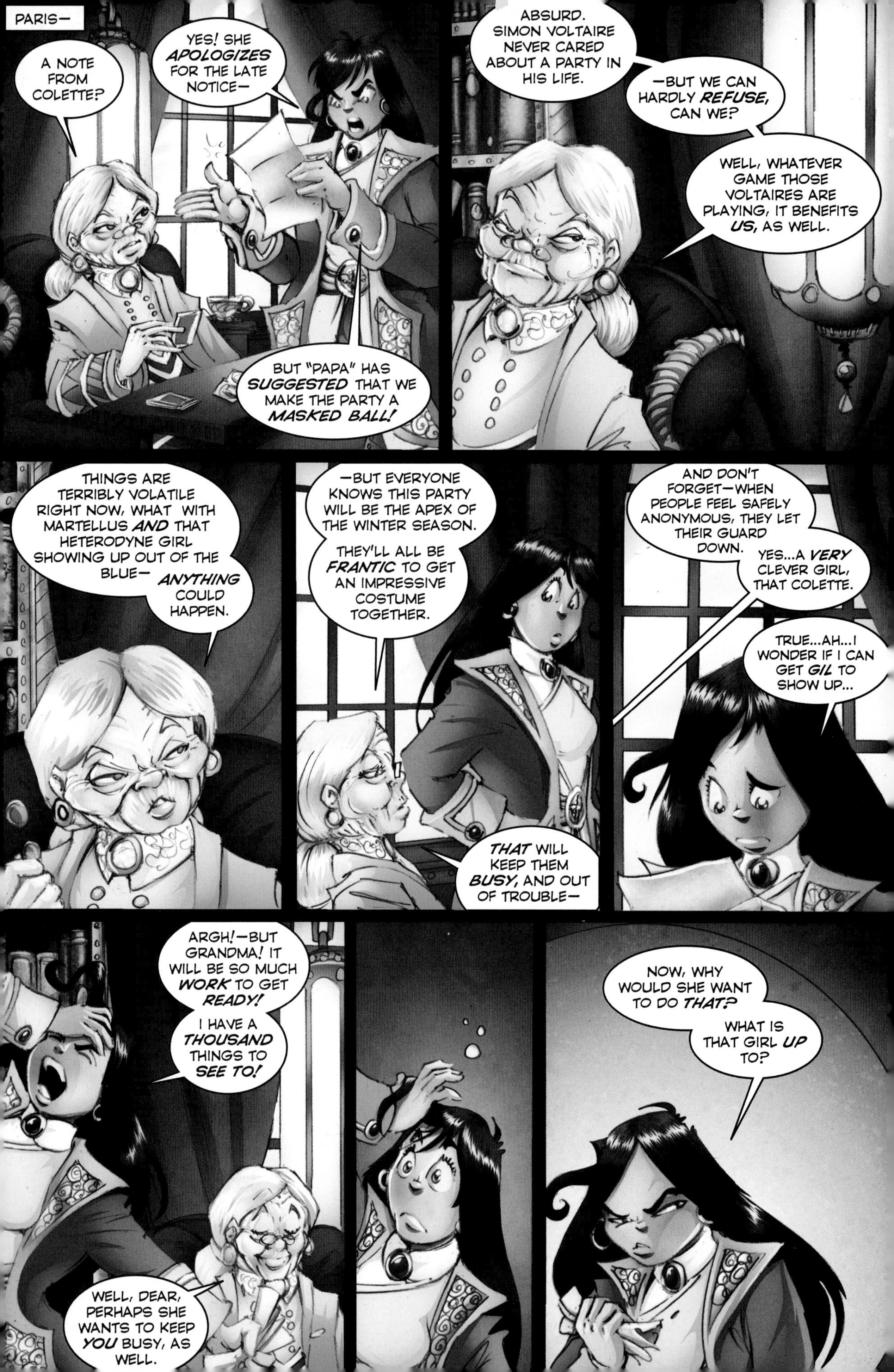
PARIS—
A NOTE FROM COLETTE?
YES! SHE *APOLOGIZES* FOR THE LATE NOTICE—
BUT "PAPA" HAS *SUGGESTED* THAT WE MAKE THE PARTY A *MASKED BALL!*
ABSURD. SIMON VOLTAIRE NEVER CARED ABOUT A PARTY IN HIS LIFE.
—BUT WE CAN HARDLY *REFUSE,* CAN WE?
WELL, WHATEVER GAME THOSE VOLTAIRES ARE PLAYING, IT BENEFITS *US,* AS WELL.
THINGS ARE TERRIBLY VOLATILE RIGHT NOW, WHAT WITH MARTELLUS *AND* THAT HETERODYNE GIRL SHOWING UP OUT OF THE BLUE—
ANYTHING COULD HAPPEN.
—BUT EVERYONE KNOWS THIS PARTY WILL BE THE APEX OF THE WINTER SEASON.
THEY'LL ALL BE *FRANTIC* TO GET AN IMPRESSIVE COSTUME TOGETHER.
THAT WILL KEEP THEM *BUSY,* AND OUT OF TROUBLE—
AND DON'T FORGET—WHEN PEOPLE FEEL SAFELY ANONYMOUS, THEY LET THEIR GUARD DOWN.
YES...A *VERY* CLEVER GIRL, THAT COLETTE.
TRUE...AH...I WONDER IF I CAN GET *GIL* TO SHOW UP...
ARGH!—BUT GRANDMA! IT WILL BE SO MUCH *WORK* TO GET *READY!*
I HAVE A *THOUSAND* THINGS TO *SEE TO!*
WELL, DEAR, PERHAPS SHE WANTS TO KEEP *YOU* BUSY, AS WELL.
NOW, WHY WOULD SHE WANT TO DO *THAT?*
WHAT IS THAT GIRL *UP* TO?

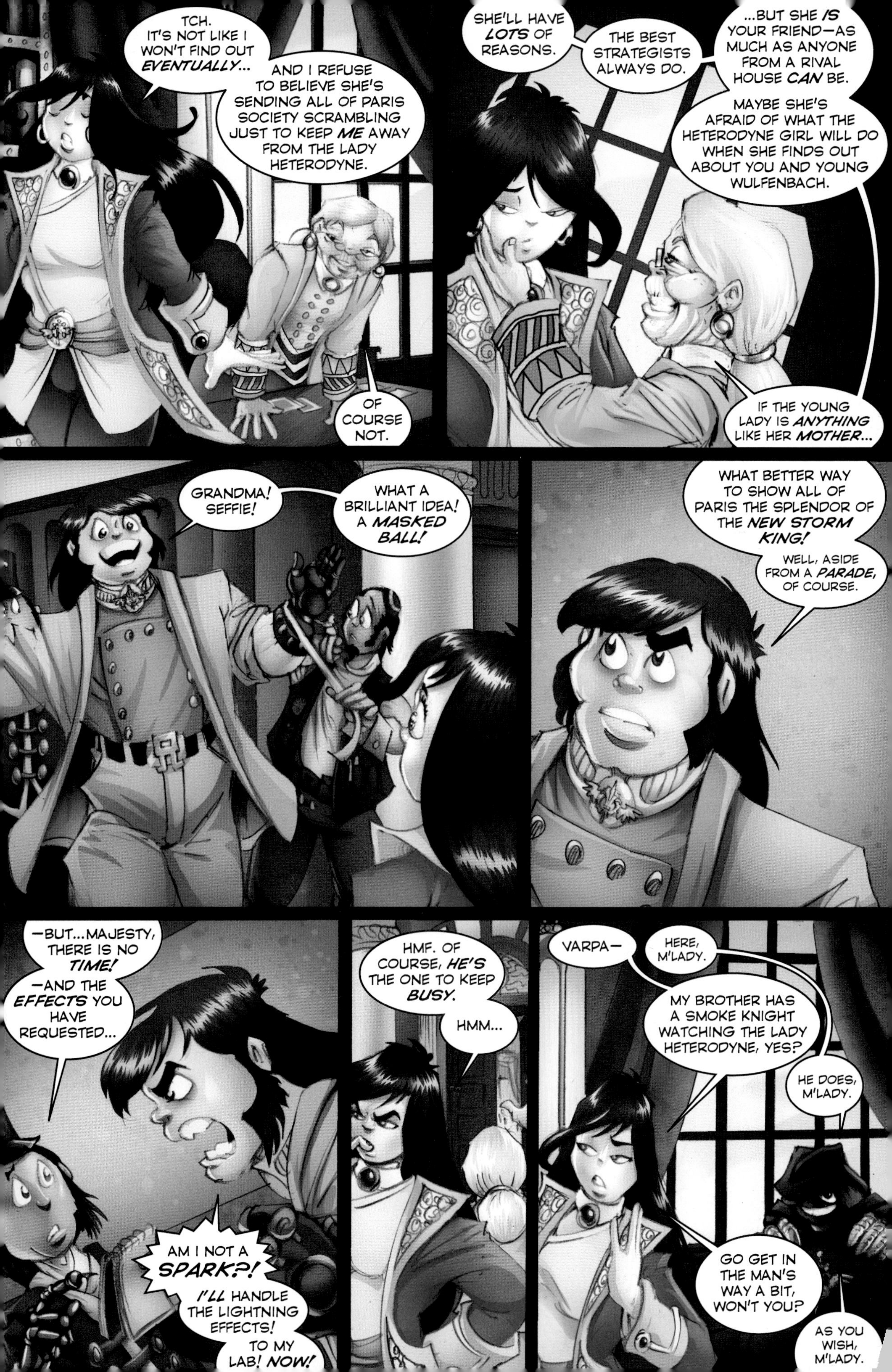
TCH. IT'S NOT LIKE I WON'T FIND OUT EVENTUALLY...
AND I REFUSE TO BELIEVE SHE'S SENDING ALL OF PARIS SOCIETY SCRAMBLING JUST TO KEEP ME AWAY FROM THE LADY HETERODYNE.
OF COURSE NOT.
SHE'LL HAVE LOTS OF REASONS.
THE BEST STRATEGISTS ALWAYS DO.
...BUT SHE IS YOUR FRIEND—AS MUCH AS ANYONE FROM A RIVAL HOUSE CAN BE.
MAYBE SHE'S AFRAID OF WHAT THE HETERODYNE GIRL WILL DO WHEN SHE FINDS OUT ABOUT YOU AND YOUNG WULFENBACH.
IF THE YOUNG LADY IS ANYTHING LIKE HER MOTHER...
GRANDMA! SEFFIE!
WHAT A BRILLIANT IDEA! A MASKED BALL!
WHAT BETTER WAY TO SHOW ALL OF PARIS THE SPLENDOR OF THE NEW STORM KING!
WELL, ASIDE FROM A PARADE, OF COURSE.
—BUT...MAJESTY, THERE IS NO TIME!
—AND THE EFFECTS YOU HAVE REQUESTED...
AM I NOT A SPARK?!
I'LL HANDLE THE LIGHTNING EFFECTS!
TO MY LAB! NOW!
HMF. OF COURSE, HE'S THE ONE TO KEEP BUSY.
HMM...
VARPA—
HERE, M'LADY.
MY BROTHER HAS A SMOKE KNIGHT WATCHING THE LADY HETERODYNE, YES?
HE DOES, M'LADY.
GO GET IN THE MAN'S WAY A BIT, WON'T YOU?
AS YOU WISH, M'LADY.

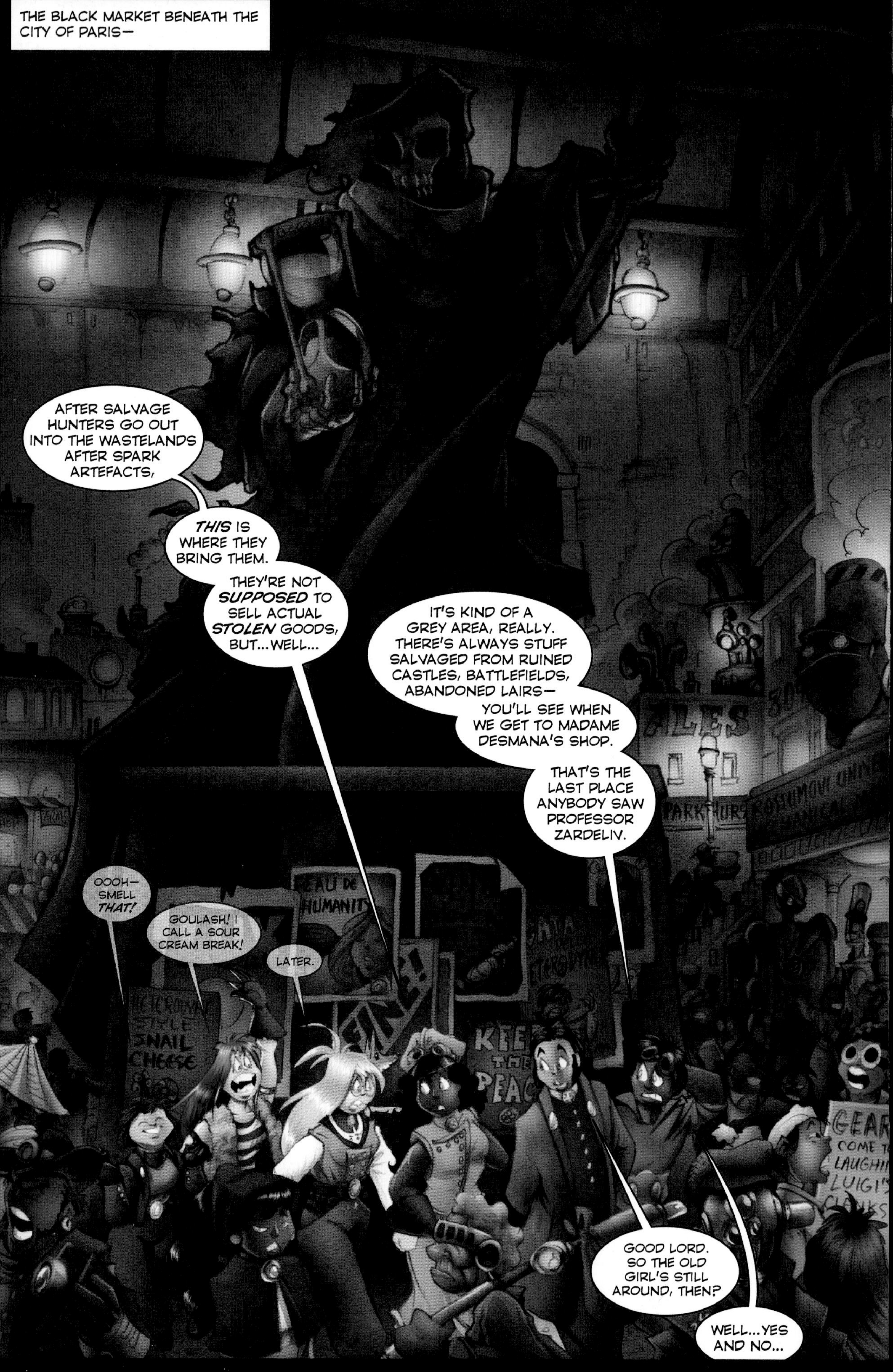
THE BLACK MARKET BENEATH THE CITY OF PARIS—
AFTER SALVAGE HUNTERS GO OUT INTO THE WASTELANDS AFTER SPARK ARTEFACTS,
THIS IS WHERE THEY BRING THEM.
THEY'RE NOT *SUPPOSED* TO SELL ACTUAL *STOLEN* GOODS, BUT...WELL...
IT'S KIND OF A GREY AREA, REALLY. THERE'S ALWAYS STUFF SALVAGED FROM RUINED CASTLES, BATTLEFIELDS, ABANDONED LAIRS—
YOU'LL SEE WHEN WE GET TO MADAME DESMANA'S SHOP.
THAT'S THE LAST PLACE ANYBODY SAW PROFESSOR ZARDELIV.
OOOH— SMELL *THAT!*
GOULASH! I CALL A SOUR CREAM BREAK!
LATER.
SNAIL CHEESE
GOOD LORD. SO THE OLD GIRL'S STILL AROUND, THEN?
WELL...YES AND NO...

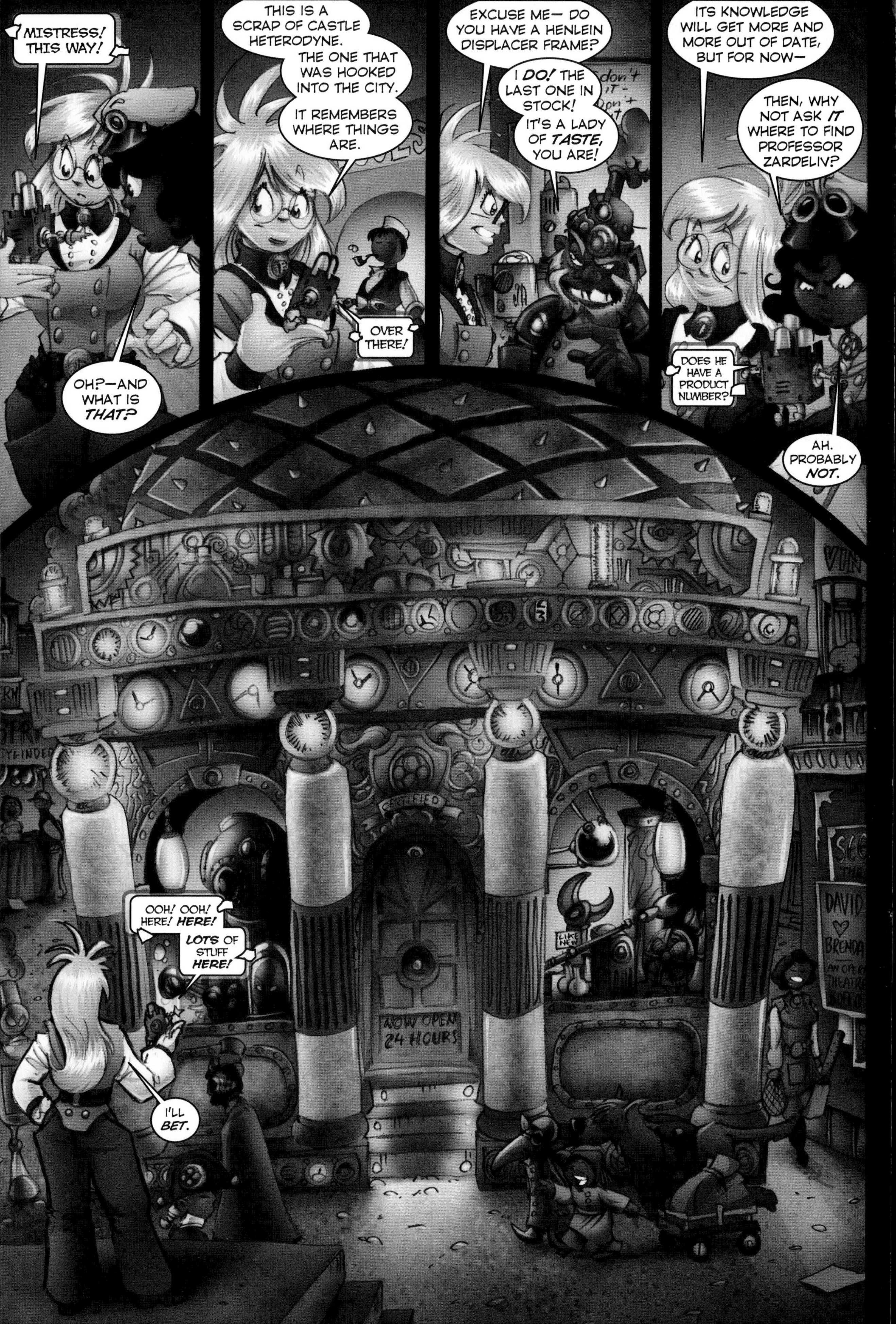
MISTRESS! THIS WAY!
OH?—AND WHAT IS THAT?
THIS IS A SCRAP OF CASTLE HETERODYNE.
THE ONE THAT WAS HOOKED INTO THE CITY.
IT REMEMBERS WHERE THINGS ARE.
OVER THERE!
EXCUSE ME— DO YOU HAVE A HENLEIN DISPLACER FRAME?
I DO! THE LAST ONE IN STOCK!
IT'S A LADY OF TASTE, YOU ARE!
ITS KNOWLEDGE WILL GET MORE AND MORE OUT OF DATE, BUT FOR NOW—
THEN, WHY NOT ASK IT WHERE TO FIND PROFESSOR ZARDELIV?
DOES HE HAVE A PRODUCT NUMBER?
AH. PROBABLY NOT.
CERTIFIED
NOW OPEN 24 HOURS
OOH! OOH! HERE! HERE!
LOTS OF STUFF HERE!
I'LL BET.
DAVID ♥ BRENDA

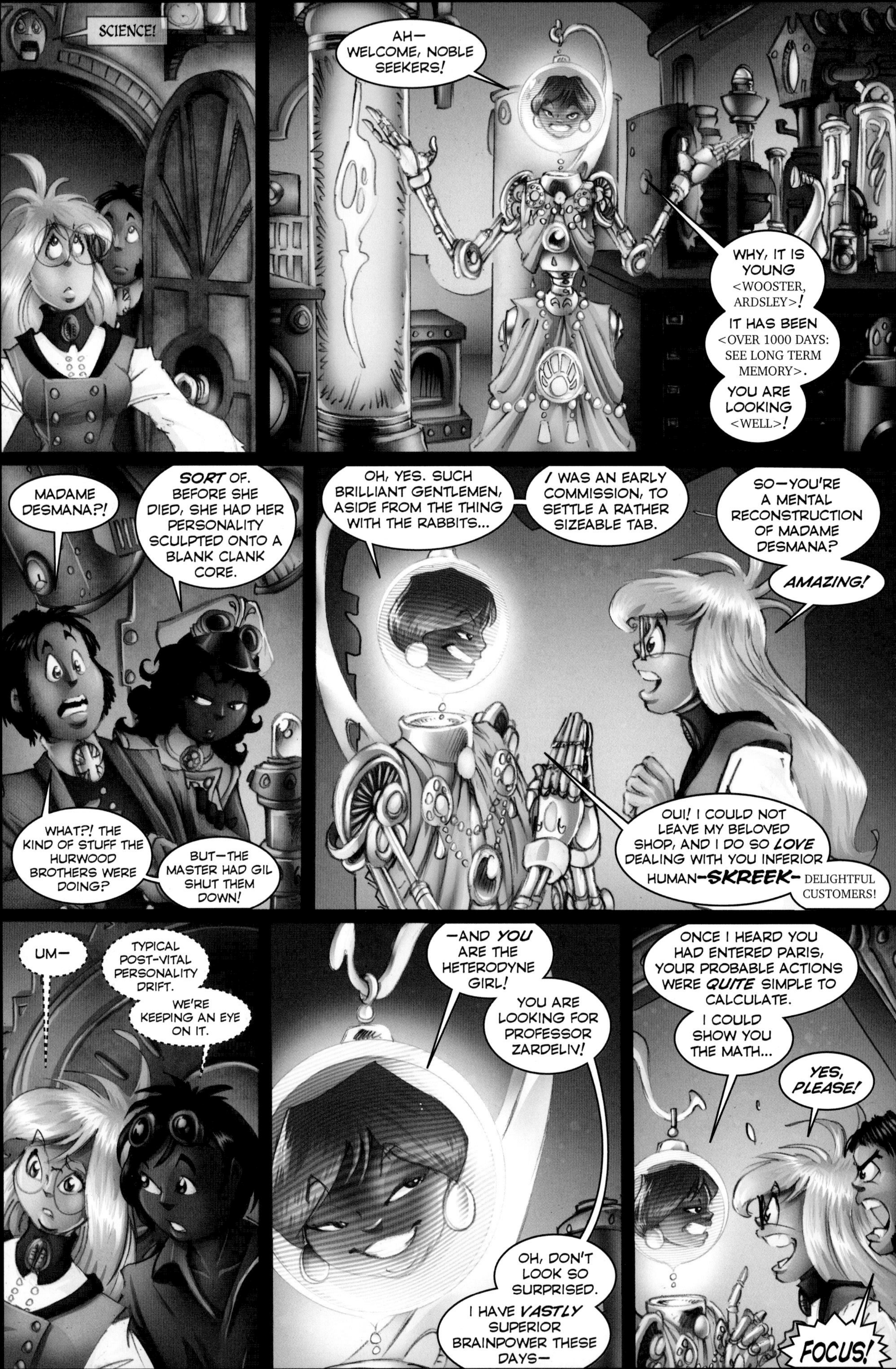
SCIENCE!
AH— WELCOME, NOBLE SEEKERS!
WHY, IT IS YOUNG <WOOSTER, ARDSLEY>!
IT HAS BEEN <OVER 1000 DAYS: SEE LONG TERM MEMORY>.
YOU ARE LOOKING <WELL>!
MADAME DESMANA?!
SORT OF. BEFORE SHE DIED, SHE HAD HER PERSONALITY SCULPTED ONTO A BLANK CLANK CORE.
WHAT?! THE KIND OF STUFF THE HURWOOD BROTHERS WERE DOING?
BUT—THE MASTER HAD GIL SHUT THEM DOWN!
OH, YES. SUCH BRILLIANT GENTLEMEN, ASIDE FROM THE THING WITH THE RABBITS...
I WAS AN EARLY COMMISSION, TO SETTLE A RATHER SIZEABLE TAB.
SO—YOU'RE A MENTAL RECONSTRUCTION OF MADAME DESMANA?
AMAZING!
OUI! I COULD NOT LEAVE MY BELOVED SHOP, AND I DO SO LOVE DEALING WITH YOU INFERIOR HUMAN-SKREEK- DELIGHTFUL CUSTOMERS!
UM—
TYPICAL POST-VITAL PERSONALITY DRIFT.
WE'RE KEEPING AN EYE ON IT.
—AND YOU ARE THE HETERODYNE GIRL!
YOU ARE LOOKING FOR PROFESSOR ZARDELIV!
OH, DON'T LOOK SO SURPRISED.
I HAVE VASTLY SUPERIOR BRAINPOWER THESE DAYS—
ONCE I HEARD YOU HAD ENTERED PARIS, YOUR PROBABLE ACTIONS WERE QUITE SIMPLE TO CALCULATE.
I COULD SHOW YOU THE MATH...
YES, PLEASE!
FOCUS!

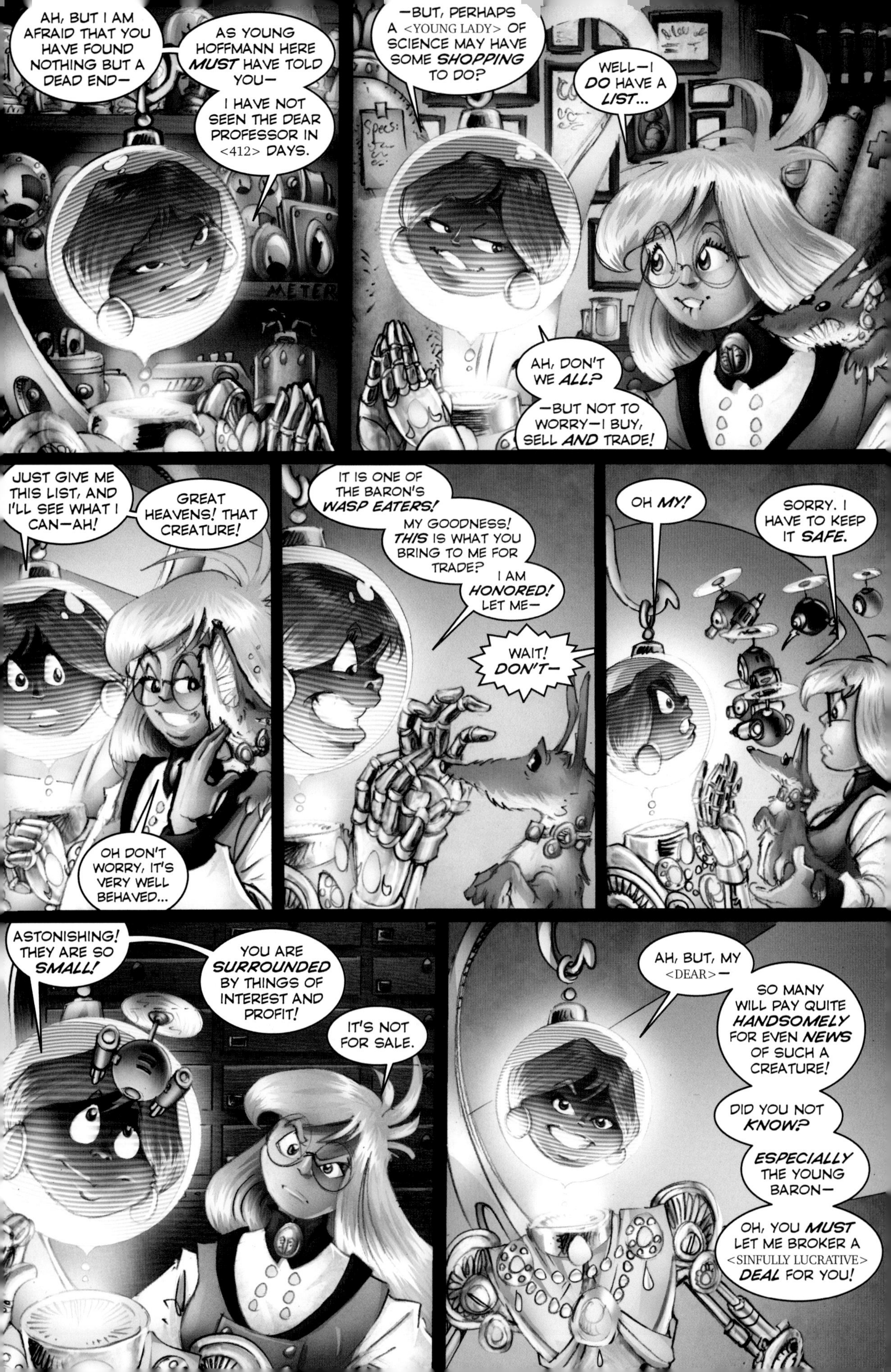

AH, BUT I AM AFRAID THAT YOU HAVE FOUND NOTHING BUT A DEAD END—
AS YOUNG HOFFMANN HERE MUST HAVE TOLD YOU—
I HAVE NOT SEEN THE DEAR PROFESSOR IN <412> DAYS.
METER
—BUT, PERHAPS A <YOUNG LADY> OF SCIENCE MAY HAVE SOME SHOPPING TO DO?
Specs:
WELL—I DO HAVE A LIST...
AH, DON'T WE ALL?
—BUT NOT TO WORRY—I BUY, SELL AND TRADE!
JUST GIVE ME THIS LIST, AND I'LL SEE WHAT I CAN—AH!
GREAT HEAVENS! THAT CREATURE!
OH DON'T WORRY, IT'S VERY WELL BEHAVED...
IT IS ONE OF THE BARON'S WASP EATERS!
MY GOODNESS! THIS IS WHAT YOU BRING TO ME FOR TRADE?
I AM HONORED! LET ME—
WAIT! DON'T—
OH MY!
SORRY. I HAVE TO KEEP IT SAFE.
ASTONISHING! THEY ARE SO SMALL!
YOU ARE SURROUNDED BY THINGS OF INTEREST AND PROFIT!
IT'S NOT FOR SALE.
AH, BUT, MY <DEAR>—
SO MANY WILL PAY QUITE HANDSOMELY FOR EVEN NEWS OF SUCH A CREATURE!
DID YOU NOT KNOW?
ESPECIALLY THE YOUNG BARON—
OH, YOU MUST LET ME BROKER A <SINFULLY LUCRATIVE> DEAL FOR YOU!

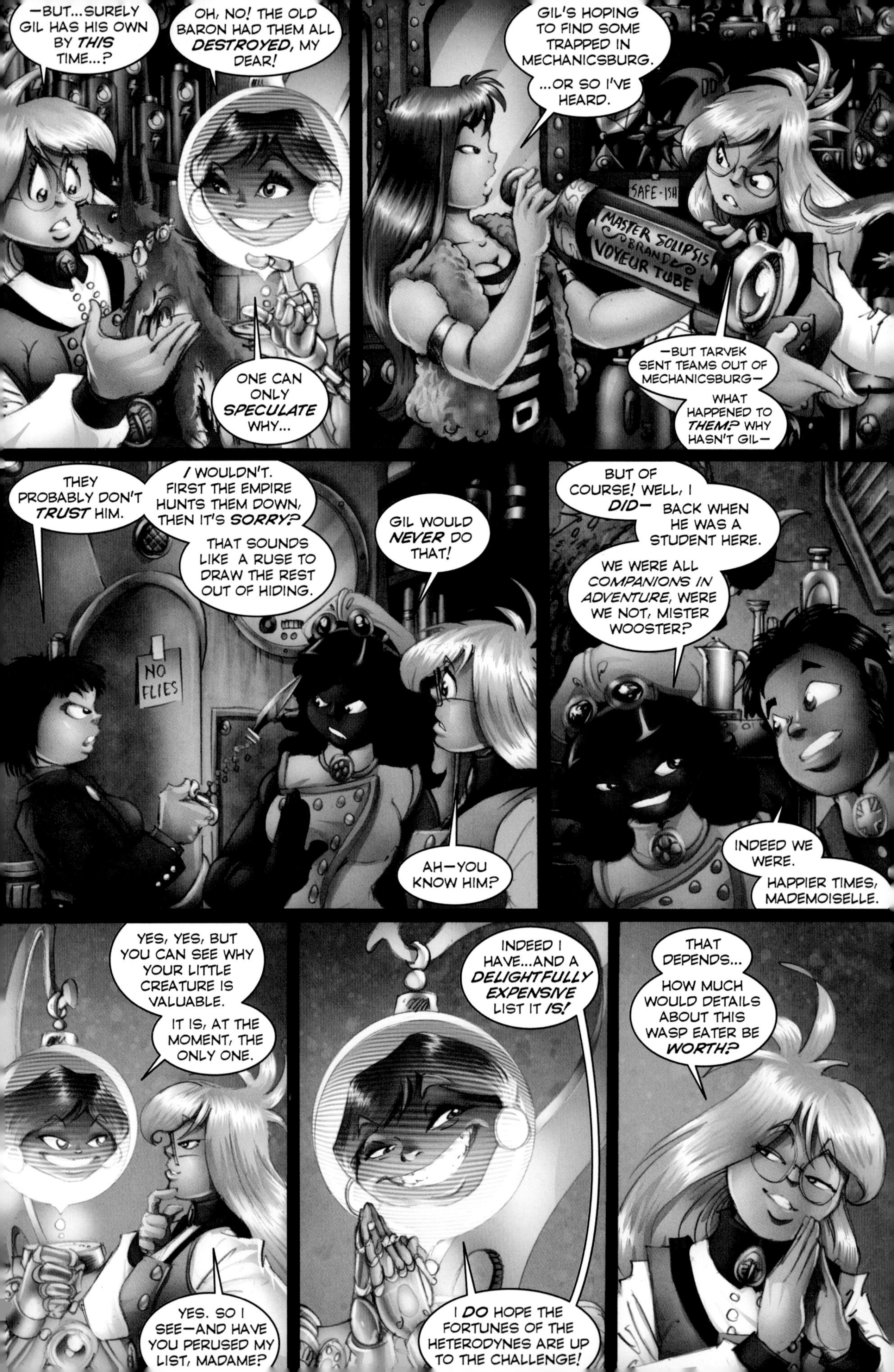

—BUT...SURELY GIL HAS HIS OWN BY THIS TIME...?
OH, NO! THE OLD BARON HAD THEM ALL DESTROYED, MY DEAR!
ONE CAN ONLY SPECULATE WHY...
GIL'S HOPING TO FIND SOME TRAPPED IN MECHANICSBURG.
...OR SO I'VE HEARD.
SAFE-ISH
MASTER SOLIPSIS BRAND VOYEUR TUBE
—BUT TARVEK SENT TEAMS OUT OF MECHANICSBURG—
WHAT HAPPENED TO THEM? WHY HASN'T GIL—
THEY PROBABLY DON'T TRUST HIM.
I WOULDN'T. FIRST THE EMPIRE HUNTS THEM DOWN, THEN IT'S SORRY?
THAT SOUNDS LIKE A RUSE TO DRAW THE REST OUT OF HIDING.
GIL WOULD NEVER DO THAT!
NO FLIES
AH—YOU KNOW HIM?
BUT OF COURSE! WELL, I DID—
BACK WHEN HE WAS A STUDENT HERE.
WE WERE ALL COMPANIONS IN ADVENTURE, WERE WE NOT, MISTER WOOSTER?
INDEED WE WERE.
HAPPIER TIMES, MADEMOISELLE.
YES, YES, BUT YOU CAN SEE WHY YOUR LITTLE CREATURE IS VALUABLE.
IT IS, AT THE MOMENT, THE ONLY ONE.
YES. SO I SEE—AND HAVE YOU PERUSED MY LIST, MADAME?
INDEED I HAVE...AND A DELIGHTFULLY EXPENSIVE LIST IT IS!
I DO HOPE THE FORTUNES OF THE HETERODYNES ARE UP TO THE CHALLENGE!
THAT DEPENDS...
HOW MUCH WOULD DETAILS ABOUT THIS WASP EATER BE WORTH?

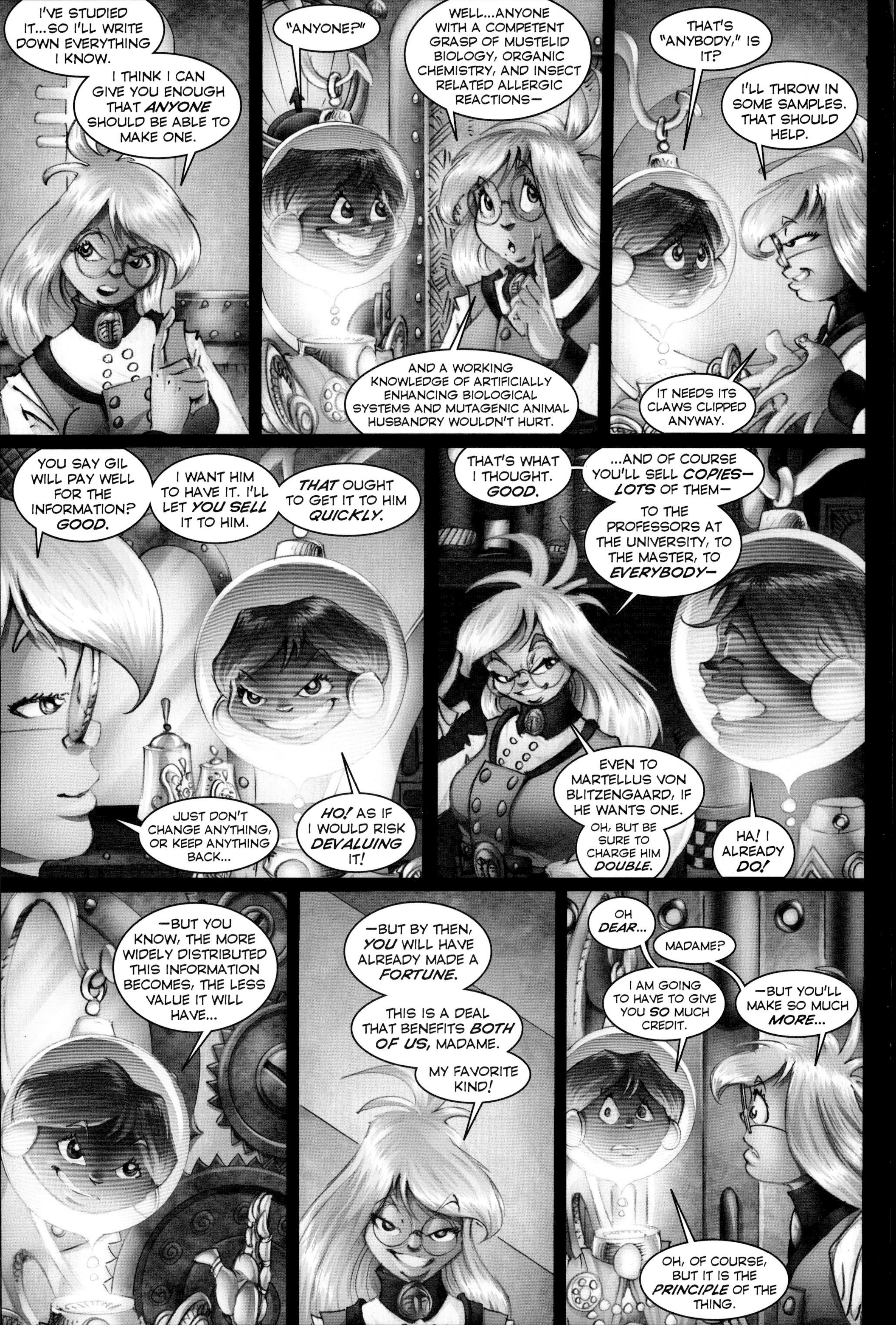
I'VE STUDIED IT...SO I'LL WRITE DOWN EVERYTHING I KNOW.
I THINK I CAN GIVE YOU ENOUGH THAT ANYONE SHOULD BE ABLE TO MAKE ONE.
"ANYONE?"
WELL...ANYONE WITH A COMPETENT GRASP OF MUSTELID BIOLOGY, ORGANIC CHEMISTRY, AND INSECT RELATED ALLERGIC REACTIONS—
AND A WORKING KNOWLEDGE OF ARTIFICIALLY ENHANCING BIOLOGICAL SYSTEMS AND MUTAGENIC ANIMAL HUSBANDRY WOULDN'T HURT.
THAT'S "ANYBODY," IS IT?
I'LL THROW IN SOME SAMPLES. THAT SHOULD HELP.
IT NEEDS ITS CLAWS CLIPPED ANYWAY.
YOU SAY GIL WILL PAY WELL FOR THE INFORMATION? GOOD.
I WANT HIM TO HAVE IT. I'LL LET YOU SELL IT TO HIM.
THAT OUGHT TO GET IT TO HIM QUICKLY.
JUST DON'T CHANGE ANYTHING, OR KEEP ANYTHING BACK...
HO! AS IF I WOULD RISK DEVALUING IT!
THAT'S WHAT I THOUGHT. GOOD.
...AND OF COURSE YOU'LL SELL COPIES— LOTS OF THEM—
TO THE PROFESSORS AT THE UNIVERSITY, TO THE MASTER, TO EVERYBODY—
EVEN TO MARTELLUS VON BLITZENGAARD, IF HE WANTS ONE.
OH, BUT BE SURE TO CHARGE HIM DOUBLE.
HA! I ALREADY DO!
—BUT YOU KNOW, THE MORE WIDELY DISTRIBUTED THIS INFORMATION BECOMES, THE LESS VALUE IT WILL HAVE...
—BUT BY THEN, YOU WILL HAVE ALREADY MADE A FORTUNE.
THIS IS A DEAL THAT BENEFITS BOTH OF US, MADAME.
MY FAVORITE KIND!
OH DEAR...
MADAME?
I AM GOING TO HAVE TO GIVE YOU SO MUCH CREDIT.
—BUT YOU'LL MAKE SO MUCH MORE...
OH, OF COURSE, BUT IT IS THE PRINCIPLE OF THE THING.

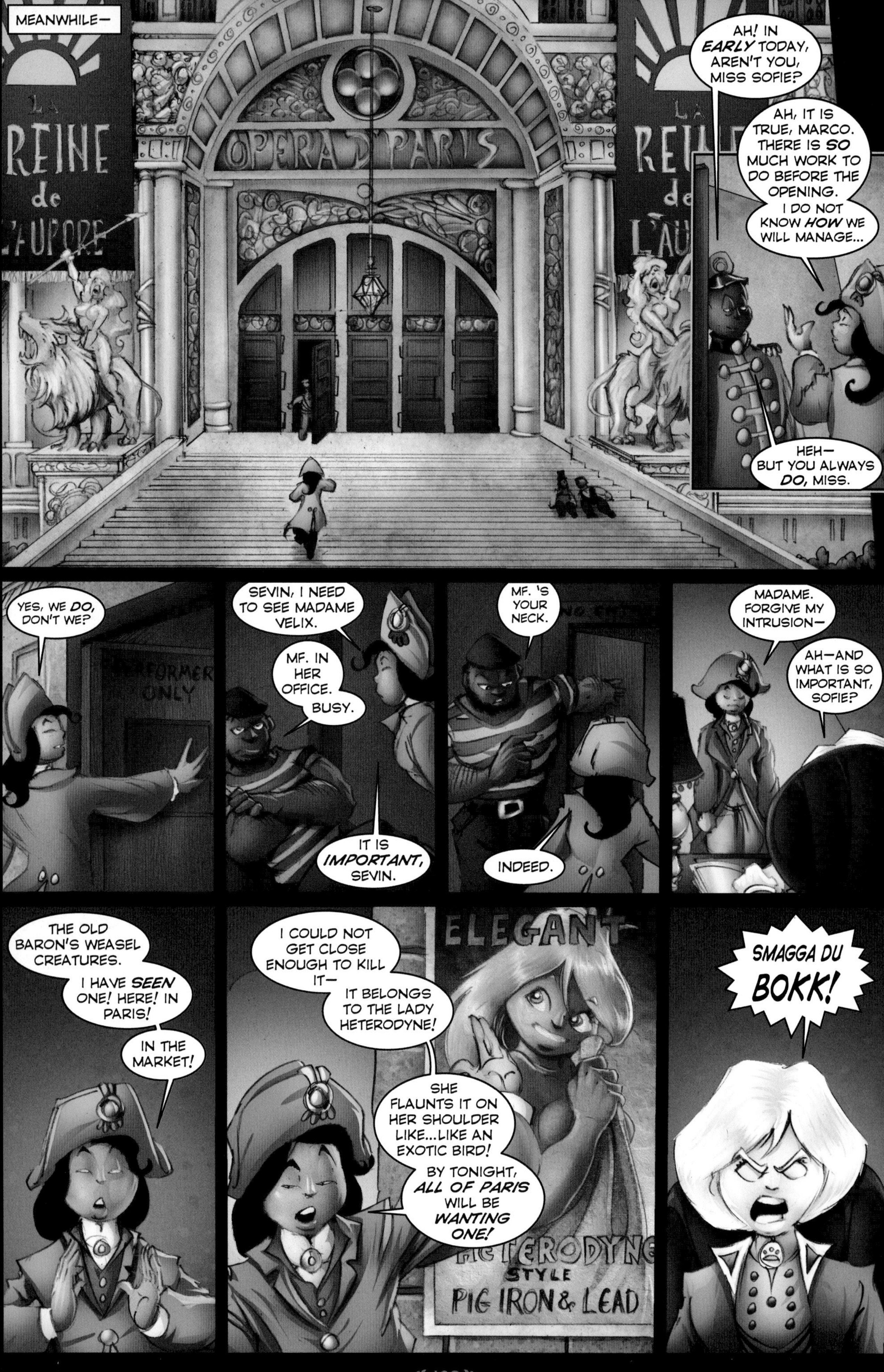
MEANWHILE—
LA REINE de L'AURORE
OPERA D'PARIS
LA REINE de L'AURORE
AH! IN EARLY TODAY, AREN'T YOU, MISS SOFIE?
AH, IT IS TRUE, MARCO. THERE IS SO MUCH WORK TO DO BEFORE THE OPENING.
I DO NOT KNOW HOW WE WILL MANAGE...
HEH— BUT YOU ALWAYS DO, MISS.
YES, WE DO, DON'T WE?
PERFORMERS ONLY
SEVIN, I NEED TO SEE MADAME VELIX.
MF. IN HER OFFICE.
BUSY.
IT IS IMPORTANT, SEVIN.
MF. 'S YOUR NECK.
INDEED.
MADAME. FORGIVE MY INTRUSION—
AH—AND WHAT IS SO IMPORTANT, SOFIE?
THE OLD BARON'S WEASEL CREATURES.
I HAVE SEEN ONE! HERE! IN PARIS!
IN THE MARKET!
I COULD NOT GET CLOSE ENOUGH TO KILL IT—
IT BELONGS TO THE LADY HETERODYNE!
SHE FLAUNTS IT ON HER SHOULDER LIKE...LIKE AN EXOTIC BIRD!
BY TONIGHT, ALL OF PARIS WILL BE WANTING ONE!
ELEGANT
HETERODYNE STYLE
PIG IRON & LEAD
SMAGGA DU BOKK!

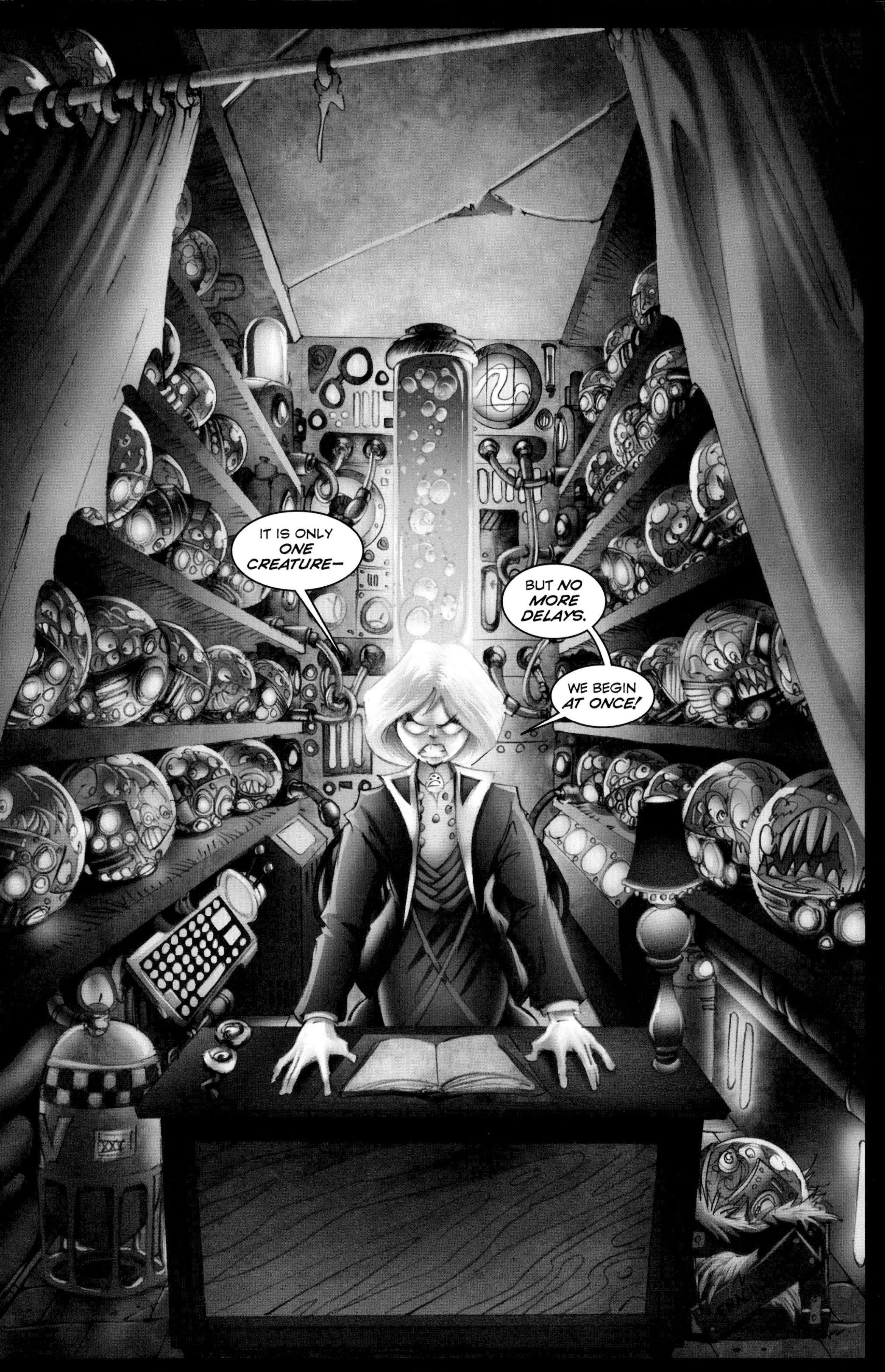
IT IS ONLY ONE CREATURE—
BUT NO MORE DELAYS.
WE BEGIN AT ONCE!

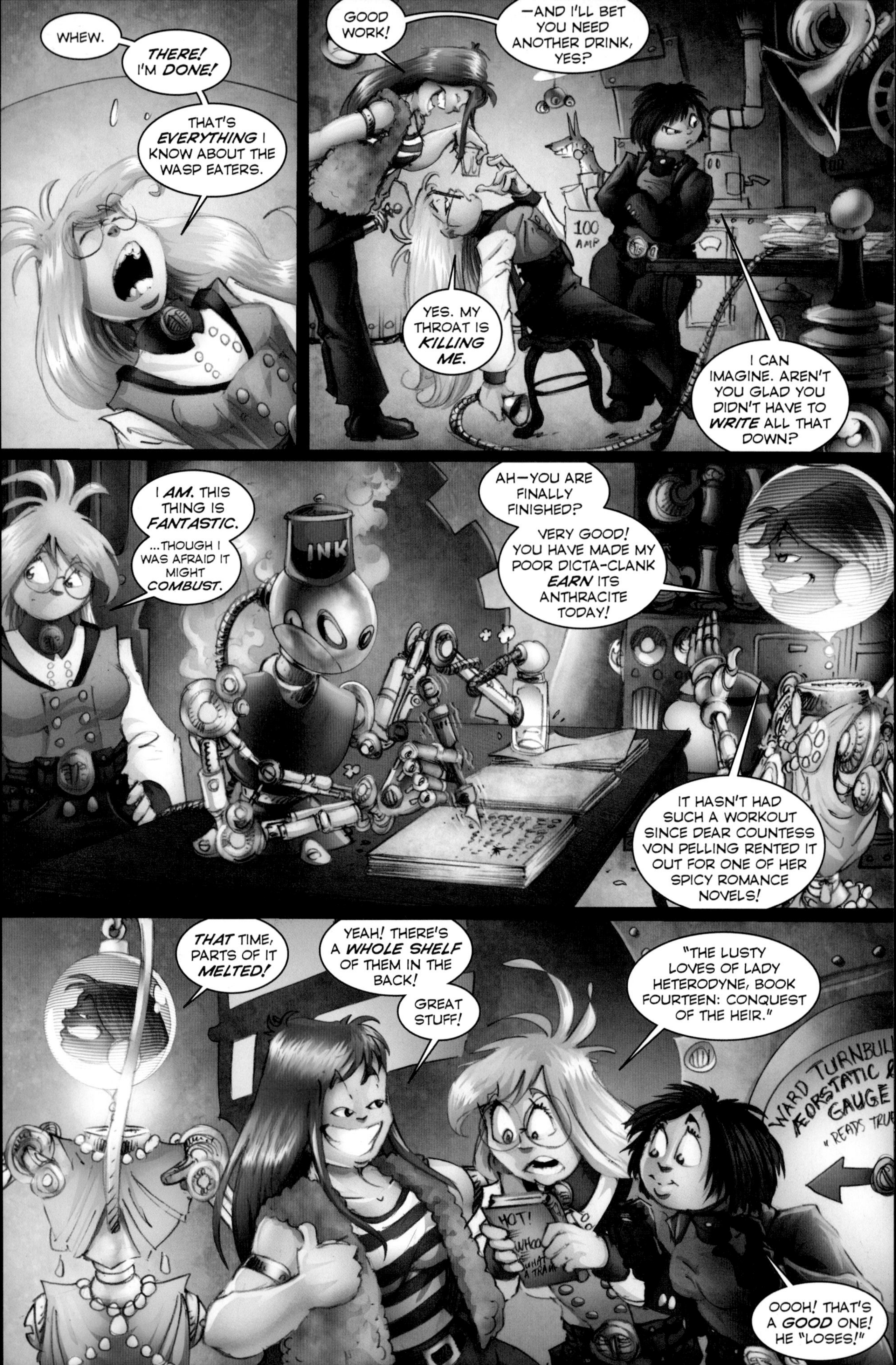
WHEW.
THERE! I'M DONE!
THAT'S EVERYTHING I KNOW ABOUT THE WASP EATERS.
GOOD WORK!
—AND I'LL BET YOU NEED ANOTHER DRINK, YES?
YES. MY THROAT IS KILLING ME.
100 AMP
I CAN IMAGINE. AREN'T YOU GLAD YOU DIDN'T HAVE TO WRITE ALL THAT DOWN?
I AM. THIS THING IS FANTASTIC.
...THOUGH I WAS AFRAID IT MIGHT COMBUST.
INK
AH—YOU ARE FINALLY FINISHED?
VERY GOOD! YOU HAVE MADE MY POOR DICTA-CLANK EARN ITS ANTHRACITE TODAY!
IT HASN'T HAD SUCH A WORKOUT SINCE DEAR COUNTESS VON PELLING RENTED IT OUT FOR ONE OF HER SPICY ROMANCE NOVELS!
THAT TIME, PARTS OF IT MELTED!
YEAH! THERE'S A WHOLE SHELF OF THEM IN THE BACK!
GREAT STUFF!
"THE LUSTY LOVES OF LADY HETERODYNE, BOOK FOURTEEN: CONQUEST OF THE HEIR."
HOT!
OOOH! THAT'S A GOOD ONE! HE "LOSES!"

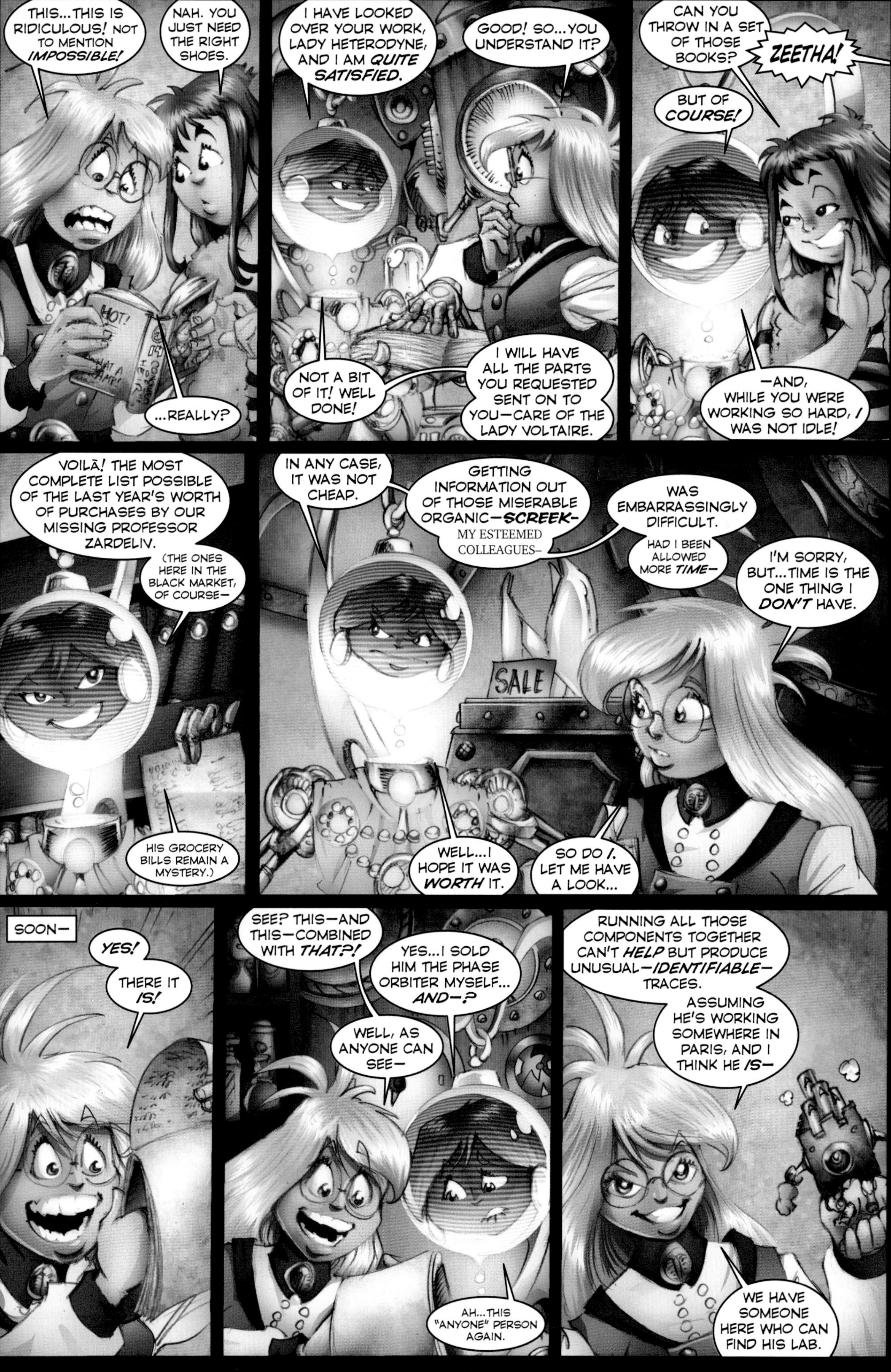

THIS...THIS IS RIDICULOUS! NOT TO MENTION IMPOSSIBLE!
NAH. YOU JUST NEED THE RIGHT SHOES.
...REALLY?
I HAVE LOOKED OVER YOUR WORK, LADY HETERODYNE, AND I AM QUITE SATISFIED.
GOOD! SO...YOU UNDERSTAND IT?
NOT A BIT OF IT! WELL DONE!
I WILL HAVE ALL THE PARTS YOU REQUESTED SENT ON TO YOU—CARE OF THE LADY VOLTAIRE.
CAN YOU THROW IN A SET OF THOSE BOOKS?
ZEETHA!
BUT OF COURSE!
—AND, WHILE YOU WERE WORKING SO HARD, I WAS NOT IDLE!
VOILÀ! THE MOST COMPLETE LIST POSSIBLE OF THE LAST YEAR'S WORTH OF PURCHASES BY OUR MISSING PROFESSOR ZARDELIV.
(THE ONES HERE IN THE BLACK MARKET, OF COURSE—
HIS GROCERY BILLS REMAIN A MYSTERY.)
IN ANY CASE, IT WAS NOT CHEAP.
GETTING INFORMATION OUT OF THOSE MISERABLE ORGANIC—SCREEK-
MY ESTEEMED COLLEAGUES—
WAS EMBARRASSINGLY DIFFICULT.
HAD I BEEN ALLOWED MORE TIME—
I'M SORRY, BUT...TIME IS THE ONE THING I DON'T HAVE.
SALE
WELL...I HOPE IT WAS WORTH IT.
SO DO I. LET ME HAVE A LOOK...
SOON—
YES!
THERE IT IS!
SEE? THIS—AND THIS—COMBINED WITH THAT?!
YES...I SOLD HIM THE PHASE ORBITER MYSELF... AND—?
WELL, AS ANYONE CAN SEE—
AH...THIS "ANYONE" PERSON AGAIN.
RUNNING ALL THOSE COMPONENTS TOGETHER CAN'T HELP BUT PRODUCE UNUSUAL—IDENTIFIABLE—TRACES.
ASSUMING HE'S WORKING SOMEWHERE IN PARIS, AND I THINK HE IS—
WE HAVE SOMEONE HERE WHO CAN FIND HIS LAB.

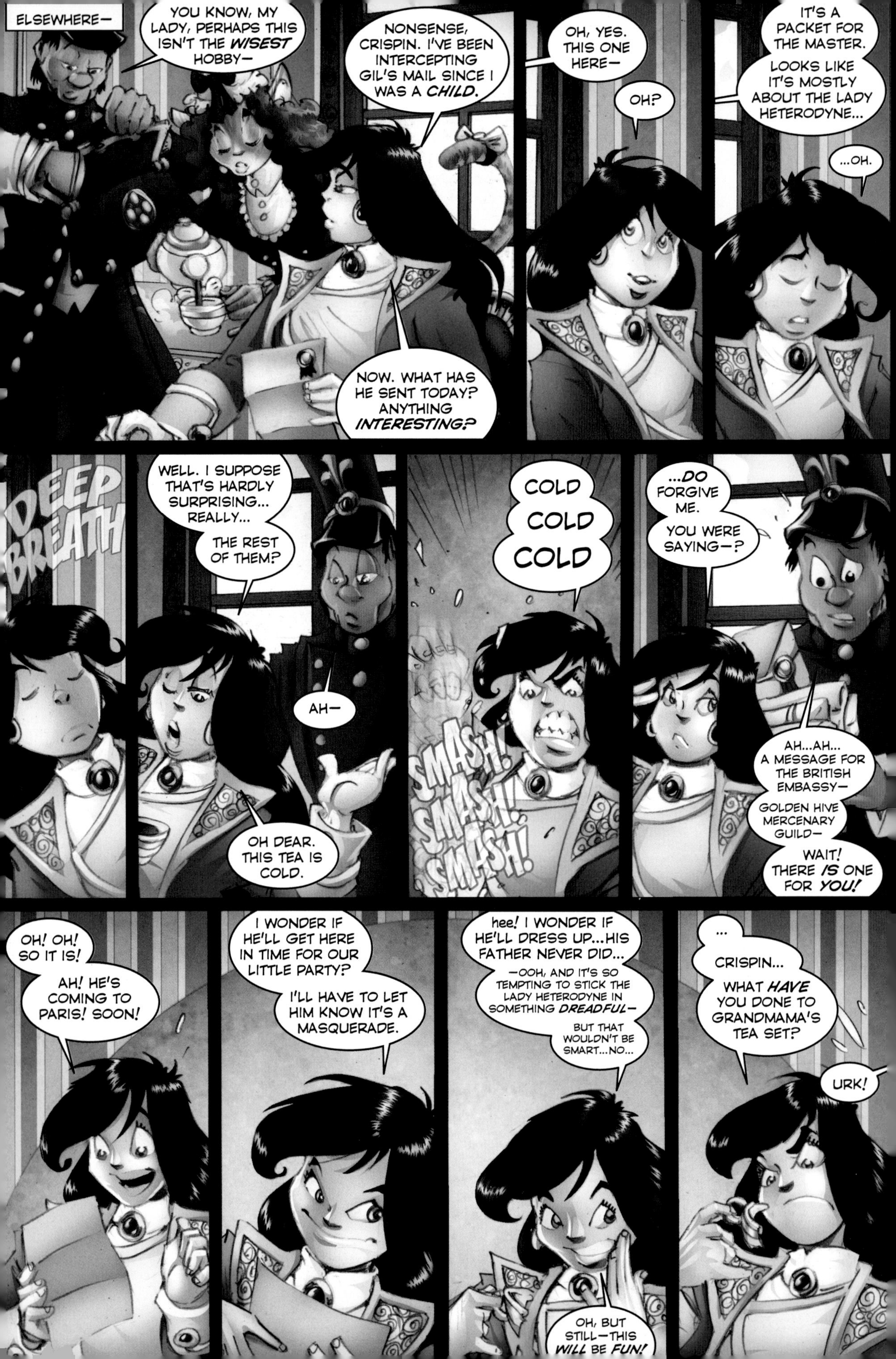
ELSEWHERE—
YOU KNOW, MY LADY, PERHAPS THIS ISN'T THE WISEST HOBBY—
NONSENSE, CRISPIN. I'VE BEEN INTERCEPTING GIL'S MAIL SINCE I WAS A CHILD.
NOW. WHAT HAS HE SENT TODAY? ANYTHING INTERESTING?
OH, YES. THIS ONE HERE—
OH?
IT'S A PACKET FOR THE MASTER.
LOOKS LIKE IT'S MOSTLY ABOUT THE LADY HETERODYNE...
...OH.
DEEP BREATH
WELL. I SUPPOSE THAT'S HARDLY SURPRISING... REALLY...
THE REST OF THEM?
AH—
OH DEAR. THIS TEA IS COLD.
COLD
COLD
COLD
SMASH! SMASH! SMASH!
...DO FORGIVE ME.
YOU WERE SAYING—?
AH...AH... A MESSAGE FOR THE BRITISH EMBASSY—
GOLDEN HIVE MERCENARY GUILD—
WAIT! THERE IS ONE FOR YOU!
OH! OH! SO IT IS!
AH! HE'S COMING TO PARIS! SOON!
I WONDER IF HE'LL GET HERE IN TIME FOR OUR LITTLE PARTY?
I'LL HAVE TO LET HIM KNOW IT'S A MASQUERADE.
hee! I WONDER IF HE'LL DRESS UP...HIS FATHER NEVER DID...
—OOH, AND IT'S SO TEMPTING TO STICK THE LADY HETERODYNE IN SOMETHING DREADFUL—
BUT THAT WOULDN'T BE SMART...NO...
OH, BUT STILL—THIS WILL BE FUN!
...
CRISPIN...
WHAT HAVE YOU DONE TO GRANDMAMA'S TEA SET?
URK!

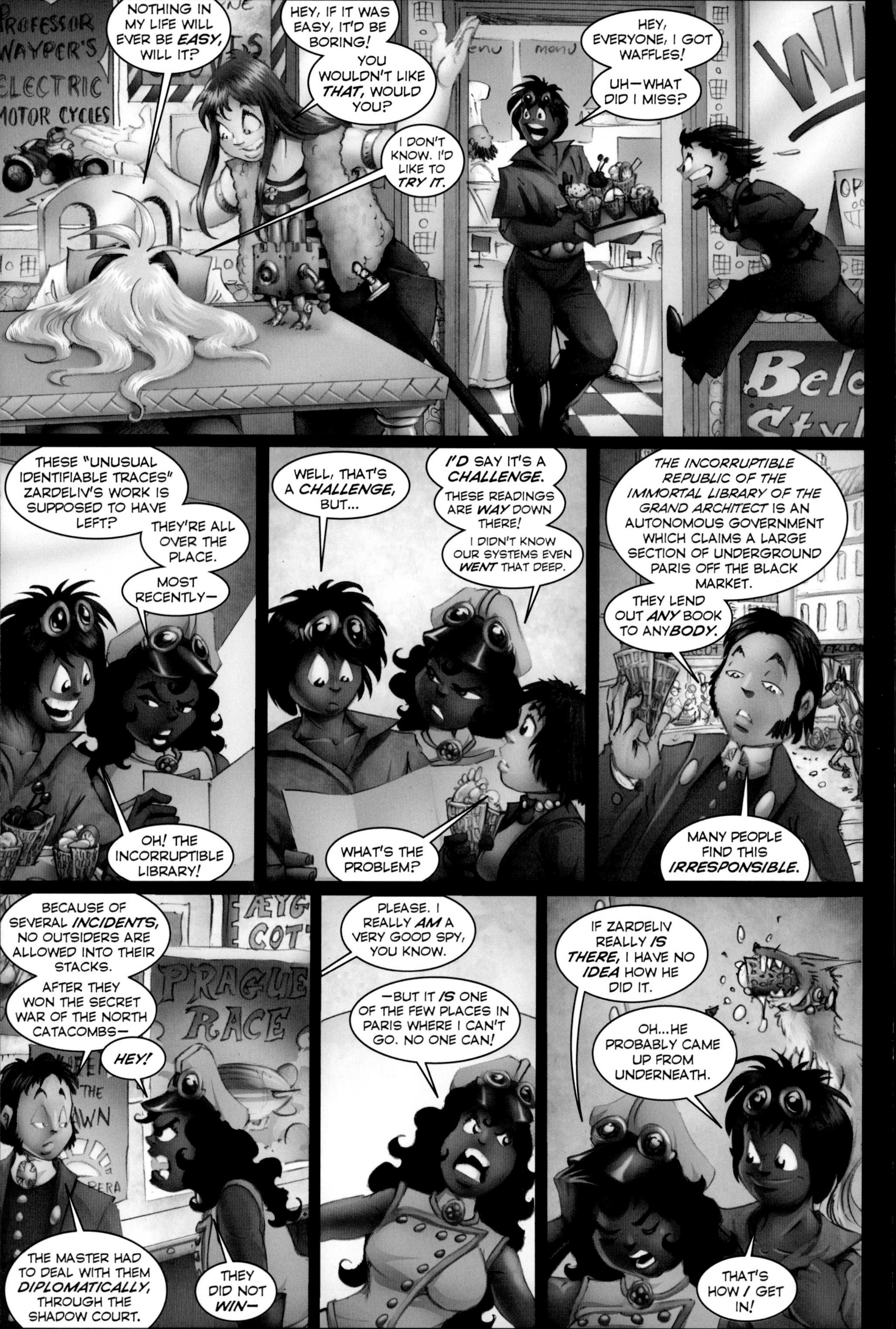
PROFESSOR WAYPER'S ELECTRIC MOTOR CYCLES
NOTHING IN MY LIFE WILL EVER BE *EASY*, WILL IT?
HEY, IF IT WAS EASY, IT'D BE BORING!
YOU WOULDN'T LIKE *THAT*, WOULD YOU?
I DON'T KNOW. I'D LIKE TO *TRY IT*.
HEY, EVERYONE, I GOT WAFFLES!
UH—WHAT DID I MISS?
THESE "UNUSUAL IDENTIFIABLE TRACES" ZARDELIV'S WORK IS SUPPOSED TO HAVE LEFT?
THEY'RE ALL OVER THE PLACE.
MOST RECENTLY—
OH! THE INCORRUPTIBLE LIBRARY!
WELL, THAT'S A *CHALLENGE*, BUT...
I'D SAY IT'S A *CHALLENGE*.
THESE READINGS ARE *WAY* DOWN THERE!
I DIDN'T KNOW OUR SYSTEMS EVEN *WENT* THAT DEEP.
WHAT'S THE PROBLEM?
THE INCORRUPTIBLE REPUBLIC OF THE IMMORTAL LIBRARY OF THE GRAND ARCHITECT IS AN AUTONOMOUS GOVERNMENT WHICH CLAIMS A LARGE SECTION OF UNDERGROUND PARIS OFF THE BLACK MARKET.
THEY LEND OUT *ANY* BOOK TO ANY*BODY*.
MANY PEOPLE FIND THIS *IRRESPONSIBLE*.
BECAUSE OF SEVERAL *INCIDENTS*, NO OUTSIDERS ARE ALLOWED INTO THEIR STACKS.
AFTER THEY WON THE SECRET WAR OF THE NORTH CATACOMBS—
HEY!
THE MASTER HAD TO DEAL WITH THEM *DIPLOMATICALLY*, THROUGH THE SHADOW COURT.
THEY DID NOT *WIN*—
PRAGUE RACE
PLEASE. I REALLY *AM* A VERY GOOD SPY, YOU KNOW.
—BUT IT *IS* ONE OF THE FEW PLACES IN PARIS WHERE I CAN'T GO. NO ONE CAN!
IF ZARDELIV REALLY *IS THERE*, I HAVE NO *IDEA* HOW HE DID IT.
OH...HE PROBABLY CAME UP FROM UNDERNEATH.
THAT'S HOW *I* GET IN!

EVENTUALLY—
—AND AFTER THAT, THEY HAD TO RE-CATALOG THE WHOLE SECTION.
—BUT THEY'RE LIBRARIANS! I THOUGHT THEY LIKED CATALOGING THINGS!
CONTEXT IS EVERYTHING, MY DEAR FELLOW.
YEAH, SO THEY REVOKED MY LIBRARY CARD "WITH EXTREME PREJUDICE."
THAT MEANS—
OH, I REMEMBER WHAT IT MEANS.
MASTER GIL TENDED TO COLLECT SUCH THINGS.
THIS IS THE LIBRARY?
NO...THIS IS THE LEFT BANK STORM DRAIN.
IT WAS DECOMMISSIONED DECADES AGO.
7017A

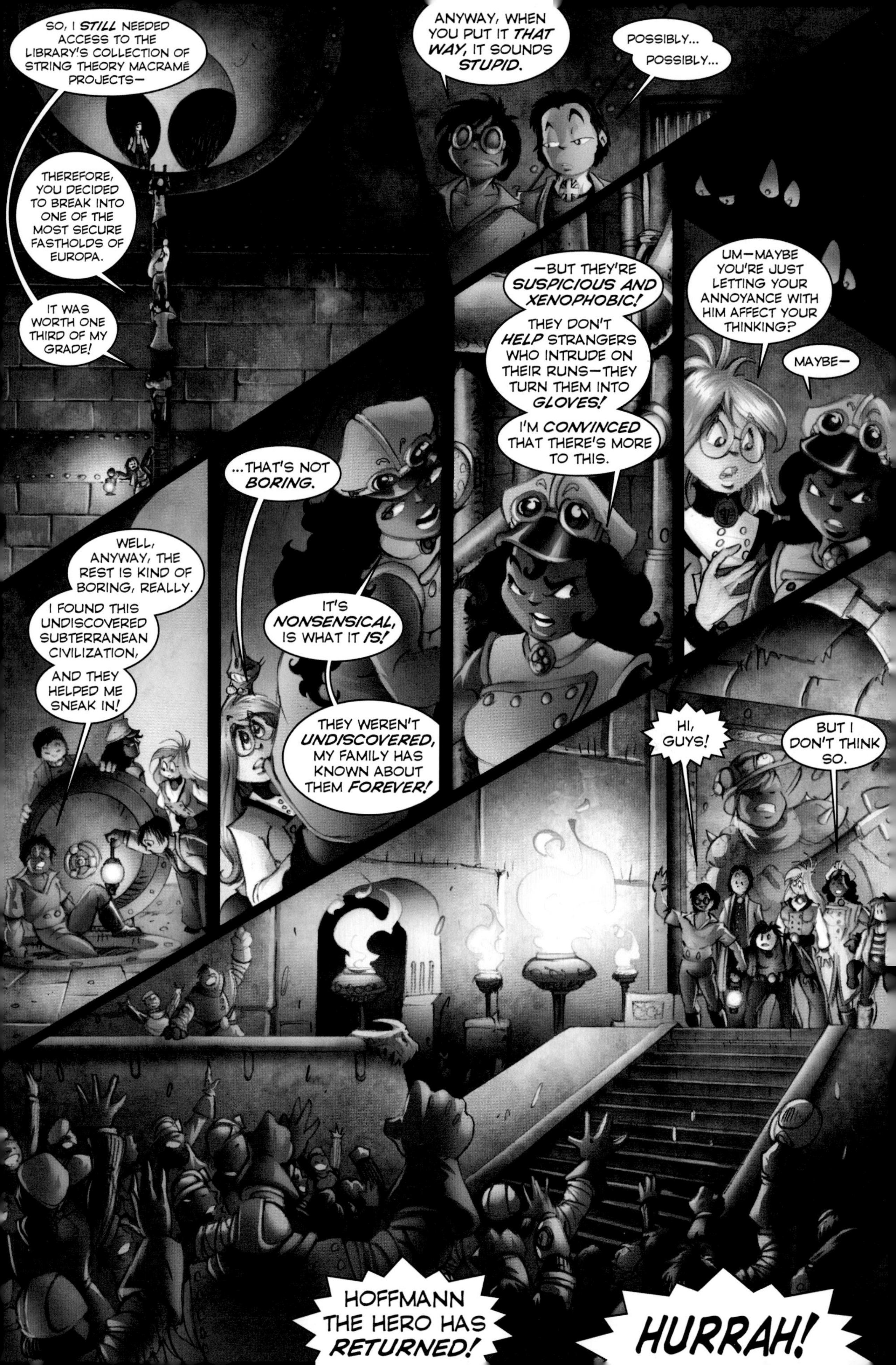
SO, I STILL NEEDED ACCESS TO THE LIBRARY'S COLLECTION OF STRING THEORY MACRAMÉ PROJECTS—
THEREFORE, YOU DECIDED TO BREAK INTO ONE OF THE MOST SECURE FASTHOLDS OF EUROPA.
IT WAS WORTH ONE THIRD OF MY GRADE!
ANYWAY, WHEN YOU PUT IT THAT WAY, IT SOUNDS STUPID.
POSSIBLY... POSSIBLY...
WELL, ANYWAY, THE REST IS KIND OF BORING, REALLY.
I FOUND THIS UNDISCOVERED SUBTERRANEAN CIVILIZATION,
AND THEY HELPED ME SNEAK IN!
...THAT'S NOT BORING.
IT'S NONSENSICAL, IS WHAT IT IS!
THEY WEREN'T UNDISCOVERED, MY FAMILY HAS KNOWN ABOUT THEM FOREVER!
—BUT THEY'RE SUSPICIOUS AND XENOPHOBIC!
THEY DON'T HELP STRANGERS WHO INTRUDE ON THEIR RUNS—THEY TURN THEM INTO GLOVES!
I'M CONVINCED THAT THERE'S MORE TO THIS.
UM—MAYBE YOU'RE JUST LETTING YOUR ANNOYANCE WITH HIM AFFECT YOUR THINKING?
MAYBE—
HI, GUYS!
BUT I DON'T THINK SO.
HOFFMANN THE HERO HAS RETURNED!
HURRAH!

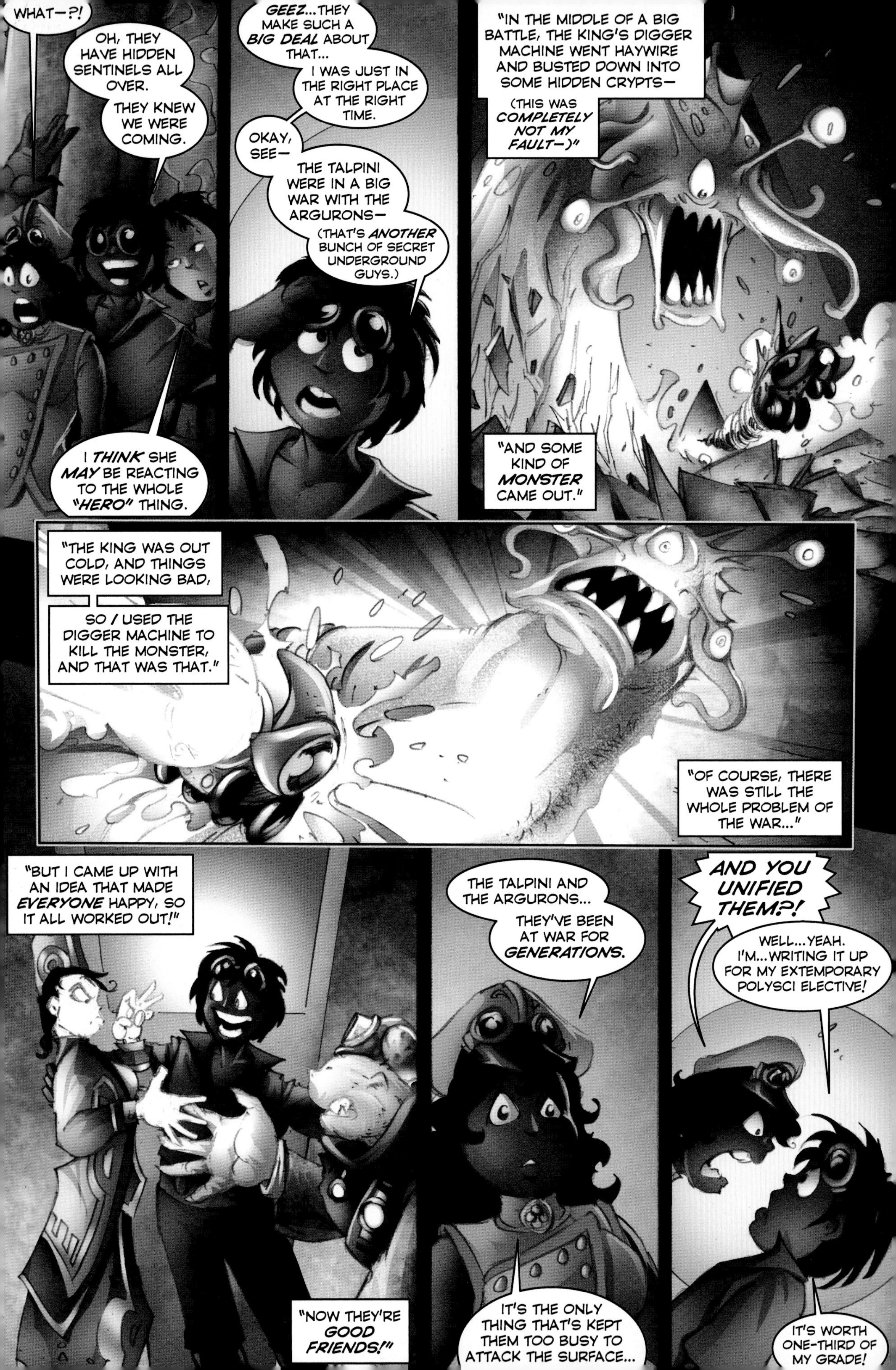
WHAT—?!
OH, THEY HAVE HIDDEN SENTINELS ALL OVER.
THEY KNEW WE WERE COMING.
I *THINK* SHE *MAY* BE REACTING TO THE WHOLE *"HERO"* THING.
GEEZ...THEY MAKE SUCH A *BIG DEAL* ABOUT THAT...
I WAS JUST IN THE RIGHT PLACE AT THE RIGHT TIME.
OKAY, SEE—
THE TALPINI WERE IN A BIG WAR WITH THE ARGURONS—
(THAT'S *ANOTHER* BUNCH OF SECRET UNDERGROUND GUYS.)
"IN THE MIDDLE OF A BIG BATTLE, THE KING'S DIGGER MACHINE WENT HAYWIRE AND BUSTED DOWN INTO SOME HIDDEN CRYPTS—
(THIS WAS *COMPLETELY NOT MY FAULT*—)"
"AND SOME KIND OF *MONSTER* CAME OUT."
"THE KING WAS OUT COLD, AND THINGS WERE LOOKING BAD,
SO *I* USED THE DIGGER MACHINE TO KILL THE MONSTER, AND THAT WAS THAT."
"OF COURSE, THERE WAS STILL THE WHOLE PROBLEM OF THE WAR..."
"BUT I CAME UP WITH AN IDEA THAT MADE *EVERYONE* HAPPY, SO IT ALL WORKED OUT!"
"NOW THEY'RE *GOOD FRIENDS!*"
THE TALPINI AND THE ARGURONS...
THEY'VE BEEN AT WAR FOR *GENERATIONS*.
IT'S THE ONLY THING THAT'S KEPT THEM TOO BUSY TO ATTACK THE SURFACE...
AND YOU UNIFIED THEM?!
WELL...YEAH. I'M...WRITING IT UP FOR MY EXTEMPORARY POLYSCI ELECTIVE!
IT'S WORTH ONE-THIRD OF MY GRADE!

SO...WHAT WAS YOUR IDEA?

WELL, I THOUGHT IF ONE OF THE TALPINI ROYALS MARRIED ONE OF THE ARGURON ROYALS...

WHA—

snurf! WE RECOGNIZE AND WELCOME *YOU,* HOFFMANN, BUT THESE OTHERS ARE *STRANGERS...*

AND I NEED NEW GLOVES!

HA HA. SO FUNNY.

OH, YES. VERY AMUSING INDEED.

HA! YOU GUYS ARE SUCH KIDDERS!

THESE ARE MY BURROW-MATES, GOLIVER!

WAIT! THERE! THE GOLDEN-FURRED ONE! *WE KNOW YOU!* AMAZING!

NEVER DID I THINK I WOULD SEE THIS DAY!

THIS IS MOLYBDENUM— THEIR HIGH PRIEST!

ER... HELLO—

OOH! OOH! SHE'S YOUR PROPHESIED HOLY ONE, *RIGHT?*

LIKE, YOUR *GODDESS INCARNATED,* DESTINED TO *RULE* YOU AND STUFF?

AH, NO... WE ARE JUST VERY BIG FANS OF HER GLOVE OIL.

HETERODYNE GLOVE OIL

NICE!

LEATHER PEPPERMINT

IT IS *MINTY!*

WELL, *THAT* WAS AWKWARD.

HEY, IT HAPPENED TO MY *COUSIN!*

A *POLITICAL MARRIAGE?* TREATING INNOCENT YOUNG PEOPLE AS *POLITICAL PAWNS?*

MAJESTY! BY YOUR COMMAND, I PRESENT THE VISITORS!

THEY'RE NOT EVEN THE SAME *SPECIES!*

AW, IT'LL BE OKAY. THEY SAID THEY WORKED THAT OUT...

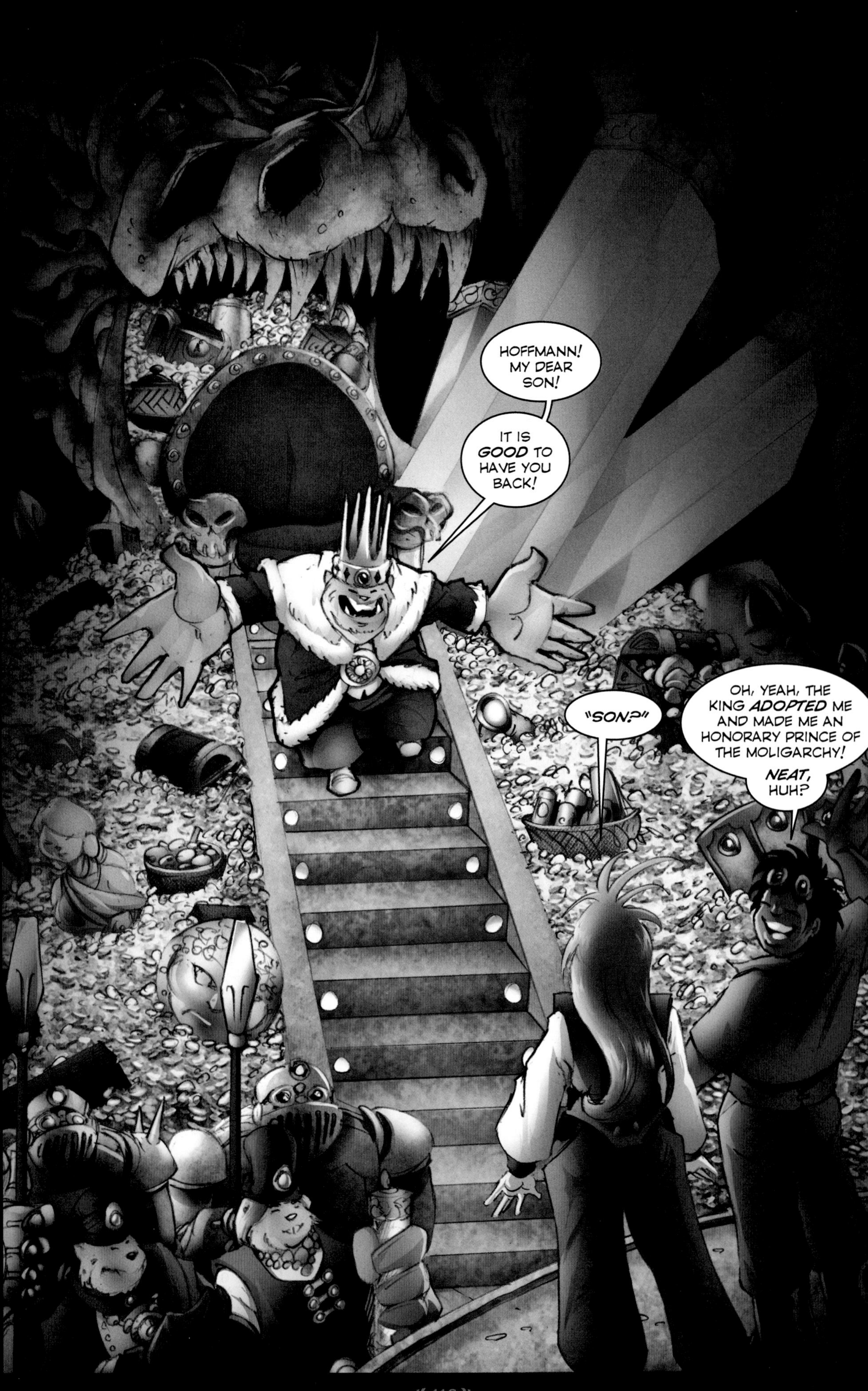
HOFFMANN! MY DEAR SON!
IT IS **GOOD** TO HAVE YOU BACK!
"SON?"
OH, YEAH, THE KING **ADOPTED** ME AND MADE ME AN HONORARY PRINCE OF THE MOLIGARCHY!
NEAT, HUH?

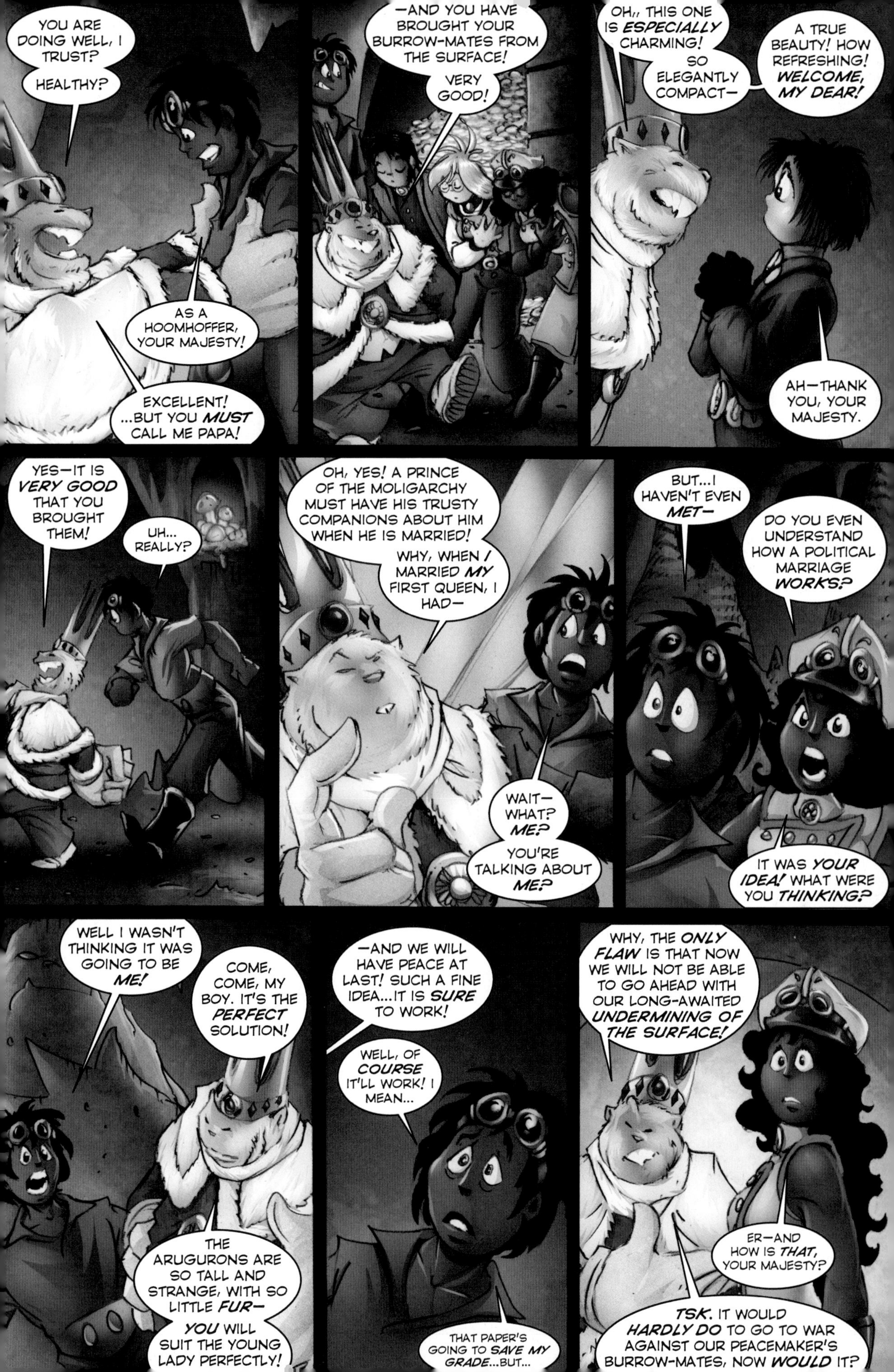
YOU ARE DOING WELL, I TRUST?
HEALTHY?
AS A HOOMHOFFER, YOUR MAJESTY!
EXCELLENT! ...BUT YOU MUST CALL ME PAPA!
—AND YOU HAVE BROUGHT YOUR BURROW-MATES FROM THE SURFACE!
VERY GOOD!
OH,, THIS ONE IS ESPECIALLY CHARMING!
SO ELEGANTLY COMPACT—
A TRUE BEAUTY! HOW REFRESHING! WELCOME, MY DEAR!
AH—THANK YOU, YOUR MAJESTY.
YES—IT IS VERY GOOD THAT YOU BROUGHT THEM!
UH... REALLY?
OH, YES! A PRINCE OF THE MOLIGARCHY MUST HAVE HIS TRUSTY COMPANIONS ABOUT HIM WHEN HE IS MARRIED!
WHY, WHEN I MARRIED MY FIRST QUEEN, I HAD—
WAIT—WHAT? ME?
YOU'RE TALKING ABOUT ME?
BUT...I HAVEN'T EVEN MET—
DO YOU EVEN UNDERSTAND HOW A POLITICAL MARRIAGE WORKS?
IT WAS YOUR IDEA! WHAT WERE YOU THINKING?
WELL I WASN'T THINKING IT WAS GOING TO BE ME!
COME, COME, MY BOY. IT'S THE PERFECT SOLUTION!
THE ARUGURONS ARE SO TALL AND STRANGE, WITH SO LITTLE FUR—
YOU WILL SUIT THE YOUNG LADY PERFECTLY!
—AND WE WILL HAVE PEACE AT LAST! SUCH A FINE IDEA...IT IS SURE TO WORK!
WELL, OF COURSE IT'LL WORK! I MEAN...
THAT PAPER'S GOING TO SAVE MY GRADE...BUT...
WHY, THE ONLY FLAW IS THAT NOW WE WILL NOT BE ABLE TO GO AHEAD WITH OUR LONG-AWAITED UNDERMINING OF THE SURFACE!
ER—AND HOW IS THAT, YOUR MAJESTY?
TSK. IT WOULD HARDLY DO TO GO TO WAR AGAINST OUR PEACEMAKER'S BURROW-MATES, NOW WOULD IT?

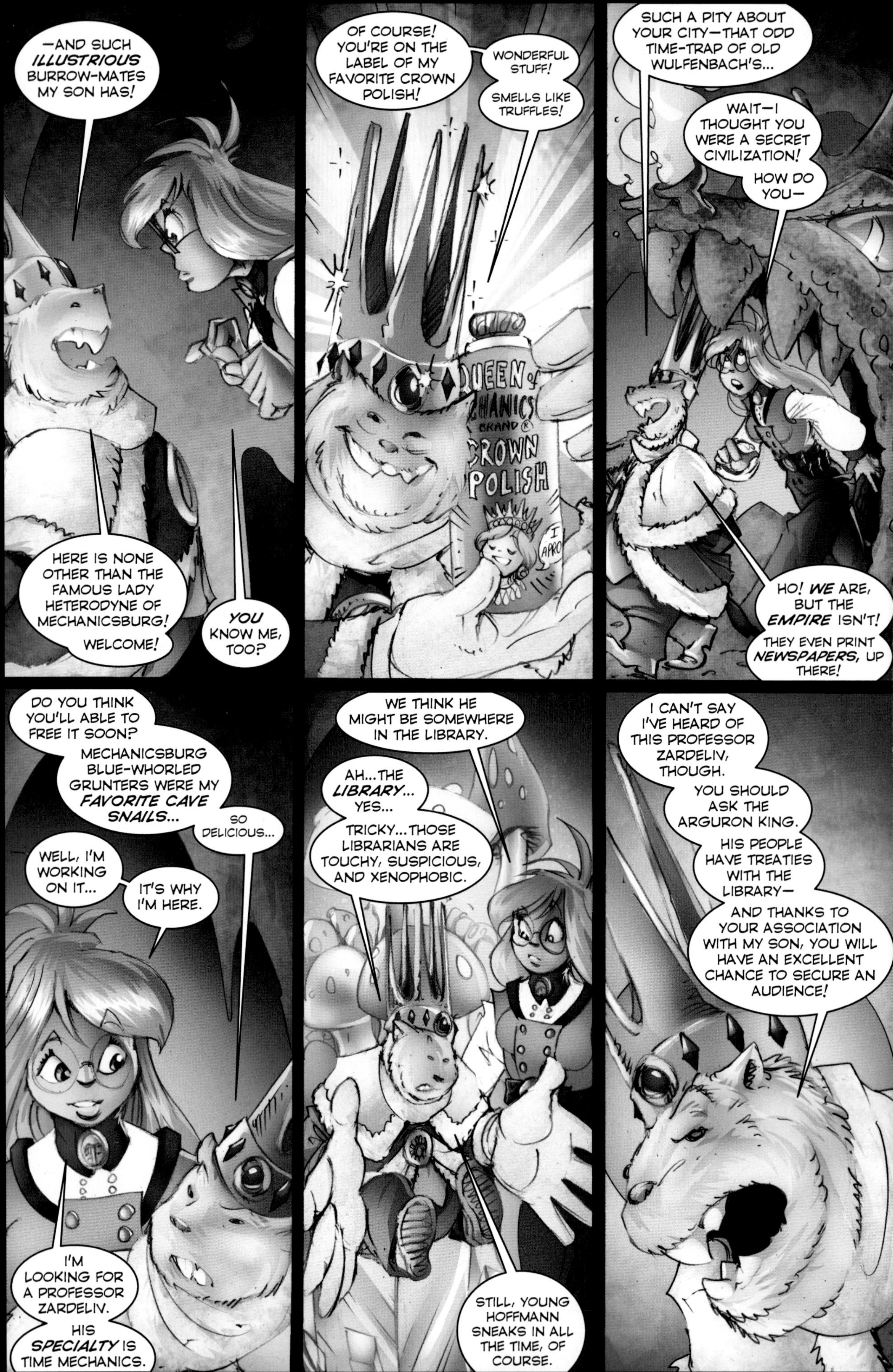
—AND SUCH *ILLUSTRIOUS* BURROW-MATES MY SON HAS!
HERE IS NONE OTHER THAN THE FAMOUS LADY HETERODYNE OF MECHANICSBURG!
WELCOME!
YOU KNOW ME, TOO?
OF COURSE! YOU'RE ON THE LABEL OF MY FAVORITE CROWN POLISH!
WONDERFUL STUFF!
SMELLS LIKE TRUFFLES!
QUEEN of MECHANICS BRAND® CROWN POLISH
I APRO
SUCH A PITY ABOUT YOUR CITY—THAT ODD TIME-TRAP OF OLD WULFENBACH'S...
WAIT—I THOUGHT YOU WERE A SECRET CIVILIZATION!
HOW DO YOU—
HO! *WE* ARE, BUT THE *EMPIRE* ISN'T!
THEY EVEN PRINT *NEWSPAPERS*, UP THERE!
DO YOU THINK YOU'LL ABLE TO FREE IT SOON?
MECHANICSBURG BLUE-WHORLED GRUNTERS WERE MY *FAVORITE CAVE SNAILS*...
SO DELICIOUS...
WELL, I'M WORKING ON IT...
IT'S WHY I'M HERE.
I'M LOOKING FOR A PROFESSOR ZARDELIV.
HIS *SPECIALTY* IS TIME MECHANICS.
WE THINK HE MIGHT BE SOMEWHERE IN THE LIBRARY.
AH...THE *LIBRARY*... YES...
TRICKY...THOSE LIBRARIANS ARE TOUCHY, SUSPICIOUS, AND XENOPHOBIC.
STILL, YOUNG HOFFMANN SNEAKS IN ALL THE TIME, OF COURSE.
I CAN'T SAY I'VE HEARD OF THIS PROFESSOR ZARDELIV, THOUGH.
YOU SHOULD ASK THE ARGURON KING.
HIS PEOPLE HAVE TREATIES WITH THE LIBRARY—
AND THANKS TO YOUR ASSOCIATION WITH MY SON, YOU WILL HAVE AN EXCELLENT CHANCE TO SECURE AN AUDIENCE!

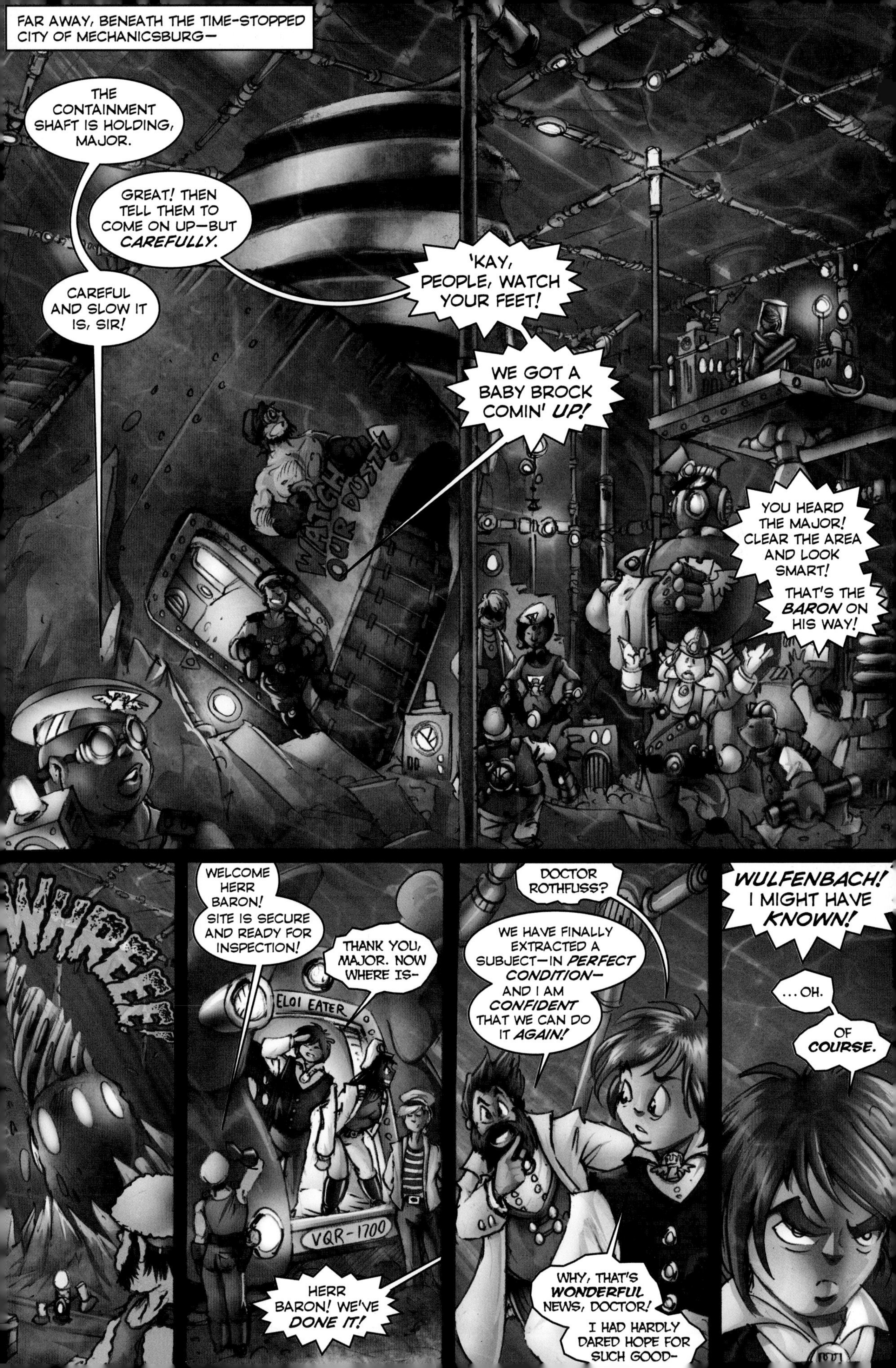

FAR AWAY, BENEATH THE TIME-STOPPED CITY OF MECHANICSBURG—
THE CONTAINMENT SHAFT IS HOLDING, MAJOR.
GREAT! THEN TELL THEM TO COME ON UP—BUT CAREFULLY.
CAREFUL AND SLOW IT IS, SIR!
'KAY, PEOPLE, WATCH YOUR FEET!
WE GOT A BABY BROCK COMIN' UP!
YOU HEARD THE MAJOR! CLEAR THE AREA AND LOOK SMART!
THAT'S THE BARON ON HIS WAY!
WELCOME HERR BARON! SITE IS SECURE AND READY FOR INSPECTION!
THANK YOU, MAJOR. NOW WHERE IS-
ELOI EATER
VQR-1700
HERR BARON! WE'VE DONE IT!
DOCTOR ROTHFUSS?
WE HAVE FINALLY EXTRACTED A SUBJECT—IN PERFECT CONDITION— AND I AM CONFIDENT THAT WE CAN DO IT AGAIN!
WHY, THAT'S WONDERFUL NEWS, DOCTOR!
I HAD HARDLY DARED HOPE FOR SUCH GOOD-
WULFENBACH! I MIGHT HAVE KNOWN!
...OH.
OF COURSE.

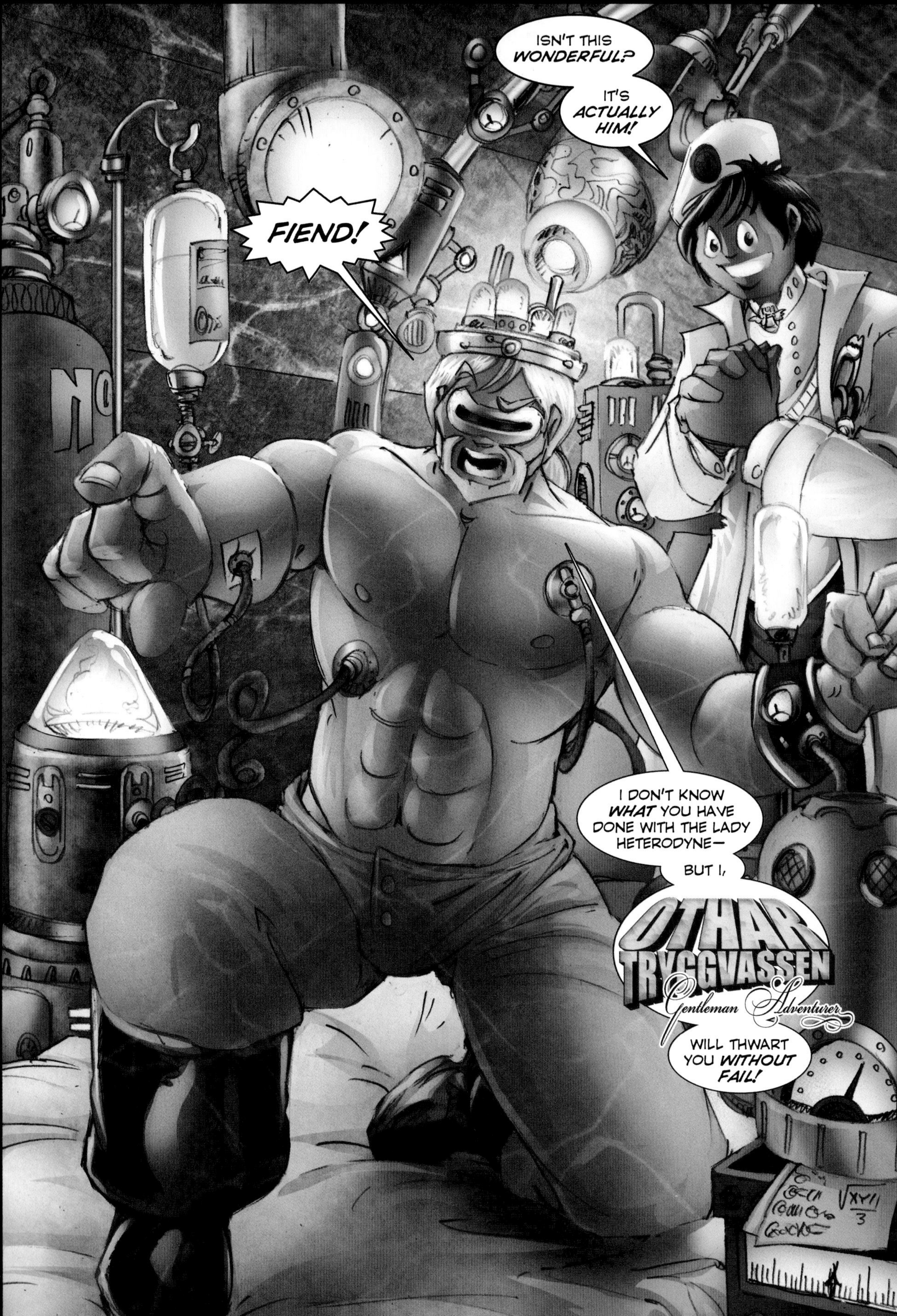

ISN'T THIS WONDERFUL?
IT'S ACTUALLY HIM!
FIEND!
I DON'T KNOW WHAT YOU HAVE DONE WITH THE LADY HETERODYNE—
BUT I,
OTHAR TRYGGVASSEN
Gentleman Adventurer
WILL THWART YOU WITHOUT FAIL!

TO BE CONTINUED IN:

GIRL GENIUS® The Second Journey BOOK 3

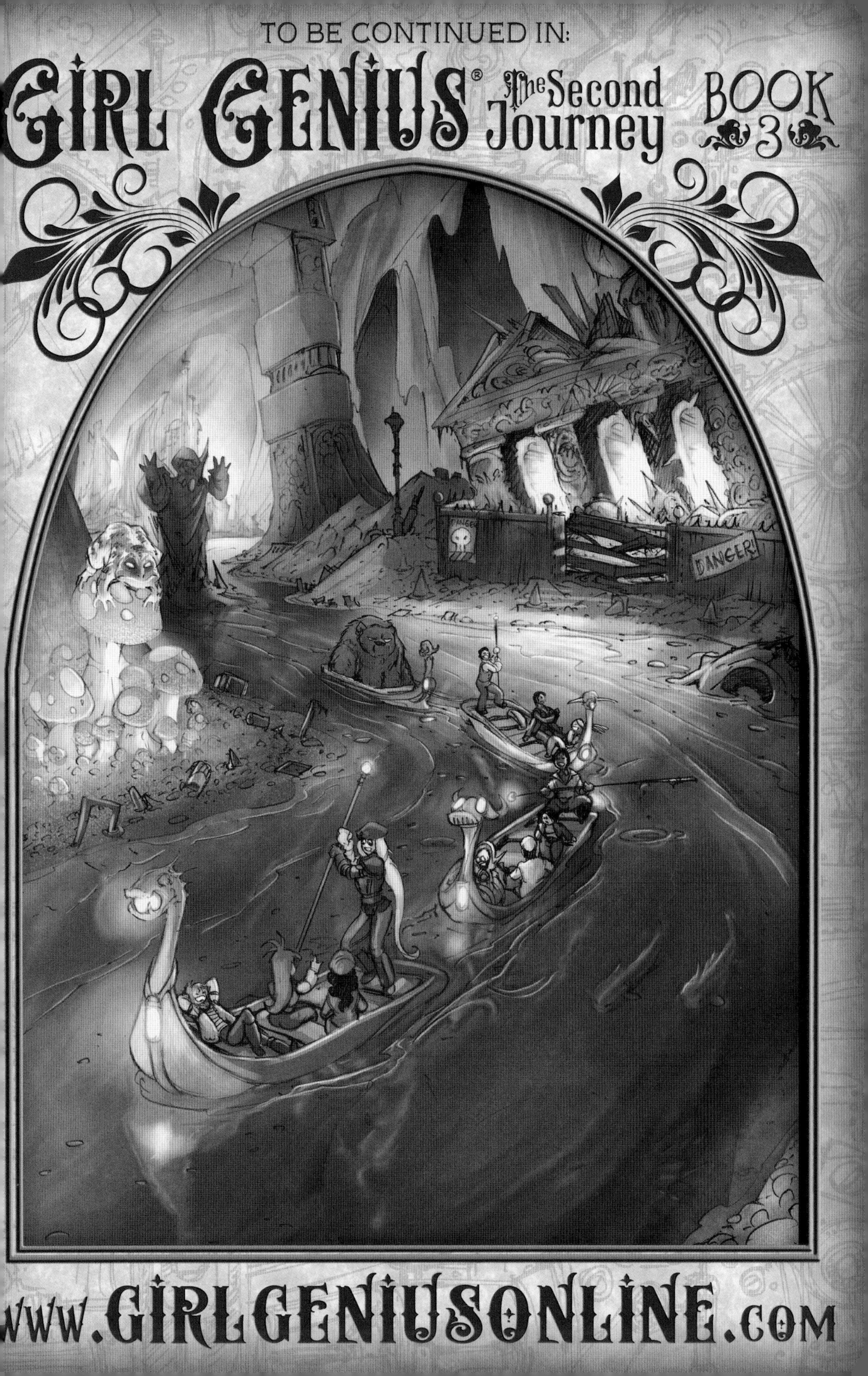
DANGER!

www.GIRLGENIUSONLINE.com